W9-CEK-863

THE FRIENDS WE KEEP

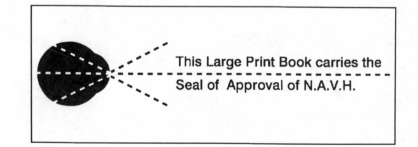

This Large Print Book carries the
Seal of Approval of N.A.V.H.

THE FRIENDS WE KEEP

JANE GREEN

THORNDIKE PRESS
A part of Gale, a Cengage Company

Farmington Hills, Mich • San Francisco • New York • Waterville, Maine
Meriden, Conn • Mason, Ohio • Chicago

Copyright © 2019 by Jane Green.
Thorndike Press, a part of Gale, a Cengage Company.

Thorndike Press® Large Print Core.
The text of this Large Print edition is unabridged.
Other aspects of the book may vary from the original edition.
Set in 16 pt. Plantin.

LIBRARY OF CONGRESS CIP DATA ON FILE.
CATALOGUING IN PUBLICATION FOR THIS BOOK
IS AVAILABLE FROM THE LIBRARY OF CONGRESS

ISBN-13: 978-1-4328-6467-5 (hardcover alk. paper)

Published in 2019 by arrangement with Berkley, an imprint of Penguin Publishing Group, a division of Penguin Random House LLC

Printed in the United States of America
1 2 3 4 5 6 7 23 22 21 20 19

ACKNOWLEDGMENTS

My publishing team at Berkley, including Ivan Held, Claire Zion, Christine Ball, Craig Burke, Jeanne-Marie Hudson, Jin Yu, Diana Franco, and Heather Connor. Angelina Krahn for doing such a wonderful job copyediting, and Ryan Coleman at The Story Factory for excellent notes.

Thomas Dolby, Keith Armstrong, and Paddy McAloon.

My board of directors: Robert Cary, Lisa Lampanelli, Emily Friendship, Sophie Pollman, and Dani Shapiro; the usual suspects: Nicole, Dina, Fiona, Shaggy, Charlie, and Fishy; my soul mates from another time: Bill, Helen, Rachel, and Steve. And a thank-you to Jason and Rena Pilalas and Ian and Debbie O'Malley.

My husband, Ian, and our children, who are each the great loves of my life.

And finally my agent, Shane Salerno, who

goes above and beyond every minute of every day.

PROLOGUE

- 2016 -

BEN

I worry that it's too late, that I should have done this years ago instead of burying my head in the sand and letting my marriage drift. My sobriety feels different this time, and these past few months I've been nostalgic. I'm praying it's not too late to make amends for the hell I've put her through, to start again.

I've been thinking about how it used to be, when we were first married, on our honeymoon when we couldn't keep our hands off each other. The hotel staff couldn't help but smile when they saw us — we were so in love. Those early years were so good. Finding the house in Somerset, trying for a baby, convinced that life would go our way, that we would get everything we ever wanted.

I hope to God it's not too late for us to get back on track. Let's face it, I'm not an impulsive man. I'm a scientist. I don't do anything impulsively, other than the years I was drinking. But I'm sober now. My doctor said one more drink would kill me. For the first time in my life, falling off the wagon isn't an option. I've had nine months without a drink, and this time I feel great. The only thing that's not working is my marriage, and I can't blame her. I've put my poor wife through hell all these years. The drinking, the blackouts, the disappearing for days at a time. I can't believe she's stuck by me, although if I'm honest, it's in name only. We've barely spoken since I started working in London. When I'm home on the weekends, we pass each other like ships in the night. I know she's still checking the bins for empty bottles of vodka. I thought I had made my amends to her for the years of pain, but it wasn't enough.

I can feel her slipping away, withdrawing so completely into herself that I don't know if there's a way to fix things. I need to do something big to try to win my wife back; I need to surprise her, to remind her of what we used to have, if there's any hope of making it through the next twenty-five years.

I lean my head against the window of the train, speeding past the London suburbs, racing past the terraced brick houses and

8

weeds climbing over the embankment, but I'm not seeing it. Not today. Every few seconds I pull out my phone and look at the screen, at the two boarding passes for Heathrow Monday morning, British Airways to Nice, where we'll pick up a Hertz rental and drive up to the Colombe d'Or, the hotel where we spent our honeymoon, almost twenty-five years ago.

I'd never been to the South of France before. My wife had, of course, but not to that hotel; her parents owned a house somewhere nearby, so this was special for both of us. The pair of us were such lovebirds, we barely left the room to explore. We spent our days getting up late and eating fresh croissants on the terrace under the huge Magritte mosaic wall, lounging by the swimming pool all day, our legs entwined, barely able to concentrate on the books we had brought. She teased me for bringing science journals, but she wasn't any more interested in the novels she had packed. We only had eyes for each other.

Her skin was so pale it was almost translucent, and her hair so red it glowed, and hung thick and long, almost touching her waist. We would stand in the pool, my wife wrapped around me like a silky coiled octopus, covering me with kisses, only

9

breaking off to look at the fourth finger of her left hand, laughing, because she said she could not quite believe we were married.

"Evil Ben," she'd say. "I'm married to Evil Ben!"

I'd laugh along with her, partly at the ridiculous nickname, but also because I couldn't believe it either. I was married to one of the most beautiful girls I had ever seen, a girl who seemed so out of my league when I first saw her at university, I didn't think I would have a hope of having a conversation with her, let alone being married to her. *Married!* I couldn't believe she was mine. I couldn't believe she had chosen *me.*

It's hard to believe we're the same people as those two lovebirds from all those years ago. It's almost impossible to believe how happy we once were. Perhaps things wouldn't have gotten quite so bad if I hadn't taken this job in London. It's never good for me to be on my own, but it was too much money to turn down. Ten more years, I thought, and then I can retire. But can we make it through the next ten years? Stupidly — *Christ, how stupid I was* — I thought that absence might make the heart grow fonder.

But that's what had happened the last

time I commuted. We had just moved to the house in Somerset, and were thinking about trying for a baby soon, but there was no pressure. My wife was thrilled I'd landed a job with such a prestigious pharmaceutical firm. It was a big promotion, and a big salary increase. And honestly? It was the perfect balance, most of the week in London and the weekends in this idyllic manor house with my beautiful wife. She loved it, too, in the beginning. She told anyone who would listen that our relationship was so good because it was part-time. We never took each other for granted, we had time to miss each other, and we looked forward to seeing each other.

But of course, I was on my own too much, and the pub was right next to my flat. Before long, I was rolling out of the pub every night, last man down. The only good thing was that my wife wasn't around to nag me about it. I'd always phone her at around nine, before I got plastered, and tell her I was going to bed. Not that she had such a problem with me drinking then, but neither of us knew what a problem it would become.

She was fine with me getting drunk on the weekends. Most of the time she'd drink with me. It was the nightly beers and a triple vodka before bed that she couldn't stand. (I never considered it a triple vodka. It was my nightly nip.) Being on my own in a London flat during the week meant I didn't have to worry about it. If I chose to have a triple vodka, or three, before bed, no one would kick me awake throughout the night because of snoring, or look at me across a table and mutter, within earshot of everyone, that I'd had enough.

After a while, I didn't want to go home. Being on my own in London made it easier to party with my best friend: booze. Until my boss intervened, telling me there were complaints that I was smelling of alcohol, and that if I didn't get myself sober, they would have to fire me. It worked. I got sober. One of many, many times.

This time around, I've been sober the whole time I've been working in London. If my colleagues invite me to the pub, I turn them down. They joke about my flat being the perfect bachelor pad, but it's lonely as hell. What's a man like me supposed to do with a high-rise luxury flat in Paddington when his wife is at home in Somerset? Yeah. Don't answer that. That's not my style. At least, it's not my style when sober. I don't want to think about all the mistakes I made while I was drinking, the betrayals I'll never be able to forgive myself for.

Nowadays the worst thing I get up to is ordering a Peshwari naan with the Indian takeout, and watching Sky News while scrolling through my phone. I now text my wife every day to say good night, at around nine p.m., but there are two differences from all those years ago when I used to phone her. The first is that I'm actually home, and the second is that she doesn't text back.

I know she knows I'm sober for real this time. I worry that she doesn't care. I'm ready to make a fresh start with my marriage. If I knew how to reach her.

How do you reach someone who has withdrawn so completely she barely looks at you even when you are together? I understand her resentment. I know that apologizing isn't enough. I have to show her I've changed. We have to find a way to start again, to stop being strangers, rattling around in an enormous country house that now feels like a prison, filled with nothing but disappointments.

Would it be different if we had been able to have children? Yeah. Of course, it would be. When I was a kid and people asked me what I wanted to be when I grew up, I used to look at them very seriously and say, "A dad." It was true. It was all I ever wanted. My sponsor thinks that's why I started drinking, but I'm not so sure. My mum was a drinker. I think it's in my blood. For years it was something I thought I could control, even before we got together. I'd get drunk on weekends only, and then the weekends stretched to include Thursdays, and then I stopped thinking about what day it was.

Now we're settling into middle age, and I'm sober, and the past doesn't matter anymore. Who do we have if we don't have each other? I don't want to divorce, I don't want to be on my own, and I don't want to start again with someone else.

I still love her, I just need to find a way to make her forgive me. You don't spend half your life with someone and not love them. It's just a bad patch, and I can't blame her. I can prove to her how different I am, how much I've grown. Am I in love with her? No. Not anymore, neither of us is. But I think we could both learn to fall in love with each other again. I think we could learn to pay attention to each other, to make a decision that we're not going to let this marriage fall apart, because right now, this marriage is falling apart.

So that's why I'm surprising her with a second honeymoon. We haven't had a holiday in years. We sit together at the kitchen table for meals, her scrolling through her phone, me reading a science journal. We barely communicate unless it's transactional — cut the grass, trim the hedges, pay the bills.

This will change all that. I'm determined. I've even booked the same room we had. How can we not rediscover each other while walking down memory lane? I'm going to print out the boarding passes when I get home, and I'll put them on the kitchen table for when she comes down tomorrow.

This is our fresh start. This is our second chance. I'm smiling as my phone buzzes, and I look down at the screen, seeing that she has texted me. This is a sign, I think, a sign that everything's going to be okay.

I'm still smiling when I open up my messages to read her text:

I've seen a lawyer. I've had enough of this sham of a marriage. I want a divorce.

■ ■ ■ ■

PART I
THE BEGINNING

■ ■ ■ ■

ONE
- 1986 -

Once upon a time Evvie would have been like these other students, she thought as she paid the taxi driver and wrestled the huge Louis Vuitton trunk out of the back of the car. Once upon a time she might have had a mother and a father just like all the ones around her now, who have driven their kids to universities, helping them decorate their rooms with colorful duvets and posters, running out to the hardware store for more picture hooks, or rods for curtains, or a kettle so they could make tea in their rooms.

Evvie no longer spoke to her father. Not since he hit her mother, knocking out two of her teeth. Two days later they were on a plane, heading to London, to her grandmother's tiny terraced house in Stockwell. It was a far cry from their old life in Brooklyn, but her mother had had enough. She went back to the bosom of her family to get her teeth and her life fixed, and she retained a divorce attorney who handled everything from overseas.

Her mother would have come with her today — her only daughter at an English university! The daughter of a Jamaican immigrant who managed, by sheer force of will and hard work, to provide her family with a life she could only have dreamed of as a child. It was a long way from the streets of Kingston, but she did it! She married the son of a wealthy white banking family, unaware they would be cut off financially once he married someone so unsuitable. But the name alone had opened doors, allowed her to give her daughter a life of privilege and opportunity.

Evvie knew her mother wasn't receiving the child support and alimony she was supposed to. She had tried to call her father herself, but those conversations never went well. Evvie knew her father was cold, but when she'd said, on their last call, that she wouldn't speak to him again, he honestly didn't seem to care. Even Evvie hadn't thought he was that cold.

They struggled for a while, but now Evvie's mom had a job at a large advertising agency. Two days off to get her daughter settled in to her university would be too much. Evvie didn't mind, she'd heard her mother telling someone, and the truth was she hadn't minded; she was so excited about going off to school that she hadn't even thought about arriving alone. She hadn't minded until she saw everyone else had their parents with them.

The taxi driver left, and Evvie was alone on the pavement, aware that people were eyeing her up and down, and worse, eyeing her trunk up and down. Oh God. She shouldn't have brought it. Who brings a giant Louis Vuitton trunk to college? But it was the only one she had that was big enough for all her stuff, and she honestly didn't give it a second thought. Until now.

She had been feeling so good this morning when she left her house. She'd been planning her outfit for weeks — the perfect baggy jeans, lace-up boots, and men's shirt. She'd gone to her mom's friend, a woman who had a hair salon in the front room of her house, who gave her a fantastic weave. A mass of tight curls cascaded down her back, leaving Evvie feeling beautiful for the first time in months.

The weight loss helped. Her mom had put her on her first diet when she was seven, leading up to the auditions for the new TV show *The Perfect Family*. Evvie had been cute and chubby, and her mother, who knew someone in the entertainment business, knew they were looking for someone slight. She put Evvie on a diet of grapes, yogurt, and a tiny bit of steak. Despite being permanently starving, Evvie lost the weight, got the part, and spent the last eleven years on the show, alienated from her regular school friends by her stardom, and isolated, too, by her weight, which yo-yoed up and down. The problem was particularly pronounced during her teenage years. She would gain weight and feel awful about herself, isolating herself at home, watching television and eating; then, as if a switch was flicked, she would wake up one day determined to lose it, knowing that the latest diet would be the key. Sure enough, the weight would drop off, and she would start going out to parties again with friends, making out with boys and feeling like she ruled the world.

Last month, having isolated herself in her grandmother's house, she read about the Cambridge diet in one of her mother's weekly magazines. Within the hour she had ordered it, and she had spent the past four weeks drinking shakes, smoothies, and soups, with a few meal replacement bars.

She had been feeling hungry, but skinny, loving seeing her hip bones emerge, loving that her 501s, once skintight with a muffin roll of fat above the waistline, now hung on her, baggy, slipping down to her hips so often she had to run to Brixton Market to buy a belt.

She had been so excited, had been feeling so great as skinny Evvie emerged, anticipating arriving at West Country University, whereupon she would meet George Michael, who just happened to be filming his new video in Somerset, and he would stop her and tell her she was the most gorgeous woman he had ever seen, and not only would he give her the starring role in his new video, but they would fall in love and live happily ever after.

She had spent so many hours lying in bed working out the precise details of this fantasy, all of which involved meeting George as soon as she arrived, that she found herself scanning the street, surprised not to see him around the corner.

Instead, two small blond girls walked past, their mouths falling open at the trunk, both of them staring at Evvie, sizing her up as she stood there, nervous for the first time, clutching a piece of paper in her hand, trying to figure out if this was the hall of residence, and where the entrance was.

She was aware of the girls staring at her,

and it wasn't staring in a good way. She felt awkward, wishing that she, too, had a friend, or family, or someone with her to help her brave her first day. She felt overwhelmed suddenly at leaving the relative safety of her grandmother's home, by starting again, yet again, somewhere so unfamiliar and new. She was about to turn her back on the girls when she decided to try something else.

"Excuse me," she said to the blondes, holding out the piece of paper with a bright smile. "Am I in the right place and do you know how to get in?"

One girl looked at the paper, while the other continued staring at Evvie as recognition slowly dawned on her.

"Oh my God," she said. "You're American? Hang on, I know you, don't I? Aren't you an actress?"

Evvie blushed ever so slightly. "I did a little bit of acting when I was a kid."

The other girl looked up, an intrigued smile on her face. "No! Are you one of those cute kids in *The Cosby Show*?"

Evvie shook her head. "I always get that. I was in the other show. *The Perfect Family*? I don't know if it even made it to the UK." She was lying when she said that, attempting to play it down, because she knew perfectly well it aired in the UK. Her grandmother used to phone her after every episode to make sure she wouldn't be as naughty in real life as she was on the show.

"I loved that show!" said the first blond girl, peering at her closely. "You were Yolanda, right? Oh my God! What are you doing here?"

"My mom's from London," explained Evvie. "Actually, she's from Jamaica, but they came to London when she was a little girl. She moved to the United States when she met my dad, but they got divorced last year and she moved back here. With me. And now I'm a freshman here." Evvie shrugged, wishing she had shut up. She always said too much when she was nervous.

"We have someone famous at our university!" said one. "Do you need help with that trunk?"

"I would love that," Evvie said as the girls looked over at the crowds of people on the street, many still unloading cars. Other students strolled by on the other side of the road, curious about this year's new students, the boys scanning them for fresh meat.

"Dan!" shouted one of the girls. "Rupert! Get over here and help get this trunk inside. This is Yolanda! From *The Perfect Family*!"

"I'm not Yolanda," Evvie corrected them,

embarrassed. "I'm Evvie. And thank you so much."

Two

- 1986 -

Her room was on the second floor. Dan and Rupert lugged the case up the stairs, down the hallway, and into a big room at the end. There, a large, dark-haired girl was refolding all her clothes and putting them away in the one closet, which she had already marked in half with masking tape.

"You must be Evelyn," she said, friendly, even though she eyed the boys suspiciously. "I'm Victoria Charles. Are these your brothers?"

Evvie almost laughed out loud. How a half-Jamaican, dark-skinned girl from America would have two fair-haired chinless wonders as brothers was beyond her, but she just shook her head.

"This is Dan and Rupert. They just helped me. Guys, thank you so, so much. Can I give you this?" She reached into her pocket and brought out the two-pound bills she had secreted there while the boys were hauling the trunk ahead of her. She had been brought up to always thank by tipping. It was the American way. The boys looked at her proffered money and laughed in disbelief.

"You're joking," said Rupert. "Are you tipping us?"

"I'm just . . . thanking you. You can have a beer on me."

"Done," said Dan, darting forward and taking the money. "Thanks very much! Have a good day!"

That last bit was said in what sounded suspiciously like a bad American accent, and Evvie knew she had done the wrong thing. Fuck. Oh well. How was she supposed to know? The boys left the room, and she heard them laughing all the way down the hall.

"Tipping isn't really the done thing over here," said Victoria, pushing her glasses back on her nose. "I think you may have just offended them."

"Oh no," said Evvie. "That's embarrassing. Fuck. Should I apologize?" She noticed that Victoria winced when she swore, and silently berated herself, taking in, for the first time, her new roommate's neat kilt and tucked-in sweater, her flute resting on the shelf, the sensible shoes lined up in the

28

wardrobe.

This was clearly not going to be a match made in heaven. Evvie had no idea what they could possibly find in common.

"My parents just left, which is such a shame." Victoria rushed in to fill the silence. "They were hoping to meet you, so I'll have to take a photograph of us and send it to them. I have a kettle" — she gestured to a kettle on the desk — "and I brought two mugs. One for you and one for me. Which one would you like?"

Evvie went over and picked up the mugs. One had a cartoon of a fluffy cat surrounded by hearts and read, *Catpuccino*. The other had a different cat and said, *List of People I Love: Cats*.

"I guess you like cats then?" said Evvie, who was much more a dog person herself.

"These are my babies." Victoria picked up a photo of two cats on a bed. "Fluffy and Buttercup. They're the loves of my life."

"Adorable," said Evvie, who had never quite understood what people could possibly find adorable about cats.

"So, which one do you want?" Victoria gestured at the mugs. This was clearly very, very important to her.

"I'll take Catpuccino," said Evvie, wondering who she might have to talk to in order to get her roommate switched.

"That's just what I was hoping." Victoria broke into a big smile. "I hope you don't mind but I have to practice my flute every day for an hour. Luckily for you, I'm rather good."

"There aren't music rooms you can practice in?"

Victoria's face fell. "There are, but not in halls. Is the flute a problem?"

"I'm sure I'll get used to it," Evvie said, praying Victoria was as good as she claimed. "Have you explored the dorms yet? Met any of the other girls?"

"I haven't. I wanted to get my room set up first. Have you?"

"Not yet but I think I might go now. Do you want to come?"

Victoria shook her head. "I'll stay and put up the posters. Look! Aren't they brilliant?" She unrolled pastel-colored illustrations of cats, complete with hearts all around.

"Brilliant!" said Evvie, backing out of the room and escaping down the narrow stairs to the common room.

The common room was very brown, very bare, and empty apart from a girl who was slouched in a chair, her feet up on another chair, watching television and quietly crying as she picked out the large round candy from a big bag and ate them, through her sobs. The first things Evvie noticed were endless bare legs, enviably long and slim, and then, as she stepped forward, a shock of thick, red hair tumbling onto her shoulders, a petite aquiline nose, and red-rimmed eyes.

"Are you okay?" Evvie said, sitting next to the girl, who was clutching sodden tissues in one hand. "Is this a sad TV show?"

"No. It's *Pebble Mill.* The only thing that's sad about it is that I'm actually watching it. My parents just left and I'm feeling homesick. Want one? I only like the round ones."

"What are they?" asked Evvie, reaching in and taking out what looked like a mini cake.

"Liquorice Allsorts, my favorite sweets. Help yourself. I'm sorry." She sniffed, regaining her composure and wiping away the tears. "I didn't mean to weep pathetically in the common room." She looked around to check that no one was listening. "It doesn't help that I've got a roommate I seem to have nothing in common with whatsoever. She's doing a degree in physics, and she's brought her pet iguana with her in a giant bloody cage that stinks to high heaven. I don't know what to do."

"Will she be playing the flute for an hour every night, and decorating the room with

31

pictures of cats? Because that's what I'm contending with."

"Oh God," said the girl, the tears replaced with a smile of disbelief as she sat up. "How in hell do they figure out these pairings? Didn't they ask us to fill out forms with our interests? I don't remember putting scaly creatures anywhere on mine."

"I definitely didn't put cats. I'm pretty sure I put George Michael somewhere on mine. And theater."

The girl's eyes lit up. "Theater? Are you studying drama too?"

"Drama and English."

"Me too!" She paused, a thought taking hold. "Don't you think it would be more sensible if you and I roomed together?"

Evvie broke into a large smile. "I think that would be totally awesome. Who do we have to speak to?"

"Probably the warden. My parents brought a huge box of chocolates for her to introduce themselves, so we're already good friends. Let's go and find her. Have you unpacked yet?"

Evvie shook her head.

"Perfect. We'll get Lizard Lady out of my room and get you in. I've got a huge bay window on the ground floor with a view of the street, so we can look out for handsome boys and invite them in for tea."

"I like the way you think," said Evvie.

"This is clearly meant to be," said the girl, now standing up and extending her hand. "I'm Maggie, by the way."

"Evvie."

"We're going to be best friends, aren't we?" said Maggie. "I can feel it."

"I feel it too," said Evvie, all insecurity and intimidation having disappeared. Now that she had found a friend, there was nothing she couldn't handle, least of all disappointing the dreadful Victoria.

Two hours later, Evvie had moved downstairs, and the lizard lady had moved upstairs with Victoria, who, it turned out, had spent her entire life dreaming of having a bearded dragon. Even though Iggy was clearly not a bearded dragon, she couldn't have been more delighted. When Evvie left her room, Victoria and her new roommate were deep in conversation about lizards the roommate had loved, and how she had looked after them.

Maggie's room was huge, and bright, and she had dragged two brown chairs in from the common room — "Shh. Don't tell anyone" — and placed them in the bay window, looking out at the street so they could indeed see all the handsome boys walking past and, in fact, everyone else.

Her bed was covered in a pretty cornflower-blue bedspread, with matching pillows, and her desk had a set of cornflower-blue stationery, pen holders, and notebooks, everything matching.

"Please tell me you're not always this perfect," Evvie said, worried that in leaving Victoria she may have left the frying pan only to jump into the fire.

"I am definitely not perfect. I just like things to look pretty. But open my wardrobe and you'll see the inner me."

Evvie had marched over to the wardrobe, flung the doors open, and laughed out loud at Maggie's clothes, stuffed into the shelves haphazardly, shoes piled up on shoes, as if Maggie had just thrown them all in there from the other side of the room.

"Did you just toss everything in here?" Evvie asked, standing aside as Maggie pulled off one of her espadrilles and launched it through the air, whereupon it landed in the wardrobe with a clatter.

"Goal!" shouted Maggie. "I wasn't Goal Shooter on the school netball team for nothing. And yes. I did throw everything in there. I couldn't be bothered to move the box from the window."

"I'm liking you more and more," said Evvie as she opened her trunk and started to unpack.

THREE
- 1986 -

Evvie's duvet was not cornflower blue, nor was it Laura Ashley. She had no idea what it was, only that her grandmother had bought it for her, therefore it had sentimental value, even though, next to Maggie's opulent quilted bed, piled high with cushions, her side of the room looked not just drab, but bare. The duvet was tan and orange, which looked terrible with the blue, and she had nothing to decorate the walls.

"This does not look good," said Maggie, surveying the room when Evvie had unpacked. "At least we have the Louis Vuitton trunk, which will make an excellent table." She had nudged it over the thin carpet to sit between the chairs in the bay window, where it did, in fact, make an excellent coffee table. "You know what this room needs? Cushions. And throws. And something for the walls. I think we should have matching beds. My mum bought two of these bedspreads, one for me and one for the guest room, so I'll just get her to send the other bedspread. And the pillowcases. You know there's a Habitat somewhere around here. Let's get the phone book and find out. I think we need to do some shopping."

Evvie paused, embarrassed. Not just that Maggie seemed so mature — she'd never met anyone who knew how to *accessorize* at their age — but that it was quite clear that Maggie's family had money. It wasn't just the quality of her clothes, although they looked expensive; it was her whole air. She acted as if she expected everything to go her way, with a confidence that seemed well beyond her years. Such was her self-possession, Evvie soon learned, that everything did, in fact, seem to go her way.

When Maggie confided in the warden, conspiratorially, that she was allergic to lizards, the warden said she would take care of it immediately. And did. And now Maggie was almost ushering Evvie out the door to spend what was likely to be serious money at Habitat, except Evvie didn't have serious money.

What she had made during her time as a child star was locked up in a trust, and without child support and alimony, her mother was working as hard as she could to put Evvie through college. There was no extra cash for frivolities like cushions and framed pictures for the wall. She thought of her father, who, now that he had divorced her mother, had been welcomed back into the bosom of his family. She thought of how much she had loved him when she was a little girl, how she thought he would always be her protector, her savior, and how he had abandoned her in every way possible. She fought the mix of tears and resentment that threatened to wash over her.

Maggie paused, noting Evvie's expression, presuming it was just about the money. "Look!" She reached into her back pocket and pulled out a credit card. "From my father. To be used for emergencies, and this room is definitely an emergency."

"I can't believe you're describing my duvet as an emergency." Evvie regained her composure and smiled.

"Is it a duvet you've had since you were a baby?"

"No. My grandmother bought it for me to bring to college."

"Would you ever, in a million years, have picked that duvet out for yourself?"

"Maybe not." Evvie started to laugh. "Okay. It's as ugly as sin. Let's go. As long as it's not expensive, I'm in. I would pay if I could, but I'm on a strict budget. My money's tied up in a trust. I don't have access to it until I'm twenty-one. I think my mom was terrified I'd turn into one of those child star horror stories and blow all my earnings on cocaine and champagne. I think she's regretting it now but my dad's one of the trustees and he won't break it."

"She sounds very sensible. Don't worry about it. My dad will be fine if I put it on the credit card. And now I want to hear more about you being a child star."

By the time the girls figured out transportation to Bath and reached Habitat, their life stories had spilled out. Maggie had, it seemed, come from the diametric opposite of Evvie's life in every possible way. She had been raised by the perfect parents, and as the only girl, was adored by her father. Her older brothers excelled in everything they ever touched, and Maggie wanted nothing more than to get married and have a life just like her parents'.

"Will you work?" asked Evvie.

"Not unless I'm forced." Maggie grimaced.

She had a plan, one that seemed to Evvie to be shockingly old-fashioned. But who was Evvie to point out that times had changed, and a woman was prime minister (even if, as her grandmother often said, there wasn't anything very womanly about Maggie Thatcher), and weren't they supposed to be having careers and taking over the world?

Maggie's plan? To attend university, and to work for a few years in something like PR or marketing, before finding a husband and settling down. She wanted a large country house, at least four children, and two Labrador retrievers, and friends dropping in all the time. She wanted, in short, a life just like the one she had had as a child in Sussex. "And why wouldn't I?" she said when Evvie pointed that out. "It was completely idyllic."

Her mother was a wonderful cook who welcomed her father home from work every evening with a gourmet meal. Maggie and her three brothers had dinner with their parents nightly, a boisterous affair that usually saw them sitting at the table chatting about everything, long into the evening. Maggie and her mother would clear the table after dinner, leaving her father and brothers to have some "boy time."

Her parents were happy, and loving, and a world away from Evvie's. Maggie's upbringing had consisted of horses, gymkhanas, and dogs, graduating to parties thrown by young farmers' organizations that ended with various apple-cheeked girls snogging drunken well-heeled young men on hay bales in barns from Cornwall to Scotland. During the sixth form there were balls, which drew from public schools across the country. Maggie had a selection of silk taffeta ball gowns and had even — oh the joy! — appeared in the society pages of *Tatler* magazine, a magazine Evvie had never heard of.

Evvie told Maggie about her own family, about her street-smart, elegant, beautiful mother who had been brought up first in Kingston, Jamaica, before emigrating to London and meeting Evvie's Waspy, preppy white father while on vacation in New York. She got pregnant, had stayed. Even though they were cut off from her father's wealthy family, he had a series of jobs, one after another. He had been doing fine until his drinking got out of control and he'd been "let go," only for his family name to open yet another door at yet another banking firm.

She didn't tell Maggie about the rages. She didn't tell her what it was like when she was a child, to hear her father come in late, slamming the door. Or what it was like to hear her mother chiding him while Evvie lay in bed, knowing that something terrible would happen, for however loving and affectionate her father was when sober, when he drank, something changed, and a temper emerged. She'd seen it lead to him losing so many of the people he loved — including, eventually, Evvie and her mother.

He was always contrite the next day — when sober. Sometimes Evvie would come downstairs and find her father on his knees, sobbing, clutching her mother's legs as he begged for forgiveness. She always forgave him, and Evvie prayed it wouldn't happen again.

But one day, he hurt her mother so badly, she stopped forgiving him. She had had enough. There was no room for begging, for forgiveness. They were on a plane, Evvie's mother's lips pressed tightly shut the entire journey so no one would see the missing teeth that had flown out when he hit her in the mouth. Evvie told Maggie none of this.

Instead she told her about being "half-caste," how she grew up in Brooklyn, going to a privileged performing arts school that was totally mixed, where none of the kids focused on whether they were black or white. And then moving to Stockwell, where her grandmother's community was entirely black, and her light skin made it both easier, and harder, to know where to fit in. Evvie felt Jamaican, American, and English. She liked ackee and saltfish for breakfast, and roast beef and Yorkshire pudding for dinner, and as much as she adored her mother, she was terrified of getting on her bad side.

"So where *do* you fit in?" said Maggie.

"Wherever I feel at home," Evvie said simply.

Habitat was empty. They wandered around the ground floor for a while, lusting after furniture and fantasizing about the kinds of houses they would have when they finally left college, before heading upstairs to the bedding department.

Wandering past the futons, they came upon a bedroom set in a bright sunshine yellow. And there, in the middle of an enormous king-sized bed, was a good-looking young man, his oxfords off and placed neatly together by the side of the bed, his legs crossed comfortably as he lay against the pillows, engrossed in a copy of Nancy Mitford's *The Pursuit of Love,* with a worn and well-loved teddy bear tucked under one arm.

"Are you serious?" Evvie held Maggie back, whispering as she pointed him out. "Is that a mannequin?"

"No. I don't think so. I think he's real." Maggie stepped toward the bed, quietly. "I think I saw his eyes move."

"His eyes are now closing," said the mannequin boy on the bed, putting the book down and closing his eyes, before opening them immediately and grinning at them. "Hello. Can I help you?"

"You're American!" said Evvie in delight.

His face fell. "Can you tell? Damn. I've been working on my English accent for months. I'm attempting to channel Sebastian Flyte, but clearly it's not working."

"The teddy bear is an excellent touch."

"Don't you think?" said the boy, propping himself up against the pillows before looking at Evvie. "Speaking of Americans, you're American. Who are you and where are you from?"

"Evvie Thompson, originally from New York, although more recently from Stockwell in London, via Brooklyn. It's complicated."

"Evvie Thompson?" He squinted at her. "You look very familiar. Is that your real name?"

"It's my mom's name. When I was a child I was Evvie Hamilton."

"I knew it! I knew I recognized you. You

were Yolanda Campbell on *The Perfect Family.*"

"How do you remember that?"

"I'm going to be an actor. It's my job to study actors and actresses. I know everything about acting, and movies. Go on. Test me."

"Quote from *The Breakfast Club.*"

" 'You ought to spend a little more time trying to make something of yourself and a little less time trying to impress people.' "

"Nice."

"Too easy," he said, pouting. "Try something harder."

"What's the name of Rosanna Arquette's character in *Desperately Seeking Susan?*"

"Roberta. Come on, girls, you can do better."

Maggie shrugged. "I'm not a big film person." She peered at him closely. "So why are you here? Are you at the university?"

"Yes. I just arrived. My parents are living over here for my father's work. He's in oil. I got here this morning to find I'm stuck on a floor with a bunch of rugby players, and my roommate is playing Led Zeppelin at high volume as he installs a series of bongs on his desk. It's hell."

"So, you decided to move into Habitat instead?" Maggie ventured.

45

"Only temporarily, sadly. I wanted to find somewhere peaceful to read, and you have to admit, this room setup is rather wonderful."

"You look like you have good taste. We're trying to do up our room. Want to help us choose pillows and throws?" Evvie had warmed to this boy immediately.

He grinned, reaching for his shoes. "Shopping is my middle name. I'm Topher."

FOUR

- 1986 -

Topher pushed the thick wedge of Welsh Rarebit around his plate with a frown, before sliding the plate away.

"I just can't," he said. "I know it's delicious but it's all so unhealthy. I tried the fruit salad yesterday thinking it would be good, but it was swimming in some kind of syrup."

Maggie grinned through a mouthful of cheese, bread, and Worcestershire sauce. "It's worth it. These breakfasts are yummy."

Evvie had already finished her slice of Welsh Rarebit, which was one slice of thick white bread with melted cheese and Worcestershire sauce grilled to perfection, with the added sin of a fried egg dripping in butter on top. It hadn't been long, but already her jeans were less baggy, and she knew she'd have to stop soon. At home, she had always helped her grandmother make breakfast every day — saltfish fritters, johnnycakes, ackee. She'd never experienced the full English breakfast, and she couldn't stop eating. It wasn't as if she could afford the freshman fifteen. Who knew when it might stop? Given her predilection for compulsive eating, a freshman fifteen could very easily become a freshman twenty-five, or worse.

She looked at her empty plate, feeling shame. She had wolfed the food down, not even tasting it, and she had been contemplating going back for more. She pushed the plate away and sat back. "I'm so full," she lied. "I can't believe I ate that much."

"Maggie? Want mine?" Topher moved his plate over to Maggie, who gratefully took it. It wasn't fair, thought Evvie. Even though it had only been a couple of weeks, Evvie saw how much Maggie ate, and yet she remained as slim as a reed. She was one of those natural athletes who thought nothing of going for a run to let off some excess energy. Maggie had said her whole family had ridiculous metabolisms; they all ate like horses and all stayed slim. Evvie, on the other hand, could easily gain five pounds just thinking about a wedge of chocolate cake.

She could feel that the switch, the switch that had to flick on in order for her to have enough self-control to diet, was slipping back. And it didn't help that Maggie always had cookies in their room. Maggie kept them just in case she felt an urge, but once Evvie discovered chocolate Hobnobs, there was no going back. They'd whisper to her from Maggie's desk drawer, and before she could even think about it, she would wolf down three, and then make herself go out so she wouldn't eat any more.

"I think we should go to Chez Jacques tonight." Topher sipped his coffee. "Apparently the food is decent. I can run in on my way to class and book a table."

Evvie blanched. She felt completely at home with Maggie and Topher, who seemed to be an almost permanent fixture in their room already, so much so that he had grabbed another chair from the common room so the three of them could sit in the bay window sipping hot chocolate and watching the world go by, gossiping about everyone. But why did the two people whom she had chosen as best friends seem to have such expensive tastes? She had to get a job, and fast.

"We can't tonight," Evvie said, relieved as she remembered their prior commitment, one that wouldn't cost nearly as much as the fanciest French restaurant in town. "It's the fresher bad-taste pub crawl, remember?"

"Oh God," Topher groaned. "The one where we're supposed to go with our residence halls? I can't go with those rugby players."

"So come with us. You've practically moved in anyway and all the girls love you. Especially Naomi." Maggie grinned. "She's desperate to lure you into her room." Naomi was a pretty Londoner who had one of the rare single rooms, tucked away under the eaves and accessed by her own staircase.

"Oh, Naomi. So pretty, and so precious, but she freaks me out." He shuddered. "Every time she sees me, she strokes my back. I can't bear it."

Evvie frowned at him. "Why not? That's sweet."

"I don't like being touched by people I don't know."

Maggie started to laugh. "You don't like being touched by people you do know. I tried to hug you the other day and you cringed!"

"I said I was sorry at the time. Don't take it personally. I'm just . . . weird about being touched."

"What is your type, anyway?" asked Evvie, who was convinced Topher was gay, but didn't feel that was something she could ask. What straight man channeled Sebastian

Flyte, complete with teddy bear? And what straight man flinched when a woman touched him? It wasn't just that; it was that he didn't seem to exude any sexual energy. But, as Maggie pointed out, it could be that he was undecided. Or bi. Or even perhaps asexual, which she had decided was the likeliest. "I think he just likes beautiful things, and beautiful people, which is why he loves you."

"I'm hardly the beautiful one," Evvie had pointed out. "It's you." Maggie was who she would like to look like if she came back in another life. But Maggie had simply snorted, so used to having been called Pippi Longstocking for most of her life, she was entirely unaware of the beauty that was emerging.

But Evvie was beautiful, too, with her café au lait skin and perfect pout, her almond-shaped blue eyes — the Hamilton gene — startling in that face. When Evvie had asked Topher his type, he just shrugged and said he didn't have one, or if he did, he hadn't figured it out yet. Maggie had given Evvie a knowing look.

And so it was agreed, Topher would join the girls' hall of residence pub crawl, starting at the King's Head that evening at eight.

"What the hell are we supposed to go as

tonight?" asked Evvie. "I hate costume things. So much pressure."

"Whatever it is," Topher mused, "we'd better decide quickly. We have about three hours to get to the thrift shop to put some costumes together."

"What are you going as?" Evvie asked him.

"I'm going to be a drunk. I bought three cans of mushy peas to pour down my shirt."

Maggie yelped with laughter. "What can I do?"

"Is there anything you hate eating?"

She paused, thinking. "I hate Marmite."

"It's a bit lame but we could make a big Marmite label for you."

"I've got it!" said Evvie. "I need pillowcases and black dye. I'm going as a pregnant nun."

The pub was packed, all the girls from Jekyll Hall and all the boys from their neighboring Coleridge Hall jammed into all three rooms in bad-taste costumes ranging from boys in suits dressed as real estate agents to a couple of pedophiles complete with greasy side parts, fake mustaches, and bags of lollipops.

Everyone was drinking pints of snakebite — lager and hard cider, sometimes with a drop of Ribena — or shots of tequila and vodka. Everyone was chattering, eyeing up the opposite sex, flirting, and getting ready for the next eight pubs. Not all would make it. Some would stagger back to their dorms, others would throw up in the street, others still would collapse in shop doorways. A handful would leave partway through, bored by the drunken behavior, and make their way back to their dorms, where they would drink tea with friends and wonder if they'd made a terrible mistake in choosing West Country when they could have gone to Manchester, Edinburgh, or Durham.

Evvie shouldered her way through the crowds standing in front of the bar. She was almost five feet ten inches in bare feet, and with heels, as she wore today (although why she chose to wear heels for a pub crawl, she would never know), she was over six feet. She liked being tall when she was slim. When she was heavy, she hated it, felt like an Amazon. But despite her jeans getting tighter, she was still feeling good as she squeezed her way through the crowds. She caught the eye of the man behind the bar and held it as she stepped toward him, proffering a five-pound note.

"Three shots of tequila please." She smiled at him, expecting him to smile back, but he scowled as he gave the faintest of nods.

"Busy here tonight, isn't it," she said, attempting conversation as he poured the drinks, but he didn't say anything.

"It looks like you could do with an extra bartender," she said, realizing that this might be the perfect job for her, the way for her to keep up with Maggie and Topher, and there was no shame in getting a job in the best pub in town. She could also, surely, keep her friends in free drinks.

The man gestured to the other room. "If you want a job, speak to Steve. He's in there."

Evvie took the drinks and gave him the money, holding her hand out for change. Usually, she would have slipped the bartender a thank-you, but not this time.

"A smile really wouldn't hurt," she said, keeping her voice light as she put the change in her pocket and gathered the glasses. "Have a great day."

FIVE
- 1986 -

"I can't stand him," said Evvie, carefully applying eyeliner as she got ready to go to her shift at the King's Head. "I don't know what I've done to him but he's just awful to me."

"I think he's sexy." Maggie grinned, pausing from singing the lyrics to a Prefab Sprout song on the cassette player.

Evvie whirled around. "You're kidding, right?"

Maggie winced. "I'm sorry. I'm happy to slightly hate him on your behalf because he's not very nice to you, but I think he's really sexy."

Evvie shook her head. "Oh my God. We are talking about Evil Ben, right? The most evil bartender ever? The guy who basically spends his life scowling?"

"I've seen him smile and it's adorable. He has these dimples that come out, and he looks like a completely different person when he smiles. I bet he's really nice when you get to know him."

"Smile? He smiles? When have you seen him smile? Oh, that's right. When he's not talking to me." Evvie sighed. "It's just me then, isn't it? He truly hates me. He's smiley with you, and he hates me. Great."

"He wasn't smiley with me. I'm much too scared to talk to him. I saw him with a bunch of professors, and he was smiley with them. I think he probably just hates all the freshers. And honestly, can you blame him?"

"Yes, I can blame him. What's wrong with freshers?"

"You know he's a postgrad student, right? He's doing some two-year program here, and he's probably just jaded. The fact that he has to work as a bartender and deal with kids is probably what puts him in a bad mood. He can't tell who's a dick and who's not, so maybe he's just horrible to all the first years. Maybe that's why I think he's sexy," Maggie mused, almost to herself. "There's something about him that I just find really compelling."

Evvie put her hands on her hips. "Objectively, even though I find his widow's peak hairline distinctive rather than sexy, he is definitely built. He has serious muscles, which is probably why Steve keeps him on

56

the job, because no one will cause problems in the pub as long as he's there. But, Maggie, honestly? I don't get how you find him sexy. He's just super unfriendly, and I have no idea why."

"He probably fancies you. That's why. I wish he'd notice me."

Evvie looked Maggie up and down. As beautiful as she was, the boys didn't seem to be attracted to her in the same way they often were to Evvie. There was something tomboyish about Maggie, a fact she attributed to growing up with three brothers. She was more likely to down pints in a drinking competition with the boys, and had absolutely no idea how to flirt.

"You don't want him to notice you. What if you fell in love and then he disappeared off to a job? Find yourself someone your own age. As to whether he fancies me, absolutely no way. On the very rare occasions he deigns to look at me, the only thing I see in his eyes is disdain. Urgh. I swear, I don't even want this fucking job anymore because of him. I went into the Golden Lion yesterday and they may need someone. They're letting me know tomorrow."

"I think you're wrong. He fancies you. Why don't you ask him if there's something you've done?"

"Because he doesn't talk to me. But maybe I will. Maybe if I get this job at the Golden Lion I'll ask him, and maybe I'll tell him what I really think of him."

"Can you also tell him your best friend thinks he's sexy and he should really take her out for dinner?" Maggie grinned, stretching out her foot suggestively, having just painted her toenails a sparkly gold.

"No. I will not allow it. If you're going to date anyone, it has to be someone we all love. Especially me."

"He wouldn't look at me anyway."

"You're not serious about really fancying him, are you?"

"I'm so sorry." Maggie made a face. "I think I have a thing for difficult men. It's really weird because my dad is so friendly and nice. Everyone loves him, but I go into this weird thing with men that are grumpy where I have to try to charm them and make them love me."

Evvie started to laugh. "That is weird."

"I know. When I was at school I was madly in love with this guy who everybody hated because he was an asshole, especially with girls. I just kept thinking that underneath there had to be this good guy who was covering up and that, duh, I would be the one to bring out the goodness and make him change."

"Of course you would think that! So, did you ever date him?"

"Kind of. We went out briefly, and I realized that if he was covering something up, he was doing a really good job, and I had no idea what it was. He dumped me after three weeks for Isabel van Dolen, this gorgeous blond Dutch girl who had just arrived in the sixth form halfway through the school year."

"So he was an asshole after all?"

"Yup. So I have awful taste in boys, which means that if I think Evil Ben is sexy, which I do, then he's probably just as evil as you think he is. I'm a terrible judge of people."

"Not all people. You knew immediately that we were going to be friends. Topher too."

"You're right. Thank you. That makes me feel better. I still think Evil Ben's rude because he likes you. Good luck. Maybe he'll reveal his true feelings for you tonight."

"Oh, ha ha." Evvie slipped her arms into her jacket and grabbed her purse. "Swing by later with Topher. I'll definitely get you drinks on the house." And with a wave, she was gone.

Six

It was ten o'clock when the group of rugby players came in. Evvie heard the noise outside the pub, and immediately went on high alert, which was what you did when you grew up in Brooklyn in the seventies and eighties.

She hadn't seen them before, this group of boys. They were clearly students, but older than first years, all enormous, and, it seemed, well into their pub crawl. They walked in singing loudly, arms around one another, as Evvie stepped back from the bar. Drunk men made her nervous, made her regress to being a scared child, waiting for something awful to happen.

She looked across the room to where Maggie and Topher were, tucked into a corner table with a couple of other girls from their hall. Maggie was looking at the boys and slightly shaking her head. She rolled her eyes and went back to her conversation. They would be safe, they weren't the target, merely other patrons, but Evvie, as the only bartender on this side of the bar, felt the danger, knew that if anything went wrong, it would be directed at her. She steeled herself as they broke into a raucous song.

It sounded like a rugby song, something about how they used to work in an old department store in Chicago, which led to chickens, which led, inevitably, to something about cocks. Evvie tensed.

They jeered and cheered, staggering in, the biggest one in the front pausing by a table on the side, where two older men sat quietly having a drink. They were locals who usually came in early during the week before getting back home for dinner, but tonight, a Saturday, they had been in with their wives, who had just left. The men were finishing up their pints before heading home.

The big student knocked the cap off one of the men, then leaned down, picked up his pint, and drained it, banging it back on the table. Everyone in the pub held their breath, but nobody said anything. The local man wouldn't meet his eye, just stood up. When the student pushed his body into him, the old man stopped for a few seconds, looking at the carpet, then walked out as the rest of the boys laughed.

Evvie took a deep breath and told herself not to be scared. This wasn't her father, about to have a fight with her mother, a fight that may or may not end in something violent. These were strangers, and they were boys, and they couldn't hurt her. But her thoughts didn't stop her heart from beating fast, the anxiety making her breath quick and shallow, a buzzing in her ears.

"Who's this then?" One of them walked up to the bar, then leaned down and sniffed. "Mmm. Fresh meat. I smell fresh meat." He turned to his friends, who all laughed before he turned back to Evvie. "Eight pints of lager and a serving of snatch."

Evvie pretended not to hear the last bit. She walked down to the other end of the bar for the pint glasses, aware that her heart was pounding.

"Oi, Whitney," he yelled. "I'll be your greatest love of all if you'll let me."

Evvie forced a small smile, as if she hadn't heard this a million times before, especially since she moved to England, where every other person seemed to think she was a dead ringer for Whitney Houston.

"Bring those beers over to us, will you." He leered as Evvie's heart sank. At least behind the bar she had some protection.

"I can't leave the bar," she said. "Boss's orders."

"What?" He leaned forward. "I don't understand you. Say it again."

"I said, I can't leave the bar. Here." She pushed the drinks toward him. "You can take them with you."

"Don't tell me what to do. I'm telling you what to do. My friends and I will be at that table, and you will be bringing us our beer. Got it?"

"I'm sorry," Evvie said, hoping her voice sounded stronger than it felt. "I can't do that." She knew that if she walked out, in her miniskirt and Converse sneakers, there would be hell to pay. At best, it would lead to lewd comments. At worst, there would be groping involved.

The student pushed himself up on his hands and lurched toward her, almost over the bar, as Evvie stepped back, now frightened.

"Leave her alone." Suddenly, Maggie was standing next to the goon in all her imperious, angry, redheaded glory.

"Well, hell-o, ginger. What have we here?" the big one slurred, as his friends laughed.

"How dare you just walk in here and steal someone's drink? And now you're sexually and racially harassing my friend. Leave her alone. I suggest you leave right now."

Evvie was impressed by Maggie's bravery, even while knowing how stupid it was for her to step forward. Maggie had no idea that she was now in the real world, no longer in the protective bubble of her perfect family. She had no idea that people didn't always do the right thing, that girls like her weren't necessarily respected or listened to.

"What the fuck do you know about it, pasty?" said the big one as his friends cheered him on.

"Fuck, she's ugly," another one shouted out. "Don't even bother talking to her, mate. You might catch something nasty."

Maggie turned bright red, but she didn't back down. "What are your names?" she said.

"Fucking *minger*!" someone shouted from the back of the gang as they all laughed.

"What does that mean?" Topher, who had also come up to the bar, whispered to Evvie.

"I'm not sure but I think it means ugly."

Topher stepped up. "Leave her alone. There's no need to insult her. And she's right, you shouldn't have stolen that man's drink, and you definitely shouldn't be threatening the female bartender. You're all drunk. You need to go home before we call the police."

The rugby players paused, their faces lighting up. "Well, well. This just gets better, doesn't it," said the leader. "Not only is he a nonce, he's a bleedin' American one as well." At that, the big drunk one stepped right up to Topher and got in his face, intimidating him with a glare before using his body to push him against the wall.

Topher flinched, but only for a second before regaining his composure and sighing. "God, this is all very tiresome. Do you want to just hit me? It's totally fine if you do, because I will file an assault report with the police immediately. Not only that, I will also bring a civil case against you. I hope Mummy and Daddy have money, because we Americans love nothing more than a court case. We *love* suing people, it's like a national pastime with us, and I have enough money and power to wipe the floor with your entire family. So go on. Please. Do us all a favor and hit me." He turned a cheek. "How about this one?"

The rugby players were faltering, the ringleader not knowing how much of what Topher had just said was true. One thing was certain, Topher wasn't scared, and they weren't used to people not being scared.

"Not the left side? I understand. It's actually not my best side anyway. Give me a good blow on the right side. I'm very delicate. I'll almost certainly have a huge black eye within minutes, and the police will definitely want it to look as bad as possible. I have high cheekbones, so if you can break one, that would be great. It makes for a much better story in the press." Topher craned his neck as the rugby player stood, seemingly trying to figure out what to do next without screwing himself over one way or the other.

"You fucking pansy," he said eventually, putting his fists down. "You're not worth my time. I might catch something nasty."

"He's probably got AIDS," called one of his mates as both Evvie and Maggie took a sharp intake of breath.

"You know you can catch AIDS by having someone infected breathe on you," said Topher. "You didn't know that? Oh my God, how close were you standing to me?"

"What the fuck is going on in here?"

The crowd parted as Evil Ben walked into the room from next door, going straight up to the ringleader. "Pete Jesperson, isn't it? What are you up to?"

Suddenly the ringleader glanced away, embarrassed, as Evil Ben looked around at them. "Damien Scanlon. Oliver Franklin.

66

Ryan McDonald." The rugby players seemed to shrink in front of their eyes, mumbling and looking at the ground.

"You know who I am, and you know that your coach is one of my best mates. I'm going to phone him tonight and tell him exactly what I've seen here. First of all, I want an apology to these freshers. Secondly, I want you to pony up some money so I can pay back my regular who you stole a drink from. I don't ever want to see or hear of any of this kind of behavior again. You're all leaving right now and going back home. Is that understood?"

The boys mumbled, and nodded.

Pete didn't meet any of them in the eye, but he handed Ben a fiver and then glanced at Topher with a mumble under his breath. "Really sorry I was rude."

"You weren't just rude," said Ben. "You need to apologize for being a real asshole."

"Really sorry I was an asshole," muttered Pete.

"And to Evvie." Maggie stepped forward. "They were all sexually and racially offensive to her."

"I'm really sorry I was sexually and racially offensive," the big one said, not meeting Evvie's eye.

"And to me," said Maggie.

"Really sorry we called you a minger."

Evil Ben shook his head in disgust. "Go on. Get out of here."

The boys left, and the entire pub exhaled in relief, the whole place having been holding its breath since the moment they walked in.

"Are you all okay?" Evil Ben looked at Evvie, then at Maggie and Topher.

"Oh my God, thank you so much," said Maggie. "My heart's still beating like a lunatic. I got really scared for a minute there. I don't know if they would have backed down, although, Topher, you were amazing."

"I need a drink," said Topher, not looking quite so brave now that it was all over. He held out his hand, which was shaking like a leaf, his face as white as a sheet.

"Are you okay?" Maggie asked.

"I just . . . That was frightening. When he pushed me I was . . ." He blinked back tears, and Maggie shot a look at Evvie, unsure what to do.

"Do you need a hug?" asked Evvie.

Topher shook his head, taking a deep breath that seemed to help him recover not only his composure, but his humor. "I swear to God." His voice was a little less shaky. "I would have fucking killed them if they'd broken my cheekbone. Thank God I'm studying theater, is all I can say. I think I deserve an Oscar for that particular performance."

"What about you?" Evil Ben looked at Evvie. "You all right? You should have come to get me as soon as they came in."

I should have, thought Evvie, even though Evil Ben was the absolute last person she would ever turn to for help.

"I'm sorry," she said. "And thank you."

"It's my job," he said, turning to leave, without so much as a smile. Evvie looked at Maggie, who seemed sad as they watched him go back into the other room.

"He hates me," said Evvie. "And you know what? We didn't even need him. Topher, you were amazing and they were already backing off. I'm not giving that asshole Evil Ben a second of the glory here. This was you, Topher. All you."

"Mostly me," Topher said. "Although I have to be really honest. I didn't get what Maggie was talking about before, but . . ." He shrugged regretfully. "That Ben is sexy. He's not very friendly, but he's got that whole taking-care-of-you thing going on."

"He did not take care of us. *You* took care of us."

"I don't know. I felt safe as soon as he appeared," Topher said.

"I know, right?" Maggie's eyes were alight. "I think I may love him. He's our knight in shining armor. And I think he may be my perfect man."

"Oh for God's sake." Evvie shook her head. "That's just because you've got brothers and you like being taken care of. You're both ridiculous. And I don't want to work here anymore. If the Golden Lion can't take me, I'll find something else. I can't stand him, and I don't want to be in the same room as him ever again."

Seven

- 1986 -

"We've brought you both something! Charlie, run out to the car and get the bags, will you?"

Maggie's mother was tall and jolly. She must have looked just like Maggie when young, and had matured into a handsome, strong woman, her face makeup-free and full of character, weathered from the outdoorsy life. She hadn't met Evvie before, but as soon as she walked into the room, she gave her a big hug as if she had known her all her life.

"It's so great to meet you, Mrs. Hallwell," said Evvie.

"You can call me Mrs. H.," she said. "That's what Maggie's school friends have always called me."

Maggie's father then seized Evvie by the shoulders and kissed her on each cheek, Maggie's younger brother Charlie flashing her a big grin as he shook her hand.

Maggie was beside herself with joy at her parents visiting, meeting her friends and seeing her new life, and Evvie felt a pang. Her own mother hadn't been there, and didn't seem all that interested in coming. Evvie knew she loved her, that she was hugely proud of her daughter being in college, but she was just so busy with her own life now.

Charlie came back in with a large bag, which Mrs. H. took, pulling out two identically wrapped parcels, throwing one to Maggie and the other to Evvie. Inside were soft plaid pajamas, a pair of Swiss slipper socks with leather soles, a huge bag of Liquorice Allsorts, and a small teddy bear.

"I know the teddy bears are silly," said Mrs. H. "And you two are far too grown-up for toys, but I couldn't resist. And, Evvie, I have no idea whether you've been brought around to Liquorice Allsorts — personally, I can't stand them — but I took a chance."

"I'm not as addicted as Maggie but I love them. Thank you. And now" — she looked at Maggie — "I can finally get to eat the round ones!"

"Enjoy them while you can. Mummy! These are amazing!" Maggie pulled the slipper socks on immediately. "I love them!"

Evvie felt tears stinging her eyes. She

didn't know what to say, unused to such generosity from anyone, let alone strangers.

"Thank you so much," she said, blinking back the tears. "This is the nicest thing anyone's ever done for me."

"I'm sure that's not true," said Mrs. H., who looked surprised but delighted when Evvie immediately gave the teddy bear pride of place, propping him on her pillow.

"So what's the plan, Pa?" Maggie flopped down on her bed, raising her legs to admire her new slippers. "Do you want a tour of the university before a very expensive lunch at the Dinham Arms?"

"We'd love a tour, and we've booked a table. We thought perhaps we could all go for a nice long walk before lunch. There's meant to be some lovely walking trails around here. Evvie, you're welcome to join us."

"Evvie won't join us," Maggie said. "She's allergic to exercise."

"Maggie!" Evvie berated her, although it was true. "I like to walk."

Maggie raised an eyebrow. "How long is the trail, darling Pa? Four miles? Six?"

"Six point six eight," he said as Maggie shot Evvie a knowing look.

"Okay. Point taken. That's not a walk, that's almost a marathon. I'm out. Anyway,

I've got a ton of homework to do."

"Liar," said Maggie, and they both laughed.

"Look." Maggie's mother drew a map out of her bag, unfolding it on Maggie's bed to show her. "We've got your hiking boots in the car and there are some lovely hills on the walk. We'll all work up an appetite!"

"Will you meet us at the Dinham Arms?" Maggie looked at Evvie hopefully. "Go on. It's meant to be the most delicious food ever."

"You're absolutely welcome," said Mr. Hallwell. "It would be our pleasure."

"If I get my essay written, I would love to."

Maggie took her parents on a tour of the campus, then a quick drive through town to show off their favorite coffee bars before they all headed to a car park a couple of miles outside of town. They pulled on their hiking boots, looping their arms into backpacks filled with water bottles, maps, binoculars, and packets of chocolate digestives just in case anyone got hungry, and off they went, through the gate marked Long-Distance Footpath.

They started off at a clip, Maggie's father, Ted, and brother ahead, she and her mother striding behind, chatting as they walked until they went uphill and their breathing became more labored.

Down through a huge meadow, with views of the Iron Age hill fort of Barbury Castle in the distance, they kept going until they spotted a couple of benches at the top of another hill, strategically placed to catch one's breath and enjoy the view. There was another hiker there, drinking tea out of a thermos, looking out at the view.

"Morning!" bellowed her father cheerfully, the first to reach the bench. "Lovely day for a walk!" He slipped off his backpack and opened it to get out his own water bottle as the other hiker turned to him with a nod, before catching Maggie's eye.

"Evil Ben," she whispered in horror, and her mother turned to her.

"What was that, darling?"

"Nothing." Maggie turned beet red as her father immediately engaged Evil Ben in a conversation about the best walks in the area.

"Do you know my daughter, Maggie?" she heard her father say. "She's a first year here. Maggie? Come and meet Ben!"

"Hi." Maggie shuffled forward, wishing her blush would go down.

"We know each other, don't we?" said

Ben. "The King's Head, right?"

"Right," said Maggie, flashing him what she hoped he would read as a warning look. The last thing she wanted was her parents knowing about the other night, and how she had been treated. "I didn't know you were a hiker," she said lamely, hoping to change the subject.

"My whole life," said Ben. "I walk when I need to clear my head."

"Nothing like it," agreed Ted. "Our Maggie's a huge walker. If you ever need company, she'll join you."

"Dad!" Maggie burst out, wishing he would keep quiet.

"What? It's true!"

"I'll definitely bear that in mind." Ben laughed, before looking at Maggie a few seconds longer than was altogether comfortable. Maggie blushed again as Ben smiled to himself and Maggie's mother nudged her.

Ben passed his thermos over to Ted. "It's Irish coffee." He grinned. "It's excellent to keep the chill out."

"Well thank you," Ted said, taking the thermos, then reaching into his pocket and pulling out Liquorice Allsorts, proffering them as Ben leaned forward to take two round ones. "My daughter and I share a not-so-secret love for them. Good job you took a round one. That's usually reserved for her." He winked at Ben as Maggie inwardly groaned. "It's a bit early for me," Ted said, looking at the thermos in his hand before letting out an easy shrug and a grin. "But why not? It's the weekend. Cheers!" He took a swig, nodding with pleasure as it slipped down smoothly. "Delicious. I wish I'd had it when we climbed Ben Nevis."

"I did have it when I climbed Ben." Ben laughed as Maggie's father's face lit up.

"You did it too? Wasn't it marvelous climbing the highest mountain in the British Isles? Young thing like you probably took no time at all. We took five hours, didn't we, Kathy?"

"That's pretty good," said Ben. "I did it in ten!"

"Ten? Aha. You didn't do the easy walk, did you? You must have done that ridge climb." Ben nodded as Ted smiled. "I wanted to do it but those days have long gone."

"It was hard, and I'm pretty fit, but it was worth it. Spectacular views from the north face. Bloody freezing at the peak though. That's where I learned about the Irish coffee!"

Ted was clearly delighted at having found a kindred spirit. "We had hailstones at about three miles. You too?"

Ben nodded. "And terrible ice as we got higher. It looked like snow but it was packed ice. I've never been so cold in my life. It's a miracle I finished it."

"I remember that weather. Awful. The wife and I want to go trekking in the Himalayas next. Ever been?"

"Not yet, but it's on my list." Ben stood then, tucking his thermos away. "I'd better get on." He shook hands with Maggie's parents and Charlie before nodding at Maggie. "It was lovely to meet you all. I hope you have a great weekend and a wonderful time when you make it to the Himalayas."

"The pleasure was all mine," said Ted truthfully. "I hope we see you again. You never know, we might run into you in Nepal."

"I hope so." Ben smiled. "Nice to see you, Maggie." He reached out and rubbed her back lightly, a gesture that felt intimate and solicitous; a gesture that was so gentle, so unexpected, it made Maggie's heart lurch ever so slightly as she stood, stunned. Who knew Ben had this soft side, not to mention that Ben and her father would have so much in common? It was a disquieting feeling, which only served to heighten her crush.

"What a lovely chap!" Ted said when Ben

78

was — thankfully — out of earshot. "That's the sort of fellow I'd like to see you with. Clever as well, bringing that Irish coffee along. I'll have to do that next time."

"He was rather handsome," said her mum. "And ever so charming." She looked at Maggie. "I think he might like you."

"Don't be daft," said Maggie, scuffing the ground with her foot and looking down so her mother wouldn't see how her heart had jumped at the possibility. "He wouldn't even look at a first year."

"I don't know," said her mother. "What do you think, Charlie?"

"Definitely fancied you," said Charlie.

"Right. And I would definitely listen to a sixteen-year-old." Maggie rolled her eyes, but inside, she couldn't stop smiling. What if they were right?

EIGHT
- 1986–1987 -

Long after her parents left, Maggie kept thinking about their walk, bumping into Ben, his hand on her back, her mother and younger brother thinking he might have been interested in her. Mostly, she couldn't stop thinking about how different he had been then than the times she had seen him in the King's Head. There he was sullen and stern, whereas he had been warm and easy with her family, charming her parents.

She had a fantasy that he might get in touch with her, even if only as a walking partner. But she didn't hear from him, and barely saw him after that weekend.

They didn't go back to the King's Head much after that terrible night. Evvie got the job at the Golden Lion, which became their regular, and by the time they did go back to the King's Head, some months later, Evil Ben was no longer working there.

Maggie still saw him around town from

time to time, but always at a distance, and he always seemed to be with other people. When Topher spotted him, he would dash back to tell Maggie where he was so the pair of them could run back out and see if there actually had been chemistry between them, to give Maggie a chance to work her magic on him and make him fall in love with her. But he was usually gone, and when he wasn't, she had always lost her nerve, so they never actually spoke after that first night.

The year passed quickly, and once exams were over, the three of them started looking at houses to live in together in their second year.

They saw two houses off the high street that were so dingy and depressing, Maggie and Topher both said they would rather be homeless than live there.

Evvie eventually found the perfect house. She overheard someone in the pub saying they were moving, and she interrupted, asking about the house. The next day the three of them walked to Castle Street with no expectations, to a terraced house that was filled with light, with large square rooms and an eat-in kitchen that had Maggie sighing with delight.

"I can cook again!" she exclaimed, hugging herself as she whirled around the kitchen. "No more pot noodles! No more crappy food! If we take this house, I promise I will cook for all of us every night."

"If we take this house?" Topher said. "There is no 'if.' This is by far the nicest house we've seen. It might be the nicest house in the whole town." He turned, taking in the spotless carpets, the simple Ikea furniture, the clean paint. "Who was it again that lived here before?"

"A couple of postgrad students," said the landlord. "One of them is leaving this year so the other decided to move to something smaller by himself. They were great tenants. Kept the place immaculate." He peered at them. "You know you can't have any parties here?"

"The only parties we'll be having are dinner parties." Topher shot Maggie a look. "We have our mother hen here to stop us from anything more raucous. Not that I would be having parties anyway," he quickly reassured the landlord. "We will be model students, won't we, girls?"

"We will!" squealed Maggie, in her excitement throwing her arms around Topher, who allowed it but shrank back, ever so slightly.

"Sorry, sorry!" she babbled. "I forgot you

82

don't like to be touched."

"It's okay." Topher attempted to laugh it off before turning to the landlord. "See? We don't even like touching other people. We're all very dull indeed."

They weren't very dull, but they kept their word about parties in their house. Anyway, it was far too nice for parties, Maggie said. Even if they were allowed, she wouldn't have wanted to risk messing up the carpets.

Instead, Evvie would make her Jamaican breakfast on the weekends, with Maggie cooking sumptuous cakes and comfort food suppers the rest of the week. Other friends would come over and spend evenings sitting around their kitchen table, talking long into the night.

Toward the end of their second year, they were adopted by a cat. He showed up one morning, meowing in the garden. Maggie opened the back door and the cat came running in, straight to the kitchen, where he kept on meowing until Maggie found a can of tuna lurking in a cupboard and opened it for him. And then, much to Topher's disgust (he was definitely not a cat person), they appeared to have a cat. Maggie adored him. She named him Colin, and he often jumped up on the sofa when she was sitting there, although he didn't like to be stroked.

It was a Saturday night when Maggie realized they hadn't seen Colin in days.

"Thank the lord," said Topher, before seeing Maggie's stricken face. "He's probably gone back to his original family," he said quickly, relieved the cat had gone, not least because he had been bitten by something a week ago and was convinced Colin had fleas.

"You never liked him."

"I could lie, but . . . you're right. Cats don't just turn up out of nowhere. He wasn't ours to keep."

"We didn't exactly lock him in."

"No, but you made it very comfortable for him."

"I'm so sad. What if something's happened to him?"

"He'll be fine. He's a feisty one. You need something to take your mind off the cat. Aren't you going to that party tonight?"

"I am. Evvie's meeting me there later with Julian."

"Julian? I thought that was all over. She said she was dumping him for good after she heard he slept with that frosh." He rolled his eyes. "She deserves so much better. Why does she put up with someone who treats her so badly?"

"I don't know. She said Julian wanted to talk, so she might bring him. I don't know that they're definitely back together. Please come. I know you said you had work but can't it wait?"

"Nope. Essay's due on Monday. Go and get ready and snog someone gorgeous. That'll stop you from thinking about the cat."

The house was dark and packed, the Housemartins and Prefab Sprout blaring from the boom box as Maggie pushed her way through. She had bought a green wrap dress at Warehouse the week before, which showed off both her legs and her cleavage. It was not the sort of dress she usually wore, but she felt sophisticated and sexy, as if she could conquer the world.

Growing up with three brothers, Maggie hadn't ever learned how to be a girl. She had never gravitated toward dolls, or pink, or flounces, but instead had climbed trees with her brothers and tumbled with them as they wrestled. She was, she told Topher, finally discovering her inner girl. Topher immediately shot back that she was actually discovering her inner middle-aged woman, for it was true, there was something mature about Maggie.

It was her maternal instinct. She was a natural nurturer, never happier than when in the kitchen, experimenting with recipes for her housemates and all their friends. Like her mother, she eschewed makeup and fancy clothes, but Evvie was trying to influence her, to inspire her to look a little more fun, a little more young. That night, Evvie helped her with makeup and hair, lending her huge dangly earrings, making her look at least a little like the young woman she was.

Maggie headed for the kitchen, sucking her stomach in. The problem with cooking so much was all the tasting. She had just made a carrot cake that afternoon, and her stomach was still bloated from licking the bowl.

There were a couple of familiar faces she passed on the way to the kitchen, but no one she knew well. She needed a drink to relax, and there, on the kitchen table, were half-empty bottles of vodka, gin, and tequila, and dozens of cans of beer on every surface. Maggie poured a liberal slug of vodka and downed it in one gulp, before pouring it again.

"I would never have pegged you for a drinker," said a voice in her ear.

She turned and found herself looking at

Evil Ben, inches from her face. Her heart fluttered as she blushed.

"There's probably a lot about me you don't know." It came out sounding more flirtatious than she had meant it to, but Evil Ben raised an eyebrow and smiled, those dimples coming out.

"Cheers," he said, finishing his beer and reaching for the tequila. "Join me?"

She nodded, aware that he was a little drunk, but not caring. He was the diametric opposite of the person she had thought him to be when she first met him. In fact, he was much more like the man she met on the bench during that walk with her parents. He looked happy, and relaxed. He was smiling, and, was she imagining it, or was he actually — oh please God, let that be the case — flirting with her? Could her mother have been right when she said he liked her?

She didn't have to wait long to find out.

"I liked your parents," he said, leading her to believe he was not as drunk as she thought he was. "They weren't what I would have expected."

"What does that mean?"

"I thought you were a posh girl. Well, you are a posh girl but your family's also very down to earth, which I like. And they're hikers. I never would have thought we'd have so much in common."

"Who knows what else we might have in common." Maggie was definitely flirting.

"Wouldn't that be nice?" He laughed, his dimples showing again as Maggie's heart flipped. "Shall we find somewhere quiet to talk?" She nodded as he took her hand, her heart leaping into her mouth. He led her through the crowds in the house and into the garden, where they sat on a low stone wall, close together, their legs brushing as Maggie felt sick with nervous anticipation.

"So what makes you tick, Maggie Hall-well? Other than hiking with your parents and almost getting into fights in pubs."

"Ha ha," she said, aware of the heat from his leg, a ripple of electricity running through her body when he pressed a little closer. "That was hardly my fault. I'm very nonconfrontational."

"I don't believe that," he said. "I think you're strong and opinionated."

"What gave you that idea? Is it just because I'm tall and a bit Amazonian?"

"Amazonian?" He laughed. "That's not the word I would have used. I would describe you as striking. Stunning, actually. And maybe just a little Amazonian. So are you strong and opinionated then?"

"I'm quite strong," she admitted. "Three

brothers will do that to you. I had to fend for myself."

He squinted at her. "What's the other side, Maggie? I think there's another, softer side. Someone vulnerable and loving."

Maggie stared at him, not knowing what to say. Of course she had that other side. Didn't everyone? She didn't expect Ben to have seen it though.

She shrugged.

"You're a caretaker," he said. "I can see that."

I am, thought Maggie. And how perceptive of him to notice.

"But who takes care of you?" he said softly as a lump unexpectedly appeared in Maggie's throat.

"Let's not talk about me. Let's talk about you," she said quickly.

"I'm not sure I want to talk," he said, gazing into her eyes. "I can think of something much more fun." And with no warning, he suddenly leaned over and kissed her as Maggie felt herself melting into him.

I'm kissing Evil Ben! she thought. This is it! The beginning of the rest of my life!

He tasted of tequila, and strawberries, but it wasn't strawberry, she knew, it was beer. So he was drunk, so what? He wasn't that drunk, he knew what he was doing, and this was huge, the happiest night of her life yet.

They sat on the wall kissing, then moved onto the ground. Evil Ben was above her, and then he was beneath her, his hands all over her, fumbling with her bra strap.

Maggie felt the cool night air against her skin, and abruptly realized this encounter wasn't just happening suddenly, but completely out in the open. Her mouth against his, she whispered, "Why don't we find somewhere inside where we can have a little more privacy."

Ben paused, then pulled back a bit. "Yes, right. That's a good idea." He seemed to think for a moment. "I'll go get us another drink. Meet you in five at the top of the stairs." And with that he was off.

Maggie headed into the house, a huge smile stretched on her face. Once she got to the top of the stairs, she shook out her hair, wondering whether she would sleep with him tonight. She would never usually sleep with anyone on the first night, but this wasn't just anyone, this was Evil Ben, and she already knew she would be spending the night with him. For just a second she imagined taking his shirt off, and inhaled sharply, a buzz of excitement washing over her. "Thank you, God," she whispered, looking to see if Ben was coming up the stairs yet.

He wasn't. She waited nearly twenty minutes, but there was no sign of him. Finally she thought she might have been mistaken, had maybe misheard, that perhaps he had said to meet him back downstairs after all. She went back to the stone wall where they had just been lying, but he was nowhere in sight. Maggie teetered across the grass on her heels, calling his name, but she couldn't find him. She walked around the garden three times before figuring he must have gone into the house, so she headed back inside, shouldering through the people in the living room and kitchen, asking them if they'd seen him.

Upstairs, she pushed open bedroom doors to where couples were writhing among huge piles of coats on single beds. "Ben?" she said, hoping to God she wouldn't find him there with someone else, simultaneously disappointed when he wasn't there.

He'd gone. Left without a trace. No one knew where he was. Maggie's happiness vanished, too, leaving her bewildered and upset, worried it was something she had said or done. It had to have been. Why else would he just disappear? Okay, so they didn't talk much beforehand, but he was flirting with her so much, he clearly did fancy her, so why would he just leave?

Where was Evvie? There was no way she could stay here by herself. Not now. She'd go and see if she could find her. Maybe she could help her make sense of what had just happened.

Evvie was behind the bar, wiping up glasses and scowling, unable to take her eyes off a table in the corner where Julian, her former boyfriend, was sitting with a group of people.

Maggie followed her gaze, seeing Julian chatting animatedly with a fresher. "I take it you're not back together then?"

"No. The bastard wanted to talk to me to tell me he was now dating that girl. And he has to damn well sit and flaunt it in here. Asshole." She shook her head in disgust before putting a bright smile on her face. "I'm trying to pretend I don't give a shit."

"Stop staring at the table then. I need to talk to you. I need advice." Evvie instantly gave her full attention to Maggie, who told her what had happened that night with Ben.

"I told you he was a dick," said Evvie, when Maggie, perched on a bar stool, had finished.

"But it doesn't make sense. You don't spend twenty minutes snogging someone and then do a runner."

"You do if you're a dick."

"I don't think so. I think something must have happened to him."

"No. You want something to have happened to him because then it won't be about you. But it's not about you anyway. You said yourself that he was drunk. God only knows what he was thinking. He probably passed out somewhere under a table and you didn't even see him. Honestly, Maggie? You deserve so much more."

"You don't know him," Maggie said fiercely. "He wasn't the Evil Ben we know. He was gentle, and sweet, and flirtatious."

Evvie looked at her skeptically. "I worked with him. 'Gentle' and 'sweet' are not words we use to describe Evil Ben."

"That's the point," said Maggie. "I think he must be really insecure or something, and drinking brought out the real Ben. Remember when I met him with my parents? There's another side to him that's lovely."

"So drinking brought out the real Ben who passionately made out with you and then disappeared? That's what you want? Someone completely unreliable?"

"There has to be an explanation. I'm going to find him tomorrow, and I'm going to ask him."

"Please don't," said Evvie. "He's not worth it. It was a drunken kiss. It meant nothing. Don't humiliate yourself further. Please."

"You're only saying that because you've always hated him. He's leaving, and we still have a whole year here. If I don't say something, I'll never know because none of us will ever see him again."

"Don't go chasing after him. You're too good for that. Please." Evvie sighed. "Oh God. I guess I'll have to be ready with a box of Kleenex tomorrow for your tears." She shook her head as she left to serve another customer.

Maggie didn't have to go chasing after Ben the next day. Topher came rushing into the kitchen, where Maggie was trying to forget about the night before by making home-made pasta. She hadn't been successful, neither at the forgetting nor at the pasta, which was thick and doughy.

"You won't believe this, but I just passed Evil Ben in the coffee shop." Topher dumped his jacket on the sofa of the house they were sharing. "He'd just ordered egg and chips, so I think he's still there if you want to go and grill him on his disappearing act."

"Oh God. I don't know now. I'm scared."

"You're allowed to rethink in the cold light of day. I think that's why it's called the cold light of day."

"No." Maggie stood up. "I'm going. I owe it to myself. I'll probably never see him again so what do I have to lose?"

Topher shrugged. "Nothing. Just all your dignity and self-respect."

"Fuck off," Maggie laughed as she grabbed her purse. "Wish me luck."

"Do you want me to come with you?" said Evvie as Maggie paused, then nodded, and the two of them put their jackets on and ran out.

"He's still there," Evvie hissed, returning to the doorway they were using to spy on Evil Ben.

"I'm going in," said Maggie, who had marched across the road before Evvie could stop her.

Evvie shook her head and reluctantly followed her in, standing at the counter and ordering a hot cross bun so she could watch.

Maggie walked over to Evil Ben, and sat down opposite him.

"Hi," she said, suddenly short of breath, nerves getting the better of her.

"Hello." He frowned at her and continued eating.

"How are you feeling today?"

"I'm all right. How are you?"

"I'm . . . fine. No, that's a lie. I'm not so fine. Do you want to tell me what happened last night?"

Evil Ben looked confused, before putting down his knife and fork with an apologetic grimace. "What happened last night?"

"You're joking, right?"

"I wish I was. It was a bit of a night. Too much to drink. I don't remember a lot. A mate apparently brought me home after I passed out." He squinted at her. "You were at the party then? Did I embarrass myself?"

Maggie stared at him. "You're serious? You don't remember anything?" What else could she say? Now was not the time to point out that they had passionately snogged, not when he was back to being the same old Evil Ben he was before she ran into him with her parents and thought there was more to him. This was the Evil Ben who had never seemed the least bit interested in Maggie, the Evil Ben who scowled and refused to meet her eye.

"I don't." He shrugged as Maggie felt her eyes welling up with tears. She turned away quickly, but not before he noticed.

"Christ. I did something to you last night, didn't I? I must have been rude. I'm really sorry, Maggie. I can sometimes be a bit of a dick when I'm drunk. I am so sorry if I offended you."

"You weren't a complete dick. In fact, you were anything but." Maggie couldn't believe that he didn't remember anything. How was that possible? He didn't seem that drunk, just tipsy. Could he be pretending not to remember? She sighed and shook her head.

"What?"

"Nothing. I just . . . I'm surprised you don't remember anything. The garden? The stone wall?" She paused. "Chatting?"

He frowned and shook his head. "I wasn't rude to you then? Well, that's a relief. But then, what did I do? Whatever it was, I'm really sorry."

"Forget it." Maggie stood up, scraping her chair back. "Have a great life." She turned and walked quickly outside, so he wouldn't see her blinking back the tears.

NINE

Toward the end of their last year, they finally got to meet Topher's mother. Maggie's perfect family had been up, and Evvie's mother had finally come, bearing roti and curry, rice and peas, and black cake, which Maggie insisted on getting the recipe for, and had made continually for about six weeks until they all begged for a change.

But Topher's parents remained a mystery until his mother announced she had a charity event in Bath and would be coming to visit. The day arrived, a Mercedes pulling up outside, driven by the most glamorous woman Evvie and Maggie had ever seen, who looked less like a mother than someone's stunning older sister.

Evvie had barely been able to say a word since she arrived. Topher's mother had sat at the kitchen table, her full-length fur flung over the back of a chair, huge diamonds glittering in her ears, peppering them all with questions. Maggie seemed to have fallen madly in love, and was chattering away, but Evvie was mesmerized, like a deer caught in headlights.

It wasn't just that Mrs. Winthrop — "Call me Joan. Please" — truly was the most glamorous woman imaginable. It was that she had a confidence that Evvie assumed could only come with money. She walked in just over an hour ago, having checked in at the Dinham Arms, her Fendi mink coat sashaying around her hips. She wore perfectly cut flannel trousers and expensive loafers, a cashmere sweater knotted around her shoulders on top of a silk shirt, and her hair was a mix of copper and blond highlights. ("My mom is a good old Irish redhead," Topher had explained before she arrived, "but she hides it expertly with blond streaks.")

But most of all, she was tiny. Evvie's mother had been slim when she was young, but since menopause she had lost her trim waistline and flat stomach. Mrs. Winthrop looked like she was twenty-five. Evvie didn't even know it was possible for women to look like that at her age.

She looked like the wealthy, philanthropically minded housewife she was, devoted to spending fortunes on herself. She was completely self-assured, and from a world that Evvie recognized distantly from her father's stories about his family, but a world she didn't know. Suddenly she felt inadequate, wishing she felt better about herself, wishing she hadn't isolated herself to study, taking sugar breaks every hour or so. All that cake may have numbed her feelings at the time, but it always led to the same self-loathing, and she was back to lying in bed every night vowing to start a diet the next day, a diet that would inevitably be broken, catastrophically, sometime midafternoon.

"You are so not what I expected," Evvie said at one point, shaking her head, breaking her gaze. "I just have to stop and say I can't believe how young and gorgeous you are. Topher never said."

"You mean, he doesn't have pictures of his family all over his bedroom?" Topher's mother waved a finger at him. "Shame on you, Topher. Why did I send those silver photo frames over?"

"I had to replace all the family pictures with photos of my friends," said Topher. "I know you'll forgive me. Especially because I even clean my own room. Can you imagine?"

Joan shook her head. "We spoiled you having Diana," she said. "You should have

100

always cleaned your room at home. I did when I was growing up."

Evvie looked from one to the other. "Diana?"

"Our live-in housekeeper," explained Topher as Evvie shook her head.

"I should have known."

Since as far back as she could remember, Evvie had done household chores, and heaven forbid she should ever question a parent. "I'm about to give you some licks," her mother would say before a series of smacks. Evvie adored her mother, and her mother adored her, but she was clearly the opposite of the indulgent mother who was sitting before her that day. Evvie's mother was the head of the household, even when married to her father. She was tough and opinionated, said exactly what was on her mind, and demanded respect. Many was the time Evvie heard, "Don't back answer me. I will put your teeth down your throat."

Evvie had no experience of being accepted unconditionally, of having a mother who might gaze at her with absolute adoration, in the way Joan Winthrop was gazing at Topher. Seeing it filled her with a sense of loss. She loved her mother, but how nice, how much easier it would have been to have a mother like this. She pictured her own mother looking her up and down, judgment in her eyes as she sucked her teeth.

"You never mentioned a housekeeper before," said Maggie. "We had a daily, but a live-in? That's very posh. You never told us you were so fancy."

"Now that you've met my mother, you know everything."

"I wish I'd worn jeans and sneakers," said Joan, looking down at her beautiful clothes. "I didn't realize West Country would be quite so casual."

"Mom, do you even own jeans and sneakers?"

"Of course. What do you think I work out in?" Joan grinned.

"You're so slim," breathed Evvie, mustering the courage to speak to her. "How do you do it? How do you stay looking so fantastic?"

"Aerobics classes three times a week," said Joan, giving Evvie a look she couldn't quite decipher. "I'm sure they have them here. They're so much fun. You girls should try it."

Evvie flushed, convinced that was a comment on her weight.

"Not that either of you need to do anything," Joan said quickly, seeing Evvie flush. "You have youth and beauty on your side.

You're perfect."

Evvie mentally exhaled. "I'm not perfect," she said, grabbing her thighs. "Look. I've gained almost twenty pounds this term. It's awful."

"It's baby fat," said Joan. "It's easy to get rid of at your age. When you get to my age it's much harder."

"I need to stay away from the sugar. All the cakes and cookies are terrible for me. Either that, or I need someone to break my heart again."

"That's the best diet ever," agreed Joan.

"I don't really want anyone to break my heart," sighed Evvie. "I seem to be drawn to losers. And no woman needs a man. I think I'm far better off on my own."

"True, the wrong man is a terrible thing. You're lucky, you girls. You're young at a time when the world is your oyster."

"Exactly! There's nothing we can't achieve. Marriage and kids are the last thing I want. I'm going to make a difference in the world." Evvie sat up proudly.

"You can still make a difference if you're married with kids," protested Maggie. "It doesn't have to be the prison it once was."

"I wasn't saying you're wrong to want that," said Evvie. "Of course we can have it all. Thank God!"

"Speaking of having it all, is anyone hungry? Can I take you all out for dinner?" asked Joan. "Apparently the Dinham Arms has a lovely restaurant."

"Yes please!" Maggie's eyes lit up. "What a lovely treat."

Later that day, when they were getting ready for dinner, Evvie came downstairs to find Joan tipping some pills into the palm of her hand before slipping the pill bottle discreetly back in her bag.

"Are you okay?" said Evvie. "Do you have a headache? Can I get you anything?"

Joan laughed and shook her head before showing Evvie the pill bottle. Dexatrim. "This is the real reason why I stay so slim," she confessed in a conspiratorial whisper. "It completely suppresses my appetite. I was very slim when younger, but as soon as I hit forty-five I started to gain weight, so I started taking this. It's amazing." She paused and looked at Evvie. "Do you want to try?"

"What will it do?"

Joan shrugged. "You won't feel hungry. It also has the added side effect of giving you lots of energy. You might feel a bit hyper, and you probably won't sleep for a while, but you're young. You don't need to sleep. I

104

can leave you these if you want. I have stacks of them in my bathroom because I'm terrified of running out."

Evvie looked at the pill bottle, excitement rising. She had no idea it was this easy, and had long fantasized about some miracle drug that would enable her to eat whatever she wanted while still losing weight.

"Just one?" She grinned.

"I take one in the morning and one early afternoon. This is probably completely irresponsible of me, but I know what it's like to not feel good about yourself. Take them. You'll love it."

"Cheers," said Evvie, feeling a thrill of excitement as she popped the pill in her mouth and washed it down with a glass of water.

TEN
- 1989 -

Evvie was lying on one sofa in the living room, Topher lounging in the armchair opposite, both of them bemoaning the fact that they would soon graduate, that three years had passed in a flash, when Maggie walked in bearing a plate of gingersnaps.

"Fresh out of the oven." She placed them on the table, grabbing two before flopping on the sofa next to Evvie, putting her feet, clad in the slipper socks from her parents, now old and faded, onto Evvie's lap.

"Evvie? Will you have one?"

Evvie shook her head.

"You never eat my food anymore. What's the matter with you?"

"I'm training myself to eat less," lied Evvie, who was by then taking at least three Dexatrim a day. The less she ate, the more successful a day she thought it was.

"But how am I supposed to show you that I love you if I can't feed you?" Maggie said with a pout as Evvie laughed and leaned forward, flinging her arms around her in a tight hug.

"Like this," she said. "Just as good and much less fattening."

"Screw the calories." Topher reached for a handful of gingersnaps. "Are you both as depressed as me? I can't believe it's over. How did we get here so quickly?"

"It's awful," moaned Maggie, cupping her hands around the mug of tea. "Tomorrow it's all over. At least the two of you will be in New York and you'll have each other. I'm going to be working in London, all by myself."

"Tons of people will be in London," corrected Evvie. "Just not us. You'll know so many people."

"But it won't be the same," she grumbled. "Who's going to protect me if drunken rugby players attack me in a pub?" Pouting, Maggie looked at Topher as they all remembered that night soon after they'd first arrived, the night that had them vowing to always have one another's backs.

"First of all, that's not going to happen. Second of all, you're more than capable of looking after yourself, and thirdly, if you need me, phone me and I'll fly over."

"You won't fly over, although I appreciate

the thought. Both of you are about to walk into the most glamorous jobs in the world, and I'm going into corporate PR. Could it be any more dull?"

"Corporate PR with a subsidized flat in Westbourne Grove. Not too shabby," laughed Evvie. "You'll be fine. You always said you only wanted to work until you found a husband and settled down to have children. Once you find roommates you'll start having fun."

"You're right. But I still want my work to be fun. And the roommates. Naomi said she's going to move to London, so she might move in with me. Apparently she knows a boy who will be there too."

"Is he gay?" asked Topher. "Are we really that easily replaced?"

Evvie looked at Topher. "I thought you were asexual."

"Ah, yes. I was. I think I just hadn't found myself yet."

"And now you know you're gay?" Maggie narrowed her eyes. "What's been going on that we don't know about?"

"You know that very handsome second year who played the Page in *Antigone*?"

"You did not!" Evvie clapped. "Daniel? The picture of innocence?"

"Oh, he's not innocent, let me tell you.

He seduced me."

"And?"

Topher shrugged. "I may not be driven by my sexual desires, but it turns out I'm not asexual after all."

"I thought you didn't like to be touched," said Evvie, confused.

"That's what I always thought too. I think it's that I don't like to be touched unless it's on my terms. I have to be in control, otherwise it just . . ." He shuddered. "Anyway. It was definitely on my terms and" — he grinned — "it was really rather lovely."

"Why didn't you tell us?" pouted Maggie.

Topher shrugged. "You were in the midst of your Evil Ben recuperation. It was all you were talking about. Speaking of whom, I saw him today."

Maggie sat up. "Evil Ben?"

"Oh no," said Evvie. "Don't tell me we're going to start this up again."

It felt like ages since Evil Ben finished his postgrad studies and left the university, and Maggie hadn't spoken about him for the longest time. Every now and then she brought him up, saying he would always be the one who got away, but they had no idea where he was, and no way of getting in touch (thank goodness, Evvie always thought). Maggie definitely deserved better than him, at least as far as Evvie was concerned.

"Where did you see him?" Evvie could see that the very mention of his name had brought a flush to Maggie's cheeks.

Topher frowned as he looked at Maggie. "I wouldn't have brought it up if I thought it would still have this effect on you. I saw him park an old green Triumph Spitfire by the King's Head, and then he and someone else went in."

"A Triumph Spitfire?" asked Evvie.

"Cool old sports car. I went over to see what it was once they'd gone."

"Who was he with?" asked Maggie. "A man or a woman?"

"Man."

"Oh, please can we go." Maggie looked from Topher to Evvie. "This can be my graduation gift from you."

"What graduation gift?"

"The one I forgot to tell you about. Please? I just want to see him again, if nothing else just to have closure."

"You had closure," said Evvie. "Remember? He didn't remember anything about the passionate garden snog you had, or he did remember, and he pretended not to. Either way, that seems to be pretty closed to me."

"Do you have any idea how British you sound when you say the word 'snog'?" Maggie started laughing. "You're coming, aren't you?" She stood up and grinned at them, knowing they would come, because that was what friendship was about. "I'm just going to put some makeup on. Be ready in five."

Maggie had pulled on her baggy jeans, and slipped her feet into boots. She was tall already, at five feet nine inches, and normally would have worn her beloved heels, but Evil Ben was only a shade taller than her, and she didn't want to intimidate him.

Evvie, on the other hand, loved her platform heels, teamed with her baggy jeans and a man's shirt, half tucked in. She had topped this off with a fedora, jauntily perched, which on anyone else might have looked bizarre, but on Evvie looked impossibly cool, particularly since she had shed all the weight she had gained and was now positively skinny.

An old high school friend sent her the pills from New York, and they worked so well, she had been recruited by a modeling agency the last time she was on the King's Road in London and had done some work already. After graduation she would be going home to New York, but this time to model, living in a shared apartment down-town.

Modeling was never what she saw herself doing, and she felt simultaneously incredulous and embarrassed, knowing that people would presume she wasn't clever enough to do anything else. If she felt she was going to be judged, rather than tell people she would be modeling, she said she would be working in the fashion industry, praying they wouldn't ask anything else. But modeling was a means to an end. Evvie knew that if she was one of the lucky ones, she had the capability to make more money than at any other job. And money would give her the freedom to do what she wanted. She wanted to start charities helping women and children who didn't have access to education. She wanted to make it easier for women like her grandmother and mother, raised in Kingston, only getting out by sheer luck and happenstance.

Her future depended on modeling, and modeling depended on staying unnaturally thin. When Maggie expressed worry about her jutting collarbones, Evvie would nod and say she definitely wasn't going to lose any more weight. At night, she would lie in bed feeling the bones on her chest, and smiling to herself.

No one knew about the pills. Maggie had once seen her taking them, but Evvie said they were painkillers for period cramps. She didn't sleep well on them, always up until the early hours, and there were times when her heart would race in a way that seemed worrying, but being this thin was worth any price. Whenever she thought about stopping them, the thought would be immediately pushed aside by the fear of gaining weight.

Evvie looked at herself in the mirror as they were leaving, and removed the fedora. There was no reason to dress up for Evil Ben.

ELEVEN

- 1989 -

Topher pushed open the door to the pub, followed by the girls, Maggie scouring the room until she saw Evil Ben standing at the bar with his friend. They were both clearly on their second, or perhaps third, pint. When they spotted him, Evil Ben had his head thrown back with laughter at something his friend had said, but hearing the door open he had turned, still smiling, and his gaze rested on Maggie.

Topher nudged her sharply. "Oh my God, he's smiling at you. Smile back!" he commanded, in a very loud stage whisper.

Maggie smiled, in a wobbly sort of way, then turned her back. "Oh God," she murmured. "I have no idea what to say. Now I'm embarrassed. We shouldn't have come."

"We can't leave now," said Evvie. "And at least he's smiling. That's actually the first time I've ever seen him smile."

"I'm going over there." Topher marched

off toward Evil Ben before any of them could stop him.

"Get drinks!" Evvie called out after him. "Pints of shandy all around please!"

"Shandy?" Maggie wrinkled her nose in disgust. "Really? Can't I have a gin and tonic?"

"No. You can't. It's much too grown-up, and you said you'd cook a farewell dinner for us tonight. The last thing we need is for you to get shit-faced. Also" — she peered at her friend meaningfully — "the last thing you need is to disappear on us and spend the night with Evil Ben."

"I would never do that," said Maggie.

"Good. Because you're an amazing cook and we want this dinner to be special. So, no going off with men, and no drinking the hard stuff until later."

"Fair point." They found a table on the side and sat waiting for Topher to bring their drinks, watching as he chatted casually with Evil Ben.

"What do you think they're saying?" Maggie leaned in, not taking her eyes off Ben and Topher.

"I don't know, but they look like they're getting on like a house on fire."

"Oh my God!" said Maggie. "What if Evil Ben's gay?"

"Don't be daft," said Evvie. "He wouldn't have snogged you, even when drunk. Plus, didn't he have a girlfriend for a while when we were in our first year? Remember her?"

Maggie did remember, because she was a redhead like herself. Maybe he likes red-heads, she had thought at the time; maybe one day he will break up with her, and then he will notice me. Maybe that's why we snogged that time, she thought now. Maybe he'll remember that I'm his type after all.

Topher came back to the table, expertly carrying three pints against his chest.

"Well?" Evvie couldn't wait. "What did you say? What did he say? What were you talking about?"

"He was actually really nice," Topher said. "I introduced myself and said I was part of the Evil Ben fan club, and that all three of us were up for it if he wanted to take his pick."

"Nooooo!" Maggie's eyes widened in horror as she shrank back.

"Of course I didn't say that. I just said that we had all seen him around for so long and he had rescued us a hundred years ago, and we never even had the opportunity to thank him properly. It seemed weird that other than you, Maggie, we had never really spoken to him, and that includes Evvie, who worked with him! Given that none of us would ever see him again, I invited him to join us for a drink. He's apparently up here to see some old friends."

"He's joining us for a drink? Are you serious?" Maggie whispered, not knowing whether to laugh in delight or throw up as Evil Ben and his friend both picked up their pints and made their way toward them. "I feel a bit sick." She looked at him, surprised that he still had the same effect on her, still made her heart flutter, even after all this time. "Oh God. What am I supposed to say to him?"

"Be your charming self," whispered Topher.

"I can't believe you did this for Maggie," said Evvie under her breath, raising her glass to Topher. "I have a whole new level of respect for you, even though there's no one I'd less want to have a drink with." She sighed, looking away.

Topher bowed his head. "I aim to please."

"Hi," said Evil Ben, pulling a stool over and sitting down. "Thanks for inviting me to join you. It's nice to see some familiar faces." He looked at Maggie then, who blushed.

His friend sat next to him and smiled at the girls, the smile clearly lingering on

Evvie. "I'm Rich Keogh."

"We all feel like we know you, even though we never really did. Well, most of us." Topher shot Maggie a look, the color of her cheeks deepening. "Obviously, you were our knight in shining armor when we first arrived, when Evvie worked here. And I know Maggie ran into you a couple of times. So what brought you back to town after all this time? And how's the work at the research lab in Hertfordshire? Sorry . . ." He trailed off. "I guess I should have warned you that you were about to be subjected to an interrogation."

"Poor Evil Ben," said Evvie, laughing. "Leave him alone."

Evil Ben raised an eyebrow.

"Evil Ben?" His friend Rich sputtered with laughter as he took a sip of beer.

"That's what we call you because you never smile," said Topher, who was doing the talking for all of them. "We'd all smile at you when we used to see you, but it seemed like you just scowled at us."

"And you were a complete dick when I worked here," said Evvie.

"You are a scowler," laughed his friend Rich. "And, mate, you can be a bit of a dick."

Ben looked at Evvie then. "Yeah. Sorry

118

about that. I was pissed off that we'd taken on another bartender in the main bar. That was supposed to be my job and they relegated me to the side bar for a pretty face."

"So you were an asshole to me? Nice."

"I'm sorry. It wasn't about you."

"He wasn't all bad." Maggie made eyes at Evvie. "He did rescue us that night."

"I did," he said. "And yet you still gave me the moniker Evil Ben?"

"It had a nice ring to it." Topher shrugged. "What can we say?"

"Evil Ben. I think I quite like it. Maybe I should add that to my CV." He took a sip of his beer before grinning at Rich. "They're right, it does have a nice ring to it."

"So, Evil Ben. If you're in Hertfordshire at a research lab, what are you doing back here?" Maggie leaned forward, emboldened by the drink, by the fact that she still felt the same way about him, and that this might be her last chance to do anything about it. She rested her elbows on the table, knowing that if his eyes dropped, he might get a look at her cleavage. Normally this was the last thing Maggie would do. Evvie was the one who tended to dress in the sexy stuff. Maggie was most comfortable in her jeans and T-shirt, not a hint of cleavage in sight.

He looked at Maggie with an amused

smile on his face. "Yes, I am at a research lab in Hertfordshire, but I'm back to see some friends. I've still got mates here, and I needed a break. This is my pre-summer holiday."

"Might be your summer holiday given what they're paying you." Rich nudged him as Ben rolled his eyes.

"I was going to say, it's not very glamorous," said Topher. "You could have chosen Ios or Majorca, and you came to Somerset? Is there something wrong with you?"

"First job out of uni. Just you wait," he said. "Welcome to the real world."

"Where are you staying?" Maggie finished her drink and placed the empty glass back on the table.

"With Rich on Queen Street."

"Otherwise known as the drinking den," laughed Rich.

"What does that mean?" Evvie frowned.

"Just that we've been doing some serious damage this weekend," said Rich.

"Are you drunk already?" Evvie peered at them both.

"We handle our liquor brilliantly," he said, turning to Ben as they toasted each other.

"I need Rich to keep me on my best behavior. As you once pointed out, I'm not always my best self when I've been drinking." He stared at Maggie as the room seemed to drop away before her.

She was swept back to that night in the garden, to Ben asking who took care of her. She remembered the kiss that took her breath away, his disappearance, and her attempts to confront him afterward. Had he remembered more than he let on? If she didn't pursue it now, she would never know. She took a deep breath. "We're having a dinner later tonight at our place. You two should come by, have some drinks later on. If you feel like it . . ."

Evvie looked at Maggie in horror. "Maggie!"

"What? You love people dropping in!"

"Do you not want me to come?" said Ben, looking directly at Evvie, who looked away. He may have been nicer today than he ever was when she worked with him, but she still didn't like him, and she definitely didn't want him at their farewell dinner.

"No. I mean, it's not that. This is our farewell dinner, the three of us. I don't think anyone else should be there."

"I didn't say come to our farewell *dinner*. I said come by. For drinks. Maybe after," Maggie said, remembering how her stomach had lurched with both the memory and the anticipation of something happening later that one evening she had spent with Evil Ben.

"We can't. Unfortunately," interjected Rich. "We have a party later on. The head of our department. Well, Ben's old department, but still."

"That sounds like fun," Topher said sarcastically.

Ben frowned. "I'm sorry we can't come. That's a really generous invitation. Couldn't we pop in?" He turned to Rich. "Just for a quick drink?"

"I don't think we're going to have time."

"I'm sorry," he said again. "It sounds like it would have been lovely. How are your parents?" he asked Maggie, who hadn't thought he remembered meeting them.

"They're good. Great. A bit sad I'm now moving to London, but my mum's planning lots of trips up to see me."

"London? So we'll be near each other? I should give you my number. There are West Country get-togethers every now and then at a pub in Elephant and Castle."

"That would be great." Maggie's smile was so wide, it was almost painful.

"Any idea where you'll be living?"

"Westbourne Grove. I've got a job in corporate PR. I've just got to find roommates."

"Nice." He whistled. "That sounds cushy. Maybe you'll buy me dinner sometime? Can I get you all another drink?"

"That sounds lovely," said Maggie, who was gazing at Evil Ben with pure adoration as Evvie nudged her.

"We've probably got to get going," said Evvie, ignoring Maggie's quick glare at her. "We've got dinner to get ready and a house to finish packing up."

"We can stay for another drink," Maggie said.

"We really can't." Evvie downed her drink as Topher frowned. "Nice to talk to you both, and I hope you enjoy your time here. Come on." She stood over Maggie, who sighed reluctantly before following Evvie and Topher out, turning to give a final wave to Evil Ben.

"Why did you do that?" hissed Maggie as soon as they were outside. "Things were just getting good."

"Because he was drunk, Maggie." Evvie sighed. "Which means something probably would have happened between the two of you, just like last time, and he would once again ignore you tomorrow. All of which is largely irrelevant because this is our farewell dinner. This isn't about other people, not even people we've had crushes on before.

We're going to prepare a beautiful dinner, and we're going to spend time together. The last thing I'm going to do is let you get off with a drunk Evil Ben just because you think it's the last time you'll ever see him."

"It's not the last time she'll ever see him," said Topher, holding up a piece of paper in his fingers. "I've got his number for Maggie. For the record, I agree with Evvie. I know you're bummed, but let's go back and enjoy this final dinner together."

"I can't just phone him when I'm in London," said Maggie, pouting like a child. "That was probably my last opportunity."

"Of course you can phone him. He wanted you to have his number, remember? There'll be a get-together for some West Country people and you'll call him and say you suddenly remembered he was there, and maybe he'd like to meet up beforehand, and then you'll fall into bed and live happily ever after."

"I wish," said Maggie, although it brought a smile to her face. "Evvie, he is nice, isn't he? Didn't you see another side of him today? He even apologized to you."

"Kinda, sorta. But not really. I mean, I definitely see what you see when he smiles. He looks less like a robot and more like a human being, and he is kind of cute, but

124

honestly? I still think he's a bit of an ass. I could tell they'd been drinking as soon as they joined us. I get the whole drinking thing when you're a student, but he's graduated. I felt like he hadn't grown up."

"That's not fair. Of course he's going to drink when he's back at his old stomping ground," said Maggie. "I suppose that means you won't be bridesmaid at our wedding?"

Evvie started laughing. "Oh, I'm sure I'll have managed to get over it by then. Let's go to Tesco and get whatever we need for tonight."

"Will you actually eat tonight?" Maggie asked pointedly, aware that Evvie's extreme slimness was mostly because she barely ate these days.

"Yes," said Evvie, and it was true. She had already decided that she owed herself one last blowout meal with her best friends. She didn't want to take two bites and push the rest of the food around on her plate like she always did. She wanted to relish the food, enjoy the dessert, and get back on track tomorrow. So she wouldn't take the third pill today, which meant she would finally have an appetite again. "Just watch me," she said, and grinned.

"Okay. You're right. Nothing was going to

happen tonight anyway. I'm sorry I was sulking. I've got food to cook and a table to set. And my friends are much more important than any man could ever hope to be." She extended her arms then, linking with Topher and Evvie, and they walked down the street, three wide, singing old Joni Mitchell songs very loudly until they reached Tesco.

That night, wine was drunk, tequila shots were knocked back, beef Wellington was consumed, and the pavlova demolished. They all got a little bit tipsy and, finally, after an evening of stories and reminiscing, a little bit weepy.

"I really love you guys," said Topher, his eyes misting up. "I can't believe I'm going back to the States so soon and I'm not going to be seeing you every day."

"I can't bear it," said Maggie. "Can we all plan to spend Christmas together, or maybe go on holiday together at the end of this summer?"

"Topher and I will be in New York," said Evvie, who was going to be the last to leave town, and still wasn't prepared to be there by herself, if only for a week. "God only knows whether we'll get vacation time. Maybe you could come and stay with us?"

"I'm not staying in your model house. Being intimidated by all the gorgeous women? No thanks." Maggie snorted. "I'll stay with Topher."

"What are we all going to do without each other?" said Evvie. "Seriously."

"We have our lives to live," said Topher. "Maybe we'll be movie stars, or supermodels, philanthropists, newspaper editors, or PR gurus. Maybe we'll find the loves of our lives. Maybe you two will get married, have kids, and maybe I'll end up in the UK. Whatever we do and wherever our careers take us, the only thing I know for sure is that I love you two and we're going to be best friends forever, no matter how far apart we are from each other. Deal?"

"Deal!" said Maggie, wiping drunken tears from her eyes. "I don't want it to end. I wish it could be the three of us just like this, forever. Wouldn't that be amazing? Evvie, you and I could open a restaurant. Cakes and Jamaican food!"

"I love it!" said Evvie. "One day, let's make it happen!"

They cleared the table, all three of them weaving slightly, occasionally stopping to put an arm around a waist, or kiss a cheek. Evvie left to go to the bathroom, and looked at herself in the mirror. She looked beautiful, her cheekbones more pronounced than they had ever been, but then she looked down at her stomach, which was distended, and painful.

She had eaten so much. The pills had somehow fooled her brain into thinking that it wasn't the pills but that Evvie had somehow changed, that her need for food had miraculously disappeared. Tonight she thought she could indulge like a normal person, but nothing about the way she ate was normal. When she took the pavlova into the kitchen, leaving Maggie and Topher sitting at the table, she quickly and quietly shoveled half of what was left into her mouth, not even tasting it. And she was already full, long before the pavlova had even been served.

She thought of that now, as she looked in the mirror, that old familiar shame washing over her. It wasn't too late to get rid of it, she thought, looking at the toilet bowl. She'd made herself throw up before, when she had overeaten, and as long as it didn't become a habit, it would be fine.

She knelt on the rug and pushed a finger down her throat, then two. It wasn't nearly as easy as people made it sound, but eventually the pavlova came up, and the beef Wellington, and when she had done as much as she thought she would be able to do, she stood up and flushed, noting how her stomach was already flatter.

Much better, she thought.

But I'm not going to do it again.

TWELVE

- 1989 -

Evvie was in a furious mood. The modeling agency had messed up her travel dates, and she wasn't leaving this Monday, but the next. The simple thing to do, as far as Evvie was concerned, was to change the flight and put her up in New York. She could see old friends, revisit some old haunts, and, if she was very lucky, stay at a swanky hotel.

But the agency disagreed. The flights were unchangeable, they said, before offering to put her up in a hotel. Evvie could have gone to London — her mother was in Jamaica to visit family, so it was just her grandmother — but Evvie couldn't think of anything more depressing than staying alone in London with no one young around.

It was Maggie's idea to get them to pay for her to stay at the Dinham Arms.

"It's gorgeous!" she kept saying. "You can use the spa all week and get them to pay for it. Bliss!"

Evvie agreed. If she was forced to stay in the UK for an extra week, why not let it be in the West Country, in full-on luxury at their expense.

She didn't tell her grandmother, who would have been devastated. Her grandmother would have wanted her safely at home in Stockwell, eating the kinds of food from her childhood that would ensure she arrived in New York several pounds heavier. Her grandmother would have taken one look at her, sucked her teeth, and declared her "crawny," before cooking up a feast of goat curry, saltfish, and bakes, all the food Evvie had never been able to resist. Other people could indulge for a day or so, and gain a couple of pounds that they shed with no trouble. Not Evvie. Evvie could easily gain ten pounds in a week. She knew it because she'd done it before. Several times. Now that she was embarking on a modeling career, that was something she definitely couldn't afford.

Far better for her to stay here, which now felt more like home than anywhere she had ever lived, even though the town had emptied out of students, she and Maggie feeling like the only ones left.

Maggie came with Evvie to the post office to ship her boxes to New York, and then, armed with one suitcase, she and Maggie took off for the Dinham Arms.

"I actually can't believe they're paying for you to stay here a week. All expenses! You are *totally* raiding the minibar," said Maggie, helping to haul the suitcase up the steps. "I'm longing to see the room. Apparently they have four-poster beds that are to die for."

"I wish you could stay too." Evvie had been trying to persuade her for the past two hours, but Maggie was flying straight to the South of France where her parents had a home in Mougins, high in the hills above Cannes. As tempting as the Dinham Arms was, the West Country could never compete with the Côte d'Azur.

The girls had eaten in the restaurant of the Dinham Arms but had never been farther than the foyer. They followed the young woman from reception up the stairs, their feet sinking into soft carpet, down a long corridor with oriel windows overlooking English gardens with clipped boxwood hedges and Gertrude Jekyll–designed beds, stopping outside a heavy wooden door.

"I've upgraded you to a suite," the woman said with a smile. "The only room we had available was unrenovated. I hope you like it." She opened the door with a flourish as

Maggie and Evvie looked at each other with wide eyes, Evvie stepping in first, pretending to be nonchalant, as if she stayed at hotels like this all the time, as if upgrades were part of her life experience.

She couldn't keep up the pretense for long, for it was the most beautiful room she had ever seen.

The Dinham Arms was a former coaching inn, bought by a wealthy local couple and transformed into a luxury Relais and Châteaux a few years previously. The students whose parents could afford it had all eaten their famous Sunday lunch in the old beamed restaurant, complete with a dessert cart that was wheeled around to each table.

But the suite! Evvie had never seen anything so luxurious. A vast four-poster bed, so high there were mahogany footstools on either side to enable guests to climb in, yards of sumptuous pomegranate-printed fabric draping over the top and down the sides, and pillows piled high.

"This is amazing," breathed Evvie, her smile almost cracking her face. "Thank you so, so much!"

"Bugger the South of France," squealed Maggie, climbing onto the bed as soon as the receptionist left. "Oh my God. I'm staying here forever." She sank back into the pillows and disappeared as Evvie walked around the bedroom, touching the glossy antique side tables, running her hands along the top of the sofa and marveling at the beauty of the fabric, before opening the door into a marble bathroom that was bigger than her bedroom at home, with an enormous tub that seemed to be a Jacuzzi, and a shower that seemed to double as a steam room.

"I feel like the princess and the pea," shouted Maggie from the bedroom as Evvie unscrewed the caps on the tiny shampoos and conditioners, body washes, and bubble baths, smelling everything and swooning. "You have to climb into this bed. It's insane."

Evvie dutifully put the caps back on, and went back into the bedroom, climbing up the steps to the four-poster and sinking down next to Maggie.

"Are you still here?" asked Evvie, reaching out an arm and feeling for her friend. "This bed is so damn huge, I think I lost you."

"What even is this?" said Maggie. "My parents have a king, but this thing is way bigger."

"Maybe it's a California king."

"What's that?"

"I have no idea. But I think it's bigger. I

can't believe you don't know, Maggie! You're the expert on fancy hotels."

Maggie rolled into the middle, her head on her elbow as she looked at her friend, frowning. "What do you mean?"

"You know what I mean. You. Your life outside of the university. I love you, and I love that you come from a different world than me, so don't pretend that you're not used to this kind of luxury."

Maggie shook her head. "I'm not from *this* kind of world. Don't you know that by now? I mean, yes, we're comfortable and we have a lovely country house, but everything's falling apart inside. Seriously, the rugs are all completely threadbare, and in winter it's so cold, you have to go to bed with a hot water bottle."

"But you have stables! And horses!"

"Because my mother is always riding. Trust me, whatever money we have is so old, it's practically disappeared."

"Oh, come on, Maggie. You're about to leave for your house in the South of France."

"You're right. I'm incredibly lucky, but our lifestyle isn't nearly as luxurious as this! I know, I sound like a posh Yah, but my family is old-school. We don't spend a penny unless we have to. Unless it's for the horses or the dogs," she mused. "Then there's no limit. Oh, or a sheep."

"A sheep?"

"We had a sheep with a twisted colon, and my mother insisted on having it operated on."

"You're so weird." Evvie started to laugh.

"I know. That's why you love me."

"I do love you. But not as much as I love this!" Evvie flopped back on the bed. "In a week's time I'm going to be sharing a New York apartment that will probably be grotty as hell. I'm going to enjoy this while I can."

"I love that you now use the word 'grotty.' " Maggie grinned.

"Remember when I had to ask you what that meant? I'm sure the model apartment will be bad."

"It will be knickers on the radiators and tampons everywhere. But soon you're going to be super famous, and then you'll stay in luxury all the time. You'll fly over to stay with me in my Westbourne Grove flat and you'll be horrified at how I live."

"I definitely won't be," assured Evvie. "By the time I'm twenty-six, I'm planning on trips to Africa to make the world a better place. I'll be sleeping in mud huts on the floor."

Maggie grinned. "I'll believe it when I see it."

"Oh, please cancel France and stay here with me. Your parents won't mind. They'll understand."

"I wish I could," sighed Maggie. "I can't get out of it. All the boys will be there, and Charlie's leaving next week to teach rugby in New Zealand for a year. This is our last family get-together. I'll phone you every day, I promise. Maybe you'll find some sexy man in town to share this bed with. It would be a pity not to share it."

"I'll do my best," laughed Evvie. "Although I'm pretty sure everyone decent has gone. Maybe I could have a fling with the local milkman."

"Desperate times call for desperate measures," Maggie said, before turning serious. "I'm going to miss you."

"I'm going to miss you too."

"Have an adventure this week and tell me everything. I'll be lying around reading and waiting to live vicariously through you. I seriously am going to call you every day, and I expect exciting updates. What's the number of the hotel?" She rolled over and looked at the phone on the bedside table. "I'll write it down. Don't forget to have fun. Oh shit." Maggie looked at her watch. "I've got to run."

Evvie walked her downstairs, where they hugged tightly, both of them laughing as they wiped away tears, unable to believe their three perfect years had come to an end. Then Maggie left and Evvie walked back up to her room, suddenly feeling very alone.

Without Maggie, the suite felt lonely and a little overwhelming. Evvie sat for a while looking out the window, with no idea what to do for the rest of the day, let alone the rest of the week.

Eventually she switched on the television and flicked around, watching the daytime talk shows. She wasn't used to being on her own, could barely remember the last time she had been. Of course there had been times when Maggie and Topher were out and she was the only one in the house, but it was never for long, and there was usually studying to be done, or some other distraction. She knew she would never be by herself for long, but suddenly a week felt like an eternity.

The daytime shows led to old black-and-white films in the afternoon, with Evvie eventually falling asleep. She woke up in the evening, disoriented, not knowing where she was, or whether it was morning or night.

Realizing it was night, and grateful that at least she managed to kill day one, she had no idea what to do for the rest of it, knowing only that she had to get out of this room that was rapidly feeling more like a prison.

Evvie had never thought of herself as someone who was not good at being alone, but it struck her that perhaps she was more of an extrovert than she realized, needing other people to energize her. But what kind of self-sufficient feminist could she possibly be if she wasn't good at being alone? How would she be able to fulfill her dreams of traveling in the third world, helping women and children with education and health, if she couldn't manage one week in a luxury hotel without a social life?

She could do this. She would have a great week, even if she had no idea what to do. She got up and opened all the cupboards in the room without thinking, before stumbling upon the minibar, the lower shelves filled with tiny bottles of alcohol, the upper one with giant Toblerones.

Toblerones. She stared at them, remembering the feel of milky chocolate melting on her tongue. She hadn't had chocolate in so long, hadn't turned to food for comfort for so long, barely at all since Dexatrim took her appetite away. She closed the minibar and walked to the bathroom, but she couldn't stop thinking about chocolate, and how it would make her feel better.

Except it wouldn't make her feel better. It would make her feel . . . nothing. That's why Evvie had always eaten, because it numbed her feelings, and it was much easier to feel nothing than it was to feel fear, or anger, or loneliness. But the numbing never lasted. Afterward, she would be plagued by guilt and shame, but she never thought about that when food was calling, as it was then; never remembered how awful she would feel until it was too late.

If she ate it now, and had one lost evening, she could start again tomorrow morning. Plus, there was always the option of vomiting. It wasn't something she did all the time, but a useful secret weapon when her willpower was nowhere to be found.

Don't do it, she told herself, shutting the door, picturing her future, photo shoots, the other models living in the apartment, all of them happily existing on Diet Cokes and Marlboro Lights. It wouldn't be worth it, she thought as the image of Toblerones lodged itself into her brain. "Distract yourself," she said out loud.

Heading to the bathroom, she poured the entire bottle of bubble bath into the Jacuzzi and turned on the jets. By the time the bath was full, the bubbles were well above the rim of the bathtub. Compared to the pathetic shower she had had to endure the last three years — more of a dripping hose than a shower — sinking into a mountain of bubbles felt like the height of luxury. She lay there for just under an hour, adding more hot water whenever it got cold, amazed that there was still hot water after forty-five minutes. In the house there was never enough hot water for one person, let alone three.

Afterward, Evvie wrapped herself in a giant fluffy robe, played with her hair in the mirror, and wondered how she was supposed to kill the rest of the night. There were inevitably a few students left, the ones who had got summer jobs, who didn't have families to return to, but Evvie didn't know anyone who was still in town.

She would go for a walk, she decided. Maybe even a run, though she had always claimed an allergy to exercise. Afterward she might grab a drink at the King's Head, see if she knew anyone there. Maybe they could do with some help. Hell, at this point, working in a pub for a few days seemed a far better option than watching television in a four-poster bed. Pulling on some leggings and a T-shirt, she clipped her hair back in a ponytail and headed out the door.

The town without its students was like a ghost town. Evvie had never realized before that half the shops closed down for the summer or were open on limited hours. With no one around to buy patchouli oil, tie-dyed dresses, and handmade wind catchers, there was little point in remaining open.

Evvie attempted a run, which quickly became a jog, which settled back into a walk, Evvie clutching the stitch in her side and breathing heavily. When the pain had subsided, she walked briskly up the high street to the King's Head, nervous about walking in on her own.

Gone were the hordes of students. A few locals were dotted around, sipping pints, but it felt deserted, and sad. She hesitated in the doorway, but couldn't bring herself to go in. It felt completely different without the students, and not a place she belonged.

Closing the door quietly behind her, she had made it halfway to the corner when she thought she heard her name. She turned, startled, to see none other than Evil Ben making his way toward her from, presumably, the King's Head. She had seen the locals, but she hadn't seen him. He, on the other hand, had clearly seen her.

Great, she thought, with a deep internal sigh. The last person she wanted to see. She had nothing to say to him. It would appear he was slightly drunk, and she braced herself, wondering whether he would be Charming Ben, whom Maggie had encountered that time with her parents, whom she had had a vague glimpse of the other day in the pub when he joined them for drinks, or Evil Ben, whom she had worked with all those years ago.

It would only be seconds before she found out.

THIRTEEN

- 1989 -

"Evvie!" He walked toward her with — somewhat bizarrely — arms outstretched, as if he was about to hug her, and with what looked like a delighted smile on his face.

Evvie took a wary step back before finding herself embraced by him in what felt like a very awkward hug. Why on earth was Evil Ben hugging her? She patted him stiffly on the back before expertly disengaging herself.

She looked at him and realized he looked altogether too happy. "Are you completely shit-faced, Ben?"

He laughed. "Not completely. We're on a scavenger hunt, and you, my dear Evvie, are exactly the woman I was hoping to see."

"Who's on a scavenger hunt, and why did you want to see me?"

"I'm on a scavenger hunt with my mates. It's Rich's twenty-fourth birthday, and this is how we're celebrating. I've been stuck on item number eight." He swayed ever so slightly as he reached into his pocket and brought out a piece of paper, handing it to Evvie to read.

She scanned the first few items, mentally rolling her eyes. *A 36C bra.* Of course. *Take a picture hugging a teddy bear.* She thought of Topher then, of his Sebastian Flyte teddy bear phase when they first met, as a pang of missing her friends washed over her that was so sharp, she inhaled deeply with a shake of her head before going back to the list. *A pair of earrings that you have to wear at the final party. Find a lightsaber. Snog a celebrity and take a picture.* Evvie looked up at Evil Ben.

"Item number eight says snog a celebrity and take a picture."

"That's why I was going to look for you. Someone said they'd heard you were here for a few days." He grinned. "You're the only celebrity I know."

"I'm hardly a celebrity."

"You were in that TV show, so you're the closest thing I could find."

"Even if that's the case, I'm not going to snog you." Evvie shook her head in disgust, appalled that he would even ask.

"Oh, go on, Evvie," Ben pleaded. "It's just for a scavenger hunt."

"Why would I do that? What's the big deal about a scavenger hunt?"

Ben shrugged. "Nothing, but I'm competitive. I was hoping you'd take pity on me. If I won, you could come to Rich's party with me. How's that?"

Evvie stared at him. Normally she'd say no. She would have no interest in going to a party with Evil Ben, but normally she wouldn't be on her own with a very long week stretching in front of her.

"Go on," said Ben. "I tell you what. Even if I don't win, you could come to the party with me."

"What makes you think I would want to go to a party with you?"

Ben paused, thinking. "Pity?"

Despite herself, Evvie laughed. "When you say snog, what do you mean? Tongues or no tongues?"

There was a long pause. "No tongues." He peered at her. "Unless you want to."

"I definitely don't want to." Evvie thought of Maggie's face if she knew Evvie was even considering snogging Ben. But this was just a game, and at least going to a party would give her something to do. A kiss, especially one without tongues, meant nothing.

"Do you have a camera?" she asked, before Ben triumphantly pulled a small disposable one out of his pocket.

"One kiss," she said as Ben whooped and fist-pumped the air.

"Here?" he asked, looking up and down the high street.

"No!" Evvie was horrified at the prospect of kissing in the middle of the street. Looking around, she saw the alleyway next to Dorothy Perkins, and pointed. "Let's go there."

Evvie walked in front of Ben, shaking her head to herself at what she was about to do. Never in a million years had she ever imagined she would be kissing Evil Ben.

They stepped into the alleyway and faced each other as Evvie suddenly felt a jolt inside her stomach. She wasn't sure what it meant, but she didn't like it. Let's get this over with quickly, she thought.

"Ready?" she asked as Ben took a step toward her, holding the camera awkwardly at arm's length. Evvie closed her eyes and tilted her head up, pursing her lips slightly, ready for the kiss. She could sense him moving closer, and she opened her eyes briefly, seeing that his face was then inches from hers, but his eyes were open, and he was gazing at her, which caused another jolt. He was not smiling, as he had been ever since he called her name, a smile that felt almost mocking to Evvie, that was completely in line with who she had always thought he was.

The smile had gone, his eyes were half-closed, and Evvie's insides were stirring. With shock, she recognized it as a dagger of lust, but before she had time to even think about what that meant, Ben's lips were upon hers, so soft, so gentle, her insides turned again as she pulled quickly away, her cheeks flushed, her heart beating a million miles per minute.

"Did you get it?" she asked, not meeting his eye, her voice harsher than she meant, to cover up unexpected feelings that made no sense whatsoever.

He stared at her, then looked at the camera, shaking his head before turning back to her. His smile was nowhere to be seen.

"I'm not sure," he said quietly. "Can we try once more?"

Evvie closed her eyes again, and this time she felt a quivering in her groin as his lips touched hers. Without thinking about it, she parted her lips as he sucked her bottom lip between his and pulled away for a second before kissing her again. She let out an involuntary sigh as their tongues tentatively met, her insides upside down, her hands automatically reaching around his back. Then Ben was pushing her against the wall, grinding himself against her as she gasped, her body responding even though her mind was questioning what the hell was happening.

"Where are you staying tonight?" Ben broke off to whisper, kissing down the side of her neck as she groaned.

"Dinham Arms."

"Can I come back there with you?" he whispered into her ear, nipping her earlobe as she shivered. Without answering, she took his hand, emotions and lust overriding whatever common sense she may have had when she left the hotel that evening, and they walked up the high street, not looking at each other, on their way to the hotel.

FOURTEEN

- 1989 -

Evvie had never understood the big deal about sex. She had had sex plenty of times, and definitely enjoyed the feeling of power it gave her, but beyond that, she was pretty sure she had never had an orgasm, and although you would never have known it from the way she joined in conversations, she had a secret worry that perhaps there was something wrong with her.

It didn't help that she was unbearably self-conscious about her body, terrified of being seen naked, convinced that however attracted men might have been when she was fully clothed, they would be disappointed in her naked. She insisted on all the lights being off, always, and used the duvet as a security blanket, hauling it off the bed to wrap herself in on her way to the bathroom. Even skinny, as she was thanks to the Dexatrim, she felt that her body would be somehow disappointing. Until now.

Every time Ben touched her, her insides would roll over, lust coursing through her body. They made it up to her room and onto the giant four-poster bed, where Ben left her top on, pulling off her trousers and her underwear, moving down her body until he was lapping between her legs. Instead of feeling self-conscious, vaguely embarrassed, worried about how she would look, smell, taste, she allowed herself to be swept away on a wave, until she was aware that someone far away was gasping and moaning, the noise building and getting louder, and it wasn't until afterward that she realized it was her.

She undressed Ben then, unable to stop kissing him, embracing him, wanting to squeeze him tight, taking him in her mouth but stopping to climb on his lap, not embarrassed when he lifted her shirt over her head, taking a nipple in his mouth as she reached down to guide him into her.

He made her orgasm again, this time inside her, allowing himself to come at the same time, and they sat, laughing softly, kissing, Evvie's arms draped around his neck, both of them covered in sweat as Evvie felt her legs shaking and tears forming that she willed away.

This is what it was all about, she thought.

I'm normal! This is why everyone makes such a big deal about sex. Finally, she understood. That wave of pleasure, so strong it was almost inhuman, the sounds that came out of her body without her realizing, the contentment she now felt, the satisfaction, the exhaustion.

"When can we do that again?" she said, grinning as he kissed her.

"I need to sleep for a bit," he said, twirling her hair around his finger. "God, you're beautiful. I am the luckiest man in the world right now. How are you feeling about this? Are you okay?"

"Am I okay? I feel amazing!" She didn't need to tell him it was the first time someone else had made her orgasm.

"*You're* amazing." He smiled. "I think I've won the scavenger hunt. And the lottery."

The smile was instantly wiped from Evvie's face as she climbed off him. "You're joking, right?" she said.

"Of course I'm joking." He came after her, encircling her with his arms. "That was nothing to do with the scavenger hunt. You're the most beautiful woman here, and completely out of my league. I've always fancied you, but not for a moment did I even think you'd look at me."

Evvie felt herself softening. "You have? I

thought you always fancied Maggie."

"Honestly? I thought you were both gorgeous. But I couldn't get involved with either of you. You were freshers when I first saw you both, and I was a postgrad student. There was no way I could get involved with freshers."

"Is that why you were so rude to me when I worked at the King's Head?"

"I didn't mean to be rude. I was so intimidated by you, I couldn't even look at you."

"Intimidated?" Evvie was stunned. She could understand people being intimidated by Maggie. She was statuesque, and well-spoken, with a confidence that belied her years. But Evvie? Evvie had never seen herself as someone who would intimidate people.

"You're so stunning. You were working right next to me, and I was terrified. I had no idea what to say to you."

Evvie thought back to those days, to how chubby she was, to how inadequate she felt, as her heart hurt. Ben had thought she was attractive. He never noticed the weight, didn't see her as she saw herself, and she felt herself flooded with gratitude.

"You were such an ass." She kissed him.

"You *have* such an arse." He moved his hands down to her butt as she laughed.

"Let's get some sleep. This is only the beginning."

When they got back into bed, Ben reached over for her and she settled in his arms. Evvie had always loved cuddling, relished the feeling of being held; up until tonight, it was the best thing about sex. But she had never been able to sleep wrapped in someone's arms, had always disentangled herself in order to fall asleep.

That night Evvie allowed herself to be held, and when she woke up the next morning, she was still tightly in his arms. It was only when the phone started to ring that she felt flooded with guilt.

It could only have been Maggie. Ben stirred with the ringing of the phone, but Evvie couldn't pick up, and let it ring and ring until it stopped. Ben slept on as Evvie looked at him, knowing how upset Maggie would be if she knew what had happened last night. Maggie had always claimed Ben as her own: her crush, hers by right.

But what right did Maggie actually have to him? One drunken snog that Ben hadn't remembered and three years of fantasizing? This wasn't high school; you couldn't claim someone who didn't want you, nor could you get upset with a friend for being with someone when you were all free agents.

And yet, this was not how friendship worked. Evvie knew that Maggie would see it as a betrayal. It may not be insurmountable, but Maggie would be hurt and would undoubtedly blame Evvie, even though this was not something Evvie had planned. My God, she had never been interested in Ben in the slightest, had actively disliked him. But the chemistry! The minute he kissed her last night, it was as if her whole body was on fire; she had never felt anything like it, and she couldn't walk away now, had to see it through to see if it was real. If it was, she would deal with Maggie. You could begrudge your best friend having a fling with your number one crush, but you couldn't hold that grudge if they turned out to be soul mates.

Evvie shook her head. There was no way on earth she and Ben were soul mates. Maybe it would be easier if she ended it now. By the time she and Maggie saw each other again, her fling with Ben would be a distant memory, a one-night stand that would be meaningless, that Evvie would be able to pretend had never happened.

Evvie drifted back to sleep, and when she woke up again, she rested her head on her hand, watching Ben until he stirred, yawning and turning over to see Evvie. She steeled herself, knowing he had been drunk the night before, expecting him to be distant or dismissive in the cold light of day, to have regrets. Evvie stiffened her back, unsure how he would be now that he was sober, unwilling to have to deal with rejection.

And then he smiled, those dimples forming as Evvie's heart flipped over. She wondered how she could go from hating someone to wanting to lick every inch of his body. He reached out and pulled her into him, nuzzling her neck.

"I have morning breath," she said when he moved to kiss her mouth.

That wasn't what she meant to say. What she meant to say was that she couldn't do this, that last night was great but it was pointless. He was going back to London, and she was going to New York, and yes, the sex may have been great, but it was only sex and there was no point in doing anything further because there was nowhere for this to go. And all the while, she would know that she was doing the right thing because if she didn't push him away, Maggie would kill her.

"I don't care," he said as his tongue touched hers, and all thoughts of Maggie, of everything, were forgotten as Evvie sighed and sank into his arms.

FIFTEEN

- 1989 -

Evvie thought about Ben all the way to the airport, and for the entire plane ride to New York. She thought about him as she looked for a driver carrying a card with her name on it waiting at Arrivals, and in the car on the way to Manhattan. She stopped thinking about him when she saw the skyline, the view taking her breath away, a shiver of excitement running through her body as she realized how big life was, how much possibility New York held.

She made herself stop thinking about Ben. There was nowhere for this to go, Evvie had been telling herself, even before she left. During those few days they had together, they didn't talk about the future. Every morning Evvie told herself she was going to end it, this would be the last time. But the chemistry between them had been so strong, she couldn't resist.

Every evening, Ben would show up at her

hotel after spending the day with his friends, not knowing that Evvie had wasted the day counting off the minutes until he arrived. He would walk in the room and she would be all over him, tearing at his clothes, the pair of them falling on the bed laughing as they rolled around, playing with each other's bodies, reveling in the heights to which they could bring the other.

Ben brought toys one night. Handcuffs, silk scarves, a paddle.

"Is this your thing?" Evvie had asked, concerned. It hadn't been either of their "thing," it turned out, other than for the fact that it made them laugh. When Ben tapped her backside with the paddle, she started giggling, and when he tried it harder, at her request, to see if it might do something for her, she let out a loud "ouch!" There was nothing sexy about it, which made them both crack up, and somehow their shared laughter, the sense of sex being fun, made Evvie feel closer to Ben than anything else.

"If I come to New York, can I see you?" Ben said on their final morning.

Evvie nodded. "And I'll come to see you if I'm in London. How about that?" She wondered why there seemed to be a lump in the back of her throat.

Evvie was about to experience huge adventures; the last thing she wanted was an English boyfriend who would get in the way. And yet, she couldn't quite believe that she probably wouldn't ever see him again, couldn't quite believe how attached she had got in such a short time.

The modeling agency had sent a car to pick her up and take her to the airport. Ben had carried her suitcases and put them in the car before taking her in his arms and holding her tight. They had clung to each other for a long time, and when Evvie disengaged, she thought she might have seen tears in his eyes.

It's not real, she told herself on the plane. It wasn't like they'd spent quality time together. They had had amazing sex, and some fun. They had even gone out for dinner on the last night, which felt like a date, even though Ben had had far too much to drink and ended up passing out as soon as they got back to the hotel room.

Her apartment was a loft in the Meatpacking District. It had sounded glamorous when the agency told her, but it was five flights up, and the stairs were dark and dingy. She arrived outside the door of 5B and pulled out the key the agency had sent her, opening the door to a huge open-plan room with exposed brick walls and floor-to-ceiling windows, through which daylight poured.

There was an L-shaped white sofa and a large distressed coffee table on which sat three empty wine bottles, five glasses, three coffee mugs, and an overflowing pile of magazines.

"Hello?" Evvie hauled her suitcases in. "Anyone here?"

"Hello!" An enormous blonde with legs like a gazelle came running into the room, flinging her arms around Evvie. "You must be Evie!"

"Evvie," she corrected.

"I am Sophie from Hamburg. We've all been waiting for you." She picked up Evvie's biggest suitcase as if it weighed nothing, and started striding toward a corridor. "You are sharing a room with me, but I have left you lots of space."

The room was big, and tidy, unlike the bedroom next door shared by Annabelle, who was Dutch, and Kat, who was English, which had clothes strewn all over the floor. By the time she had unpacked and put her clothes away, she had stopped thinking about Ben, and by the end of her first week, after late-night getting-to-know-you chats with her roommates, and appointments with hairdressers, bookers, and photographers, her old life at West Country University felt like it had happened to someone else, many lifetimes ago.

It was a whirlwind, and a wake-up call after a sleepy Somerset university. Everything was bigger and brighter in New York. Every night, the girls would try on one another's clothes before heading out to a club. There was more champagne than they could drink and cocaine to kill their appetites and sober them up, and everywhere they went, there were dozens of creepy old men willing to keep them in drinks, drugs, and occasionally expensive presents, mostly just for the privilege of their attention.

After six weeks, Evvie got her first official modeling job. Dressing to get ready, she pulled on some pants from Kat that she had borrowed a few times before. They had always been a little big, but as she shrugged them up and tried to fasten them, the material stretched, the button refusing to meet the buttonhole.

Evvie groaned. It wasn't like she'd been eating — living with three other girls who didn't eat did wonders for her dieting. All of the girls were going to extreme measures to stay skinny, and Evvie's Dexatrim combined with the odd line of cocaine at the parties they went to was proving magical. So how was it possible that these pants didn't close? She grabbed a safety pin and pinned them together, wondering if she might have been bloated from something she ate.

She forgot about it once she arrived at the photo shoot, until a change of outfit and the photographer instructing her to jump off a box with her arms high up in the air. As she launched herself, the military jacket she was wearing popped open, the button clattering to the floor and spinning into a corner, revealing Evvie's nonexistent breasts. Except they were no longer nonexistent; they seemed much fuller, and rounder than usual.

"Fantastic!" shouted the photographer, who kept on shooting as Evvie frantically pulled the jacket over her breasts, silently and shamefully vowing to eat nothing for the next two weeks.

That night, it was Kat who voiced the one thought Evvie had been refusing to allow herself to think.

"I think you're pregnant, love," she said after Evvie got home from the shoot, looking her up and down, her eyes coming to a final rest on her stomach. "It's not the trousers. You're putting on weight in that pregnancy way. And look at those bosoms! You didn't have those when we all moved in."

"Fuck," whispered Evvie, the color draining from her face. Ben had used protection. They used condoms, every single time. Except for that first time, when neither of them was prepared for how lust would carry them away. But even then, they were careful. Ben pulled out. It couldn't be that. Evvie said as much to Kat, who looked at her with skepticism.

Fuck.

Kat accompanied Evvie to the Planned Parenthood clinic the next day. All the while, Evvie stayed firmly in denial. She kept thinking that it couldn't be, there could not be any way she was pregnant after one time; this wouldn't be possible. It certainly wouldn't be *fair*.

The nurse at Planned Parenthood was gentle, and sympathetic. She gave Evvie armfuls of leaflets to look over while they waited the few days for the blood test to come back.

But it didn't help.

"I feel sick," said Evvie as soon as they walked out, her face as white as a sheet.

"Do you need to throw up?" Kat asked,

glancing at a nearby trash can.

"No. I just mean I'm scared. I'm also hungry. Can we get some Baskin-Robbins?"

Kat started to laugh. "Are you joking? God, you really *are* pregnant. I can't eat that stuff. I've got a shoot tomorrow. I've been eating cotton balls soaked in orange juice for the last two days."

"You have?" Evvie looked at her in horror.

"I have. It's awful. But I was feeling so bloated, and someone said that's what the girls do to stay thin. I still haven't met anyone else who's actually done it, and it's so disgusting, I think it may be an urban myth."

"You look great. And your boobs are practically flat. Try living in this body." Evvie stuck out her expanding breasts. "I'm getting ice cream. Screw the photo shoots."

The phone call from Planned Parenthood came a few days later. The results were in, and they were positive. Evvie was told to come in as soon as possible to discuss options.

Two days later, the abortion was booked, with Evvie's only question being whether or not to let Ben know. She tried to tell herself that it was none of his business — her body, her future. She wished she was able to run it by Maggie, who had always steered Evvie in the right direction. But of course Maggie was the last person she could confide in.

"If I were him, I would want to know," said Kat. "It's a courtesy. He's still half-responsible, and even though he doesn't get a say in what you're going to do, I think it's the right thing to tell him."

Evvie waited until everyone was out, until she knew she would have complete privacy. She got out her Filofax and turned to *C,* her heart pounding as the phone was picked up.

It wasn't a great connection, and she had trouble hearing the person who had answered the phone.

"Ben?" she asked, unsure.

"No. Hang on. Who's calling?"

"Evvie."

She heard the man yelling for Ben, then footsteps and a dull murmur, until it was quite clearly Ben's voice saying hello. For a second she felt relief, and pleasure, before remembering why she was phoning.

"This is a surprise," he said. "I didn't expect to hear from you while you're in New York. Unless you're in London?" It's irrelevant, thought Evvie, but his voice sounded hopeful.

"Can't you tell from this awful line? I'm

in New York."

"Oh. How are you? How's the modeling?"

Evvie took a deep breath. "It's all good but I have some news. I'm really sorry to phone with this but . . ." She paused. How were you supposed to deliver such momentous news, even if it would only be temporary? "I'm pregnant," she said quickly. "I just wanted to let you know that I've scheduled an abortion for next week."

There was a long silence.

"You're what?" said Ben.

"Pregnant. I know. It sucks."

"But . . . I don't understand. How could you be pregnant?"

"The first time? When we didn't have a condom? Remember?"

Another silence, and Evvie knew he didn't remember, that he had had too much to drink. "You pulled out," she said quietly. "I never thought this could happen."

"You're pregnant," he said again as Evvie's heart sank, not knowing what to make of this reaction.

"I'm not asking anything from you. I don't want money, I'm taking care of everything. I just thought you should know."

"What if I don't want you to have an abortion?"

"What?" Evvie didn't think she'd heard

properly.

"I know it might be crazy, but what if you had the baby? What if I got a job in New York, or you moved to London? What if we tried this out? You and me. And a baby. I know we don't know each other well, and this sounds nuts, but I have a good feeling about us. I think we could do it. I think we could make this work."

Evvie was silent. This was the very last thing she ever expected to hear. She had no idea what to say.

"I know it sounds crazy." Ben's voice was rushed, heightened with what sounded suspiciously like excitement. "But I think we could do this. I've always wanted children, and obviously, this isn't planned, but this could be the best thing that's ever happened to us."

Us, thought Evvie. There is no *us.* And there couldn't be an *us,* not when she was at the very beginning of her adult life, when having a baby would change everything. She didn't want a baby, and as much as hearing Ben's voice gave her a pang that felt like missing him, they barely knew each other. Bringing a baby into the world would be the last thing either of them needed.

"This isn't what I want," said Evvie. "I'm sorry. I really am, but I can't have a baby.

Not now."

"But it's not just about what *you* want. What about me? What about what I want? This baby is half mine. This isn't a decision you can make by yourself."

It's not a baby yet, thought Evvie. It's a collection of cells. I refuse to think of this as a baby or I don't know if I will have the strength to do what I need to do.

"I'm sorry," said Evvie. "It is a decision I can make by myself, and it's a decision I've already made."

"Don't do this," said Ben, his voice now hard. "You can't do this. If you go through with this, Evvie, I will never forgive you."

"I'm sorry," she whispered as a long silence fell. And because neither of them knew what else to say, she put down the phone.

■ ■ ■ ■ ■

PART II
THE IN-BETWEEN
YEARS

■ ■ ■ ■

Sixteen

- 1992 -

Topher eased his eyes open and looked at the clock. It said 3:32, and for a few seconds he was completely disoriented. Was that 3:32 in the morning or in the afternoon, and if it was in the morning, why was there daylight visible through the bedroom blinds, and could it be possible that he had been asleep for a day and a half?

Of course not, he realized. Last night was the usual danceathon at Club USA, doing lines in the bathroom that kept him wide awake and dancing until the early hours, getting back to his apartment sometime around ten. In the morning. *Shit!* Wasn't the audition for that soap today? Jumping out of bed, he grabbed his planner, letting out a sigh of relief that he'd got it wrong, the audition wasn't until tomorrow, as he gratefully crawled back into bed and sank against the pillows. He couldn't go out tonight. This audition was for a major role in a long-running soap, and Topher's agent had said that not only was he perfect for it, they were excited to meet him. He would not fuck it up by going clubbing tonight. No way, no how, because even when he would tell himself he was only going for an hour, a quick drink, it always seemed to turn into an all-nighter.

At least he was alone, he thought. No one to get rid of, nothing to regret on that front. So much of the New York gay scene had been decimated by AIDS, the ones who were left were determined to squeeze every last inch out of life. Topher was among them. He was young and pretty, and although decidedly not into one-night stands or casual flings, he loved being admired, and no one was a better flirt.

He needed food, he thought, a sudden craving for one of Maggie's perfectly pale homemade French omelets. He hadn't spoken to Maggie much, nor Evvie, which would be ridiculous if not for the fact that Evvie's modeling career had taken off and she was hardly ever in New York. When she was, they would try to get together, but the clubs and bars they frequented were not the same, although Topher was still always surprised that they didn't see each other more.

There was a diner on the corner, but Topher didn't want diner food; he craved homemade. He could be in and out of Gristedes and back home cooking in twenty minutes. He pulled on sweatpants and sneakers, threw on last night's T-shirt, and gave his teeth a cursory brush before grabbing his wallet and taking the elevator downstairs, running his hands through his hair in a bid to make himself more presentable.

"Afternoon, Topher," said Louis, the doorman, grinning. "Big night?"

"Always," said Topher, raising a hand as he passed him.

In Gristedes he pushed the small cart around, trying to figure out what he wanted. Eggs, naturally. Emmental. Mushrooms. Spinach. Garlic, because why not. Sourdough bread. A Viennetta as a treat. He'd try not to eat the whole thing.

He was aware of someone close to him, and looked over to see a man peering into his cart.

"That looks like a delicious seduction dinner," said the man, who was a little older than Topher, and extraordinarily cute.

"Hardly. It's my hungover-from-too-late-a-night-at-Club-USA recovery breakfast," laughed Topher.

173

"You need more greens," said the man, looking into Topher's eyes. "And more protein. In my book, bacon makes everything better."

"Bacon!" Topher laughed. "How could I have forgotten the bacon?"

"I'll get it for you," the stranger said, turning toward the refrigerators. Topher watched him walk. Nice butt, he thought, smiling when he realized the man had turned and caught him looking.

"I'm Larry," said the man when he got back. "This bacon is the best."

"I'm Topher. I guess you must live in the hood?"

"Next block. I'm pretty sure you do too because I've seen you around before."

"One block east."

"It's nice to meet you. How do you feel about inviting neighbors over for breakfast?"

"*You're* forward," Topher said, acting surprised.

"You can't ever be forward with neighbors. I'm just being neighborly. Also, I'm a very good cook. I could help make the job easier. I'll bring my Sunday papers."

"You're sure you're not a serial killer who picks up young men by pretending to live in their neighborhood?"

"This is who I am," said Larry, bringing a

business card out of his pocket and handing it to Topher, whose face lit up as he read it.

"You own the Muscleman gym? I love that place. I wish I could afford the membership."

"Let's talk about special rates over breakfast," Larry said with a grin, taking Topher's cart and insisting on paying for all the food, before they walked side by side back to Topher's apartment.

"I never do this," said Topher as they sat down to perfect omelets made by Larry, who had also made himself right at home, opening all the kitchen cabinets to find the pans, whisks, and spoons.

"You never invite strange men back to your apartment? Come on. Do you think I was born yesterday?"

"I don't invite them back for breakfast. Or is this lunch?" Topher looked at his watch. "I guess it's pretty much dinner. The early bird special."

"I don't usually get invited to cook in strange men's apartments, so we're equal."

"You invited yourself," said Topher, who was astonished at how easy it was to be around Larry. He was twenty-nine, six years older than Topher, a Penn graduate who spent his first few years working in finance, until he made enough money to buy a failing gym, which he then turned into Muscleman, the hottest gym in the village.

"I did. I've seen you around and I wanted to meet you, and what better way to get to know someone than over a meal. Eat your spinach." He nodded over at Topher's plate, and Topher did as he was told.

"So . . . no boyfriend?" Topher asked, wondering why someone as clever, cute, and accessible as Larry might be in a position to come to his apartment on a Sunday afternoon, seemingly with no other plans or commitments.

"He died," Larry said simply. "It's okay. It was two years ago. I'm trying to get on with life, but no one serious since then, no."

Topher presumed, as was always presumed when someone gay died before their time, that it was AIDS, but he didn't want to ask. Not that it would change his view of Larry; half his friends were positive. It had become a fact of life that was not shocking to Topher and his friends; it just *was*.

"You?" Larry asked.

"Footloose and fancy-free," said Topher. "And happy that way," he added, just in case Larry had the wrong idea.

After lunch, they washed up together, idly chitchatting in the kitchen, all the while Topher realizing he was finding Larry more and more attractive.

"Newspaper time." Larry put coffee on as if he belonged there, then went to the living room, sinking into the sofa, feet on the coffee table as he unfolded the Sunday *Times.* "I'm really sorry," he said to Topher. "You're welcome to fight me for it, but I always start with Style."

"I'll make do with Arts," said Topher. "Just this once." He hesitated, not knowing where to sit, until Larry patted the sofa next to him. Topher sat down, aware that their legs were touching, but Larry didn't turn and kiss him, or move a hand to his crotch as Topher thought he might.

Instead, Larry just sat there, completely comfortable, as he immersed himself in the paper. Topher read his own section of the paper, inching his upper body slowly toward Larry's, until soon, he was leaning on him. He looked over and met Larry's eyes. Larry smiled at him, then went back to the paper, and Topher felt his whole body relax as he leaned into this newfound friend with a contented sigh.

SEVENTEEN

- 1992 -

Sometimes, when Topher showed up for an audition, everything was wrong. He couldn't always put his finger on it, but it would start the minute he rolled out of bed. He felt uptight, out of touch with himself, and nothing went his way.

And then there were other days, like this, when he woke up feeling great, full of energy, excited about life, knowing that he would charm everyone he met that day, that life would go his way.

What Comes Around was one of the most successful soap operas of the decade, and Topher was in the lobby of a small television studio in Midtown, right on time, waiting to be called in to audition.

There were three other men dotted around, all of them looking over the same script, all of them there for the same audition, all of them good-looking men, roughly the same age. The part was for Rip Wallington, the long-lost son of the wealthy patriarch of the Wallington clan, a boy who had been banished to England but who was returning to steal his father's secret mistress and create general havoc on the show.

One of the men sitting there gave Topher a smile. He looked familiar, and Topher wandered over.

"You're here for the part of Rip?" he asked, sitting down.

"We all are. Did I see you at the Jungle last week?"

"Friday night?"

He nodded.

"Then you did. Great bar, right?"

"I loved it. I'm Alec."

"Topher."

Just then the door opened and a woman stood there looking at a clipboard. "Topher Winthrop?"

"Nice to meet you. Good luck." Topher smiled at Alec as he stood up, knowing he would bump into him again, and recognizing that Alec was giving him that look that said under different circumstances, had they had more time, Alec probably would have suggested they meet.

It was a good audition. Hell, maybe it was the best audition Topher had ever had. He had never imagined himself on a soap, so he wasn't particularly attached to the outcome. He wasn't nervous, felt confident, and read beautifully. Although the script wasn't particularly humorous, there was one line that made Topher laugh, and he played it for humor, bringing a laugh out of everyone in the room.

"You were fantastic," said the girl with the clipboard as she led him back out. "They loved you!"

"I'm sure everyone here is fantastic," Topher said conspiratorially.

"Not like you. You would be a perfect Rip. Good luck."

She called Alec in, and as he walked past Topher, he muttered, "Jungle this Friday?"

Topher just smiled. Under different circumstances he would have agreed, but there was something about Larry that he couldn't get out of his head. He didn't want to play the field or complicate things. He wanted to see whether there could be something with Larry, whether he was as good as he seemed.

Over the next couple of weeks, he and Larry fell into an easy routine, meeting after work for a quick bite to eat at a neighborhood restaurant, or Larry cooking Topher dinner at either of their apartments. After three weeks, Topher started to worry that Larry wasn't attracted to him, that he had read this all wrong. He assumed it was perhaps the start of a beautiful friendship, the easiest one Topher had ever had, but not more, because Larry hadn't made a move.

And Topher, who had spent his life avoiding intimacy, avoiding being touched, found himself craving Larry's touch. He had thought about kissing Larry, or reaching over and placing an unsubtle hand on his crotch as they sat together after dinner, but the prospect of rejection was one he couldn't handle. And so he waited.

Topher's agent finally called, bubbling with excitement. Topher had got the part of Rip Wallington! They had known from the minute he walked in that it was him, and they wanted him to come in on Monday and meet everyone.

Topher was thrilled to have steady work, even as he hoped he wouldn't remain a soap actor forever, rather that it would be a stepping-stone to greater things. But still, it meant a modicum of fame, which was exciting, whichever way you sliced it.

He phoned Larry to tell him the good news, and Larry immediately suggested a celebratory dinner that night. But Topher was tired and in need of a night at home, so Larry came over instead, to cook something suitably celebratory.

It was lobster. They were alive when they arrived, in a polystyrene box with ice, carried in by Larry, who immediately filled a huge pot with water and boiled it. Topher offered to plunge the lobsters, but much to his mortification instead dropped one beast on the floor when it unexpectedly moved a claw. It scuttled into the corner as Topher shrieked and climbed up on a stool.

Larry laughed until tears ran down his cheeks. "I wish I had a camera," he said, wiping the tears away as he helped Topher off the stool. "*I'll* put the lobsters in the pot."

"I'm sorry. I didn't think it would be a problem. God knows I watched our housekeeper cook enough lobsters when we were up at the Vineyard, but I just couldn't do it. I'm too much of a wuss."

"A very cute and talented wuss," said Larry affectionately, retrieving the lobster and plunging it into the boiling water with no compunction whatsoever. Topher watched, impressed, wondering, hoping, that he and Larry would become more than friends sometime soon.

It happened that night. Topher was washing up after Larry had cooked dinner, the two of them puttering in his tiny galley kitchen, when he became aware of Larry standing behind him. They weren't touching, but there was something different in the air, a heaviness as if time were standing still. Topher's breath caught in his throat.

Larry didn't say anything. Topher felt the heat emanating from Larry's body as his own body started to respond. Slowly, and gently, he sensed Larry moving closer, before feeling Larry's soft breath on his neck, and then, like the softest of buttery kisses, felt his lips in the same place. Topher didn't move. He stopped washing the bowl he had been holding, setting it down gently in the sink, not moving, his entire being focused on the feel of Larry's lips on his skin.

All he could hear was the sound of his own breath echoing in his ears; all he could focus on was the feel of Larry's mouth on him. He turned as if in slow motion, and they stood, foreheads touching, breathing heavily, Larry not moving, not doing anything else, until Topher couldn't stand it anymore, and leaned forward until his own lips were on Larry's. And then they were kissing, as Topher felt his entire body turn to liquid gold.

Larry stayed over, and in the morning Topher was woken up by the sound of Larry laughing, his head appearing over the wall of pillows Topher had erected once Larry was asleep.

"What the hell is this?" Larry said, tossing each pillow, one by one, across the room. "How did the Great Wall of Pillows appear once I was sleeping?"

"I'm sorry." Topher was embarrassed. "I don't like to be touched when I'm not expecting it."

"You didn't seem to mind last night." Larry grinned over the one remaining pillow.

"I definitely didn't mind last night." Topher's stomach lurched as he flashed back to Larry's face above him, dipping down to lick his ear. "Maybe it's a sleeping thing," he lied. "I'm weird about suddenly finding an arm or a leg touching me while I'm asleep."

"Noted." Larry flung the last pillow to the end of the bed. "I'm not in a rush. I like you."

"I like you too." Topher felt a flush of pleasure.

"I mean I really like you. I want to take this slow. I'm in no rush. If you don't want to be touched unexpectedly, I won't touch you. We don't need to erect the Great Wall of Pillows every night."

Every night? Topher couldn't stop smiling

as he exhaled in relief at finally finding someone who seemed to understand him so well.

EIGHTEEN

- 1994 -

It was Maggie's first day at her new job, and she had no idea what to wear. She had worked in corporate PR where black was the order of the day, but she was certain that her boring little black suits wouldn't be chic enough for Les Jolies, the French cosmetics company she would now be working for. She was leaving corporate PR for consumer PR, and not for just anyone, but for one of the biggest cosmetic companies in the world. For the first time she would be exposed to the magazine industry, and the glamorous beauty editors who worked there.

She was terrified of getting it wrong. Fashion had never been her thing. The black suits she was able to get away with for years had been an enormous relief — like wearing a school uniform (which she had also loved). She had never needed to think about it — a black suit, a collared shirt, and sensible low heels.

A tour of her new office after she had accepted the job showed how wrong that would be in this world. It was like the cast of *Friends* had met the catwalk. Maggie's heart sank when she realized how she would have to start dressing.

Since then she had hit Joseph (for the expensive stuff) and Miss Selfridge (for the non-), and her work wardrobe now consisted of some jewel-tone crushed velvet bootleg pantsuits, with a few strappy dresses to be worn over silk T-shirts.

For her first day she had decided on a burgundy velvet suit with a black strappy camisole underneath (no one would ever see it was a camisole, for Maggie was determined never to remove the jacket, no matter how hot it got), and a black velvet choker. Her hair had been newly cut into choppy layers à la the "Rachel." This morning she had styled it just like Rachel on *Friends,* hoping that she could scrape it back in her usual bun by the end of the week.

She felt both glamorous and like something of a fraud. She'd even bought a burgundy lipstick to match the suit, and every time she caught a glimpse of herself in the darkened window of the tube, she thought she looked like a clown.

She was wrong. Within twenty minutes of walking into the office, five people had come up to her and complimented her on the suit, asking where she got it from.

"Your desk is here," said Linda, her boss, who marched through the office at a rate of knots, despite her four-inch heels. She led her to a small cubby with a blank wall facing her. All around, her fellow executives had decorated their cubbies. Their own walls were sophisticated and glamorous, covered with photographs of models, shots of beauty products, and inspirational messages. Maggie spotted Evvie on four different walls, and smiled to herself. This was clearly a sign that she was in the right place.

"I'm throwing you in at the deep end a bit." Linda handed Maggie a stuffed file with a laugh. "It's sink or swim here, I'm afraid. We've just announced a partnership with Swerdling, the pharmaceutical company. They've developed a revolutionary skin cream that actually stimulates the collagen in your own skin to not just make you look younger but actually reverse the aging process. We've been working on a new campaign to launch this, so I want you to familiarize yourself with it. Once you've read it, you can type up your own ideas to add to the campaign." She paused, seeing Maggie freeze. "Don't worry," she said. "No pressure. Just if you think of anything we haven't already covered. Let me have your notes by the end of the day."

By lunchtime, Maggie's head felt ready to explode. She had read through half the notes, keeping a notebook by her side, constantly stopping to scribble down ideas. The revolutionary ingredient was derived from fish, and it was scented with French lavender. There was a historic hotel just outside of Grasse, near Maggie's parents' home in the South of France, that had fields of lavender that were harvested for the perfumers in Grasse. Maggie had already phoned them and, in her immaculate French, negotiated a heavily discounted rate for the press trip she was going to propose to Linda.

She had written down Evvie as the face of the product, delighted that she had an inside track, hoping it might score her brownie points on her first day. And, thanks to her corporate PR background, she realized that scientific journals were the one item nobody had thought about. She had researched the journals, including those published in America, Australia, and throughout the major markets in Europe, proposing profiles on the scientists who had developed the ingredient.

At around one, a girl called Kelly came over to her desk. "We're all going to drop in to the launch of our new lipstick color," she said. "It's at the roof gardens in Kensington. I'm really sorry, because normally we'd ask you to come, but the receptionist is off sick and we need someone to stay and man the phones. Would you mind terribly staying just this once?"

"That's fine," said Maggie, who was relieved. The last thing she wanted to be doing was milling around with a group of strangers at a launch she knew nothing about.

"Do you know where the cafeteria is?" Kelly continued. "If you want to run down and grab something, we'll be here for another fifteen minutes. Also, we've all been invited to a film premiere Tuesday next week. Make sure you can come."

"Great." Maggie got up, realizing that Kelly felt guilty, picked up her purse, and, promising not to be long, headed downstairs to grab a sandwich to eat at her desk.

She was standing in the checkout line when she felt a tap on her shoulder. Turning, she took a sharp intake of breath as she found herself looking into the eyes of Evil Ben.

"Maggie?" he said as she tried to compose herself, amazed not only that he remembered her name, but that she still felt exactly the same lurch looking at him as she felt all those years ago.

"Oh my God. Ben! What are you doing here? Do you work here?"

"No. My company is developing something for Les Jolies, and we have a big meeting here today."

Maggie narrowed her eyes. "You don't work for Swerdling, do you?"

"I do! How did you know?"

"I just started in the PR department of Les Jolies today. I've spent the morning reading about the ingredients in Radiance and, naturally, all about Swerdling."

He gave a wry smile. "What a small world. It's been years since I've seen you. Wasn't it just before you graduated?"

"It was."

"You look good," he said, eyeing her suit. "You've become . . . trendy."

"You mean I wasn't trendy before?" she teased.

"You *were* a bit jolly hockey sticks." He shrugged. "Not that that's a bad thing. I've always liked posh girls. Now you look very

Les Jolies."

"Thank God." She wasn't sure what to make of his comment about liking posh girls. "My transformation last week worked." She paused. "You might be able to help me with some ideas I have for some features around Swerdling. Is there any chance we could chat sometime? Maybe you could tell me a bit more about the company."

"I'd like that." Ben looked at his watch. "I have to run now, but . . . how about Friday night? We could go for a drink. I have a four p.m. meeting here that should be done by six. How does that sound?"

"That sounds great." Maggie attempted to wipe the grin off her face, with little success. "I'll meet you in the lobby."

"Done. It's so good to see you. Really." He reached out and squeezed her arm, and in an instant she was swept back to the time they had run into him while hiking, and he had rubbed her back, or touched her back, just before he left. She had the same feeling just now as she had had that day — it was a sense of safety, of being taken care of, and she liked it just as much as she had back then. And then he was gone, leaving Maggie's heart racing as she headed back upstairs and immediately flicked through her

Filofax until she found the number she was looking for.

Maggie hadn't spoken to Evvie in ages. She had tried to stay in touch, but Evvie had become so successful, was traveling all the time, that the messages Maggie left on her answering machine were never returned. Maggie sent Christmas cards, and very occasionally, Evvie would phone, but it was always while Maggie was at work. It felt more and more like they were ships that passed in the night, the close friendship they once had — more like sisters than friends — a distant memory.

But who else would understand the thrill of what just happened? Who else could share in the excitement? Maggie's roommate, Lola, was lovely, and they were close friends, but she knew nothing of Evil Ben. Her other friends wouldn't have understood. She picked up the phone and punched in Evvie's number, astonished when there was a click, and there was Evvie's voice, saying hello.

"Evvie! It's me!" She paused, expecting Evvie to know exactly which "me," but when she heard nothing in response, she clarified. "Maggie."

"Maggie! I haven't spoken to you in so

long! What a great surprise! How are you doing?"

"You're never going to believe this. I had to phone you because you and Topher are the only two people who understand how momentous this is, but I just started a new job at Les Jolies, and you will never believe who I bumped into in the cafeteria."

There was a pause. "Evil Ben?" ventured Evvie.

"How did you *know*!"

"A good guess. How does he look?"

"Exactly the same except even more handsome, if that's possible. Not that he's really handsome, but cute."

"You still fancy him then?"

"I know. It's crazy. All these years later and I swear, my heart lurched in exactly the same way. And guess what? We're going out for a drink on Friday night! Wouldn't it be so bizarre if something happened? I mean, can you imagine if now he and I actually got together for real?"

There was a long silence.

"Evvie? Are you still there?"

"Yes. I just had a premonition. You're going to marry him."

"Don't be ridiculous. There's no way in hell that's going to happen. It's just a drink. Or maybe a bit more. I haven't even snogged anyone in ages, and Evil Ben remains the best kiss I've ever had, so yes, I'm definitely up for some snogging."

"It's going to be more than snogging," said Evvie. "Listen, I really want to stay and chat but I have to leave for a magazine shoot. It's really good to hear from you and let's try and speak more regularly, okay?"

"Definitely." Maggie was a little taken aback by the brevity of the conversation. "Shall I call you after . . ." But suddenly there was the dial tone, and Evvie had gone.

Ben was on his third pint, Maggie on her second gin and tonic, all the formality that had marked their initial conversation now dulled by the alcohol, and perhaps their mutual excitement at being together. At least, that's what Maggie hoped. She had never been good at realizing when people liked her, but she could feel the chemistry, and the giveaway sign was that neither of them had stopped smiling since the moment they met.

Evil Ben had clearly matured, relinquishing the scowl that defined her memories of him. Either that, or he liked her. He truly liked her.

She was telling him about her roommate, Lola, and her parents' menagerie of dogs, cats, and chickens in Kent, much like, she laughed, her own parents' home in Sussex.

"A group of us are going to stay at Lola's next weekend while her parents are away. I love living in London, but every now and then the noise gets too much for me and I need my dose of the country."

"I feel the same. I miss the West Country all the time."

"Me too. Those were the happiest days of my life. Would you ever move back?"

"That's the plan," he said. "When I have enough money, that's where I'd go. Fresh air and lots of hikes. What could be better? Speaking of hiking, how are your parents?"

Maggie laughed. "I can't believe you even remember my parents. They're great. I don't see them very much right now but I speak to them every week. My brothers are scattered all over the place. One's in Australia, one's in America, and the youngest, who you met, is in Glasgow."

"Glasgow? And the others are in America and Australia? Poor sod! How did he draw the short end of the stick?"

"It isn't!" Maggie laughed. "He loves it."

"Do you still hike?"

"Not in London. Unless a shopping trip along Westbourne Grove counts."

"Depends on how big a backpack you

needed."

"Big. Let me tell you, I had to completely reinvent myself for this job. I have to pretend I'm trendy." She sighed. "It's hell. I have to keep a stack of magazines in my bedroom for inspiration. I've got no idea what I should be wearing. This is when I wish Evvie still lived with me."

Ben's face grew serious. "Are you still in touch with your old friends? Do they come to London ever?"

"Sadly not really. I do speak to them occasionally, but I haven't seen them in ages. I miss them." She lost herself for a few seconds, thinking of Topher and Evvie, before shaking her head with a smile to bring herself back to the present. "What about you, Ben? Do you still hike?"

"Not as often as I'd like to. Hey! We should go hiking sometime. I've never found anyone to come with me, and much as I like hiking alone, I suspect it would be much more fun with you."

"I'd love that!" He wants to see me again! she thought.

"What about next weekend?"

Her face fell. "I can't. That's the weekend I'm going to Lola's in Sussex." An idea dawned. "There's a big group of us going.

If you wanted to come, I'm sure there'd be room."

"I'm not good with people I don't know. But thank you. A group of strangers, even with you, is never my idea of a good time. But let's make a plan to hike. Can I get you another drink?"

"I'm fine. I'm already getting a bit light-headed. I probably shouldn't have used the straw."

"Beginner's mistake." Ben grinned. "What about something nonalcoholic? I'm going to get myself another beer."

"A Diet Coke would be lovely."

An hour later, Ben insisted on seeing Maggie home in a cab. He left his car — an MG Midget, which, Maggie pointed out, was a decent upgrade from the Spitfire — as Maggie wouldn't let him drive. He had had too much to drink, and when she hailed a cab, he told her a gentleman would insist on seeing her to the door.

Two hours later, Ben was sprawled on the sofa in Maggie's living room, watching *Eurotrash* on Channel 4, while Maggie, unable to stop smiling, cracked eggs into a bowl for one of her omelets, hoping the food would soak up some of the alcohol. She wanted to keep pinching herself — Evil Ben was in her living room! Evil Ben was here!

He was drinking the coffee and the big bottle of water she had set on the coffee table. She kept moving to the doorway to look at him, marveling at how comfortable he seemed, his shoes off, his legs up on the sofa; marveling at how right this scene felt.

She melted a large knob of butter in the pan and whisked the eggs, adding seasoning and chives she snipped from the pot on the windowsill. When the butter was sizzling hot, just about to brown, she tipped the eggs into the pan and quickly, quickly, using the back of the fork tines, scrambled the eggs before turning the heat down to low and setting the omelet back on the gentle flame to cook through, making sure the top stayed perfectly creamy. Folding the omelet onto a plate, she added a toasted brioche, before bringing it into the living room, to Ben.

"That looks delicious." Ben sat up, reaching for the knife and fork. He ate quickly, and quietly, other than constantly looking at Maggie and proclaiming this the best omelet he had ever eaten in his life.

It's what I do, thought Maggie. Food cooked with love. I show the people I care about that I love them by feeding them. Then she rebuked herself for thinking that when it came to Ben. She didn't love Ben;

she hardly knew him.

"Is there room for me?" she said, when he had finished.

"There will always be room for you." He smiled before patting the seat next to him as Maggie curled up. She didn't resist when he took her legs and pulled them onto his lap, resting his hands absent-mindedly on her shins, with no idea of the effect it was having on Maggie, who could hardly breathe. They sat together for a while, appearing to be perfectly comfortable, even though Maggie was feeling ever so slightly nauseated, the butterflies in her stomach taking great leaps every time he moved. He had had plenty of alcohol, but rather than seeming drunk, he seemed softer, sweeter, his defenses down. This was the Ben who rubbed her back, who squeezed her arm, who would, she thought, take care of her.

On-screen, the host, Jean Paul Gaultier, visited something called the Tickle Factory.

"Oh God," said Maggie. "That sounds like hell to me."

"Which bit?"

"Tickling. I hate being tickled."

"Oh, Maggie." Ben turned his head from the television and looked at her, a twinkle in his eye.

"What?"

"Oh, Maggie, Maggie, Maggie."

"What?"

"You should never have told me that." He raised his hands as Maggie yelped, pulling her legs off his lap and inching away from him on the sofa, but it was too late. Suddenly his hands were everywhere, tickling her as she laughed hysterically, while begging him to stop.

He did stop, both of them breathing heavily, Ben suddenly on top of her, his face inches from hers. They were both smiling, until the smiles slid off each of their faces as they gazed into each other's eyes.

"Are you drunk?" Maggie whispered, remembering once upon a time when she found herself in a very similar situation, not wanting to ever have that happen again.

"I'm very definitely sober," he whispered back, tipping his head forward until his lips were on hers, and Maggie's whole body shuddered with an electrical current she didn't know it was possible to feel.

NINETEEN

- 1995 -

"Too scrawny," her mother kept saying, sucking her teeth and shaking her head every time she looked at Evvie over the past two days.

"You want me to stop modeling?" Evvie would ask, and they would both start laughing, for Evvie's mother couldn't have been more proud of her daughter. Everywhere she went she got Evvie's picture out of her wallet, and everyone told her Evvie had clearly got her good looks from her mother.

"I wish you'd come and visit more often," said her mother, walking Evvie to the fancy car that had pulled up outside the house in Stockwell.

"I wish you'd come and visit me! I've got a fabulous apartment downtown and there's more than enough room for you."

"New York was another life," said her mother. "I like it here, and the only place I like traveling to at my age is Jamaica."

"Your age. You're still young, and vibrant. You've been living with Granny too long."

"You're telling me." Evvie's mother patted her stomach and laughed. "My stomach is testament to that."

"And now you see why I don't come and stay more often," Evvie teased.

"Nothing wrong with that," said her mother, allowing Evvie to put her arms around her and give her a tight hug before waving her off, standing outside her house until the car was long gone.

Evvie's life was going even better than she expected in every area except romantically. At twenty-seven years old, she was one of the world's best-known models. She was not merely a model, but a supermodel who rubbed shoulders with the rich and famous and who was, in fact, rich and famous herself.

She was supposed to have it all, but when Maggie phoned her last year to tell her that Evvie would never believe who she had run into in the cafeteria at her new job, who she was having drinks with later that week, Evvie had felt her heart plummet. She knew she was going to say Evil Ben. And as soon as Maggie did, Evvie felt sick, knowing, beyond a shadow of a doubt, that Maggie would end up marrying him.

Evvie had had plenty of relationships, but she picked horribly. She used to joke that if you put a thousand nice guys in a room with one fuckup, she'd find herself leaving with the fuckup, except it wasn't that funny because it was true. From time to time she had thought about Ben, wondering what-if, wondering if things might have been different with him. All these years later, there was still no one with whom she had had the same chemistry, no one who had turned her on in the same way, and there were times, late at night, when she would lie in bed and wonder whether anyone might ever make her feel that way again.

And now, he was marrying Maggie. Evvie was, naturally, in the wedding party, and she had no idea how she was supposed to act when she saw this man again. She thought she had prepared herself by armoring up. Protecting herself from the pain of this weekend's wedding by cloaking herself in exquisite clothes, and jewelry that he could never have afforded to buy, in a bid to prove she was invincible, incapable of feeling remorse; in a bid to show him, perhaps, that she was so far out of his league, he could never hurt her.

Evvie made sure she looked her best. She

had had a nose job years before, her nose now perfectly streamlined and petite, and thanks to ever-changing hair extensions, she had a mane of thick, glossy caramel hair, down to her waist. She was no longer Evvie Hamilton, merely *Evvie,* and the world knew her by that name. There was Naomi, Christy, Linda, Tatjana, Cindy, and Evvie. And no one could compete.

When Evvie went out around her neighborhood, it was easy to be invisible. With no makeup, in sweats and a baseball cap, no one gave her a second glance. But she didn't want to be invisible at Maggie's wedding; she wanted Ben to see all that he didn't have. After that amazing week they had had together, she never believed he would really stay away. She thought they had had something special, that he would have flown out to see her. And if not immediately, she had thought, maybe a bit later. She had harbored a fantasy of him coming out perhaps a year later, when they were both a bit more settled, a bit more mature.

The abortion put an end to that, even though for the longest time afterward she couldn't believe that he never got in touch. Not to see how she was, not to say hello. Nothing. It was as if Ben had disappeared. As if she were dead to him.

Soon, she stopped thinking about him, and when fame and fortune came knocking on her door, she could have had, and indeed did have, any man she wanted. That most of them were alcoholic, addicted to drugs, or abusive was not her fault. Her picking mechanism was broken, she joked to friends; she was better off on her own. Sometimes, late at night when she was lying in bed alone, she would wonder about Ben, wonder whether he might have been her soul mate, whether the timing had been all wrong, whether things might have turned out differently.

She also soon learned fame and fortune were not what they were cracked up to be. Evvie had thought the money would give her freedom. She thought fame would make her feel loved. Neither had lived up to her expectations. Every time she wanted to do something for herself, work would get in the way. A job that paid too much money to turn down; an appearance at a gala that she had to make, even though she was exhausted and had planned to take her mother to Jamaica for a luxury vacation at Round Hill. She could never say no to a job, knowing her years at the top of this business were finite, terrified that there was always some-one younger, more beautiful, waiting to take her place.

There was an old saying that when you're famous, your trajectory went something like this: *Who's Evvie? Get me Evvie! Get me Evvie but cheaper! Who's Evvie?* Evvie was at the height of her "Get me Evvie!" phase, but she thought it would be different for her. She thought that it was only the beginning, that it was going to go on and on, that the sky was the limit. The most successful supermodels were being offered parts in music videos, in movies. Given that she had already acted as a child, movie roles seemed a sure bet in the foreseeable future.

Evvie was used to putting on a million clothes, a million faces, but the one face she had no idea how to pull off was the one of the girl whose best friend was marrying the man that Evvie still wondered about.

She knew she'd had no choice about the abortion — she would have had no career, no future, no independence, and she was twenty-one years old, too young to be able to handle the kind of responsibility that came with being a single mother. Except over the years she had thought about what Ben had said, that she wouldn't necessarily be a single mother, that they could do it together, that it was something he didn't just want, but that he was excited about.

She still remembered the eagerness in his voice.

Here she was, in the car on the way from the airport, feeling sick about seeing everyone again. She'd spoken to Maggie before the wedding, had seen Topher from time to time in New York, but had not spoken to Ben since he told her he would never forgive her.

She got out a compact mirror and checked her makeup, newly applied on the plane as they were preparing to land. She was getting ready for the paparazzi who would undoubtedly be waiting, she told the stewardess, rolling her eyes with a smile. But it wasn't for the paparazzi; it was for Ben.

She would use her beauty and her clothes as armor, rise above it and refuse to let anyone see how much she hurt.

Evvie was determined to show nothing, to give nothing away. She would be friendly and slightly cool at the wedding. Her allegiance was to Maggie, after all. Her allegiance should always have been to Maggie. If it had been, she wouldn't have gone through all the heartbreak and be in this mess now.

The car pulled up in front of the hotel, and Evvie looked around at the idyllic countryside, suddenly aware of how inappropriately she was dressed. This was a country village in Somerset, and she was decked out in fur, jewelry, heels, and inch-thick makeup, as if she were about to hit a club in New York. She was doubting herself again, realizing it had been years since she felt this insecure. She sat in the car a few minutes longer, taking deep breaths, eventually pulling her hair back in a ponytail and trying to wipe the eye shadow off. It didn't do much, other than perhaps tone down the glamour a tiny bit. She sat there just wishing Ben hadn't taken up quite so much space in her head again, after all these years.

Evvie got out and thanked the driver, who lugged her suitcases into the lobby. She had three, all huge, matching Louis Vuitton trunks.

"No!" A tall flurry of red hair and freckled skin came dashing toward her. "You're still traveling with the giant Vuittons!"

Evvie was embraced in Maggie's arms as her eyes filled with tears. The one person she had tried not to think about when she thought about Ben was Maggie. It was so good to see her, to rock back and forth with her in the lobby.

"I can't believe you're here," crooned Maggie, refusing to let her go. "I have to buy all the magazines to see you now. It's been years. Oh, Evvie, I'm so, so happy you came."

"I'm so happy I came too," said Evvie, meaning it for the first time. "Is Topher here? I tried to get on the same flight but I had a booking and couldn't make it earlier."

"Do I hear my name being taken in vain?" Suddenly, Topher was there, wrapping his arms around both Maggie and Evvie in a group hug as Evvie forgot about Ben for the first time in hours, reveling in being back with her old friends.

"I hope you're ready for champagne, because I just ordered us a bottle of Cristal in the bar," Topher said.

"You're so fancy." Maggie giggled, looping an arm through each of theirs and marching them through to the bar. "I feel like we're the three musketeers."

"We are, and you're the fancy one this weekend," Topher said. "You look absolutely gorgeous."

"Do you think?" Maggie asked. "I've been detoxing like crazy to try to get a glow, and I had my eyebrows dyed last week. You don't think they're too heavy?"

"You look the most beautiful I have ever seen you," said Evvie, for it was true.

"I can't believe you're marrying Evil Ben." Topher shook his head. "What an insanely small, crazy world it is. Do you make him smile more than he used to?"

Maggie snorted, the champagne coming out of her nose. "Do you remember how serious he was! Remember how much you hated him, Evvie?" Maggie laughed, missing Evvie's flush. "He is so not who we thought he was. He's really kind, and thoughtful. And . . ." She lowered her voice. "He is rather excellent in the sack."

"Too much information," said Evvie, desperately wanting to change the subject.

"Are you kidding?" Topher frowned at her. "I want all the grisly details."

"I want the details on the dress," lied Evvie as Maggie went off on a tangent describing finding the perfect dress.

"So where is the groom?" asked Topher, after a while. "Do we get to see him before the rehearsal dinner? Is he going to be nice to us or will he be grumpy?"

"You'll see him tonight and of course he'll be nice to you. He can't wait to see you again. Evvie, every time I bring home a magazine that you're in, he steals it from me. I know you never really knew each other, but I think he's so proud by some kind of osmosis."

Evvie swallowed hard. That was the first thing Maggie had said that hurt. What went through his mind when he looked at pictures of her? Did he feel sadness, or regret? Or worse, anger? Or would it be worse if it were relief? And why did he look at her pictures? She forced a smile.

"That's so cute," she said eventually.

"Isn't it? I wish you guys lived here. I wish the three of us could see each other every day. Thank God I've found Ben or I'd definitely get you to agree to a pact to live together again."

"I'd live together again," said Topher. "I may be loving New York but I'll always be a committed Anglophile. I'd be over here in a heartbeat if I didn't have the soap opera. And I don't mind agreeing to a pact. Frankly, I think it's a great idea. Not that anything's going to happen to you and Ben, but if, for whatever reason, we all find ourselves on our own at sixty, how about we live together again?"

"Sixty?" Maggie asked, askance. "Our lives will practically be over. How about fifty?" She turned to Evvie, who laughed.

"Sure. I'm in. But you definitely won't be on your own. You're marrying Ben. Topher and I will be the old maids living together."

"I very much hope I won't be on my own at fifty, but just in case, shake." Maggie extended a hand, and they all shook, with large grins on their faces. Maggie looked at Topher. "I can't believe I haven't asked you anything about your job on that soap opera!" Maggie clapped her hands. "Tell us everything. Are you hugely famous? Do you love what you do?"

"*I* love what he does," said Evvie. "I watch that show every damn day. Topher is amazing. You are so good, and I'm dying to know who killed Cassandra."

"My lips are sealed." Topher laughed. "Seriously. We sign contracts and we are not allowed to say anything. But between you and me, let's just say you should be keeping an eye on Clay."

"Do you have legions of women sending you fan mail?"

"I do," he said. "And a few gay men. Larry's more bothered by the gay men than the women, but he trusts me."

"Tell us about Larry," Maggie said. "I'm so sorry he couldn't be here."

"So is he. And so am I. You'll meet him another time. He's wonderful."

"He *is* wonderful," said Evvie, who had met him the few times she'd managed dinner with Topher in New York. "Best of all, he loves Topher as much as we do. And he takes care of you, right?" She turned to Topher, who flushed with pleasure. "He was incredibly sweet with you. I don't want to say paternal, because that would be creepy, but he definitely puts you first."

"Is it awful to say my ego enjoys that?" Topher laughed. "Although, honestly, we take care of each other. It's really something special. I didn't think I would find something this comfortable, and easy, and . . . right. I'm happy."

"What about you?" Maggie looked at Evvie. "What's going on in your romantic world? Are you still dating rock stars? And is it true what I read about you and Richard Gere?"

"I couldn't possibly say!" Evvie put a hand to her chest but then she laughed. "The truth is, much of that is just the product of my PR firm. Generally I'm having the same disastrous relationships with the same old disastrous men."

"Disastrous how?" asked Maggie.

"You name it, I've dated it! I just seem to have this unerring ability to find men who will treat me badly, because they're either addicts or narcissists. I have no idea why. I keep thinking that this time I've got it right, but every time he turns out to be a mess." She noted Maggie's sad face. "Do *not* feel sorry for me. I'm happy. Honestly, I don't know that I'm very good at relationships, or maybe I'm not very good at picking good men. Either way, life is much less complicated when I'm single."

"I understand that. But I think it's because you haven't met the right man. And you will. Look at you. You'll find someone amazing, and maybe it will be in the last place you expect. I mean, my God, who would have thought I would end up getting married to Evil Ben! Evil Ben!" Maggie started to laugh as Evvie tried to join in, wishing she didn't feel so awkward, wishing she could push away the very real thought that, had things been different, it could have been her.

"What makes him right for you?" Evvie didn't know if she should have asked, but she couldn't help herself.

"It's funny. We may be from very different backgrounds, but we're very similar people. We both love the countryside, and fresh air, and both of us are introverts. We want the same things out of life — a big family, a house filled with animals and kids. And he makes me feel safe. I'm a caretaker, I always have been, and he adores that, and" — she shrugged, lowering her voice — "as I may or may not have already mentioned, the sex is great!"

Topher burst out laughing as Maggie's

phone rang. "Okay," she muttered after answering, her face falling. "No? Today? Do you have to? But . . ." There was a silence while she listened. "Okay," she said eventually before hanging up with a frown.

"Everything okay?"

"I'd hoped Ben might drop in earlier to see you both. But he says he's caught up in the pub with his friends, who are determined to give him a special send-off. God, I hope he's not getting drunk."

"The night before the wedding? It's unlikely, surely," reassured Topher, but Maggie continued to look unhappy.

"Look, if you can't beat them . . ." Topher waved the waitress over and ordered another bottle of champagne, with some tea sandwiches to "soak up the alcohol."

Later that day Topher came to collect Evvie from her room for the rehearsal dinner. She was in a full-length silver crochet dress, her hair in a low chignon, and her makeup was far more subtle than she had worn earlier.

"Wow." Topher whistled when she walked out, her skin glowing. "You look like a supermodel."

"Ha ha," said Evvie, nudging him with her shoulder as they walked toward the elevator. "You don't look so bad yourself, all scrubbed up and in a suit. Brioni?"

"Oh you're good." He smiled.

"They're paying you well."

"I'm very lucky."

They passed a large gilt mirror on the wall and paused. "Look at us." Evvie sighed. "We'd make a beautiful couple. Wouldn't it be fun? We'd have separate bedrooms and I'd never bother you for sex."

"Well that's a relief, because it's highly unlikely I'd respond. Even if you were my type, which, quite clearly, you are not, I'll always take a cup of tea and an early night over sex. I think in another life I must have been Boy George."

"Even with Larry?"

"God, yes! That's one of the things I love so much about him. He's just as happy to climb into bed with the newspapers. I'm sure it's why it works so well."

"You don't have sex?"

"Darling, I don't remember the last time we had sex. That's not really what our relationship is. It's friendship, and partnership, and love. If anything, it's much more than sex."

"No idea what you're talking about." Evvie laughed. "Which is probably my downfall. My relationships are always about mostly sex." She didn't say that it was the only time she felt powerful, the only time she knew what to do in order to feel loved.

They walked into the dining room for the rehearsal dinner, and there, right by the doorway, was Maggie, chatting with someone they didn't know while she stood arm in arm with Ben. He looked up as they walked in, and his eyes met Evvie's. Everything about him, his face, his body, was so familiar to her that she inhaled sharply as her stomach flipped over.

Topher turned to her. "You okay?"

"I . . . Look at Maggie!" She covered up. "Look how beautiful she is."

Maggie, hearing her name, turned, stunning in a pale pink chiffon dress, the tiniest of roses embroidered all over the bodice, a radiant smile on her face.

"Look who's here, Ben! You remember my old friends Topher and Evvie."

"It's good to see you." Ben shook hands with Topher, then turned to Evvie, giving her a hug, and Evvie knew that she was wrong, that no matter how many years it had been, there was something about his smell, the chemistry that still seemed to be there, that continued to make her weak at the knees. As he hugged her, he rubbed her back as her heart lurched. This was what she remembered about him, how tactile he was, how affectionate, how these small gestures made her feel loved. She quickly disengaged.

I should have told Maggie, she thought, stepping back, wishing she had come clean at the time, although who knew if she would be here if that had been the case. But perhaps better for her not to be here. It was . . . painful.

"Congratulations," she said, forcing a neutral smile. "It's lovely news."

"It's been a long time," said Ben. "It's been ages since we saw each other. Years, no?"

"Something like that. What a funny, small world that you and Maggie should cross paths again, and now, well! The two of you!" She used every acting skill she had to be bright and happy, as if she were genuinely thrilled.

"I don't deserve her," Ben said, suddenly serious, looking at Evvie intently, in just the way he had all those years ago, and her heart fluttered. He was about to say something else, but Maggie slid next to him, her arm up around his neck as she kissed him. Evvie visibly winced with pain, relieved that no one saw.

"I still can't get over it," said Maggie. "Evil Ben! Who would have ever thought?"

"Who would have ever thought," echoed Evvie, looking from Maggie to Ben, feeling that Ben had been about to say something about their time together, the fact that Evvie had an abortion, that Ben said he would never forgive her. But the moment had passed, and Maggie led him away to other guests, leaving Evvie pretending to have a good time.

"Am I imagining this or was there . . . something . . . between you and the groom?" Topher leaned over and whispered in her ear.

"You're imagining it," she snapped, and he didn't say anything else.

She wouldn't think about Ben again, she decided. After this weekend she would put the past to rest. She wouldn't see him and Maggie together, not after this weekend. It was too painful, but they had an ocean between them, which made drifting apart an easy choice.

She would miss Maggie, but the truth was it wasn't the Maggie of today that she would miss, it was the Maggie of their university days, a Maggie she really didn't know anymore. Of course they still had a shared history, but it was in the past, and they didn't necessarily have anything in common any longer.

Except Ben. But only one of them knew
that.

TWENTY

Maggie shook Ben until he stirred, aware that she was being rough, that her shaking barely hid her resentment at how badly she slept thanks to how loudly he snored. He had a "work thing" last night, which meant the same as it always did when he had a "work thing." He'd roll home in a taxi very late, or in the early hours of the morning, and stumble into their bedroom, crashing into walls and doors, before eventually collapsing into bed and snoring so loudly it felt like the whole house was shaking.

She kept telling him to sleep in the spare room if he was drunk, but he was always too drunk to remember.

So Maggie would lie next to him grinding her teeth, furious with him for being so drunk, wondering why he couldn't do what most normal people did, go out for one drink and then stop. Ben just didn't seem to be able to stop.

"Wake up, Ben," she said, her voice harsher than she intended. "We've got the appointment to see the house in Somerset at eleven thirty. You have to get up."

He opened his eyes and smiled at her, pulling her into his arms, and even though she didn't want to, she felt herself acquiesce, and as she did so, her anger disappeared.

"Don't get your hopes up too much," he murmured into her hair. "Remember what happened last time."

"I have no hopes up at all." Maggie thought back to the last house they had seen, two weekends ago. It was an old rectory in Frome that looked charming in the brochure, huge square rooms in need of a little modernization, lovely grounds. In reality, it was decrepit and dark, and those huge square rooms turned out to be so by virtue of a very clever camera lens.

They got up to shower and dress, Maggie quickly making a bacon roll for Ben to eat in the car. She got in the car first, moving the papers on the passenger seat to make room for herself. Ben now drove an Alfa Romeo Spider, still passionate about old sports cars, whereas Maggie would have been happier with a Volvo wagon. She picked up the papers and was about to put them on the back seat when she noticed a flyer from a nightclub, offering two drinks for the price of one on the next visit.

Maggie had never considered herself a jealous woman. Nor a particularly possessive one. She didn't mind that Ben went out with the lads after work, and didn't even mind when he got home late. He was moving up within the ranks of his company, and even though she was still working, they had been talking about starting a family in the foreseeable future. Ben's salary was reaching a point where her working was not a necessity, hence they were looking to move to the country.

But Ben's drinking was becoming a problem. And it was not just the drinking; there was a part of his life that felt secretive. This nightclub, for example. When did he go to a nightclub, and what did he do while he was there?

They had started arguing about his drinking, even though Maggie couldn't figure out why it bothered her so much. It wasn't as if he became unpleasant, angry, or violent. If anything, he was looser, more affectionate, loving. She should've been thrilled when he put his arms around her, but instead, she was flooded with white-hot fury.

She had started watching him to see how much he drank, trying to keep her voice level as she told him perhaps he ought to slow down. She had started checking the vodka bottle in the freezer, not going as far as to mark it to see how much he drank each day, but coming close. She didn't need a marker to know.

How ironic, she found herself thinking, that for so many years she thought she needed looking after, she deserved to be looked after, in just the way her father looked after her mother, and yet here she was, the one responsible for looking after Ben, for this was how she saw it: it was her responsibility to stop him from drinking, her responsibility to make him sober.

She watched Ben leave the house, locking up and making his way down the street to the car. However much he drank, he never seemed particularly hungover. He got in the car, his smile fading as he saw the look on Maggie's face.

"When were you at Ministry of Sound?" She tried to keep her voice neutral, not wanting to fight all the way to Somerset.

Ben sighed. "It was a late night last night. I didn't want to go but the boys insisted. I didn't stay long. I don't even like that bloody house music. I had one drink, then I came home."

"So what time were you home?"

Ben paused, and Maggie knew it was because he was debating whether or not this was a trick question. Was she awake and did she hear him come in? Was this something else that would lead to a big row?

"I honestly don't know."

"Was that because you were drunk, by any chance?" She couldn't keep the sarcasm out of her voice.

"I had a few, yeah. It was the boys. I can't not drink. I wasn't drunk though."

"You always say that, and I know that's not true. When you're drunk you snore so loudly, you almost bring the house down."

"Exaggerate much?"

"Don't take the piss out of me. I'm worried about you. I'm worried about your drinking. You're going out with the boys more and more, or to work events that end later and later, and every time you get home drunk."

Ben gritted his teeth, keeping his eyes on the road as he headed toward the motorway. "Most of the time you're already asleep when I get home, so how would you know?"

"Because even when you're home you're drinking. Do you not think I don't realize how much vodka you're going through?"

"God, Maggie. What are you? My mother?"

"No. That's the point. I don't want to be your mother, but that's exactly what I feel like. You're not being responsible. We're talking about having children, but how can we have a family when you're so irresponsible?"

Ben shook his head. "I've just got another promotion at work, and I am doing a very good job of supporting us. I know you work, too, but let's face it, your money is a nice addition rather than being necessary. Please don't accuse me of not being a good provider, because that's not true."

"You're twisting my words. I'm not accusing you of that. I'm saying that I'm worried about your drinking."

"What are you saying exactly? That I'm an alcoholic or something?"

Maggie took a deep breath. "I didn't say that. You said that. Do *you* think you're an alcoholic?"

"Of course I'm not a bloody alcoholic. Have you seen me miss a single day of work? Am I ever hungover? And the last time I was on antibiotics, I didn't drink for ten days and it was easy. I didn't even think about it. Do you think an alcoholic would be able to do that?" Ben's voice was rising in irritation now, and Maggie instantly backed down, not wanting to ruin this day, and thinking about what he had just said. He had a point. He was not hungover, and surely alcoholics can't just stop drinking because of medication. Perhaps she was overreacting. Perhaps she was making too big a deal of it.

"I'm sorry," she said eventually. "You have a point. I just . . . worry about your health."

"I'm in the prime of health." His voice softened, both of them wanting to redress the balance. "Look!" He brandished his right arm, flexing his muscles as Maggie finally smiled. "Would an alcoholic be this fit?"

"Okay, okay." She placed a hand on his arm. "Let's not talk about it anymore. Let's enjoy the day." She leaned her head back and looked out the window as they drove. The Spider was supposed to be a shared car, one that was only really used on the weekends, or in the evenings when they went out for dinner. Maggie rarely used it herself. She hated stick shift, and even though she recognized it was cool, she would have preferred something low-key. Not that either of them drove often. Normally, they both walked to the tube station and took the tube to work. They only ever used the car when they went somewhere together.

The dirty brick houses lining the way to the M25 soon gave way to fields lining the M3. Leaving the motorway for the A roads just outside Warminster, Maggie felt her heart lift. This felt like home, driving through the pretty country villages, pausing at the roundabouts, roads she remembered from university days. They turned off the radio as they pointed out places they had visited years ago.

"I think this is it," said Ben finally, looking down at the map on Maggie's lap as he turned left down an old country lane.

"This is gorgeous." Maggie looked out the window at the fields and the high hedgerows on either side. "A proper country lane. Apparently all this land used to belong to the house, but the owners needed money sometime in the seventies, so they sold it off."

"Do you know who they sold it to and what they've done with it?"

"The estate agent said it was owned by a local farm. Look! That must be the gate!"

The house was down a long driveway flanked by old hedgerows — elder, hawthorn, and beech tumbled together in a mass that formed a canopy over the narrow road. At the end, emerging from the tunnel of plants, was dappled sunlight and an old split rail gate.

Maggie frowned. "Are you sure this is in our price range? This is like something a rock star would live in."

"I know!" Ben turned to her, as disbelieving as she. "It must be awful inside. We mustn't get our hopes up. The house is probably terrible."

The car pulled through the open gate onto a sweeping gravel driveway, the stately house standing at the end, bathed in sunlight as if spotlighted by a talented lighting director. With stone mullion windows and a heavy wood gothic door, the entrance was flanked by spiraled topiary yews, beautifully clipped box balls flanking the driveway. Wisteria clambered up the left wing of the house, almost to the gabled roof, and the two of them pulled up and just stared at the house, both with huge grins on their faces.

"This is beautiful," said Ben, shaking his head. "We can afford this? If this was our house, I'd wake up every day feeling like I owned the world."

"Isn't it stunning?" Maggie took in the three classic gables, the four chimneys, the beauty of the house and the freshly mown lawns, and she felt a swell of happiness. "I would be happy if we lived here too." She squeezed his hand and got out of the car. "That must be Robert, the estate agent."

She gestured to a black BMW parked discreetly on the side.

The man came out to meet them, explaining that he had been inside making sure all the lights were on and everything was open.

"Remember," said the estate agent, "you have to use your imagination. The house would be transformed with paint and modern furniture, but as you can see, the Jacobean front elevation is one of the prettiest in the area, and the slate roof was renovated five years ago, so that's in excellent shape."

Maggie didn't have to use her imagination. The house dated back to the seventeenth century, with some later additions, and was everything she had ever dreamed of. The hallway was large and square, a handsome staircase leading upstairs, heavy wood-paneled doors opening onto a gracious living room with a large stone fireplace and windows everywhere, including deep window seats tucked into two oriels, sunlight flooding into the room.

She didn't say anything, just walked around unable to wipe the smile off her face, occasionally looking at Ben, delighted to see that he had the same smile. The kitchen was large, with dated wood cabinets and a terrible linoleum floor, but there was a giant old Aga, which made her heart beat faster.

"Just a lick of paint," said Robert as Maggie turned to him with a skeptical look.

"I think the kitchen needs a little more than that," she laughed, turning to Ben. "Cabinets are easy though. The layout is perfect, it just needs new cabinets and countertops and maybe a new floor. Possibly a butler's sink. Is that a conservatory?"

"That's one of the more recent additions," Robert said, leading them out to the conservatory. "I believe it would be very easy to get planning permission to knock through. This wall between them is not a permanent wall, and that would give you the dream kitchen."

It would, thought Maggie, wrapping her arms around herself, not trusting herself to speak, not wanting the estate agent to know quite how much she had already fallen in love.

They moved through the house, to the drawing room painted a dark red, the "den" a dark green, through various rooms that seemed to be filled to bursting with the detritus of childhood, and then upstairs. Every bedroom was large and light, each with a fireplace.

They moved outside, to the stable block

and guest cottage, the barn that had been used as a playroom that could become a lab for Ben, thought Maggie, if he ever decided to work from home.

The lawns were clipped and neat, but the trees and bushes and hedges were over-grown. The house felt like it was a solid, happy, much-loved family home that had been neglected in recent times.

"Do the owners still live here?"

"They don't. They moved to a town house in Bath."

"So they must be keen to sell?" Ben perked up.

"I would definitely make an offer," said Robert.

"A low offer?"

"The thing with a low offer is that you can always go up." Robert laughed.

"Would you mind if we wandered around again?" said Maggie. "Maybe just the two of us can walk around the house?"

"Of course," Robert said diplomatically. "I'll wait in the kitchen."

Back upstairs, Maggie pulled Ben into the master bedroom, and closing the door, she looked at him and let out a silent squeal. "I love it," she said. "I love, love, love, love it."

"I do as well," said Ben, who looked a little scared. "But this is a big house. It's huge. I can't imagine just the two of us living here."

"But that's the point. It's not going to be just the two of us. I feel like this is all meant to be, that this house is a happy family house and it's waiting for people like us to come here. Can't you just see children running around that lawn? Imagine our sons playing soccer right there!" She pulled Ben to the window that overlooked the back lawn. "And our daughter will have picnic tea parties right there. Can't you see it, Ben?" She looked at him then, startled to see his eyes were glimmering.

"I can," he said and nodded, gazing around in smiling wonder. "I really can. You could get horses. We have stables!" He grinned.

"Maybe I will. What do you think? Lord and lady of the manor. Kind of."

"Not bad for a working-class boy from Lancashire," said Ben. "Although this is pretty normal for you. Just bigger."

"True. But much bigger. This is a proper grand manor house. Do you think it's too big for us?"

"Not when we fill it with children and dogs. Shall we do it? Shall we make an offer?"

"We'd be happy here," said Maggie, sitting on the window seat and looking out the large bay window in the master bedroom. "This feels right." She looked at him. "You're ready to commute?"

"I'd have to stay in London a couple of nights a week, but I think we should do it." He sat down next to her and put his arms around her. "You?"

"Yes. Let's do it," she said as they both hugged each other tight.

Whatever challenges they had faced, however difficult Ben's drinking might have been over the last couple of years, she knew this would be a fresh start. Clean, country air and old-fashioned values. No Ministry of Sound. No pubs on every corner. The quiet country pub was the sort of place they'd go to for Sunday lunches after a long hike. This was perfect. This was everything she'd ever dreamed of.

TWENTY-ONE
- 1998 -

Evvie had just returned from a shoot in Jamaica, bringing her mother and grandmother along for an all-expenses-paid holiday. They stayed at Jamaica Inn, which her grandmother pretended was much too fancy for her, but Evvie knew she loved it.

"Come back to New York," she'd pleaded with her mom on the penultimate day, knowing she wouldn't come. "I have so much room and I'm living on my own now. You've never seen my place. Just change your flights. I'll pay for everything."

"Don't bother me," said her mother. "I'm going back to Stockwell."

"You can't say I haven't tried," sighed Evvie, who went through this every time she saw her.

Evvie was on her way back to her open-plan loft in the Meatpacking District, not too dissimilar to the one she once lived in with roommates when she first came to

New York, except bigger, brighter, and much tidier. The exposed brick walls were flooded with light from the giant floor-to-ceiling windows, her furniture a collection of things she had gathered during her travels.

Enormous white sofas that were as big as beds were piled with Indian hand-blocked pillows. Leather poufs from Marrakech were scattered around the Balinese door coffee table, and antique wicker lounge chairs sat on either side of the fireplace on top of an ivory and pale pink dhurrie rug.

It was an eclectic and beautiful blend, what Evvie liked to think of as "boho chic." There were objects she had collected from all over the world, hand-carved African sculptures, painted pots from Tunisia, antique *suzanis* thrown over the backs of chairs.

Everywhere she looked, she saw a memory, and no matter how glamorous her trips, returning home was always something she looked forward to most of all. The agency had sent a car to pick her up from the airport, and as it rounded the corner, her heart sank, for there was the familiar figure of Patrick, leaning against the wall, scrolling through his PalmPilot.

Evvie's first instinct was to tell the driver

to keep on going, but she couldn't avoid him forever. It wasn't as if she hadn't expected him to show up. Being in Jamaica was a much-needed break from him, and she had done her best to put him out of her mind. A year ago, when she met him, she had thought he might be the One, this charming, funny venture capitalist who owned a vineyard on the North Fork and loved the outdoors.

He didn't show his other side until nine months in, until Evvie was truly smitten, could see a future with him. They had been having an argument one night, Patrick's jealousy getting the better of him. He was convinced she had spent the evening flirting with a photographer at a party they had been to.

Evvie had laughed in disbelief at Patrick's rage. The photographer in question was gay, in a well-documented long-term relationship, and Patrick, who was almost frothing at the mouth by the time she had laughed, slapped her. Evvie's hand had risen to her face in shock as she stared at him, eyes widened, unable to believe what just happened.

Patrick was horrified, immediately apologetic, disgusted that he had done such a thing. He swore it would never happen again as he wept, with great heaving sobs, and Evvie, who was shaken to her core, then had to reassure him that he wasn't the most terrible man in the world and that these things happen, and she would forgive him. But if it ever happened again, she said, she would be gone.

It happened again. Of course it happened again. He pushed her, body-slammed her into a wall before screaming in her face. He sobbed that time as well.

Just before she left for her next shoot, Evvie booked the vacation with her mother and grandmother to join her. She needed to feel as safe as she could, needed the break, and the only bad thing about the trip was knowing it would be over, that she would be coming home to Patrick. Two days before the vacation ended, she e-mailed him to tell him it was over.

And here he was, outside her building. She would have to confront him sooner rather than later, but didn't want to be left alone with him. She leaned forward to the driver, reaching for her wallet and pulling out a crisp hundred-dollar bill.

"I need you to do something for me. I need you to escort me up to my apartment, and not leave until that man has gone."

The driver turned around, seeing the

money, and nodded. "Of course, ma'am. Anything you need."

He parked and opened the door as Patrick looked up, coming over immediately.

"We need to talk," he said as Evvie steeled herself, determined not to show her fear.

"I've said everything I need to say. I don't know why you're here. It's over, Patrick."

"Evvie." Tears sprang into his eyes. "I love you. I've never loved anyone like I love you. I know I have some issues but I've started seeing a therapist, and she says she can cure me. You have to give me another chance."

Evvie looked in his eyes then, marveling at how irresistible she had once found him. Now, she was mostly scared.

"No," she said. "I'm glad you're getting the help you need, but I don't feel safe around you anymore. It's over."

Patrick roared in fury and came toward her as she cringed, and the driver stepped forward, using her suitcase to create a barrier between them, ready to wield it as a weapon if needed.

"Sir, if you don't leave her alone, I am calling the police."

"What for? I haven't fucking done anything," sneered Patrick. "Yet," he added menacingly, looking at Evvie, who was shaking. But he slunk off down the street, turning around to call Evvie a cunt as he left.

The driver came upstairs, asking if he could call anyone to be with Evvie.

"I'm fine," she said, even though she wasn't. "I have very good locks and a security system. Thank you."

She put on *The Miseducation of Lauryn Hill* and let the music relax her, dancing as she unpacked, with a large glass of wine in her hand. She had a video security system, and when Patrick didn't return, after a few hours she started to unwind. He was a classic abuser, so like all the men she ended up dating. Handsome and charming, until he wasn't.

She showered and put on the men's boxer shorts she usually slept in and a stretchy camisole top, and had just made herself a cup of tea (she didn't drink the builder's tea of old anymore — now it was mint tea, with a slice of lemon rather than copious amounts of milk and sugar), looking forward to lying on the sofa and watching some television before crawling into bed, when the phone rang.

She jumped, presuming it was Patrick, nervous about picking up the phone lest a string of abuse come barreling down the line. If that happened, she would hang up and leave the phone off.

"Evvie?" The voice was familiar, but it wasn't Patrick. She breathed a sigh of relief as she tried to place it.

"This is she," she answered cautiously.

"It's Ben," he said. "Ben Curran. Maggie's husband."

Her heart pounded as she forced her voice to sound normal. "I know who you are, Ben."

"How are you?"

"I'm fine." She looked at her hand holding the phone, noting it was shaking, unsure now if it was because she was expecting Patrick to be on the line, or if it was because it was Ben.

"I'm in New York just for tonight and wondered if we could get together. I know you're probably busy, but Maggie sends her love and said I should call you, and . . ."

He stopped talking and there was a long silence. "Evvie," he said eventually, pain evident in his voice. "There are things I need to say to you."

More silence as Evvie thought about her early night, knowing she should stay home, should do as she planned, going to bed, but before she could stop herself, she found herself asking, "Where are you staying?"

"The Mark Hotel."

She looked at her watch. "I'll meet you in

the bar at eight," she said, before hanging up the phone.

She decided to dress down to see him. At his wedding, she had been ridiculously overdressed, standing out like a sore thumb, and tonight she wanted to blend in, to be comfortable and cozy: she wanted to feel safe today, at least in her clothes.

She took off her pajamas and pulled on her oldest long-sleeved T-shirt, worn soft and thin, with her most faded jeans and scuffed leather boots. Her hair was pulled back in a bun, and she deliberately kept her face free of makeup. Whatever tonight was about, she decided, for her it was about honesty, and she couldn't be honest if she covered herself up with artifice of any kind, be it jewelry, makeup, or designer labels.

She got there early, wanting to have the upper hand, taking a deep breath as she walked into the small dark bar off the reception area. She ordered a vodka martini, drinking it down quickly — Dutch courage — then ordered a second one to sip slowly.

Ben walked in, squinting in the darkness, looking for her. She watched him for a while, wishing her heart didn't still ache after all this time, then raised a hand and watched his face light up as he came to greet her.

Two kisses, one on each cheek, as if they were just old friends from college, as if he were just the husband of a girl who had once been one of her best friends.

"Can I get you another?" he asked, gesturing to her drink, sliding onto the bar stool next to her.

She shook her head. "I'm fine for now."

He ordered a Manhattan and grinned at her, shrugging his shoulders. "When in New York," he said, and she smiled back, although her grin felt forced. She was nervous, and uncomfortable, and unsure of what he was doing there.

"How's Maggie?" she asked.

"She's good." He nodded. "Great, actually. We're good. We moved to Somerset and it's been great for both of us."

"I'm glad you're happy together." She didn't mean for it to sound sarcastic. Of course she wanted Maggie to be happy; she loved her. She just wished her friend's happiness wasn't so painful for her; she wished that Maggie had been able to find the same level of happiness somewhere else. She stared into her drink, unable to look at him.

"I'm so sorry that I . . ." Ben said finally.

Evvie turned to look at him, cutting him off. "So sorry that what? That you said you wouldn't forgive me? That you didn't think about what my life would be like if I'd had a baby? That you were completely selfish, only thinking about yourself, and then punishing me for not doing what you wanted, even though it would have meant giving up everything in my life?"

"No. That's not what I was about to say. I was about to say I'm sorry that I told you I would never forgive you. I forgave you almost instantly. I wanted to come and see you, but I didn't think you would want anything to do with me."

"What?" Evvie stared at him.

"I shouldn't tell you this. I suppose it's water under the bridge now, but . . . I fucked up. I fucked up in every way imaginable. I fucked up by not telling you what I felt about you, and then trying to emotionally blackmail you to be with me."

Time stopped as Evvie stared at him. "What do you mean, what you felt about me?"

"What do you think I mean?" Ben sounded angry. "Don't make me say it. You know exactly what I'm talking about."

"I have no idea what you're talking about. None. If you had feelings for me, you knew where I was. Why didn't you pursue me instead of saying you would never forgive me?"

"Because I was devastated by the abortion. And devastated at losing you. And I had no idea how to tell you. You were embarking on this modeling career, and everything in your life was going right, and I didn't think you wanted me. If you did, you would have said something."

"That's bullshit." Evvie turned her body to face his. "First of all, when someone says they'll never forgive you, you believe them. Why would I have said anything when you had already made it clear? You had your grant, your future, and both of us had talked about pursuing our dreams. We never talked about compromising and finding a way to be together. I presumed it was a few days of pleasure, and that was it. Now, all these years later, you're telling me it was something more? What the fuck, Ben?"

"I thought you were too good for me. I thought you wouldn't have wanted me, not once we had left West Country and were in the real world. Let's face it, Evvie. You could have any man you wanted. Why on earth would you even have thought about me?"

"Are you fucking kidding me? I loved you. I love you. I couldn't have done anything differently. You needed to come after me."

There. She'd said it. She sat back, shocked. Embarrassed, a part of her unaware she even felt this way, but as soon as she said it, she knew it was true. She busied herself rustling around in her bag to pay for her drink and leave as Ben put his hand on her arm. She looked down at his hand, remembering it so well, remembering what his hand, his fingers felt like on her body, inside her body, and then she looked at him, and he had tears in his eyes.

"I loved you too," he said, but he didn't take his eyes off her, and Evvie wasn't sure for a while whether he had said *loved* or *love.* She sank back on her stool, deflated and confused, knowing exactly what his gaze was saying.

"Please don't do this," she whispered. "We can't. Not now. You're married to Maggie."

"I love my wife," he said, his voice trembling. "It's true. Maggie is wonderful. You have to understand that I love her . . . but not a day has gone by when I haven't thought about you."

He reached over then and touched her cheek, cupped her chin, as Evvie trembled. After Patrick, after every abusive boyfriend she had ever had, here was the one man who had only ever made her feel safe. Then every thought she had disappeared as she felt, once again, that buzz of electricity, before Ben leaned forward and kissed her.

They walked to the elevator in silence, staring straight ahead. As they stepped into it, Evvie steadied herself, every muscle and fiber in her body tingling and buzzing, feeling more alive than she had in years.

Outside the door to Ben's room, she paused, feeling him pressing up behind her, his breath on her neck. She closed her eyes briefly before turning and kissing him the way she had wanted to ever since she saw him on his own wedding day.

Their lovemaking — and it was lovemaking — was intense and fast. There was no foreplay, Ben was inside her, and she started crying as he moved back and forth. He kissed away her tears. Later, much later, when both of them had slept a little and awakened to find it was still dark, still night, when Evvie realized that this was not a dream but that Ben was beside her, gazing at her just as he once had, they made love again. This time it was slow, and languorous, and loving and lustful, and when she came, she heard her own voice shouting from somewhere else, and it was only afterward that she realized the only time this had ever happened before, this intensity, was with Ben.

"How was that?" Ben said.

"It was transcendental," she sighed, before

frowning again. "Oh Christ, Ben. What are we doing? What are we going to do?"

"I want to be with you," he said. "I love Maggie, but not like you. I know it will be hard, but she will be fine. She's an amazing woman, and it could be so much worse. At least there are no children. I can find work here. I can move to New York and we can start again over here."

"We can't," said Evvie, her voice catching. "I can't. Maggie would never get over the betrayal, and honestly, I would never be able to forgive myself. I know we're barely in touch, but still, she's someone I love. I couldn't cause someone I once knew so well this amount of pain. I don't want to be the other woman. It would be different if you weren't married, but I can't be responsible for breaking up a marriage."

"So that's it?" Ben looked at her, shocked. "We have this one incredible night and we both go back to our lives as if nothing has happened? I'm willing to tell Maggie. I'm willing to give this a shot. Maggie wants children but we haven't started trying yet. If we're going to do this, now's the time."

"I can't. I can't do this. I could never live with myself, knowing I stole you from Maggie."

"You didn't. This, us, existed before Maggie."

"But you're married. And we barely know anything about each other. Sure, we have amazing chemistry, and it feels like love, but who knows whether we would actually be able to sustain a relationship. We had a fantasy week together when we were children, but we don't know each other. I can't blow up your marriage when I have no idea what the future would hold. I can't do this to myself and I can't do this to Maggie. I won't do this to people I love."

"But you love me."

"It's different. Maggie doesn't deserve this. I can't do it." She took a deep breath before looking at him. "This is closure, Ben. We will never do this again."

Even in the semidarkness, Evvie could make out the stricken look on his face. And she realized then that she was the one who had to be strong through this, resolute; she was the one who had to make sure this never happened again.

"We aren't meant to be together, Ben. Perhaps back then, had either of us got in touch with the other, things would be different, but we are where we are. You cannot leave Maggie for me."

"What if I left Maggie anyway, and after a

period of time, we got together."

"No. Because I would always know. I'm sorry."

Evvie left soon after that. She gave him a last lingering kiss, and started crying as soon as she closed the hotel door behind her. She sobbed as she came down in the elevator, and waved away the concerned concierge as she walked through the lobby and over to Madison to find a cab.

She sobbed all the way home, and through the rest of the night, back in her apartment, feeling as if her heart had truly broken and that life would never hold anything good, anything to look forward to, ever again.

Five weeks later she was on a modeling job, and in a furious mood. Usually she was able to turn it on for a photo shoot. However she may have felt waking up in the morning, there was something about the cameras being focused on her, a photographer (usually handsome) telling her how beautiful she was, how great the pictures were, that built her up and brought out her bubbly side. But today she couldn't snap out of the funk.

"Honey." The deputy fashion editor of the magazine they were shooting for was present for the shoot, and took her aside. "I have no idea if this is not enough sleep, or your hormones acting up, or whatever the fuck else it might be, but I am sending you out for a walk, and I suggest that when you come back, you have decided to wake up on the other side of the bed."

Hormones, thought Evvie, realizing she was premenstrual, except . . . where was her period? And she remembered this from before. Her boobs were big, and her jeans were tight.

She went for that walk, straight to the Duane Reade on the corner, where she bought a pack of pregnancy tests. She came back to the studio and headed for the bathroom, peeing on the stick while sitting on the toilet, numb, not thinking about anything.

The line was blue. Evvie found herself smiling. Surely this couldn't be. And this would be terrible, this wasn't what she wanted at all, but she was smiling as she pulled the second test out of the box and peed on the second stick, and that, too, produced a blue line.

Evvie wrapped the tests in toilet paper and put them in her bag. She couldn't quite believe it and knew she'd have to keep looking at them to make sure she wasn't dreaming.

Or was it a nightmare? She washed her hands and looked at herself in the mirror, thinking that she wasn't ready for a baby, that she hadn't ever thought about this. But even as those thoughts flitted through her mind, she saw that she was smiling, and she wrapped her arms around herself and hugged herself, and it was the first time in five weeks she had felt happy.

"Thank God for that," said the fashion editor when she walked back in. "You've reset?"

Evvie had nodded, and the rest of the photo shoot went swimmingly.

She wouldn't be able to tell Ben. Obviously she couldn't hide a baby from Maggie, even though she was barely in touch with her these days, but she could play with the dates, tell everyone the baby came early, or late, or something to throw Ben off ever knowing. She would figure it out. And she was in New York, far away from Somerset, where Maggie and Ben were living. No one would know. She would keep the father a secret from everyone, say it was just a one-night stand.

As she had anticipated, Ben phoned her, the first time they had spoken since she left his hotel room nine months before.

"Is it mine?" he asked, his voice filled with a mixture of hope and fear.

"It isn't," she said. "I'm so sorry. The baby is a month early. I had a boyfriend when we . . . met . . . in New York. I've checked the dates. I'm absolutely sure."

Ben was skeptical. "How can you be so sure?"

"Because," she lied, "quite apart from the dates not matching up, I had my period right after you left. It's a physical impossibility. I'm sorry."

Ben had sighed with what sounded a little like relief, a little like disappointment. "Thank God," he said finally. "I couldn't bear it if . . ."

"It's definitely not yours," she said, with all the conviction she could muster. It was fine, she told herself. Because she'd make sure Ben never saw the baby.

Jack was the image of Ben. From the moment he was born, it was like looking at a tiny Ben. When she sent out announcement cards, she made sure it was an artful shot of Jack swaddled in a blanket, fast asleep, his head turned so you could barely make out his features, let alone what he looked like.

She deliberately removed herself from her friends. She had the odd phone call with Topher, but allowed barely anything with

Maggie. She let the friendships drift, immersing herself in raising Jack, in a love that was unlike anything she had ever known, unlike even the love she had for Ben.

Her love for Jack was all-consuming, filling a hole she had been unaware of having. Over time, she stopped thinking of him as a miniature Ben, but simply as Jack, remembering only that he would never be able to meet her old friends, and she would never be able to do what everyone she knew was doing, sending Christmas cards with pictures of their children.

The older Jack grew, the more like Ben he became. He had Evvie's coloring, her hands and feet, but everything else was Ben. Everything else had to be kept a secret. Maggie could never know, and so, over time, their friendship became birthday cards and Christmas cards, then just Christmas cards (generic, no pictures of children anywhere in sight), and then, nothing at all.

TWENTY-TWO
- 1999 -

Topher opened the medicine cabinet and avoided looking at the left side. Larry's razor was still there, his deodorant, his cologne. Occasionally, when Topher was feeling particularly morbid, he would pry off the lid of the cologne and inhale deeply, allowing himself to be swept back in time, but it had been two years since Larry died, and he was trying to do it less. He couldn't bring himself to clean it out though. Not quite. Larry's pill bottles were still there, the cocktail of drugs they had prayed would work, Crixovan, Viracept, the protease inhibitors that were seeing incredible results, but not for Larry.

He had been the picture of health, until a small red lesion popped up on his inner thigh. They both pretended it was nothing, until more appeared, and within a few months Larry was a hollow-eyed skeletal shadow of his former self, dying in Topher's arms in a quarantined section of the hospital.

His funeral was mobbed by everyone who had ever been to his gym, and many who hadn't. Larry had been beloved by everyone who knew him.

Topher pulled out his own deodorant and examined himself in the mirror. How lucky he was to have escaped; God knows which gods exactly were looking out for him, but someone, some of them, had to have been.

Topher looked good, as he should, for a soap opera star at the top of his game. He had just been offered a part in a movie with another up-and-coming actress, Kate Hudson. His agent was convinced this would be the beginning of his transition from soap opera star to proper superstardom.

But Topher wasn't so sure. He didn't want to move to Los Angeles and give up the relative anonymity he had in New York. Here, people recognized him, but they left him alone. He liked walking everywhere, couldn't imagine driving in LA, even though he had great friends there, friends whose wooden house built into a hillside in Laurel Canyon was one of his most favorite places in the world.

He didn't think he wanted superstardom. He loved being on the soap, but it was grueling, and every day felt much the same. If anything, he thought he might like to try theater, and where better than New York for theater? He turned to look approvingly at the muscles in his back. He hadn't been back to Muscleman since Larry died. He went to the cheap gym on the next block, and pushed his body to its limits in a bid to assuage his grief.

His exterior didn't match his interior, that was for certain. Handsome and now buff, he looked as if he were ready to take on the world, but inside he still felt numb, still felt, ever since Larry died, that his own life wasn't over, exactly, but that he would never be as happy or fulfilled again. Topher was thirty; even though logic told him he had a whole life ahead of him, he still spent much of his time living in the past. It was easier than living in the present. Two years on he had learned to live with the grief, and a few close friends helped, the most unexpected of whom was Benedict, whom Topher was meeting for lunch today.

Topher had first met Benedict soon after he moved to New York. He had been invited out to a wealthy writer's Hamptons beach house. (Oh, the irony! The writer, while published and successful, was in fact a trust-fund baby who would never have been able to afford his lifestyle on writing alone.) To-pher was then a young pretty boy new to the scene, eye candy for the older gay couples that mixed in this wealthy circle, moving from Upper East Side apartments to the Hamptons in summer, and Palm Beach in winter.

Topher took the jitney out to the Hamptons, his bag packed with shorts, polo shirts, and a copy of *American Psycho* by Bret Easton Ellis, the more gruesome scenes of which he had to read with his eyes half-covered, skimming paragraphs so the images wouldn't lodge themselves into his mind forever.

He had taken a cab out to what he thought would be a simple beach house, but that turned out to be a beautiful old shingle estate, with immaculately clipped high privet hedges and a heavy wooden gate that opened automatically for the beat-up taxi.

A crowd of men were already sunning themselves by the pool, steaks and freshly picked corn from the farm down the road starting to sizzle on the grill when Topher arrived. He greeted his host, George, waved at the crowd of men, noting that the vast majority were quite a bit older, a few twinks his age scattered among them, before he went upstairs to change.

His bedroom was in the attic, undoubtedly one of the more modest rooms in the house given that he peeked into a giant bedroom on the second floor. The attic bedroom was small, under the eaves, with whitewashed floors and a woven cotton blue and white rug, a pretty blue and white quilt on the double bed, and a selection of excellent beach reads on the old wooden nightstand. Topher adored the room immediately, far preferring it to the grand chintzy bedroom he had glimpsed downstairs. He put his clothes away, neatly folded, pulled on a pair of swimming trunks, and looked out the window to where the glimmering water of the pool beckoned.

Groups of men were standing chatting, gales of laughter shimmying up to Topher's attic window. They were standing around the barbecue, a couple sitting on the edge of the pool, cooling off with their feet in the water. On the far side of the pool was an older man, very tan, in bathing shorts and a loose white shirt. He had a tumbler of something like a gin and tonic on the table next to him, reading glasses perched on the end of his nose, and he was buried in what looked like — Topher recognized the cover — a biography of Sarah Bernhardt. *He* looks interesting, thought Topher, who skipped down the stairs and stood on the edge of the pool, aware that he was young and trim and quite probably invited because of his pretty looks, before climbing onto the diving board and executing a perfect swan dive.

He didn't look at the older man in the white shirt, but hoped that he had made a splash, in more ways than one. Topher swam underwater until he reached the other side, knowing he would emerge at the feet of the man who might, if luck was on his side, have unglued himself from his book to watch Topher.

Topher emerged from the water, running his hands over his hair so it sat sleekly on his head like a seal, flashing a wet grin at the man, who was indeed now looking.

"Well," said the man, revealing a handsome smile. "This day suddenly got an awful lot brighter. I'm Benedict. Who are you?"

Benedict claimed Topher as his for the weekend. They went to bed together that night, and a handful of times afterward, but the chemistry between them was less sexual than platonic (as it so often was for Topher), and as the sexual part of their relationship fizzled out, they quickly became close friends, with Benedict taking an almost paternal, mentor-like role in Topher's life.

He was a theater producer, part of an elegant old-world New York, with a glorious Upper East Side apartment filled with heavy, swagged silk curtains and round tables, layered with chintz tablecloths edged with tiny silk pompoms, the grand piano covered with silver-framed photographs of Benedict with every famous actor and director imaginable.

Topher was an excellent companion for Benedict, who he quickly started calling Dickie, the only one who was allowed to call him such a frivolous nickname. They saw each other regularly, until Topher met Larry, at which point he saw Benedict less, largely because he was busy learning to be in a proper relationship, and because Larry wasn't comfortable in Benedict's sophisticated world. Topher still saw Dickie from time to time, during the day if he had a day off, when Larry would be at the gym.

When Larry died, Benedict showed up at the funeral, and came back to the apartment for the service. When everyone left, Topher was desperate for them to stay, desperate not to be left on his own with his memories and his grief, and Benedict stayed. He didn't ask if he was wanted, he just cleaned up quietly and then pulled out the sofa bed, telling Topher that he was staying and wouldn't take no for an answer.

That weekend, Benedict picked Topher up and drove him up to his country house in Litchfield, Connecticut. It was a gracious old house on North Street, with a large wraparound porch that held a swing and a deep wicker sofa. Dickie sat Topher on the sofa, made fresh lemonade, tucked a blanket around his legs when it became chilly, and sat, quietly, saying nothing as Topher sobbed.

Benedict picked Topher up every weekend that summer, and by the end of the summer, Topher started to feel like he was almost human, all of which he owed to Dickie, who never asked anything of him, never made a move, never expected anything in return. Once, Topher had started to kiss him, not for any reason than he thought it was what Dickie must have wanted, presumed it was why he was being so nice to him, but Dickie had calmly pushed him away, smiling, saying that wasn't what their relationship was about. And Topher felt relieved.

Since then, they met for lunch every week. Often, Topher would accompany Dickie to the theater, and Dickie, knowing that Topher had bigger ambitions, would introduce him to everyone for when he was ready to leave the soap opera. It wasn't what you knew, he always said, it was *who* you knew.

But the security of the soap opera was something of a relief for Topher, once Larry died. He wasn't ready for another change, other than perhaps something to alleviate his loneliness. He missed having another body in the apartment. He missed having someone to talk to, someone who would help with paperwork, and contracts, all the things Topher hated. Of course, his agent helped, but Larry had always talked everything through with Topher, often picking up on small things the agent had missed.

Topher missed companionship. He could have reached out more, to old friends, but in the beginning they had all reached out to him, and he had been so sick with grief, he hadn't wanted to see anyone. They had all left him alone after a while, leaving messages saying they were there for him for whatever he needed, and he should get back in touch when he was ready. By the time he felt ready, it had been too long. He didn't know what to say to those friends he hadn't spoken to for months (in some cases over a year) so he didn't call, instead withdrawing, his life outside of work becoming more and more isolated.

Dickie was the only one who refused to

leave him alone. When Topher told Dickie he wasn't feeling well and had to cancel lunch, Dickie would just show up, knowing the doorman would let him in. He'd lean on the buzzer until Topher had to open the door, insisting on Topher getting dressed and coming out. Topher never wanted to go, but afterward, when he was back home alone, he was always glad he had been out.

Today they would be going to Michael's for lunch, which Dickie loved, for he ran into everyone he had ever known. At night, they would often go to Orso for a pre- or post-theater meal; Dickie treated it like his own personal party, moving from table to table to greet, hug, and charm.

Today, Topher decided on a jacket but no tie, soft leather Italian driving shoes, and no socks. He slipped some small black-and-white portraits into his jacket pocket — wherever he went there were fans, especially midwesterners on vacation in New York who would be in Times Square, and he tried to have something on hand to sign and give away. This was what he was frightened of giving up, he realized, if he left the soap opera. The validation, the recognition that he was someone who mattered.

Dickie insisted on dessert, as he always did,

a cappuccino for him, a mint tea for Topher. He stirred his three sugars into his cappuccino and looked at the table in the way he did when he was preparing for a serious conversation.

"Oh dear," Topher said, attempting to preempt whatever it was he suspected he had done wrong. "You have your serious face on. Whatever I've done, can I just apologize now so we can move on?"

Dickie smiled, the creases around his eyes now deep from the sun. In his early fifties, he had only grown more handsome, and many was the time Topher had wished for a greater libido, or more chemistry, or something that would make their relationship romantic. But it didn't seem that it was something either of them particularly wanted, so he chose instead to admire Dickie as a fine figure of an older man.

"You've done nothing wrong, darling boy. But you're right, there is something I wanted to talk to you about. As you know, I have been rattling around in my large apartment for some time, ever since Felipe left."

"Ah yes, the handsome Felipe." Felipe had been a "friend" of Dickie's who had lived in one of the guest rooms for the past six years. Their relationship had been platonic (although no one quite believed there weren't *some* benefits), and wasn't quite understood by anyone. They weren't sure if Felipe took care of Dickie, or if Dickie took care of Felipe. Dickie had a cook, and a cleaner, so there were no domestic duties, and it was rumored he lived rent-free, so if there was no sex, and Dickie swore there was no sex, then it was friendship, companionship, which would have been understandable had Felipe not been so handsome (and, it was rumored, something of a gold-digger). He had in fact left after starting a romantic relationship with a wealthy real estate investor in Palm Beach, and now lived with him in old Palm Beach grandeur on a water estate.

"You know Felipe and I didn't have a romantic relationship. In fact, he had his own dalliances that he kept private, and I, occasionally, had mine."

"You did? You've been keeping things from me!"

"Oh, there's nothing to tell. They are, after all, only dalliances. An old bachelor like me doesn't want to get involved with anyone romantically, not now. I'm too selfish and too set in my ways, but, I do like having company in my home, and it has to be the right kind of person. I have been thinking of you, rattling around in your own apartment . . ."

"My apartment isn't big enough to rattle around in," said Topher.

"You know what I mean. I have been thinking about both of us, living on our own and not really enjoying living on our own, and I have been wondering if you might consider moving in with me. This isn't about romance, or sex, but, as it was with Felipe, companionship. I like having someone to sit opposite me in the mornings to chat about what we're reading in the newspapers. I like hearing someone else moving around the apartment. The guest suite has its own entrance should you wish to bring people back and have more privacy, but I have thought about this a lot, and I think that our personalities are very well suited."

"Our personalities *are* very well suited." Topher sat back, surprised at the proposition, never thinking this might be a living arrangement he would want. He was one of the biggest soap stars on television, more than capable of looking after himself, financially and otherwise, and yet he, too, missed the conversation, coming home to someone, having someone to talk to.

"You would have your own life, Topher. I don't expect rent, and there isn't much I ask. Occasionally cooking on the weekends, accompanying me to events if you want to come. Mostly, I like having someone around at home. You're so young that I am also prepared for you to meet someone and leave. I wasn't surprised when Felipe left, but for now, at least, I thought we could perhaps take care of each other. It would alleviate my loneliness, and I thought it might alleviate yours."

Topher sat and thought of his apartment. Of the closets still filled with Larry's clothes, the memories that crowded into every square inch. He thought of bringing men back to Dickie's apartment, but he couldn't quite see it. That wasn't something he tended to do. In fact, the older he grew, the more he thought he might not be a sexual being at all. Asexual, he thought, at times. A lover of beauty, which was always enough.

"Yes," he said, a smile spreading on his face. "I think that's an excellent idea."

Twenty-Three
- 2005 -

The alarm woke Maggie with a start, Ben still snoring beside her. Today was the last day of her fertile window, the four days when Ben's sperm, such as it was, was most likely to survive, and they had had sex every day, even though neither of them was particularly in the mood. Sex had become something of a chore since Maggie started tracking her fertility. If she wasn't ovulating, there was no possibility of pregnancy, and if there was no possibility of pregnancy, she wasn't interested.

They had had perfunctory sex after lunch, after which they both fell asleep. She let the alarm continue buzzing, reaching for her BlackBerry to see if anyone had e-mailed her while she was asleep, cursing as she knocked the large amethyst crystal off her bedside table. She looked over, but Ben hadn't stirred. He'd take a while to wake up, hence leaving the alarm buzzing.

She hadn't meant to nap today — they had a party at their neighbors' house at three — but she'd slept terribly the night before. Ben had been snoring heavily, which always made her nervous. He only snored like that when he'd been drinking, but since his latest bout of sobriety ten months ago, he hadn't snored, not like he did last night. He had started coming to bed after her. Last night, after she had taken her temperature and checked her ovulation testing kit, they had gone upstairs and had sex. There was little foreplay, and afterward she lay on the bed with her legs in the air, resting against the headboard, visualizing strong sperm swimming their way to her egg. When she had first done this, years ago, Ben had laughed, lying on the bed with her as she inched her feet farther up the wall. Last night, after Maggie had shifted to put her legs in the air, Ben had gone to the bathroom, put his clothes back on, and went downstairs to watch television.

When she woke up at two a.m. because of his snoring, she crept downstairs to go through the rubbish bins, hating herself every second. She had no idea what she would do if she found, as she expected to find, empty bottles of alcohol; she didn't know if it would result in a fight, or in her expressing her disappointment, feeling more like his mother than his wife.

This was his third time getting sober, and this time, she thought, until last night, this time she thought it was different; this time it was for good. He wasn't just going to meetings, he had a sponsor, and they met for breakfast twice a week. He was happier than he had seemed in years, less volatile, and she had started to relax, letting go of the need to monitor his drinking. It had been months since she was on high alert, all her senses heightened, furtively monitoring how much he was drinking.

The relief she felt when she didn't find any evidence of alcohol in the early hours of the morning was overwhelming. She went back up to bed, slipped in some earplugs, and allowed herself to feel hopeful before drifting back to sleep, knowing they had one more day to have sex, one more day this month to create a child.

All of their friends had children, as did all of their neighbors here in Somerset, where everything seemed to revolve around children. So many of the fathers worked in London during the week, the wives bonded together Monday to Friday out of boredom, desperate for adult conversation, and Maggie, who had initially felt like she belonged because they were trying for a baby and it would surely only be a few months before she was granted entrance to the same club, was beginning to dread their parties.

She was now singularly focused on becoming pregnant, trying anything and everything, no matter how esoteric. She had recently read an article in a women's magazine featuring three women who had been trying to get pregnant for years. None of them had any luck until they each saw a healer who pronounced their homes had "bad feng shui." All of them had moved furniture, painted walls, and filled their homes with strategically placed mirrors and crystals, leading to all three of them getting pregnant.

Maggie hadn't told Ben. She did the research by herself, finding a feng shui expert, and soon their bed was moved across the room, with various mirrors and crystals hanging from windows. It hadn't worked.

She got up, turned on the shower, and went to wake Ben. "We've got the birthday party in half an hour," she said, finally managing to wake him. "We can be a bit late, but we have to be there."

"Did you finish the cake for them?"

Maggie thought of the Barney dinosaur

cake she had made for Emily and James Sullivan's baby, who, at a year old, went nowhere without her soft Barney toy. Maggie had made a chocolate cake glazed with a dark chocolate ganache, topped with a Barney dinosaur romping through a field of candied violets. It was beautiful enough for the adults to swoon, and Coco would love the Barney on the top. Everyone would be happy.

"Cake is ready, and I made tiny Barney cupcakes as well. Come on. Time to get up and jump in the shower."

"Did you enjoy that?" Ben said suddenly. "Our . . . session."

"Our *session*?!" Maggie burst out. "Do you mean sex?" Maggie started laughing. "Did you?"

He shrugged. "I miss you," he said, his face now serious. "I mean, it was fine, but I miss us kissing. Taking our time. It's always a quickie these days, and it always feels like . . ." He sighed. "I don't know. It feels like it's a job."

"It won't be like this forever." Maggie planted a kiss on his nose. "I'm feeling really good this month. The fact that we've both given up coffee is going to boost our fertility. I can feel it."

"I hope you're right." Ben pulled her

down for a deeper kiss, but Maggie pulled away.

"Not now!" She got up, slapping his hand away with a smile as she headed to the bathroom. "We've got a party to go to."

"It's amazing!" Emily flung her arms around Maggie when she saw the cakes. "And cupcakes too! Maggie! You're fantastic!"

Her mummy friends crowded around, oohing and aahing at the gorgeous cakes. "Would you make a cake for me?" said one. "That's so much better than the one I had," said another, who seemed aggrieved about it. "Can we have your number?" one said to Maggie.

"How the hell do you have time to make cakes like this?" said another.

"No children," Emily explained, before Maggie had a chance to say anything. "No sleepless nights. No small creatures pulling on you all the time."

"Oh my God!" said the woman who had asked how she had the time. "No wonder! We would all be making cakes like that if we didn't have children!"

Maggie smiled a stiff smile, wishing she could crawl into a hole. She felt deficient enough already, the only woman her age at these kinds of parties who didn't have children. The last thing she needed was for anyone to point it out publicly. Even though she knew Emily didn't mean to intention- ally shame her, that was nevertheless how she felt. She excused herself and went outside to the garden, where a bar had been set up to serve the adults. Maggie walked past the fathers, gathered around with beers in hand, and went to the bar to take a Pimm's. She wouldn't ordinarily drink in the afternoon. She wouldn't ordinarily drink if Ben was around, saving her white wine spritzers for nights out with the girls, but after that conversation, she needed a drink.

She downed half on her first swig, and finished the drink by her fourth.

"Another Pimm's?" The bartender grinned. "You look like you needed that."

"Yes please," she said, wondering how quickly she could leave. She saw Ben on the other side of the garden, deep in conversa- tion with one of the dads.

What she didn't notice, however, was his hand behind his back, hiding his third can of beer.

Twenty-Four
- 2008 -

Evvie was lying in bed leafing through magazines when Lance came in from the bathroom. She pretended to immerse herself in her magazine, not wanting to look up and meet his eye, very aware that after four years, the honeymoon period was definitely over. Recently he had started looking her up and down when she was naked, or in her underwear, a look that seemed suspiciously like disdain, which had begun making her self-conscious and nervous.

It had to be about her weight. Admittedly she had put on weight recently, but isn't that what's supposed to happen when you're forty and — finally — happy? She believed Lance loved her; she believed that their marriage was real, based on friendship and trust, that she could finally relax and start enjoying herself a little.

If that meant eating dessert, or allowing herself to have cake when she met friends for tea, or having a late-night bowl of cereal topped with yogurt, honey, and nuts while watching a movie, so what? Isn't that what normal people did? Isn't that how normal people ate? If it meant she had taught their cook how to make jerk chicken, coco bread, and patties, what was wrong with that? Normal people ate patties and dumplings in between meals, surely?

That Evvie had no idea how normal people ate didn't occur to her. Her entire life had been spent either overeating or restricting. Twenty-odd years of crazy dieting for her modeling career had taken their toll, and the pendulum now seemed to be swinging the other way. Judging from Lance's recent passive-aggressive comments, it was beginning to show.

Evvie paused at a picture of a model she had known well when she was young. A model who had a comeback career now that she was in her early fifties, her mane of blond hair now white, a handful of crow's-feet around her eyes, but as beautiful as she always was. She had instigated a trend for older models. Lance climbed into bed beside Evvie, glancing over at the picture.

"Who's that?"

"Arabella. We used to work together a million years ago."

"She still looks fantastic. Look at that figure! How old is she? She must be younger than you."

Evvie flinched at the barb. "No. She's much older. She looks great though."

"You used to look like that," said Lance. "You should get into shape again. And stop with the late-night snacking."

The words made her angry and tearful. She still carried shame about eating, about being seen eating, and shame about ever having been, or being, overweight. Lance's comment burned. She felt her ears and cheeks grow hot. She didn't want to eat the cereal at night. Lying in bed each night she told herself that tomorrow would be the start of a new day, that tomorrow she would begin the day with a smoothie, eat nothing but salads, and snack on fruit if she had to snack on anything at all.

Her mornings started well, but by mid-afternoon she was starving, and the cakes, the cookies, the furtive eating when Lance was at work and the housekeepers were on the other side of the house were both shameful and comforting. And every night, just like tonight, she lay in bed feeling her stomach growing more round, her breasts heavier as she vowed that she would start again tomorrow.

She knew that Lance wasn't happy about it, but this was the first time he had said something outright, and she had no idea what to say, wanting only to bury herself under the covers and weep.

"Put the magazine down," Lance said. "We need to discuss this."

"Are you joking?" Evvie then turned to look at him. "You want to discuss my occasional bowl of late-night cereal as if it's a serious issue?"

"The late-night cereal isn't an issue, but I don't want to be married to a fatty."

Evvie gasped in horror. "First of all, are you really that superficial? And secondly, I'm hardly a 'fatty,' as you call it. So I'm not model thin anymore. I'm forty years old and a mother. I'm not supposed to be rail thin."

"I'm just telling you what I'm attracted to. It has nothing to do with superficiality. I like my women to be thin. You have always been thin, but the last few months you've been gaining weight, and I would like to see you get back to your best self."

"What if this *is* my best self?" Evvie's voice was bitter, filled with disbelief that they were even having this conversation.

"Let's just hope for your sake that it's not," he said.

"I hope you're kidding," Evvie said. "Are you actually fat-shaming me?"

"You can call it whatever you want. I'm telling you that in your role as my wife, you have to look a certain way, and I not only don't want you putting on any more weight, I want you to lose the weight you've put on. What is it, ten pounds? Fifteen?"

"I don't know," said Evvie, which was true, as she had been avoiding the bathroom scale ever since her clothes started to feel tight. She blinked back the tears that had started to form, incredulous that her husband, the man she thought was her knight in shining armor, was turning out to be more controlling than she ever would have dreamed.

She should have known better. She should have known that you don't get to have this kind of success, this kind of money, without being some kind of control freak, without being used to having everyone around you do everything your way.

When she met Lance, she was the single mother of a six-year-old boy. Since the day Jack was born, Evvie had devoted herself to being his mother. She worked sporadically, modeling, doing catalog work, but because she couldn't make it to the go-sees, couldn't travel at the drop of a hat anymore, the work slowly dried up. She found herself an ex-model and a single mother, willing to do whatever she needed to do to work.

The early days were easy. She had money to burn, dressed Jack in gorgeous Bonpoint outfits, the best of everything. She barely worked, and when she did, she found a network of babysitters to come and look after Jack. But every second away from him was hell.

Jack was the perfect baby. He was beautiful looking, with caramel skin and large brown eyes, and strangers would sigh over his dimples and adorable smile. His personality was equally sunny, and Evvie knew she had been blessed.

She left her downtown loft for a smaller two bedroom on the Upper West Side, and then, when the merry-go-round of private school craziness was about to start, decided to leave New York and head out to the suburbs. There, the schools were free, and a small yellow bus would pick her son up and drop him off at the end of the road every day.

She needed to be careful with money by that time. She was plowing through her savings rather than making more, and her bank account was dwindling. She needed to find somewhere with great public schools, and she wanted fresh air for Jack, a place where he could grow up bicycling.

She found a small house near the railway station in Westport, Connecticut. She started taking on work as a style consultant, helping women organize their closets, co-ordinating their wardrobes, shopping with them at Mitchells and the Darien Sport Shop. She was always elegant and im-maculately put together, even though the designer clothes in her own closet were years old.

As Jack grew, so did her expenses. She needed more work, and when her friend Kim opened a local coffee shop and asked her to help out, she said yes, relieved. It turned into a regular job to supplement her freelance income.

This wasn't the life she would ever have chosen for herself, she often thought. She remembered her stardom, the years she spent modeling, lavishing money on ridicu-lous bags and shoes and fur coats that were gradually sold off, one by one, after Jack was born. But there wasn't a thing she would change about her life, given the wondrousness of Jack.

She was pretty happy, if not rich, the day Lance walked into the coffee shop, impossible to ignore. He carried himself with an air of authority, was charming and brimmed with an appealing confidence. He was not her type at all — she had always gone for pretty boys, whereas Lance was older, and heavier set. But she found him compelling, and once he established himself as a regular, she would look forward to him coming in. It wasn't just his air of authority and his charm, it was that he seemed like the kind of man who would look after you, take care of things. She may have thought she relished her independence, but being a single mother was hard; part of her was clearly more tired of struggling on her own than she had realized.

She knew nothing about him then, had no idea who he was. All she knew over the course of the year was that she served him cappuccino with extra foam, and he went from wearing a wedding band to not wearing a wedding band. And he was clearly fascinated by her. He asked her very early on if she had been a model. He recognized her, he said. If she was busy serving someone else, he would wait off to one side, until she could help him. He was patient, and always polite. He was charm personified.

She mentioned one day that her son loved hockey, and the next day he slid an envelope over as he was leaving. Once he was gone, she opened it to find ten tickets to a New York Rangers game, and not just stadium tickets, but a private box.

Jack was beside himself with excitement. He brought all his friends. They arrived at Madison Square Garden to find free sodas, burgers, and french fries delivered to the box, and as much candy as they could eat.

Evvie was speechless at the generosity. The next day she tried to thank Lance when he came in, and he said the only thanks he would take would be if she agreed to have dinner with him.

"You're not married?" she asked, confirming what she realized she had grown to hope was true.

"Not anymore. Separated."

"Separated leading to divorce, or separated as a temporary measure?"

"Divorce papers were filed last week."

She couldn't hide her smile. "Then that's a yes."

One week later, Lance picked her up at home, and it was only when she walked outside to his Maserati parked on the street that she learned he had built his own hedge fund and lived on Beachside Avenue, the most expensive street in town. Now she understood his air of authority, and why she felt safe with him, as if he would take care of her. Of course. A man like him was used to taking care of things.

He didn't take her to a fancy restaurant. He took her instead to a lobster shack in a pretty coastal town an hour's drive away. They tied bibs around their necks and cracked their claws, and when a stream of juice squirted onto his beautiful cashmere blazer, he laughed. They both had french fries, and when she left half of hers uneaten, he gobbled them up unapologetically.

Evvie had fun. More fun than she had had in years. He was a wonderful storyteller, and surprisingly self-deprecating. He didn't ask her lots of questions, which she liked. Evvie had never liked talking about herself, and she appreciated that he didn't quiz her about how she ended up a single mother and why the father wasn't involved. He talked about his own kids, all five of them, from two different marriages, the youngest one a junior in high school, the rest all grown and flown.

"Two marriages and counting," Evvie mused out loud. She couldn't help herself. "That's . . . *impressive.*" She didn't mean *impressive,* she meant *concerning.* Two marriages surely meant there would be little point in another date, in a future. What kind of prospect could a man be who had two marriages behind him? Third time's a charm, she found herself thinking.

She mentally berated herself. For God's sake, she thought. This is one dinner, not marriage.

"I know." He grinned. "I'm a terrible proposition. My first marriage was one that absolutely should not have happened. It was my parents' choice, not mine, doing the right thing, making other people happy, et cetera, et cetera."

"Making other people happy?" Evvie gave him a cool stare. "You don't seem like the sort of man who cares about making other people happy."

"Hmm. Now how am I supposed to take that statement?"

"I just meant you seem like someone who is very self-possessed and used to getting his own way."

"I am now, but I also come from a family that had firm expectations, and I wasn't quite so self-possessed when I was younger. I was more inclined to do what my father wanted me to do. So I married the girl he wanted me to marry, and it didn't work out at all. We hated each other for years, but surprisingly, we have recently become friendly again. She seems to have forgiven me."

"Forgiven you for what?"

"For not making a go of a marriage that was making us both miserable."

"And your second wife?"

"She ran off with the electrician."

"You're serious?"

"Completely. She is living with him in Fairfield. Poor bastard. She is one crazy bitch." Lance got a steely look in his eye. "I'm sorry. I shouldn't have said that. Let's not talk about her. Tell me how a stunning woman like you ends up working at the coffee shop."

"Thank you for the compliment, even though it implies there's something wrong with working at a coffee shop . . ." Evvie had laughed, despite her discomfort.

"I applaud anyone with a good work ethic, and you've certainly got that. I just see you doing something else. If you were working in a high-end clothing store, that I could understand. Or being a rich man's wife."

Evvie let out a bark of laughter. "Is that an offer?"

Lance grinned. "If you play your cards right."

Evvie hooted. "That, my friend, may be the best offer I've had in years." She blushed. "I'm kidding. In all seriousness, I'm not proud and I have a son to support. A friend asked me to help her, and while I'll admit I didn't expect it to turn into something so regular, I love it. I still do style consulting, and every now and then I do the odd modeling job. It suits me. I get bored if I'm stuck doing one thing."

"Does your son's father help?"

Evvie had smiled and shaken her head. Jack's father had no idea he even had a son, which was exactly the way she wanted it. "He's not in the picture."

By the end of the night, Lance had made her promise to come and edit his wardrobe. It was clear from his Brunello Cucinelli cashmere jackets, Hermès ties, and John Lobb shoes that he didn't need her, but she wasn't going to turn the invitation down.

"Come on Sunday," he said. "Bring your son. We can have brunch. And bring your swimsuits — I have a pool that no one uses anymore. I bet your son would love it."

That Sunday, they pulled up outside huge wooden gates on the most expensive street in Westport. The gates slowly drew inward as Jack exhaled with an audible "whoa" muttered almost under his breath.

"It's big, isn't it?" said Evvie, who had been to many houses equally grand when she was at the height of her modeling career.

"Mom, this is awesome. Who lives here?"

"Just a friend. A man I know from work."

"Does he have a wife?"

Evvie couldn't suppress a smile as she gave her son the side-eye. "Why?"

"Could you maybe get married to him? Then I'd have a dad and we could all live here!"

Evvie laughed, even while feeling a stab of remorse. It wasn't often that Jack said anything about not having a father. It would come out unconsciously, in comments just like this, when Evvie realized how much he wanted a man in his life.

"I think it's a bit early for that," she said carefully. "We're just friends. But it's interesting that you said that about having a dad. Is that something you want?"

Jack shrugged then, but she continued looking at him, and he nodded. "Maybe," he said. "If it was someone nice."

She reached over and ruffled his hair, her heartstrings pulling as she thought about what he had said. Evvie had always given him everything, but the one thing she hadn't given him was a father. He so rarely brought it up that she thought she had done a great job, had left him wanting for nothing, until times like these when his desire was exposed.

They pulled up a winding driveway, past a tennis court, past a caretaker's cottage, past outbuildings and vast metal sculptures, to a cobbled courtyard in front of a huge white house, the blue-gray water of Long Island Sound a huge vista behind it.

Jack's eyes were wide. "Mom, is this a *palace?*"

"I think it's about the closest thing to it that we're ever going to get, so yes, I'd say pretty much."

Jack was awestruck. "Did you see the basketball court when we drove in? And the tennis court? And you said there's a swimming pool too. I bet he has a boat as well!"

The front door opened and Lance strode out in jeans and a polo shirt, a wide smile on his face as he extended his arms to welcome them.

He's really attractive, thought Evvie suddenly. Why hadn't I ever noticed quite how attractive he is before now?

They got married six months later. For the first few years, it was perfect. Evvie had never been taken care of in quite this way. She hadn't ever wanted to be taken care of, had valued her independence and self-sufficiency, but now that she was, she found out how much she loved having nothing to worry about. Whatever she wanted, Lance provided. He was lovely with Jack. She went from worrying about money all the time, to never having to think about it. She went from worrying about everything to feeling safe. Until recently, when she caught him looking her up and down, judgment in his eyes, when the calm, reasonable, loving man she had married had, at times, seemed to disappear.

When he first lost his temper with her, she was able to ignore it, even laugh at it, but it had been happening more and more, and it was beginning to wear her down. The last couple of times had been genuinely frightening.

Last week he had been so angry, he threw his keys across the room. It wasn't at her, would never have hit her, but his face was twisted in rage, and she had flinched never-theless, terrified, thrown back to being a little girl, afraid of her father's rages.

Now, lying in bed, listening to Lance's comments about her weight, the only thing she kept thinking was, Don't make him angry; whatever you do, don't upset him. She closed the magazine and looked down at the cover. "Are you saying you wouldn't love me if I got fat?"

"I'm saying let's not go down that road and find out." He said it without looking at her, before reaching over and switching off the light on his nightstand. Within minutes he was gently snoring as Evvie lay in bed, stunned at the threat behind his words.

She had heard about his notorious temper at work, how he kept everyone on a tight rein, but she never thought he would apply those same unreasonable conditions to her. She was his wife, and not just his wife, but *the One*. She was different; she was the soul mate, the one he had spent his life waiting for. At least, that's what he used to tell her when they were first married.

Evvie lay down, her eyes open, thinking about her life as her husband snored beside her. These comments and his recent anger were jarring and upsetting, but not enough to leave, she thought. Not when she was able to provide Jack with the kind of life that would be unimaginable without Lance. He offered both of them safety and security, and up until recently, what felt like unconditional love. She just had to be a little better, a little thinner. Then everything would be perfect again.

TWENTY-FIVE

- 2009 -

"You've done it again, haven't you!" Karen threw her arms around Maggie. "Honestly, I don't know what we did before you came along. What did we do without her, Pete?" She turned her head to her husband, standing in the doorway of the pub. "How did we manage?"

"Badly," he shouted, coming over and patting Maggie awkwardly on the back as Karen released her.

"The village fete was perfectly fine before I came along," Maggie said, flushing with pride because, although it was perfectly fine, it was really for the pensioners, and since Maggie got involved, the whole village now showed up.

It was Maggie's idea to have a petting zoo and pony rides for all the small children in the village. There was already a baking competition, but Maggie redid the categories so it wasn't all Black Forest Gateau and

Victoria Sponge, but Puddings, Pies, Cakes, Biscuits, Pastry, and Bread (she had won the cake category two years in a row).

She gently suggested getting rid of the white elephant stand, given that it was usually filled with secondhand rubbish that no one wanted, and instead found local craftspeople to set up stalls, and her neighbor Emily, who was a graphic designer, designed beautiful flyers that they posted on everyone's front door to ensure the best attendance ever.

"What did I do?" Maggie asked, laughing as she perched on a stool in the pub. Karen and Pete were the landlords, and had become Maggie's closest friends through her involvement in the village fete. Even though they were a bit older, they had never had children, and as a result, Maggie never felt the need to explain. They didn't ask, presuming perhaps that Maggie and Ben, like themselves, had chosen not to have children.

"You sweet-talked that grumpy old Charlie into donating his ice cream van for the day. Everyone's over the moon! We've all been trying to get him to do it for years, but he always refused unless we paid him! How did you do it?"

Maggie grimaced. "I would love to tell you it was my beauty and charm, but I paid him.

This is out of my own pocket though. It's my donation to the cause."

"As if you don't already donate enough," said Pete, pouring her a gin and tonic and sliding it over the bar. "What about you, love?" He turned to Karen. "Usual, or are you in the mood for something more exotic? Pineapple, perhaps?"

Karen and Maggie both caught each other's eye and giggled. They had gone on a girls' night out last week in Bath, and both had had far too much to drink. Karen had a penchant for piña coladas, and had been drinking them as if they were mother's milk.

"I wish we *had* piña coladas here, if that's what you're implying," said Karen, laughing. "Maybe we should do that? Have a cocktail night once a month? What do you think, Maggie? You and Ben would come, wouldn't you?"

Maggie nodded, because Karen didn't know about Ben's drinking . . . *issue*. Maggie couldn't tell anyone about Ben's drinking, nor how difficult things had been between them over the past year. She wished she could, but as much as she loved Karen and Pete, this was a small village, and news traveled like wildfire, particularly gossip.

The only person she had been able to confide in was her mother. She spoke to her every day, sometimes crying on the phone at how incredibly lonely she was.

"This will pass," her mother said. "No marriage is good all the time. The most important thing in marriage is kindness, and Ben is a kind man. Even if he's drinking again, he will stop. He always does. You just need patience."

Maggie hadn't phoned her mother in three weeks. Not because she didn't need to talk, but because she was fed up with her mother's insistence that this wasn't a big deal, that all men drink, that Maggie's deep loneliness was something that she could, and should, live with.

"Here you go," said Pete, and suddenly a piña colada, complete with maraschino cherry and paper cocktail napkin, was in front of Karen.

"What? How did you . . ." Karen started laughing as Pete grinned, which made her laugh all the more.

"I do love you, Pete," she said, leaning over and kissing him on the lips.

"I know how to make my wife happy," he said, winking at Maggie, who loved seeing how sweet the two of them were together, even amid her own sadness at not having the same sort of marriage.

Things had become harder and harder

over the last few years. IVF hadn't worked, and after a while, they stopped trying. They had talked about adoption, but Maggie adamantly refused, without giving him an explanation why. Ben had pointed out all the wonderful stories there were, but Maggie wouldn't listen.

They had each shut down, to the point where there was less and less to say to each other. Ben had his work, his hiking, and Maggie had her cooking. She didn't hike with him anymore, let him go off with his hiking club on the weekends, while she went to Karen and Pete's, or out with other friends.

When they were together, if they weren't talking about something logistical to do with the house, Maggie felt they would run out of things to talk about. Ben didn't seem to mind, but she hated it. Sometimes, when Ben was on his way home for dinner, she would make a note of things that had happened to her that day that might interest him, or maybe make him laugh. Anything to avoid the silence.

On the rare occasions they went out for dinner, she would see other couples, a few their own age, some much older, who would sit there in silence, looking around the room or — presumably — eavesdropping on the lucky people who did have things to say to each other. Maggie never noticed those people until about two years ago, until she realized that unless she put in the work, they stood a very good chance of becoming one of those couples.

For a long time, she blamed the drinking. Ben would manage a few months sober, sometimes a year, before one drink would derail him, and the chaos would start all over again. It always started with one drink. Ben could handle one drink, but before long it would be a vodka to start, then a second and third, before "splitting" a bottle of wine. Or two. Maggie only ever had a glass, at most, and she tried not to drink in front of Ben.

She found herself saying things at the beginning of the evening like, "Please don't drink too much," or the more passive-aggressive, "Drinking again, I see?" and the evening would devolve into resentful silence other than commenting about the food.

When Ben went into AA, as he did every once in a while, usually when she'd find him passed out on the stairs night after night, Maggie always hoped that sobriety would bring the easy, chatty conversation that had defined their courtship and the honeymoon years of their marriage.

But Ben was an introvert, one who might have been very good at pretending to be an extrovert, but he lived in his head. It didn't occur to him to share his thoughts with Maggie, who could happily burble away to anyone. After a while, she ran out of things to say to Ben. He didn't seem that interested in stories of her life in the village, and although he was interested in politics, Maggie wasn't particularly, and she didn't have the will to learn about it.

She tried to find other ways to fill the silence. In the evenings they would often eat dinner with the radio on. She would scour the *Radio Times* to find a play, or a show she knew he would like. If there was something on the telly they would have a TV dinner, but Maggie hated that, didn't want to get into that habit.

After dinner she would go to her little office and check her e-mail, Ben going to his own office, coming to bed long after she was fast asleep.

She could smell the alcohol on him when he came to bed. And she had never been lonelier in her life. She wished her mother's words were true, but even if this passed, even if he got sober yet again, she had no doubt her life would always be this roller coaster.

She would sometimes try to think of what they once had in common, but it was getting harder to remember. Most of the time, she thought they were hugely mismatched from the beginning. Had she not harbored such an enormous crush on him, had she not worn rose-tinted spectacles every time she looked at him, perhaps she would have seen it.

"Where is that husband of yours, anyway?" said Pete. "He was good fun at the lock-in last Saturday."

"Oh, you should have been there," said Karen. "We had Simon from the grocer's on the piano all night. We didn't leave until the early hours. Your Ben was the life and soul of the party!"

Did he drink? Maggie wanted to ask, but of course he was drinking. He was only ever the life and soul when he was drinking.

If she wasn't so scared of being on her own, of the enormous changes divorce would bring, she would leave him. Instead, she harbored her resentments and wounds, and lay in bed dreaming of an easier, happier life.

Twenty-Six

- 2010 -

Dickie always came along when Topher did the chat shows, particularly the morning shows, as there were always producers there that Dickie had known from way back when. He enjoyed the whole process, arriving early, sitting in the greenroom, hopefully running into a thespian or two that he had once worked with.

They had arrived at the *Today* show early that morning, Dickie thrilled when Stephen Fry entered the greenroom, here to talk about a new movie. They had worked together years before, and Stephen generously offered to help Topher with his memoir in any way he could.

Topher still couldn't believe he had a memoir out today, a memoir in which he finally outed himself, mostly because the rumors online had been growing out of control. Perez Hilton had been dropping hints in blind items for months, which at first had terrified Topher — would he ever get work as a straight actor again if the world knew he was gay? — and then became tiring.

His publicist had come up with a strategy involving Lori Lenone, a hot young female singer from Australia who was looking to build her profile in the US, and the two of them staged a "romance," kicking off on the island of Nevis, where they were photographed with a long-lens camera while relaxing at the private and luxurious Montpelier Plantation, lying on sun beds and kissing, Lori straddling his back to rub sunblock into his shoulders, leaning down to plant a kiss.

The paparazzi had been planted, as had the moves. They were photographed holding hands as they strolled along the sands at sunset, gazing into each other's eyes over lunch at the Four Seasons, unable to keep their hands off each other as they waited for dinner at Bananas Bistro.

Everyone picked up on the story, given that the gay rumors were at their height, but after a couple of months, Topher phoned his agent and said enough. He couldn't stand the vacuous conversation with Lori anymore. Their lack of chemistry, even for a friendship, had gradually morphed into not being able to tolerate being around each other, and when his agent suggested a breakup followed by another staged romance, Topher said no.

He was forty-two years old, and no longer interested in living a lie. So he was gay. So what? It mattered to him more when he was young, when he thought he might be interested in a Hollywood career, but as a soap star who was signed up to play Agador in *La Cage aux Folles* on Broadway for a six-month run during the sabbatical, he didn't care anymore.

His only stipulation was that he come out on his terms. It was his brilliant agent who not only suggested the memoir, but got a huge bidding war going, which, in itself, was an excellent publicity move.

The publisher had offered a ghostwriter, but Topher's ego wouldn't hear of it. He fancied himself a writer, even though he hadn't written anything since college. But the idea of being a writer appealed to him. He had taken to going to the New York Public Library after filming, settling down in a quiet corner to get his book written, breaking it down into chapters, going back as far as he could remember. He couldn't remember much. And the words didn't flow in the way they did when he had imagined writing. Most of the time he would sit and stare at the blank screen, sighing. He would jot down memories, but it was so hard to put the words together, and the memories he had were few and far between.

In the evenings, when he wasn't out with Dickie, he would read other memoirs, trying to figure out how other people managed to do it. Surely it couldn't be as hard as it seemed.

Writing, and remembering, were the hardest things he had ever done, far harder than acting. Dickie kept trying to persuade him to use a ghostwriter, but Topher was convinced he could do it, even when all the evidence was pointing otherwise.

He was in a small bookstore in Maine when he stumbled upon a self-published memoir. At that point he was reading every memoir he could get his hands on, and even though he had never heard of the author, the writing was beautiful. Topher saw now what his book needed. Phrases as beautifully constructed as these. He wrote them down, peppering them throughout his book to remind himself, and suddenly it got easier.

It wasn't a long book, but he finished it, finally, and with much relief. The literary ambitions he had held when his agent first suggested a memoir had well and truly disappeared. He never wanted to write anything again as long as he lived.

The book was out that morning, and the preorders were through the roof, thanks to the *National Enquirer* running a piece about Topher being gay.

Topher was taking a sabbatical from the soap in order to do a thirty-city book tour before his theater engagement, kicking off with an interview with Ann Curry on the *Today* show. In truth, he suspected he wouldn't return after the sabbatical. He had been on the show for years, and it was time for a new challenge, kicking off with the memoir. He wasn't even sure he wanted to continue acting, but his publicist had made him swear he would never say this publicly.

Three publicists, one from the publisher together with the two from the soap, were with him, everyone excited about this interview, knowing that an interview like this on a show like this could propel the book up to the top of the bestseller lists.

Dickie and Stephen were still deep in conversation, both sharing stories that had everyone in the greenroom in stitches, Topher remaining quiet, leaving the room for hair and makeup (he was used to that, a bit of foundation to smooth his skin, concealer for the shadows, wax for his hair), worrying a little about what they would ask him.

And then there was no time to worry, they called him in and sat him on the sofa, and Ann reached over and shook his hand, and was so warm, so gracious, he instantly relaxed, and it was clear that she hadn't just read the producer's notes, but had read the book, and he thanked her profusely right before the cameraman started counting down to the end of the ad break when they were both going live.

"And with us today we have Topher Winthrop, who you will all recognize from one of my favorite soap operas, *What Comes Around.* He was in the news last year for his romance with Lori Lenone, and now he's trying something completely different." She reached next to her and held up a copy of his book. "Topher has written a memoir, *Behind the Scenes,* and Topher, I have to tell you, I could not put this book down. You talk about your first love, your mother, and your childhood in Greenwich, Connecticut, and what it was like going into acting. We follow Topher through his early days acting in New York, and there's lots of juicy gossip from, literally, behind the scenes of *What Comes Around.*"

"Nothing I can be sued for though," Topher interjected as she laughed.

"I would hope not. But what is so fascinating for all of us is that you have used this memoir to come out as gay, which is incredibly brave, especially as you have been plagued by online rumors for some time now."

"Oh, we're going there immediately?" Topher laughed.

"We're going there." Ann laughed in return.

"The truth is, I wanted to do this on my own terms, and I couldn't write a memoir without writing about the one huge thing that everyone questions about me. I had reached an age where I thought, I want to be real. I want to be known for who I am, including my sexuality, and if it puts people off or they don't like it, that's okay with me. You can't please all of the people all of the time."

"You must feel lighter, not keeping this secret anymore?"

"I never really thought of it as a secret because it was only a secret in my professional life, but yes, it's great to have been able to be as honest as I was in the book, and for it to be so well received."

"That's right. *People* magazine called it 'beautifully written and compelling from first page to last,' and Lauren Weisberger of *The Devil Wears Prada* fame said, 'It's gossipy and fun, and I couldn't put it down.' That's some high praise indeed, and well deserved. I was very interested in your childhood. You were born to some privilege in the tony town of Greenwich, and much of what you write sounds like you had an idyllic childhood."

"I really did," said Topher, who found he was on high alert. This was exactly what he didn't want to talk about. He had written it, of course, but had regretted this particular chapter, and wanted to remove it from the book completely, but his publisher wouldn't allow it.

A compromise was reached, where he kept a couple of paragraphs in the book, but didn't go into as much detail, and he hoped, how he hoped, that it wouldn't be a talking point when it came to publicity.

"And yet in chapter four you mention you had a tennis coach who only gave private lessons to boys, and that you realized years later how inappropriate his behavior was." Her face took on an expression of extreme empathy. "You don't write much more about that, and I wondered whether that was a hard decision, to put that in the book."

Topher nodded. "It was a hard decision.

Even years later it's hard to think about. It's hard to even talk about, and I didn't want to dwell on that. It wasn't a formative issue of my childhood, just a dark spot in what was otherwise pretty wonderful, and I have chosen to move on and live the life I have in spite of that."

"Which is so commendable. I wonder whether you ever thought of expanding on the issue of childhood sexual abuse? There are more and more adults who were victims of this kind of thing, and often it is helpful to read about what happened to others — it helps us realize that we're not alone."

"I think in mentioning it at all, I have hopefully done that." Topher said nothing else, and kept the smile on his face, but it was clear that he was done with that topic.

"And I understand you will be appearing on Broadway at the end of the summer, which is a first for you. Can you tell us more about that?"

Topher's shoulders relaxed as he talked about the play, and then it was over, and he was back in the greenroom being congratulated on a great interview.

"Come back anytime," said the young producer who showed them out. "We'd love to have you back when your show is opening. Ann loved you. Really, you're welcome to come on the show whenever."

They thanked him as they headed outside; back in the town car, Dickie looked at Topher with concern.

"It was fine. She's lovely."

"Were you okay about the question about your childhood? The . . . abuse?" Dickie's voice softened as he said the word, knowing how reluctant Topher was to discuss it, even though he had finally admitted what Dickie had always suspected.

"Of course I wasn't," said Topher, turning to look out the window. "I knew it was a mistake to keep that in. Now it's going to be all that everyone focuses on."

"Maybe it's you that could be focusing on it a little more? I know you don't like talking about it, but maybe this is an opportunity for you to perhaps see a therapist? You were a young boy, and it wasn't your fault, and there was nothing you could have done to stop it. It was about power, and although you think you are perfectly fine and you have moved on, I believe that what you have actually done is switch off your sexuality, because you are terrified of it. I have someone you could see, who I think would be of enormous help, and I say this because I love you, and because I want you to embrace all of yourself. I want you to be the fullest person you can be."

Topher turned from the window and looked at Dickie, before his face crumpled as he broke down in sobs.

Twenty-Seven

- 2015 -

The bathroom light was flattering, casting a soft, dewy glow as Evvie turned around so her husband could fasten the catch at the back of her neck. As he did, he looked her slowly up and down and she resisted the urge to cover her body with her hands.

There was absolutely no denying the weight gain anymore. This former model, once skinny and tall, was now insulated by a thick layer of flesh. Her thighs rubbed together when she walked, her stomach was rounded and full, her breasts had become large enough that she couldn't wait to get home every night to take her bra off, her shoulders aching from the weight.

She was both horrified and relieved by her changing figure. The more weight she gained, the more Lance left her alone — other than to point out, as he was surely about to do, how *fat* she was, how *disgusting.* The passive-aggressive barbs had stopped long ago, replaced with disdain. His words still stung, but the knowledge that he no longer wanted to sleep with her, the protection the weight afforded her, was ample compensation for any sting she may have felt.

"You are enormous," he whispered in disgust, shaking his head as she felt her breath catch in her throat.

Evvie would lie in bed at night and rest her hands on her belly, stroking the curves. She would walk into the bathroom and lift her pajama top, cup her heavy boobs, rub her rounded stomach, and think that if she weren't in her midforties, she might be mistaken for being pregnant. And as much as she hated it, she recognized that she needed it, even though she struggled with her reflection in the mirror.

Her face had lost the sharp cheekbones of her youth, and although still exquisitely beautiful, she didn't feel it; all she saw was her round face, her thick neck, the rolls of flesh around her back.

None of her old clothes fit. For the gala that night, she had bought a dress in a size she had never thought she would wear. She had been praised and rewarded for her beauty for her entire life, for her slimness, how perfect she was. And now? Now she had to buy her clothes online.

Once upon a time, men on trains would stop and stare at her, valets would rush to park her car, free gifts from beauty companies would arrive at the house. When she gained weight she became invisible, and the attention stopped, and when it stopped, as her marriage was disintegrating, Evvie's confidence disappeared, leaving her quiet and withdrawn, a shadow of her former flirty, fun, sexy self.

She missed her old self. She pined for her confidence, for who she used to be when she knew she was beautiful and understood the power that came with that beauty, but that beauty wasn't worth the cost of giving up the only thing that brought solace to her loneliness, the only thing that protected her from Lance. Her excess weight kept him well away from her, and as a result, Evvie, who now both hated and feared her husband, would continue to eat for as long as she could.

In the beginning Lance had insisted she diet, bringing in personal trainer after personal trainer, forcing her to work out in their home gym. She would lose a pound or two, but it always came back on, and she always found a way to get rid of the trainer. It was easier to blame hormones and early menopause rather than the cakes she had started buying and eating in secret.

Her weight enraged Lance, but she couldn't stop eating. In every other area she tried not to displease him. She would tiptoe around him trying to make him happy, terrified of setting off one of his rages.

Over the years the rages became more and more frequent, more and more terrifying. Often, they started with derision, maybe teasing her size, poking a roll of flesh in her back. But they escalated quickly into verbal assault. At times like those, there was no shadow left of the man she had met. He became a completely different person.

He didn't hit her, but she always expected him to. He loomed in her face, his jaw clenched in fury, unrecognizable in his ferocity as he spat out terrible things, hateful things, found her weakest spot, and went in for the kill.

Evvie had always thought she was strong. She had always been a fighter, and in the beginning, she had fought back. She screamed as loudly as Lance, got in his face, flounced out. But his rage was greater than hers, and eventually it wore her down — the never knowing what would set him off; the terrible, wounding things he said; the fear of saying or doing the wrong thing. As the years went by, she became more and more reserved. As the years went by, she withdrew so completely, she forgot who she had once been.

Her real concern was Jack. Lance never went after Jack, but Evvie tried to protect her son from hearing, or seeing, how Lance treated her. She had done a good job, she thought. The rages almost always happened when Jack was at boarding school, and even when he was home, it was always behind their closed bedroom door. Jack didn't know. She was sure he didn't know.

Tonight was one she had been dreading. A gala at Sotheby's, where she would be paraded around on his arm as he leered at other women with his male business associates.

Now, as they stood in the bathroom, he grimaced as he looked at her breasts, his eyes narrowed. Her heart started pounding in frightened anticipation of what he might say, of what he might do.

"A morbidly obese wife," he sneered. "Jesus Christ. How in the hell did I end up with such a disgusting pig of a wife? It's time you had a gastric bypass. I don't know why we didn't do it earlier. We'll get you looking halfway decent again. I'll get Doris to make an appointment on Monday. I can barely even look at you now."

He walked out of the bathroom then, and Evvie exhaled, unaware she had been holding her breath. She looked at herself in the mirror, trying to drown out his voice with more positive messaging of her own.

"You are strong," she whispered. "You are a wonderful mother. You are smart and capable. You are a good person. You are beautiful.

"Don't let him get to you," she whispered to herself. "You know why you're heavy. And you are better than he is. You deserve more." She rolled her shoulders back, shook out her hair, and despite wanting to crawl into bed, she plastered on her best smile, and slipped on her shoes.

The cocktail hour at the gala was interminable. The rooms were packed, the music blaring, people yelling to be heard over it. The stark white walls of the gallery were hung with works by Degas, Monet, Manet, Toulouse-Lautrec, Seurat, Sisley, all of the greats, but everyone was ignoring the paintings, too busy looking around to see who was who, and what they were wearing.

The gowns were magnificent. Jewel colors draped around aging women who were size zero, their tan, bony shoulders exposed in silks and satins, their hair sprayed into coiffed helmets, their cheekbones unnaturally high and round as they chattered excitedly with their friends. They were accompanied by husbands in black tie, many of whom appeared to be thirty years older than their wives, until you looked at the wives' hands, bejeweled and wrinkled, the only giveaway of their age. The men stood together as the women admired their dresses, showed off their jewels, subtly eyed each other up and down to make sure they were wearing a more expensive, more exclusive outfit, a bigger necklace, better jewels.

Through it all, Evvie stood, and smiled, air-kissed people she knew, made small talk with the wives of Lance's colleagues, even though she knew they did not think much of her, these New York society matrons. She knew they judged her and found her inferior, the ex-model, half-black, once-single mother who would never, ever be good enough for them.

She became aware of a woman staring at her, a woman who seemed to have been staring at her throughout the evening. She was an actress Evvie vaguely recognized from a popular television show. She was petite, and pretty, and worked on. Her lips were pouty in the artificial way that immediately told Evvie they had been plumped, her breasts the sort of large melons Lance loved. Her arms were toned and tanned, and her hair a waterfall of glossy blond.

Evvie found herself catching the eye of the blonde enough times that she was wondering if perhaps they had met, or — unlikely — that Evvie had done something at some time to offend her, for her gaze seemed hostile. But then, standing in a circle of people, chatting (although Evvie never felt as if she was standing *in* the circle, but always just outside), the blond woman was there, and they were being introduced.

"Ally, do you know Lance Colton and his wife, Evvie?" Carl Steenberg said as the actress shook her head. "Lance, Evvie, I'm sure you know the actress Ally Majors."

"Good to meet you," said Lance, shaking her hand.

"How do you do?" said Evvie, surprised by the firmness of Ally's handshake. She looked so delicate, as if she would be one of those people who limply placed their hand in yours before sliding it away. But in fact she looked Evvie straight in the eye and gripped her hand, shaking it firmly.

"So lovely to meet you," Ally said to Evvie. "I can't take my eyes off your dress. It's absolutely beautiful."

"Thank you so much." Evvie wanted to warm to the compliment, yet there was a lack of warmth in the woman's tone. "I loved the show you were in, with Rob Lowe. It was one of my favorites."

"God, that was a long time ago. But thank you. It was huge fun."

"Will you excuse me?" Evvie needed to get away. "I must visit the restroom." This was the trick she always used to get away when she was uncomfortable, excusing herself to go to the restroom, or to get another drink, or to get some air — anything for a few moments of peace by herself.

She wandered through the crowds, aware that curious eyes were watching her, that there were people wanting to say hello. She stopped to greet Rena and Jason Pilalas, and Ian and Debbie O'Malley, before excusing herself, performing an old trick from her modeling days, walking off and keeping her eyes trained on the middle distance so everyone became a blur, a smile on her face, careful to avoid making eye contact.

Just as she reached the other side of the room, she turned and saw the group of people she had been standing with, the actress, Ally, now deep in conversation with Lance. As she watched, her husband reached over and placed a hand on Ally's backside, pulling her slowly up against him. Ally smiled the most intimate of smiles, dancing her fingers up his arm, before removing it and looking around to check that no one had seen.

Her eyes landed on Evvie's. She immediately composed her features into a cool gaze before whispering something to Lance. It was obvious that they knew each other very well, that they had *known* each other — Evvie guessed in the biblical sense — for some time.

Ally started walking toward Evvie, who turned on her heel and left for the bathroom, hoping the actress wouldn't be able to follow her in the crowd. She headed downstairs, to the quiet bathroom, moving quickly. Once there, she locked herself in a stall, taking deep breaths.

So her husband was having an affair. How did she feel about it? Neither shocked, nor surprised, nor upset. Resigned, perhaps. And maybe relieved. In fact, she felt something she hadn't experienced in a long time: a smattering of hope. If he was involved with someone else, perhaps he would leave her alone. Perhaps he would spend even more time away. This certainly explained why he had been spending so much time in the city as it was.

The door to the bathroom opened, and Evvie heard her name.

Damn.

She walked out of the stall and faced Ally, who was standing there prettily, her hands on her hips.

"So. You know."

"That you and my husband are having an affair? I do now."

"I'm sorry you had to find out this way, but it's not just an affair. He is in love with me."

A glimmer of hope sparked in Evvie's chest. "And how do you feel about him?"

"The same," Ally said, in a monotone. "He says you will never divorce him, but I don't believe that to be true. I understand you've gotten used to the lifestyle, but why would you want to stay married to a man who no longer loves you? Why not get out now, while you are still . . . relatively young . . . and have a chance to be happy yourself, and to let him be happy."

"You want to marry him?" Evvie asked, trying to hide a smile of disbelief, of . . . relief. Maybe this was the hand of God reaching down and opening up the tiniest of exit doors.

"I do. And he wants to marry me."

"Why has he not said anything to me?"

"Because he knows you will fleece him."

"I have no interest in fleecing him," Evvie said. "If you want him, you can have him."

Ally's mouth fell open. "That's it? It's that simple?"

"I don't have the energy for the fight," Evvie said. "He's yours. You can tell him that I've taken the car back to the house, and I will be out by morning. Good luck," she said, wanting to add, *You'll need it.* But she refrained. She was too selfish to warn the woman about what she was getting into. And she doubted Ally would listen. Evvie had heard the rumors about Lance, and had chosen to ignore them herself.

This was clearly not what the actress had been expecting. She stared at Evvie, lost for words. Holding her head high, Evvie walked out of the building, and to the corner, where she texted her driver. Within minutes, she was inside the car and pulling away from the curb, and Evvie realized the dream she had been dreaming for years seemed to have unexpectedly come true. She started to smile as a great weight lifted from her shoulders and the smile turned to a laugh, and soon she was laughing so hard, it brought tears to her eyes.

TWENTY-EIGHT
- 2016 -

"It's so beautiful," said Karen, wide-eyed, at Emily's house. "I don't know how you did it."

"I had help," said Emily. "I'm much too busy with the children, but I definitely had a big hand in everything. My decorator came up from London, but I was forever e-mailing her things I'd seen and loved."

The men were in the living room with drinks and nuts as Emily gave Karen and Maggie a tour of their newly renovated kitchen. After ten years in the house, Emily had decided the kitchen was completely outdated, and they had knocked through into what had been the den, to create a giant kitchen and family room.

Maggie had loved the old kitchen. It had been cream, with butcher-block countertops and a large Aga, which Maggie had never fully understood, given that Emily never cooked.

The new kitchen was stark and modern. The bleached wood herringbone floor was, to Maggie's mind, the most beautiful thing about it. There was an island now, ten feet long, with a huge slab of marble waterfalling over the sides. The flat-fronted cabinets were black, and the splash backs a polished horizontal slatted wood. It looked like it had just stepped out of the pages of *House & Garden.* Maggie missed the old Fired Earth tile splash backs that reminded her of a sunrise. This wasn't a kitchen she would want to cook in, however beautiful it may have been. The thin brass stools at the countertop repelled rather than invited — the whole room was a triumph of form over function.

Two women in white shirts and black trousers were bustling around the kitchen getting food ready.

"Something smells delicious," said Maggie. "Is it lamb?"

"Lamb stuffed with pine nuts and apricots. And a Moroccan couscous. I've found the most fabulous caterer in Bath. I'll give you her number."

Karen burst out laughing. "Have you tasted Maggie's cooking? No offense, but she doesn't need a caterer!"

"You never know," said Emily. "What if

she and Ben are having a party?"

Ha, thought Maggie. Nothing would be less likely. Now that Ben was working in London again, they socialized less and less. She only saw him on the weekends, and they hadn't been invited anywhere for ages. This, Emily and James's dinner party, was the first event they had been to together in months.

"I'd kill to have a kitchen like this," said Karen, her eyes still wide. Maggie thought of Karen's own kitchen above the pub, dated but well used and well loved, copper pots and pans hanging from hooks drilled into the brick wall above the range.

You wouldn't, thought Maggie, eyes darting nervously toward the living room as a burst of laughter came through from the men. Ben was drinking again. She didn't know this until tonight, when James offered him a vodka and he accepted, saying, "Just a small one." He didn't meet Maggie's eyes.

She had given up trying. In the old days this would have set her on high alert, would have ruined her night, but she didn't care anymore. He had been looking terrible, the whites of his eyes yellow, his whole body seeming bloated. He had been to the doctor months ago, and had returned saying he was fine, and would be going to a meeting that night. She presumed the doctor told him to stop drinking, but he didn't say anything more, and she didn't ask.

"Those boys!" Karen rolled her eyes at the burst of laughter. "A few drinks in them and they're wild. That Ben." She shook her head affectionately as she looked at Maggie. "He's the life and soul. I don't know how you're not exhausted!"

"Me neither." Maggie gave a tight smile.

One of the ladies looked at her watch. "We're ready to sit down when you are."

"Great," said Emily. "Let's serve the first course in about ten minutes."

Maggie had lost count of how much she had had to drink. In the old days she refused to drink in front of Ben, lest it encourage him or pull him off the wagon. These days she didn't care; it was easier to get through a night like this when she had something to take the edge off.

There was a new woman in town who apparently sold marijuana edibles. They were all the rage among the yummy mummies, according to Karen, who said she'd long ago eschewed the witching hour glass of wine for a gummy bear or a pot lollipop.

Karen had bought some lollipops and given a couple to Maggie, but she hadn't tried them. Her only experience with weed had been long ago at university, and all she could remember was falling asleep.

Her drug of choice, if you could call it that, was red wine, and tonight she had had just enough to be able to ignore Ben, who was laughing so hard, he was wheezing. But everyone around the table, apart from Maggie, seemed hooked on every word of the funny story he was telling.

". . . so the woman in the comments section said how horrific foxes were, and that no one would be saying that if a fox had massacred their chickens and turkeys, and a man wrote underneath . . ." Ben couldn't speak for a few moments, loose with laughter as he wiped the tears from his eyes. " 'My chickens are cunts.' "

The table exploded into raucous laughter, except for Maggie, who managed a wry smile. She had laughed out loud when she read the original David Sedaris story, but it wasn't quite as funny for her, coming from the mouth of her husband, who, at that moment, was shaking with laughter so much that he spilled his red wine.

Maggie looked around the table, at everyone having a great time, all of them adoring Ben, whose introvert tendencies went AWOL when he drank. She excused herself to go to the bathroom, and as she passed Ben's chair, he reached for her.

"My beautiful wife," he crooned, holding out his hand as she sidestepped his grasp.

"Sorry!" she lied. "Desperate for the loo."

By half past eleven, Maggie was done. James had broken out his vintage whiskey collection, and Maggie didn't want to watch her husband get legless.

"I'm fine, I'm fine. Too much red wine and a bit headachy," she said, kissing Emily and thanking her.

"I'll put Pete in charge of getting Ben home safely." Karen put her arms around Maggie and gave her a tight hug. "Not that he's much better. Boys will be boys, eh?" She laughed as Maggie attempted a smile.

"You don't need to put Pete in charge of Ben. It's fifty yards away!" said Emily, who was herself a bit tipsy. "I'm so glad we did this. Your husband is hilarious. We ought to do this much more often. How long has it been since we got together? I think it's been years! We definitely won't leave it this long again!" She gave Maggie another hug before Maggie stepped out the door, grateful for the cold air as she walked home.

She fell asleep as soon as her head hit the pillow, but woke up, sometime later, thinking she had heard a bang. She turned the light on in the hallway and called out.

"Hello? Ben?" There was no answer. She walked downstairs, seeing the front door was wide open, and the grandfather clock in the hallway said it was twenty past one. She closed the door and locked it, knowing that the bang must have been Ben.

She found him in his office, his "nightcap" spilled all over the floor, Ben slumped against his desk, blacked out, with vomit on his shirt.

Maggie stood in the doorway, looking at her husband. In the old days she would have forced him awake, taken off his clothes and thrown them straight in the wash, scrubbed the carpet clean, and helped him upstairs to bed. She would have been furious, upset, would have insisted they have "a talk" in the morning, when he was sober.

This time she felt nothing. She backed out of the room, turned off the lights, and closed the door. Let Ben clean up his mess when he finally woke up.

■ ■ ■ ■

PART III
PRESENT DAY

■ ■ ■ ■

Twenty-Nine

- 2019 -

Maggie paused in the hallway, where silver-framed photographs clustered on a polished walnut table, and picked up her wedding photo. There they were, her little group, Evvie and Topher, she and Ben looking so young, so unprepared for what the future would bring. She should have put the photograph away after the funeral, but she felt too guilty. Her penance was keeping the photograph out, pretending that their marriage had been perfect, that Ben had been perfect, even now, three years after his death.

Much of the time Maggie still couldn't believe Ben was dead. Oh, what irony, that he was on his way out to try to surprise her in a last-ditch bid to save the marriage, just as Maggie had decided to leave. They had been unhappy for so many years, this house that they had both once loved feeling like a prison, a constant reminder of what they didn't have, neither children nor, as time went on, anything that bound them together, until the wedge between them became insurmountable.

Ben dealt with it by falling off the wagon more times than Maggie could remember. She knew each time he had started drinking again, and every muscle in her body would tense as he lay beside her snoring, as the same old patterns started again, her monitoring the alcohol everywhere in the house, him lying about where he had been and what he had been doing.

The warning signs were there, early on, about his drinking, but Maggie had had no experience with life, no experience with alcoholism. She chose to see what she wanted to see, turning blithely away from everything that might have been a red flag.

By the time his doctor told him his liver was shot, that one more drink could kill him, Maggie didn't much care. And when the news came, that he had collapsed on the train on the way home, his liver having finally failed him, she felt guilty that she had just sent him the text about wanting a divorce. But she had mostly felt relieved.

And still none of their friends knew the truth about what killed him. Maggie didn't want them to know just how imperfect their marriage was, what a disaster Ben had become by the end. Years of brief sobriety before drinking again, the whites of his eyes turning yellow with jaundice, Maggie having to regularly phone work and make excuses for him. Her official story was that Ben died from a heart attack rather than alcoholic liver disease.

She looked at the wedding picture, feeling nothing. That couple, that happy, young couple with dreams of a family and years of joy, felt like strangers, like they had nothing to do with her.

When Maggie ran into Ben that day in the cafeteria, years after leaving university, it had seemed like fate. Maggie had phoned Evvie as soon as she got home, shrieking at the coincidence of it, and Evvie had said, "This is meant to be. You're going to marry him."

Maggie knew she had been right. It *was* meant to be, and they were happy in the early years, happy even when life stopped going their way, when they both had to accept they wouldn't have children, they weren't being given the life they thought was their due.

But the happiness didn't last. Ben's drinking put paid to that. When the police showed up at her door, gently informing her that her husband had collapsed on the train on the way home and hadn't made it, Maggie looked at them in disbelief. She had been dreaming of divorce for years, had sometimes, in her darkest moments, thought how much easier life would be if Ben just had a fatal heart attack, then berated herself for even thinking that.

And here were the policemen, telling her that her darkest thoughts had come to pass. Initially, after the disbelief came relief. She didn't have to dread his coming home on the weekends, the dark cloud that seemed to fall on her shoulders every Friday morning when she woke up. She didn't have to lie in bed grinding her teeth, filled with fury at her husband who was stumbling around downstairs, drunk.

She felt . . . relief, until the shame kicked in. What would she tell people? The truth? That Ben was a high-functioning alcoholic who often passed out on the stairs on his way up to bed, more times than she could count? That she had become the last thing she had ever wanted, a cross between his mother and a detective, attempting to sniff out every drop of alcohol he consumed? Would she tell them his doctor had warned him his liver would fail if he carried on? Or would she lie, say he died of a heart attack?

She went with the heart attack.

After the shame came the guilt. Why hadn't she done more? Or less? Was she too hard on him, or not hard enough? Wasn't it her responsibility to check he was going to meetings when he said he was, to check in with his sponsor? Should she have carted him off to rehab as soon as he started drinking again? Should she have kicked him out properly, or left him herself? What could she have done differently? For surely she should have, could have, would have done things differently if she could turn back the clock.

Maggie spent months second-guessing herself, overwhelmed by guilt at not having done the right thing, at letting her husband go years ago, even though she knew she was no match for alcohol. Every time someone asked how he died and she responded with "a heart attack," she was engulfed by shame and guilt afresh.

While Ben's unexpected death may have brought her some peace after all the years of chaos, the peace was always tied together with guilt.

Initially, her friends gathered around, but soon they got on with their lives, leaving Maggie with no idea how to get on with hers. She should have been free, she was free, but secrets are hard to keep, especially from your closest friends, and soon she found herself withdrawing.

Her saving grace, she often thought, was the house, a house she loved as much as the day she first saw it, even though it was far too big for her, and every check she had to write for the upkeep was a painful one.

Her days were peaceful now. She did the occasional catering for people from home, but she pulled out of organizing the village fete after Ben died — she wanted to see people less, not more, for everyone was filled with questions as to how a young, seemingly healthy man could suddenly drop dead of a heart attack.

When Ben was alive, Maggie always thought there was nothing lonelier than being married to an alcoholic. But she was lonelier now. At least then she had a purpose, even though it was not one she relished. Now she found that she was drifting aimlessly, unsure of what to do with a life that was not what she ever expected.

She still spoke to her mother most days, her mother who had been trying to convince her to sell up and move somewhere that was not so isolated.

"Bath is divine," she kept saying. "You'd have a lovely time in Bath. So beautiful and there's so much to do! Buy yourself a little flat and reinvent yourself."

But Maggie couldn't imagine doing any such thing.

So it was, almost three years after Ben's death, Maggie found herself going through something of a depression. It came on slowly, characterized initially by a listlessness that was unfamiliar to her. Maggie had always been a ball of energy, but suddenly she was staying in bed all day. She didn't think of herself as depressed, didn't cry, wasn't consumed by dark thoughts in the way she had always thought depressives were. But nevertheless, she stopped caring about all the things that were once important to her.

She had loved gardening, but wasn't interested anymore. The hedgerows were overgrown, and the topiary yews had completely lost their shape, with weeds covering half the gravel driveway.

E-mails would show up in her in-box, which she would read but somehow never get around to answering. Bills would go unpaid, and the washing machine stayed broken for weeks, her clothes unwashed. It was easier to hide in bed and watch television, wait for the world to pass her by.

Her mother was convinced it was the

house, that she needed a change. "If you insist on living in that enormous house, darling, get lodgers. Something so you aren't so lonely. Or get a job. You need something to do all day."

Maggie could barely contemplate getting out of bed, let alone going for a job interview. And even if she wanted to work, was there anyone who would employ an almost-fifty-year-old woman who hadn't worked in over twenty years? What could she do? She could cook, and she was still eminently presentable. She made an excellent first impression. Maybe she could be a receptionist somewhere? Each time she thought of this, she shuddered and burrowed deeper under the duvet. In theory, she knew it would be good for her — being out in the world, around people, having office workers she could lunch with. If only she could drag herself out of bed.

Her bright spot had been Jasper the cat, who used to curl up with her in bed, but Jasper had reverted to his barn cat roots and spent most of the time outside. She got up to feed the chickens, but that was it. Days went by when she saw no one, talked to no one other than her mother, and was seized by what she was refusing to think of as depression, instead calling it "inertia," which she worried would never go away.

Maggie heard the doorbell from the safety of her bed and hoped whoever was ringing it would leave if she just ignored it. But by the third ring, she was forced to get up, thankful she was in her version of pajamas — sweatpants and a T-shirt — and went downstairs.

It wasn't as if she didn't have to get up anyway. Tonight was her university's thirty-year reunion in a hotel in London. She didn't go to the tenth or the twentieth, but neither did anyone else she cared about. Tonight both Evvie and Topher would be there, and Topher had insisted she come. It was the one thing she had looked forward to in months. Maybe years.

But she wasn't anticipating anyone coming over, and suspected it might be one of her neighbors. She only knew Emily and James, was friendly with them when they first moved in, but a disagreement over tree height — they had refused to cut down their cypress trees, which now blocked the views from Maggie's house — had led to them ignoring each other.

It was probably one of the other new neighbors, complaining. She didn't remember their names. All of them looked alike to her, bright young thirtysomethings, newly-weds, with babies and toddlers, gorgeous wives with long glossy hair, fur-trimmed parkas and Hunter wellies, all of them suddenly descending on their tiny village outside of Bath. Why were they *here*? It wasn't commutable to London, but because a couple of celebrities had bought nearby, suddenly Frome, and their little village just outside, was the topic of articles in magazines like *Vogue* and *Tatler*, bringing scores of aspirational bright young things with their four-wheel-drive baby buggies, full-time nannies, and Range Rovers.

A group of them lived in the houses that led up to Maggie's own manor house. Once it had been land belonging to the house, before it was sold off to the local farmer years ago. He built one house there, bought years ago by Emily and James, and had promised not to develop any further. When he died, however, his son immediately sold it to developers, who swiftly came up with proposals to build five large houses, in traditional style, which horrified both Maggie and Ben (during a period of sobriety when he still cared about these things). Ben was fighting it, fighting for the open space, when he died, and Maggie had neither the energy nor the will to keep on fighting once he was gone.

It was astonishing how quickly the houses went up. One day there were fields, and the next, it seemed, large stone houses with immaculate gravel driveways on which sat Range Rovers and shiny Teslas, clipped privet hedges, and little children on electric scooters in the road.

Maggie didn't mind the children. She loved having children in the vicinity, loved hearing the peals of giggles, even the occasional cry as one fell over, and thought she had become accustomed to the houses. It was the adults that she struggled with.

They were all perfectly *nice,* these young women whose husbands had worked in finance in London, who seemed to have retired at an ungodly age — what, thirty-five? Younger? — to start their own businesses and move out to their dream homes in the country. All of the husbands described themselves as *entrepreneurs,* and all seemed pleasant enough, clean-cut, fresh scrubbed, handsome. Until, that is, there was that first knock on the door requesting if maybe she would consider trimming the hedges so the landscaping would fit the rest of the street.

Maggie hadn't even known that they owned the actual road that led to their manor house before Ben died. Nor the hedges that abutted it. She certainly never imagined she would be dealing with these annoying neighbors. But the road itself was indeed hers, which included the hedgerow.

The hedgerow had always been wild. It was a country lane, and the shrubs and trees on the sides had been left. Perhaps twice in all the years they had lived here Ben sent a gardener to clip them back ever so slightly. But they loved the wildness; it was what made it a country lane.

Unfortunately, the wild hedgerow didn't match the neatly trimmed privet flanking the new houses on the other side, nor, in one case, the rather complicated topiary yew that filled the front garden.

The new houses might have been pretty if they didn't look quite so *new*. Everything about them was perfect, and the neighbors were not happy with the wild hedgerow they had to face when they pulled out of their driveways or looked out their windows. They had all gathered together, it seemed, shortly after they moved in. Of course they were friends, the yummy mummies, their children attending the same nursery schools, the women getting together for a glass of wine in the afternoon while their children were fed and bathed by nannies.

Maggie would hear them on occasion if

she went out on walks. Shrieks of female laughter, the clinking of glasses. Before the others moved in, she and Ben were invited to Emily and James's, but because they were older, and because they never had children, once the younger families moved in, they were forgotten about. Now, even if she received an invitation, she wouldn't go. It wasn't that she wanted to be un-neighborly, but she had no interest whatsoever in these young mothers who seemed to her as if they thought they owned the world. Perhaps they did. God knows, Maggie had no idea what it was like to have the sort of money that afforded full-time nannies, fabulous cars, and what looked to her like designer clothes. What did Maggie care; she hadn't been shopping for years, until she lost so much weight after Ben died, she had to eventually buy some trousers that didn't threaten to fall to her knees as she walked. Even before that, fashion had never been her thing. Evvie used to attempt to style her at university, because Maggie was always most comfortable in long skirts and ballet flats.

She had clearly never been a yummy mummy herself. If she passed them, they would exchange friendly-enough smiles, a brief wave, but invariably sometime after that a husband would be dispatched to inquire politely about the hedgerow. Or the gravel on the road. Would they mind re-graveling it so it didn't have bare patches all over it? Would she please do something about the terrible mess that was the road, and which they just didn't understand wasn't terrible at all, but was, in fact, what living in the country was all about.

Maggie did mind. It was the country, she tried to explain, and the road had been like this for decades, probably longer. In fact, they were lucky that anyone at all had ever thought to put gravel down, as it was really supposed to be a dirt road.

They understood, they lied, but the new houses were so pristine, it just seemed so out of place. They would pay for it them-selves, they offered, all the new neighbors, and she wouldn't have to worry about it.

"But I would have to look at it," Maggie had said. "I don't want the hedgerow clipped into tight submission. This is the country and it is supposed to grow wild. I love that it's wild. I cannot give anyone permission to touch it."

On principle, Maggie now refused to touch the hedgerow, even though it was looking wilder than it ever had before. She got a slightly twisted sort of pleasure know-ing that its present state would so annoy the neighbors. She thought she probably ought to feel bad about that, but she couldn't. There was something about the smugness of these new people that was irritating, and if this was the only victory she could have, it was better than nothing. At least it gave her something to care about.

Opening the door, Maggie stood impassive in the doorway, nodding a hello at the neighbor. He was handsome, she thought. She would give him that, although they were all handsome, these young husbands. They had the confidence you had when you were in your thirties, before life became a grind, throwing obstacle after obstacle in your path, taking away the things you loved and making you realize that the only way to ease the hardship was to move through it.

"Yes?" She arched an eyebrow, preparing for the onslaught.

"Hello!" He gave her his most charming smile and moved in to kiss her on each cheek as she tried to place him. Oh God, she thought, it was James. How long had it been since she last saw him?

"I haven't seen you in ages. We've been worried about you. Emily keeps saying she wants to have you over. Also, you ought to meet the new people in Wisteria Hall. We're thinking about doing drinks."

Maggie nodded, registering that it was nice of them to make this overture, even if they were still refusing to cut down the bloody cypress. As to new neighbors, she'd been in such a haze, she didn't even know new people had moved into the latest house to be built.

Wisteria Hall, she thought, wondering which one of the houses it was, realizing it must be the one — of course, for the developers had little imagination — with the wisteria growing over the pergola that was attached to the barn. The developers gave each of the houses grand-sounding, if somewhat ridiculously cliché names, all the better to attract the wealthy buyers. It worked, clearly. Wisteria Hall, Willow Farm (this one had a small man-made pond and a couple of hastily planted willow trees), Chestnut Hill Manor (the hill was particularly clever, she thought, given that the land was almost entirely flat, and fill had to be brought in to create the hill), Acorn Hall, and Meadowview Farm (which, true to its name, did actually have a view of the meadows, no cypress trees in its way).

"I'll get Emily to text you. I'm so sorry to bother you like this," said James. "I hope I haven't caught you at a bad time." Maggie shrugged, realizing she looked as if she had just rolled out of bed. Unsurprisingly. "Some of the neighbors have been complaining about noises early in the morning. We have all been woken up the last couple of weeks at around five in the morning by what sounds like a rooster crowing. We've all got together to discuss it" — of course you have! she thought — "and we think it might be coming from here." He waited for Maggie to acknowledge his words, but she merely looked at him.

"Is it coming from here?" he prompted, the smile now seeming more forced.

"I'm sorry," Maggie said. "I don't understand what you're asking. You think I have a rooster?"

"Well. Technically, I'm *asking* you if you have a rooster. I'm hoping the answer is no because although, granted, we live in the countryside, I think you'll agree that the houses are now far too close together to make roosters a viable pet."

Maggie burst out laughing. "I'm not sure that anyone would consider a rooster a pet. They are livestock, and I think you'll find that you are no longer in Notting Hill, or Barnes, or Shoreditch, or wherever you moved from before you lived here, but in the country, where every other building has cows, horses, goats, sheep, dogs, chickens,

351

and yes, roosters."

James Sullivan shifted uncomfortably. "Well, that may have been true until now, but the road association has met, and, hang on, I'll read it to you." He drew an iPhone out of his pocket and started to read from the screen, clearing his throat with some discomfort, it seemed. ". . . we are all in agreement that animals, or livestock, that impede the peace and serenity of those who live here, may not be allowed."

Maggie frowned. "What road association?"

"The one the developers set up."

Maggie let out a deep sigh and smiled at him. Poor man. He was so young. He really thought some fake road association was all he needed. "James." She shook her head. "James, James, James. I have lived here for over twenty years, and for almost all of that time, I have had animals of some kind. In fact, the space that is now occupied by Wisteria Hall, and indeed all the other somewhat ridiculously named houses, was, until just before you and your lovely wife moved in, occupied by horses. I don't really care what your road association bylaws say. I am not part of the association, and in addition to owning livestock, unless I am very much mistaken, I own the road and can keep it in any way that I see fit. I have to be really honest here, James. Had you knocked on the door and simply asked if I might consider getting rid of the rooster, I might have said yes. But that you chose to come over and throw some makeshift rule in my face has only served to piss me off." Maggie stood up straighter, feeling emboldened. Perhaps the only good thing to come out of widowhood was that she no longer cared what people thought of her; life was too short. "I'm afraid the only thing I'm willing to do is to direct you to Boots, where I believe you'll find they have some excellent earplugs. I recommend the wax ones rather than the foam. They keep out the noise much better. Bye-bye now," she said, not giving the man on her doorstep a chance to say anything else. "Say hello to Emily for me, and do let me know if you ever want fresh eggs. The rooster has friends."

Shaking her head, Maggie walked through the house, her bare feet making soft thumps on the limestone floor. She felt a certain pleasant satisfaction until she paused by the large mirror in the corridor, reluctantly turning her head, a reflex she hadn't been able to master, even though she knew she wasn't going to like what she saw. She had never cared particularly about her looks, but while married she had done the basics, dyed her hair to keep the gray roots at bay, brushed it, smoothed Oil of Olay moisturizer over her face, neck and décolletage, just as her mother and grandmother before her had done.

Since Ben died, she didn't see much point in making an effort. Not that she made an effort for Ben, not for a long time, but she still felt she had to keep up appearances as, quite literally, lady of the manor. Not anymore. Her hair was no longer the vibrant red of her university years but was now a dull, faded umber streaked with fine lines of steel gray. Her eyes were punctuated by shadows, and deep folds around her mouth pulled her face down, folds that had not been there three years ago. These days, when she looked in the mirror, she saw her grandmother staring back, and not her grandmother in the prime of her life when she was a great beauty, but her grandmother toward the end, when she lived alone, riddled with dementia, in her grand old house in Somerset.

Maggie looked as old as she felt. She paused and examined her hair, scrutinizing the frizzy split ends, the gray roots. Would she have time to dye it before the reunion tonight? She hadn't even considered it, but she knew it would be the first thing Evvie noticed. She looked at her watch. She could. No time for a hairdresser, but if she ran to the supermarket, she would definitely be able to manage a home dye job before driving in to the reunion.

Their thirty-year reunion. She hadn't seen any of them in years, although Topher had been at the funeral. Not that she remembered much about it. Evvie wrote, but unsurprisingly couldn't make it. Not that she expected her to. Once upon a time they had both been her closest friends in the world, her family, but that was many lifetimes ago. She and Evvie had lost touch completely. She had missed her for years, but didn't expect anything from her now. It was another thing that felt like several lifetimes ago.

And yet today, she had to admit she felt excited to see them again. She wasn't even sure until precisely this moment, looking at her hair and deciding, on a whim, to dye it, that she was going to be able to get herself to go, although she hadn't told Topher that, had lied and said she would definitely come, even as she was thinking up palatable excuses to use on the day. She wasn't sure if her desire to see her old friends could overcome her inertia, but she found that it had. She found the idea of revisiting them, and perhaps a bit of the person she used to be before she met Ben, the first thing in a long time that she actually felt a desire for.

She passed the kitchen table and grabbed a handful of raspberries from the fridge, pouring them into a small bowl. On the kitchen table were stacks of bills that she hadn't been able to face, and she picked them up, resolving to pay them after she picked up the hair dye.

Clucking as she walked out the back door, she called, "Hello, girls," and laughed as the chickens appeared, running along the path, half jumping, their wings flapping in excitement as they saw her, the prospect of treats one they looked forward to every day.

Fluffy pushed her way to the front, except it had become apparent in the last few weeks, not just to Maggie but it would appear to the neighbors as well, that Fluffy, a small white Bantam Silkie, was a rooster. Maggie thought she had bought only female chicks, but Fluffy, with his extravagant tail feathers and recent crowing, clearly slipped through the cracks.

Poor neighbors, she thought. She herself had been woken up at five in the morning, but she couldn't possibly get rid of Fluffy. What was one supposed to do with a rooster, she wondered, particularly this one, to whom she was already attached?

She scattered the raspberries, using the opportunity to attempt to pat Fluffy, who expertly hopped out of her reach, even while managing to grab a raspberry at the same time. She laughed, then went back into the house to grab her car keys, this time with a smile on her face.

Thirty

"Honey? Did you want almonds on the oatmeal as well?"

Topher was in the kitchen of the luxury flat they had rented in Kensington. There was no response from the living room, so Topher tipped a few out from the packet he had picked up at Marks & Spencer at Heathrow, sprinkled them on the oatmeal (which was called porridge in England, which was so delightfully Dickensian, he laughed out loud as he put the box in his basket), added just a sprinkle of brown sugar, and no butter. Benedict had to watch his cholesterol.

He brought the bowl into the living room, with his own hard-boiled eggs and grapefruit, passing Benedict, who had his legs up on the chaise longue. His reading glasses were on the tip of his nose as he perused last weekend's *New York Times.*

"Come on, Dickie," said Topher. "Breakfast is ready."

Benedict looked up. "Oh! I didn't hear you. I was lost in this fascinating article about the Trumps."

Topher groaned. "No. I can't. I need a break from politics."

"This isn't politics," said Benedict, getting up slowly and making his way to the dining table in the sunny bay window. "This is family dynamics."

"I just don't want to think about it while I'm over here. If you want to talk about the queen, that's fine with me, but no politics."

"Why would you want to talk about an old queen when you already have this old queen sitting by your side?"

"You're *my* old queen," said Topher affectionately, reaching out and rubbing Benedict's arm, "which makes you very dull. I already know everything about you."

Benedict smiled at him. "You are good to me, darling boy. What would I do without you?"

"You'd probably find some other lovely young man to accompany you to the theater and look after you."

"I might. I definitely wouldn't have the good health I have today if it weren't for you. I do love you."

"I know," said Topher, picking up the Arts

section and sliding it out to read while he ate his own breakfast. "I love you too. Go ahead and eat your breakfast while it's still hot."

Benedict stirred his oatmeal, and did exactly as he was told.

"So, are you excited about seeing your old friends tonight?" he asked.

"I'm dreading the reunion, but I can't wait to see the girls. I haven't seen Maggie since the funeral, which was . . ." He paused to think. "God! Three years ago. That's terrible. What kind of a friend am I that I haven't seen her for so long when she's dealing with such loss. Do you know her mother contacted me through Instagram?"

"I thought you weren't doing Instagram anymore."

"I'm not. I just go on from time to time to check. But Maggie's mother messaged me and apparently Maggie's been in a deep depression. She said I had to convince her to come to the reunion, so that's why I did. And I've got a job to do tonight."

"The job being?"

"Her mother wants her to sell the house and move to an apartment in Bath, but I told her I couldn't push that on her if she didn't want it. I do think she needs to get out more though. And maybe take some antidepressants."

"Do you think she'll talk to you about that, given how long it's been?"

"I don't know. I'm hoping that we'll all fall back into the friendship we've always had, but maybe that's too much to ask. Oh God, Dickie! I've imagined having this wonderful catch-up, but what if we've all changed too much and we have nothing in common anymore?"

"Then you've all changed too much and you have nothing in common anymore. That's okay. That's life."

"I know, I know. You're right. Meanwhile, to be superficial, I'm going to putter around Westbourne Grove this afternoon, see if I can find a blazer. I don't like the one I brought at all," said Topher as Benedict finished his breakfast. "You'll be all right here by yourself?"

"Stop treating me like I'm elderly," said Benedict.

"You are elderly." Topher grinned.

"Age is a state of mind."

"That's my point exactly. You've been referring to yourself as an old man for the past thirty years."

"You haven't known me for thirty years."

"Close enough."

Benedict reached out and patted Topher

on the arm with an affectionate smile. "We make a good pair, don't we?"

"We do," said Topher, leaning over and kissing him on the cheek.

"I have plans myself, as it happens," said Benedict. "I'm meeting an old friend for a walk around the gardens at Kensington Palace, and then, while you are at your reunion, I shall be joining him and his wife for dinner at their house."

"You're quite sure you don't want to come to the reunion?"

"And have everyone think I'm your grandfather? No thank you. But you have a wonderful time, and let things unfold the way they're supposed to. You can't force a new friendship on an old one if you've grown apart. Did you talk to Simon about it?"

Simon. The wonderful therapist Topher had been seeing for years. The wonderful therapist that gently led Topher back through his childhood, that encouraged Topher to drag up memories he had pushed far, far down in order to never have to think of them again. Simon, who had incorporated EMDR therapy to deal with what he termed Topher's post-traumatic stress disorder, who made sense of why Topher hadn't thought of himself as a sexual being, why he had "switched off" his sexuality, why he found it safe to be with men like Larry, who was happier going to bed with a cup of tea, and Dickie, who asked nothing of Topher other than companionship.

They had spent years working through it, with Simon gradually encouraging Topher to open up the side of himself he had shut down. Topher had read about Grindr on Queerty and *Joe.My.God.,* but hadn't been interested, until Simon helped him feel safe enough to explore.

And explore he did, much to Dickie's quiet delight. Dickie had always had his own discreet partners, had always encouraged Topher to have the same, and it made no sense to him that Topher didn't, until Topher wrote the memoir, and during the course of the writing, told Dickie about his greatest shame, asking him whether or not he ought to include it.

Simon was a godsend, for not only had Topher been able to fully embrace his sexuality, he had become wiser, and calmer. He seemed far more comfortable in his skin without the constant need he had carried around when younger, the desire to be seen and loved.

More recently, they had spoken about Topher's mother, who again lived in the UK, and who Topher was planning to visit while here. His relationship with his mother had always been good, if superficial. He had never spoken to her about his childhood abuse, and she had never brought it up, not even after she phoned to congratulate him on the book, telling him how beautifully written it was and how proud she was.

It was not unusual for Dickie to ask what Simon thought, for Simon had become the third party to their relationship, even though Topher had been transitioning out of therapy, getting ready to finish and handle life on his own.

Topher arched an eyebrow at Dickie. "Of course I talked to Simon about it. I talk to Simon about everything. And you know exactly what Simon said."

"Was it 'don't worry about it and take it as it comes'?"

"And that's why you love him. Because he always parrots you. Or maybe it's the other way around."

"And what does Simon say about seeing your mother and the struggles you've had with that recently?"

Topher paused. He had always adored his mother; she was the one person in his life who could do no wrong, until therapy unlocked the memories he had been suppressing for years, and with them a growing resentment toward his mother that he didn't know how to handle. Talking to Simon as often as he did didn't seem to help. Simon had suggested a gentle confrontation. Topher had wept in Simon's office saying how could she have not known, how could she have not noticed how quiet he was when he returned from his lessons, how introverted he had become.

"He has suggested gentle honesty. Keeping it in the 'I' sentences, as in, 'I felt hurt and abandoned when you didn't notice what was going on.' "

"You're ready for this?" Dickie looked concerned.

"As ready as I'll ever be." Topher kept his voice light, even though he was dreading this conversation. But until it happened, he knew he'd never be able to fully heal.

THIRTY-ONE

- 2019 -

Evvie's friend Sophie was out when she arrived at Sophie's London flat, ready for the reunion that evening. Evvie found the key hiding under the potted plant and let herself in, lugging her suitcase up to the top floor. Her packing habits had never been good, and she was paying for it again. She always tended to overpack, preferring to have everything she might need, just in case.

When she was married to Lance, they had drivers and staff who would carry their bags. She never had to carry a case up four flights of stairs. If she ever forgot anything, or found they were invited to something for which she had nothing to wear, she would pop in to a local designer store and think nothing of spending thousands on the perfect outfit. It had to be said, as a former model, Evvie couldn't help but have fun shopping. Everything looked spectacular on her, before she gained weight.

Now that Evvie was no longer comfortable in her skin, money was tight, and shopping wasn't nearly as enjoyable, Evvie brought everything she might possibly need, including much she probably wouldn't. Three pairs of (very stretchy) jeans, two pairs of high-heeled boots (one black, one tan), sandals, silk T-shirts, wraps, sweaters in case it got cold in the evening, makeup, toiletries, and hair products. So many hair products! In the old days, the modeling days, she straightened it, but more recently she couldn't afford those keratin treatments and Brazilian blowouts, and her natural curl had come through. Who knew curls would require even more products than having straightened hair?

She carried all that up those steep stairs in what looked like an unassuming house off the main drag in Shepherd's Bush, up the rather dismally lit hallway, along the stained carpet, putting her key in the lock and turning it to find herself in a beautiful flat that belied its somewhat insalubrious entry.

The floors were a sanded oak, very pale, in a herringbone, and the apartment had minimal furnishings. It was very white, very open thanks to almost every wall being knocked down, with high ceilings that had been vaulted into the roof, and limewashed beams above her head.

There were white, furry flokati rugs strewn about, and the odd midcentury-modern pieces Evvie recognized — the Eames chair, the Saarinen tulip table. The only spot of color was from the books that lined one wall, stretching from floor to ceiling, with a ladder on a rail that moved from side to side.

On the floor was a piece of paper with an arrow: *Your room is that way.*

Evvie hadn't seen Sophie in years. They'd lived together in New York, when they were both in their early twenties, modeling, partying, borrowing each other's clothes, and coming home to stay up all night chatting.

Now Sophie had married, divorced, and had a daughter, Helena, who was the same age as Jack. When the kids were very young, Sophie came to Connecticut to stay with Evvie, but they hadn't seen each other since. But, as with most true friends, Evvie knew that despite the distance, the friendship would be the same as it ever was. She also knew that Sophie was at work. After all these years, she had gone back to the career she had when she finished modeling — a booker in an agency. She specialized in older women, "women like you, Evvie, if you ever found yourself in the UK more frequently and decided to go back into business." Evvie had laughed, not wanting to tell her about the extra forty pounds she now carried, the weight she was convinced would leave as soon as her divorce was finalized, and quite possibly it would have left her, had menopause and hormones not conspired to devastating effect.

Evvie unpacked, put her clothes away, sat on the bed, and texted Topher, but there was no response. She hovered over Maggie's name, instantly guilty, ashamed of the secret she had kept, further ashamed at not being here for Ben's funeral. She wanted to come, she *planned* to come, but her own devastation was too overwhelming. She wanted the closure but suspected her grief would reveal everything she had worked so hard to keep secret, and so she stayed away.

She sent her condolences in a handwritten card that might have been from anyone. She wasn't surprised when she heard nothing back. They had been friends a long time ago, so long ago that Evvie wasn't sure they would have anything in common anymore, other than Jack, who Maggie must never know about. Every time she thought about it, she felt a wave of nausea, but it mingled with excitement at seeing Maggie again, and more, at the three of them being together again. There was no reason for Maggie to suspect anything, she kept telling herself, pushing the thought out of her mind.

She phoned Jack, but he couldn't talk; he was in a meeting about a new app his company was developing. So Evvie pulled on her boots and a jacket, wincing at how tight the jacket was, the sleeves now covering her arms like sausage casings, before taking the spare key, going downstairs, and slipping it back under the flowerpot.

It was only as she left the flat that she realized how unsettled she felt. She loved flying into Heathrow, felt instantly at home, but Shepherd's Bush wasn't her neighborhood, the buildings weren't familiar to her, and suddenly she felt that she had been wrong about England being a new home; maybe she wasn't at home anywhere. Maybe, when you leave the country in which you were born and raised and try to make a home somewhere else, you can never go back. And if that new place wasn't home . . . maybe the rest of her life would be spent drifting, trying to find a place that was her own; maybe she would never find a place to call home again. She shook her head to dislodge the thought, and walked up the street to find a decent cup of coffee.

Thirty-Two

- 2019 -

Maggie felt a burst of what might be excitement, what might be nerves, as she drove up to the hotel in Kensington. Parking the car in the underground lot, she made her way up to the banquet hall.

There were people everywhere, milling around the lobby, striding purposefully toward the lifts, and she searched their faces in the hopes of seeing someone familiar, but none of them looked like people she once knew.

She hadn't been out in months, and she was astonished at the noise, the people, the energy, and more, astonished that rather than scaring her, it was exhilarating. This was the first time since Ben died that she had felt alive.

Signs were dotted around pointing the way to various events held in various conference rooms and ballrooms — clearly their reunion was not the only thing happening here tonight. She hesitated, suddenly wanting to turn around and run back to the door, drive home, and crawl into the safety of her bed, wondering why she was braving a reunion that suddenly seemed overwhelming to her.

"Maggie?"

She heard her name from across the lobby, and squinting through the hordes of people, she saw a figure so achingly familiar, a prick of tears came to her eyes. Tall, as vibrant as ever, heavier than she remembered, but the smile was still the same. She would know that smile anywhere. As she watched Evvie walk toward her, the weight, the wrinkles, the years dropped away, and it was Evvie, looking just as she always looked, standing right there.

With a smile on her face, Maggie threw her arms around Evvie, squeezing hard, both of them pulling back to look at each other, both laughing, before hugging each other again.

"Oh, Maggie," Evvie said, and she was crying this time. "I'm so sorry. I'm so, so sorry."

Maggie knew she was sorry about Ben dying, about not showing up for his funeral, about losing touch; she was sorry for all of it but none of it mattered. What mattered was the overwhelming feeling of love she had for her old friend, and when they finally disengaged, they stood for a while, grinning at each other, each drinking the other in.

"You look amazing!" Evvie laughed. "Look at you! You haven't aged a year. How do you do that? How do you look so fantastic?"

"Are you kidding?" burbled Maggie. "You're the one who hasn't aged. Your skin! You look twenty-five! I look terrible. Honestly, if you'd seen me this morning, I was an aging hag. I couldn't inflict my gray hair on you lot so I dashed to the chemist and did a home dye job."

"First of all, my skin is only great because I'm enormous."

"Evvie!" Maggie's face fell. "You're not enormous. You're beautiful. Are you really still hung up on your weight? We're fifty. You need to get over it."

"Honey, it's okay. I'm learning to deal with it, finally. As my mama always said, once you hit forty, you have to choose face or figure, and I guess I chose face. Secondly, no way that's a home dye job! Really? It's amazing. I can't imagine you, or any of us, with gray hair. The only one of us I *can* see with gray hair is Topher, who would probably look even more handsome and distinguished."

"Topher! I've missed him so much. Do you see him often in New York? You must, you live so close to each other."

"I should but I don't, which is awful. Somehow life just gets in the way."

"Oh, Evvie. I can't believe we lost touch." Maggie linked her arm through Evvie's. "I can't believe I lost touch with everyone. Seeing you makes me feel young again. I want to hear everything. What are you up to, how is your life . . . ? I know you went through a horrible divorce, but you must be doing okay now, you look so happy. Let's go up and find the reunion. You can tell me all about it as we walk."

"There's something I have to say to you first." Evvie stopped and looked at Maggie. "I'm so sorry about Ben. I should have come to the funeral. I wanted to come but . . . There is no excuse. I am so sorry and more, sorry that I wasn't there for you." She blinked away unexpected tears.

"Thank you," said Maggie. "It means so much to me that you have said that. It was . . . complicated." She stood still, wanting to tell Evvie about Ben. She hadn't told anyone other than her mother, but she wanted to tell Evvie. And Topher. She didn't want to keep his secrets anymore.

"Complicated?"

"It's a long story and one I'm going to tell you, but not tonight. Let's have this night and then I'll give you the full story next time. Which means there'll have to be a next time. Deal?"

Evvie wanted to know now, but she knew Maggie well enough to know she wouldn't be pushed.

"Tell me all your news," said Maggie, changing the subject. "Tell me about Jack!"

"No! I want to hear your news first. Topher said you lived in Downton Abbey. Girl, how did you manage that?"

"It's not Downton Abbey." Maggie rolled her eyes with a smile. "It is lovely, though, a very pretty manor house that is entirely too big for me. It was entirely too big for the two of us. If we had known that we wouldn't have children, we would never have bought it, but I'm glad we did. We both fell completely in love with it as soon as we saw it. I think Ben could never believe that he could actually afford a house like that. It meant a lot to him . . ." She trailed off, a sudden image of Ben passed out in the hallway downstairs flashing in her mind.

"Anyway." Her voice was immediately, falsely, bright. "Tell me about your son. Do you have pictures?"

Evvie paled. "I'm a terrible mother," she

lied. "Everyone always asks to see pictures and I've got nothing. I do have his baby picture as my screensaver, but that's it."

"Let me at least see that." Maggie held out her hand for the phone as Evvie handed it over, knowing that with his face half-turned into his blanket, he was unrecognizable. "Oh, he was adorable. What a cutie. How old is he now?"

"Twenty-one, and entirely self-sufficient. He's living in Oakland, just outside of San Francisco, working for a tech start-up. I can't actually believe I have a grown son who fends for himself."

"Does he look like you? I bet he's gorgeous."

Evvie smiled. "He is gorgeous, and he looks a little like me." She didn't say any more, couldn't say any more.

"Am I . . . allowed to ask about the father?" Maggie remembered Topher once saying that the father wasn't involved, that he thought the father may not even have known that he had a son, and that Evvie never discussed it.

"You can ask," said Evvie, "but that doesn't mean there's anything to tell. It was a long time ago, and at the time I thought it was a terrible mistake and would ruin my life, except for the fact that of course Jack has been the best thing to ever happen to me."

"I hope I get to meet Jack one day," said Maggie.

"If you're ever in San Francisco, I'll make sure it happens!" Evvie lied.

"How do you cope, with him being so far away? Haven't you ever thought about moving there?"

"I have. I think about it all the time, but the truth is, San Francisco isn't my place. I spent some time in LA when I was young and I hated it. I can't see myself on the West Coast, even though I miss Jack hugely. I keep hoping he'll come back to the New York area, but I don't think it's likely. I have to let him go. I have to fight every day not to drive him mad with texting, or phoning, or going to see him. He was always my happy place, especially when I was married to Lance, and in some ways that wasn't a great thing for him. It gave him too much responsibility. It's better that he's far away. He needs to find his feet, build a life without feeling like he has to look after his mother."

"It's still so weird thinking of you as a mother," said Maggie. "I still see you as a nineteen-year-old with furry slippers sipping giant mugs of hot chocolate and taking all those weird slimming pills."

"You knew about those?"

"Of course I knew. We were worried as hell but figured you were old enough to look after yourself. Oh my lord, is that Topher?" Her face lit up as she called out his name, spying him at the front of the signing-in line.

"Get over here!" He gestured for them to come to the front, his American accent even more distinct than it was all those years ago when he let his Anglophile tendencies get the better of him, adopting a slight mid-Atlantic drawl.

"We can't queue jump," Maggie said, noting that everyone in front of them was turning to look at them.

"Of course you can. Get your asses over here now."

"I can't believe you just did that," Maggie mouthed to Topher, following Evvie mutely to the front and pretending not to see people stare as Topher squeezed her arms and then flung his own around her.

"I am capable of much, much worse," he murmured in her ear, and she instantly forgave him. He hugged Evvie as they all signed their names in the book, then walked into the big room, heading straight for the bar, but pausing as Topher held them back.

"God, this is all a bit sad," said Topher, frowning at the lack of decoration, lack of . . . anything. There were a few groups of people standing around the edges of the room, picking at the buffet tables, with a small line developing at the bar. "Where are the balloons? Where are the streamers?"

"Where do you think you are? The United States?" Evvie started to laugh. "The fact that there's a reunion at all is a bit of a miracle. You didn't expect them to spend proper money on it, did you?"

"I did! God knows they've all seen enough American movies to know how it's done. Balloons, streamers, and a live band."

"And punch!" Maggie laughed again. "Where's the punch? They always have punch in those American films."

"I'm not seeing punch." Topher eyed the bar. "I *am* seeing boxes of wine though. Urgh. This is all depressing."

"Hi!" A woman in a patterned lilac ball gown came over to them. "Oh my God! Look at you all! You all look amazing!"

They all looked blankly at her, Evvie wondering if perhaps she might persuade the woman to hire her for a wardrobe makeover, because that ball gown looked like something out of 1986.

"It's me! Victoria Charles! We were room-mates for about ten seconds!" She looked at Evvie, whose mouth opened.

"Oh my God!" Topher's face lit up. "Victoria! Look at you!" He gave her a hug. "Guys." He turned to the others. "You remember Victoria! You loved cats, right?"

"I did! I actually run a cat rescue now."

"I can't believe you're here," said Evvie. "You look exactly the same."

"Victoria!" Maggie hugged her as Victoria beamed. "Look at you! That dress is spectacular!" she lied smoothly.

Victoria giggled. "I couldn't believe it still fit. I wore it to the graduation ball! Can you believe it? Good old Laura Ashley!"

"I can't believe it," said Evvie, who, other than recalling her Catpuccino mug, had only one other vague recollection of a large, jolly girl who had drunk too much at the graduation ball, collapsing in a toilet stall, her lilac-patterned Laura Ashley skirts billowing out around her. "You kept it all these years!"

"I never throw anything away," Victoria said proudly. "You never know what comes in handy. I still have my cat posters from university in the downstairs loo! Not to mention my clothes. Who would ever have thought I could fit into this dress after all these years?"

"You'll be wearing it everywhere now,"

said Topher. "It's very in, the eighties retro thing."

Victoria's face lit up. "That's what I thought. It's very Downton Abbey."

"Indeed," said Topher. "Victoria, if you'll excuse us, we have to go and find drinks."

"Make sure you come back and we get some proper chatting time! It was so great to see you." Topher already had an arm around the waists of both Evvie and Maggie as he steered them away.

"I hate to say this," Maggie whispered as they walked off, "but who in the hell was that?"

"You don't want to remember," said Topher, looking at Evvie. "Catpuccino anyone?"

"Oh my God! That roommate! Now I remember!" Maggie began laughing, realizing with a start that she was feeling something she hadn't felt in years. Happy.

"Fuck, I think I hate reunions," said Topher, looking around the room. "I mean, this is the only one I've ever been to. But this all feels desperately sad. I have a terrible memory, and nobody here looks the slightest bit familiar. And I don't want to be accosted by any more people like that Catpuccino girl. Also, this swirly carpet is depressing me."

"Oh, stop," said Evvie. "So it's not the Four Seasons. Get over it. We don't have to stay all night, but at least this got the three of us together. Let's go find drinks."

"But that's my point. Everyone else is irrelevant. We should go and find somewhere lovely to have drinks where we don't have to make small talk with people we don't remember."

"We can't leave immediately. But I would be willing to leave in an hour," Maggie demurred, ever the proper girl her mother raised.

"How about half an hour?"

"Forty-five minutes?" Maggie grinned. "I had forgotten how difficult you are."

"I'm not difficult, I'm wonderful. I just don't see the point in making small talk with people I haven't seen in thirty years. There's a reason I haven't seen them in thirty years."

"You've barely seen us in thirty years," said Maggie.

"That's different," Topher said. "And you know it."

"Let's just make a little bit of small talk, and we'll leave as soon as we can."

THIRTY-THREE

- 2019 -

Fifteen minutes later they were sitting in a tiny, candlelit bistro off Kensington High Street. Wooden pews as seats and the dark lighting made it cozy, although, as Topher put it, "cozy in a very nineteen eighties kind of way." They all declared it perfect, then, for their reunion night.

"I couldn't handle it," said Maggie, after ordering a gin and tonic. "Other than you lot, I didn't even remember anyone."

"I feel the same. Isn't that awful? Although did you see Julian Maple?" Evvie asked.

Maggie frowned. "Julian Maple who you had that terrible one-night stand with?"

"Yes! Julian Maple who was ridiculously good-looking even though he was a bit of an ass."

"I didn't see him," said Maggie. "How did I miss him?"

"You wouldn't have recognized him. I did a double take when I saw his name tag."

"What does he look like?"

"Nothing like he used to. Kind of doughy and dull."

"Everyone looked like that to me," said Topher. "Is that awful? It just . . . God, it wasn't exactly a glamorous reunion."

"It wasn't exactly a glamorous university," Evvie reminded them with a laugh. "Other than the English and drama departments, it was all a bit sad."

"The science department was good," Maggie said quickly, and they all nodded, embarrassed, remembering Ben, before Maggie sighed. "But do we look like the rest of those people? Because the thing that horrified me most was that half of them looked my mother's age. We don't look like that, do we?"

"I hope *I* don't look like that," said Topher. "Or my dermatologist is getting fired."

"Dermatologist? What do *you* need a dermatologist for?" asked Maggie.

"It's a New York thing," explained Evvie. "Most of the women our age are doing fillers, Botox, other stuff to make them look young."

"No wonder you look so good," said Maggie.

"I did all that when I was married. My husband insisted." She made a face, a frown with some real bitterness behind it. "I haven't touched it since. This" — she craned her chin out and stroked her skin — "is all courtesy of my Jamaican mother, and weight gain. My grandmother died at ninety-six and I swear, she looked sixty-five. She also always said that extra weight made your skin better as you got older."

The waitress came over and took their order.

"Fondue!" Maggie shook her head as she left. "I haven't had fondue since a school skiing trip. This feels rather decadent."

"It's lovely." Evvie relaxed. "I can't believe how lovely it is being all together again. I can't believe how it's as if nothing has changed. Honestly, I was nervous about seeing you all. I thought, what if we have nothing in common anymore? But I feel as relaxed and comfortable with you both as I always did."

"I feel the same," said Topher. "I live with Benedict, and I love him, but it's not my home. If I'm really honest, other than Larry, who really was my home, the only other people and place I felt most myself was with you guys."

"We know each other so well, that's why," said Evvie. "And we lived together so well. If we hadn't got on when we lived together, then it wouldn't be the same, but we had so much fun. And yeah, it does feel like no time has passed."

"Wouldn't it be lovely if we could live together again?" Maggie said dreamily, downing her drink quickly when the waiter interrupted to ask if they wanted another round. They all did. "Didn't we once make a pact that said something like that? When we were all fifty we would live together again if we were on our own. You could all move in with me!"

"That sounds perfect," Evvie laughed. "As long as your house is big enough for us to retreat. When Topher gets on my nerves I have to be able to disappear until he stops annoying me."

"You mean when you get on my nerves," Topher said archly. "Co-living. I like it. But I'm not on my own. I have Dickie. Can I bring him with? You're going to love him."

"If you love him, we'll love him, so yes. He can come. I love the sound of this." Maggie clapped her hands. "I know it's only a fantasy, but wouldn't it be amazing? We could do our own thing, work, do whatever we do during the day, but all come together for a big evening meal."

"That really would be like being back at college. I'll be in charge of the music. I'll make sure Prefab Sprout and the House-martins are playing in the background." Evvie couldn't believe she even remembered the music they used to listen to.

"The Housemartins!" they all said at once, laughing at the memory.

"Can I be in charge of the gardens?" asked Topher. "I'm slightly obsessed with gardening of late, even if it is only in theory, but I do think I'd be an excellent gentleman farmer. Would I get to wear a tweed waistcoat?"

"Honey, you can wear whatever you want," Evvie said.

"Oooh, oooh, ooh! Let's make this happen!" Maggie shouted suddenly, realizing that she was a little bit drunk, but she was also happy. Truly happy, being with these friends, reverting to who she was before she met Ben, who she was before denial, guilt, and shame locked her away and made her feel like she was living a shadow of a life. "You would bring my house back to life, and my mum will finally get off my back about finding a bloody flat in bloody Bath!"

There was a brief silence.

"Seriously, guys," Maggie said, leaning forward. "Could we actually do this?"

"It would solve my loneliness," said Evvie, without thinking.

"You're lonely?" Maggie sat up in astonishment, and then, unexpectedly, felt a lump in her throat, and before she could do anything to stop it, tears were falling.

"I'm sorry." She wiped the tears away with her sleeve. "It's just . . . this is so nice. I've been so miserable for such a long time, and being with you two makes me feel happy again. I can't think of anything I want more than the two of you moving in with me right now. If you're serious, it would be life changing for me."

"Oh, darling." Topher put an arm around her. "You've been that bad since Ben died? I'm so sorry I haven't been in touch. I had no idea. You guys were so perfect together, I can't even imagine what —"

"We weren't perfect," Maggie said. "We were as far from perfect as anyone you've ever met. On the day he died, I texted him to tell him I was leaving him and wanted a divorce." She started crying again now. "Our marriage was a disaster. We looked like the perfect couple, with the perfect house and the perfect marriage, but it was based on deceit and lies." She was sobbing, and Topher comforted her by rubbing her back, and Evvie sat back, stunned, trying to take in what Maggie had just said.

■ ■ ■ ■

Their marriage was a disaster? What did that mean? Now was not the time to ask, but it was all Evvie could think about as she sat next to her, watching Topher calm her down.

Eventually, Maggie's sobs subsided into hiccups. "Oh God." She smiled. "Too much gin. It always makes me emotional. I'm so sorry."

"Don't be sorry," said Topher. "I think our plan to live together is an excellent one. I'm serious!" He looked at Evvie. "Come on, Evvie. We did make that pact, and you're dying a slow death on your own in Westport. I've spent my entire adult life dreaming of moving back to England, and now my mother's in Weston-super-Mare, so this would be perfect. I know this started off as a fantasy, but why the hell not? Isn't life too short? Let's at least explore it. Frankly, I could do with a new adventure. And maybe your house really could be perfect, Maggie. Why don't we all come up and see? If nothing else, I'm desperate to see your house."

"Really?" Maggie's eyes lit up. "Are we really exploring this?" She looked at Evvie, who broke from her reverie to shrug and nod.

"Let's do it!" she said, clapping her hands, a fire now in her eyes. "Come up! When? Tonight? Tomorrow? Wouldn't it be amazing if this actually worked?"

Thirty-Four

- 2019 -

Maggie shut the car door and headed toward Topher, who was already standing in the station car park, to give him a hug before turning to Evvie, who was sitting on a bench with an elegant older man, his hands resting on a silver-topped cane.

"That's Benedict?" She gestured to Benedict as she looked at Topher.

"Yes, that's him. He's been dying to meet you."

"He's so elegant!" She approached the bench and extended a hand to Benedict, telling him how lovely it was to meet him. Benedict ignored her outstretched hand and stood up, giving her a big hug.

"I can't possibly not hug you." His voice was filled with warmth and graciousness. "I feel like I know all of you, and I am so happy to meet you finally, after all this time."

Maggie stepped back, blushing slightly. Of

course he was gay, and old enough to be her father, but the combination of his good looks and charm was instantly disarming. He kept them amused all the way to Maggie's house, with stories of what he'd been up to in London.

They turned down Maggie's lane, through the gates, as a silence descended. Maggie parked and turned to them. "Well, here we are. Home."

Evvie got out of the car, her mouth hanging open. "Are you fucking kidding me? This is your house? You live here?"

She slowly swiveled, taking in the golden manor house, the overgrown topiary yews, turning around to see the old wooden gates now creaking their way closed. "This is like something out of a movie. I feel like I'm in *Brideshead Revisited.* It's gorgeous."

"This is breathtaking," Dickie agreed. "The classic English country manor house."

"It's beautiful but a little high-maintenance, and the decorating's very old-fashioned now," said Maggie, looking at her house with fresh eyes as she beckoned them into the hallway, where they all stood, swiveling around to take in the oak paneling, the chintz curtains, the sweeping staircase. She had spent the last twenty years in love with this house, while simultaneously apologizing for it. Pretending that it was a burden, that they couldn't really afford it, that she was slightly embarrassed. But seeing it now, taking in its beauty, she stopped talking. She had said enough.

"First of all, *anything* this size is going to be high-maintenance," said Evvie. "Between all of us, spreading the work, it becomes . . . practical. If we all lived here, it would probably be entirely manageable. As for redecorating, that's easy. I'd love to help. We can get rid of all the chintz and get some lovely Swedish grays and neutrals in here. And we'll fill it with new memories."

Topher turned, taking in the large inglenook fireplace in the hall, big enough to roast a large animal. "I already love everything about this house. I want to live here starting right this second. I'm not joking. This is heavenly, and I'm ready to move in tomorrow."

"You know what I think?" Maggie laughed. "I think it's time to put the kettle on. It's chilly in here anyway. Let's build a fire in the den, and we can talk about it some more. Nothing needs to be decided today."

"Of course it's chilly in here," said Topher. "It's an English manor house. There would be something wrong if it wasn't chilly."

Maggie turned to go to the kitchen, followed by Evvie, as she told Topher and Benedict to feel free to explore — Topher looked like he'd explode if he didn't get to see it all immediately.

Walking into the kitchen, Maggie felt an energy and levity in the house that hadn't been there for years. She had had the same sensation as she did arriving back at the house just a few moments ago, seeing it with fresh eyes. It wasn't her tired old kitchen filled with the ghosts of children she never had and a husband she had lost, but a large, sun-filled room with a limestone floor, cream kitchen cabinets, and a kitchen table large enough for ten people. It was a room crying out to be lived in, and loved. It was a room begging for people sitting around the table, for laughter, for bottles of wine being opened, for huge casseroles being cooked and served at the table.

She had not served this house well, she thought. She had blamed the house for all that had gone wrong in her life, and for the first time today, she knew that this house did not deserve it.

The kitchen was a beautiful room, as it was a beautiful house, a house she and Ben bought because it felt like a house that needed to be filled, with children, with people, with animals. And it was only today, for the first time, with her dearest, oldest friends right behind her, that she realized this was what was meant for the house, this was what the house had been waiting for: her family of choice.

Already, it felt like a completely different house; already, it felt like a new home.

By the time they brought tea into the living room, complete with Maggie's buttermilk scones (they were hiding in the freezer, but defrosted beautifully), Topher had built a fire, Benedict looked completely settled in the battered old leather wing chair next to the fireplace, and Evvie had started to feel excited. She wasn't worried about keeping Jack a secret, for Jack, with his life in Oakland, was so far away from this, it felt probable that even if she lived here, never the twain shall meet.

"Are those Liquorice Allsorts?" Evvie slid a glass jar over, filled with the multicolored candy. "Maggie! I haven't had these since college! I can't believe you still eat them."

"Help yourself," said Maggie. "I'll even let you have the round ones in a bid to tempt you here as soon as possible. What's your plan?"

"I'm going to get out of my condo as quickly as I can," said Evvie, picking out all the round candies with a grin. "I never want to leave this place."

"I was just saying the same thing to Dickie," said Topher. "I think we should sell the apartment in New York, and maybe buy another small pied-à-terre just to keep a toehold in the city. I said I wasn't zipping over to see my mother later," said Topher, kicking off his shoes. "We might never leave either."

"Where did you say your mother's living?" asked Maggie.

"Weston-super-Mare. She was somewhere else in Somerset after my father died and she moved back here, and then had a sketchy boyfriend for a while who lived by the sea. She gave everything up to move in with him. He left her in the lurch a couple of years ago, and she's still in the house."

"Oh my God, that's terrible. Is she okay?"

"She is more than okay. She's the femme fatale of Weston-super-Mare, which is all a bit disconcerting. My father dying seemed to give her a completely new lease on life. Right now she has three boyfriends, apparently, and she's a pensioner."

"Your mother was so fabulous," sighed Evvie. "The most glamorous woman I had ever seen." Also the woman who got her hooked on diet pills, thought Evvie. An addiction that took years to break.

"She was lovely," said Maggie. "I always liked your mother. I like having the older generation around. It keeps us grounded. I've barely seen my parents since they moved to Cornwall. I love the idea of having someone's parents around, even if they're not mine. I'll adopt anyone's family if I like them."

"My mother will be delighted to hear that," said Topher, wincing at the discomfort of what was coming between himself and his mom. "It probably would be a good thing to be close to her, not to mention, live in this fabulous house with my oldest friends." He turned to Maggie then, noting her eyes were glistening. "Are you crying?"

"Only very slightly," she said. "I just . . . I love you guys. I can't believe we're back together again. I can't believe we lost one another for so long, and I really can't believe that we're considering this incredible adventure. I just feel . . . you really are the only people who know the real me, and you really are my family, the family I've chosen. I just wish we'd all done this years ago."

Topher and Evvie reached out to hug Maggie.

"I'm so glad we're all here," Maggie said when they disengaged. "We probably couldn't have done this years ago. We definitely couldn't have done this when Ben was around. Or your ex-husband." She looked at Evvie. "Perhaps we all needed to go through the stuff we went through to bring us here today. Right, Evvie?"

Evvie couldn't meet her eye. "Right," she said, looking past her to the house, knowing that disaster was likely to strike, but she couldn't stop it now. It was too late. She wanted this, these people she loved, all back together, more than she wanted to keep hiding, more than she wanted to keep secrets.

It's too late to change the past, she thought. Maybe it was time she chose happiness rather than secrets. She took a deep breath.

"What do you think?" she asked. "How soon can we make this happen? I'm going back to the States on Monday, but how soon can we all move in?"

THIRTY-FIVE

- 2019 -

Weston-super-Mare was relatively quiet, the tourists having left for the summer, but the Royal Hotel was busy, filled with well-dressed people having tea.

Dickie stood up with a mild stretch and took his cane. "I'm going to leave the two of you alone while I go on a sea walk," he said.

"Don't go on your own," said Topher's mother, who had been at her most charming and gregarious, flirting with Dickie for the past hour as they had tea. "We'll come with you."

Dickie shot Topher a quick look before bestowing his most charming smile on Joan. "I'm going to leave you and Topher to have some mother-son time. I know he's been wanting you all to himself."

"We don't mind, do we, darling?" Joan turned to Topher.

"There *is* something I want to talk to you

about," Topher said, much more nervous than he should be. This was no longer the loving but grand, perfect mother of his youth. She was still beautiful, still impossibly elegant, but when they picked her up he was shocked at how fragile she was.

It was the first time he had seen her as an old woman. She would be horrified to hear that, but her lipstick had twice smudged onto her cheek during tea, and he had to gently wipe it away for her, plunging into a role reversal he wasn't expecting. He drove up here feeling nervous about confronting her, with a tinge of leftover anger, but found it had dissipated over tea to something more akin to sadness.

They bid Dickie goodbye as Joan called the waiter over. "Can you bring us our scones please?"

"You want more scones?" Topher was stunned. "You already had two scones."

His mother looked confused. "I did?"

"With cream and jam," he added as Joan waved the waiter away. "Are you okay, Mother?"

"My memory isn't what it was," she said, attempting to laugh it off.

He was slightly disturbed by her words, but too focused on what he had to say to really think about them. "Mother, did you actually read my book?"

"Of course, darling. It's wonderful."

"Do you remember the chapter in which I talk about the tennis coach?"

"Tennis coach?" She frowned. "I'm not sure I remember that bit."

"Did you read it or did you skim it to find the bits about yourself?"

His mother chuckled. "I did start it, darling, and I really enjoyed it, but my book club insisted I read another book, so I had to put it aside and I haven't had a chance to pick it up again. I will soon though."

Well, that explained why he hadn't heard from her, thought Topher, regretting his recent anger, his presumption that she hadn't cared, or didn't believe him, thought he was being overdramatic.

"Do you remember I used to have tennis lessons with Coach Patrick?" Given her admission that her memory was terrible, he had no idea if she would remember, but she lit up.

"Of course! Twice a week. You were very good, darling. You should never have given it up."

"Do you remember that I became very quiet and I didn't want to go?"

"Oh, I do! You made such a fuss. You kept saying that you hated it, but I knew you'd thank me later. Tennis is such a wonderfully social sport. Everyone should learn to play, and aren't you happy now that you had those lessons?"

"Mother, the reason I wanted to stop the lessons was because Coach Patrick was abusing me."

There. He said it. The words were out. He watched his mother's face as she took in what he said, but she didn't understand.

"What do you mean, Topher?"

"I mean he was sexually abusing me. That's why I didn't want to see him anymore. I have been seeing a wonderful therapist because it's clear that I have had PTSD for years, and I couldn't get better until I dealt with it. And part of dealing with it is talking to you about it. I've never been able to tell you. I tried when I was young, but I always felt that you steamrolled me into continuing the lessons. I felt completely powerless, and I felt abandoned when you didn't listen to me."

His mother said nothing, just looked at him blinking.

"So I've harbored a lot of suppressed emotions. I've been pretty angry because I felt that you enabled it. I tried to have a voice and I wasn't allowed to have a voice and I'd love to know what . . ." He stopped as a tear trickled down his mother's cheek.

"I had no idea," she whispered, stricken. "Oh my God, Topher. I had no idea. I feel sick."

Her shock was genuine, and Topher reached out a hand, the vestiges of his resentment disappearing. "It's okay, Mama," he said, realizing that it was. "Look at me. I'm fifty and I'm fine. I'm better than fine. I have a wonderful life despite pushing all of that stuff down. I've spent the last little while dealing with it in therapy, and I needed to talk to you about it."

"Oh my God, Topher. Your father never liked him. He said he didn't trust him, and I ignored both of you. I'm so sorry. I will never forgive myself."

His mother was in tears now, which was the last thing he expected. Several people were looking at them, the handsome middle-aged man and the elderly woman now in tears. "Please don't say that. It's fine. I just needed to . . ." Needed to what? he wondered. Punish her? Make her aware of her culpability? Guilt her? He didn't know, but he did know that this was, just as his therapist suggested, closure. Her tears, her distress were all the proof he needed that she truly didn't know, that she was doing the best she could, and he put his arms around her and gave her a hug.

"Can I get you a brandy or something?" he said when they disengaged, but she shook her head and pulled out a bottle of pills from her bag.

"These are better for me. Xanax. This will calm me down."

He remembered all the pills over the years, the uppers, the downers, the sleeping pills, the antianxiety medication, and he shook his head with a smile. "You haven't changed. Still pill popping."

"Still pill popping." She handed him the bottle to help with the lid, washing down a pill with lukewarm tea. "Darling boy." She took his hand, staring at him with pure love in her eyes. "What is it we were just talking about?"

THIRTY-SIX

- 2019 -

Back in New York, tired suddenly of the hustle and bustle, dreaming of a golden manor house in the country, Topher sat with his back against the wall in Sant Ambroeus, busy checking out all the young, beautiful people crowded in there for coffee, pastries, brunch.

"I do love it here," he said to Benedict, who leaned forward to try to hear him above the din of excited conversation. "Even though I can't wait to be lord of the manor, it makes me feel young again, being around all these gorgeous things." He gestured to the table next to them, five teenagers, each more beautiful than the next, the girls with long, shiny swinging hair, perfect pouts, in the kind of distressed sneakers and fur-collared bomber jackets that screamed wealth. Their Celine and Hermès bags were flung on the floor, their privilege, and comfort in that privilege, oozing from every pore. They sat, each of them on their phones as they stared at their individual screens and tapped quickly with their thumbs, occasionally reaching out an arm to pick at french fries in the middle of the table.

"This is one of the places I'll miss most when we leave New York. I can't believe we're leaving! Oh, Dickie, I'm so excited. I can't believe things are happening so fast. We've already sold the apartment and it didn't even go on MLS! And I loved that little apartment we just saw downtown. It's busy, buzzy, and the perfect pied-à-terre for when we visit."

Benedict looked down and stirred his cappuccino. "What about the one on Sixty-Eighth that we saw first? I thought that was rather lovely."

"It was beautiful, but too big, honey. We only need something tiny. We're not going to be here much, now that we're moving to England, and we definitely don't need a dining room!"

Benedict said nothing, kept stirring his coffee. "The dining room would make a wonderful library, though, and I like having space. I think the other one is just too small."

"We can keep looking," said Topher. "Just because we got an offer on our apartment so quickly doesn't mean we have to rush and buy another immediately. I love the one we just saw, but we both have to love it. We can wait until spring if you want — I'm sure much more will come on the market then."

Benedict looked at his watch, an elegant Patek Philippe bought for him by his own father many years ago. "We ought not be too long," he said. "Cookie is taking me to the theater this afternoon."

"Cookie again?" Topher was surprised. "You've been seeing so much of her lately! Don't get me wrong, I adore Cookie, but I might start to get jealous."

Benedict smiled at Topher over the rim of his coffee cup. He and Cookie had been friends for forty years. She was married to a hedge fund manager who, one morning three years ago, didn't wake up. She found herself with no children and more money than she knew what to do with. She bought a smaller apartment in New York, kept the apartment in Aspen, the house on Nantucket, and started producing theater. Her last show had been a huge hit, the kind of hit that comes along once or twice every decade. Now she often relied on Benedict as her walker, her chaperone to the various galas, shows, and dinners at which she found herself on a nightly basis.

She had other walkers, but she and Benedict were longtime friends, and recently Benedict seemed to be seeing her more than usual, and not just as a chaperone. They were having lunch together fairly regularly, and sometimes afternoon tea.

Topher adored Cookie. She was a character from a bygone era, tall and as thin as a rail. She only ever ate three mouthfuls before pushing the rest around her plate. Ironic, given her name. She was the most naturally elegant woman he had ever known, and that was saying something, given his own mother. Cookie had closets filled with couture clothes from the sixties and seventies, which she still wore, and that still looked fabulous. Her basic uniform had remained the same for forty years: straight pants and a thin cashmere sweater, in every muted color imaginable, with the same Manolo Blahnik d'orsay shoes (again, in a variety of colors). But her jackets, scarves, shawls, and cardigans were exquisite, and her jewelry had been written about in *Vogue* many, many times.

And yet, despite her wealth, her beauty, her sophistication, Cookie was the most self-deprecating woman Topher had ever known, with a dirty sense of humor that always had Benedict wiping tears of laughter from his eyes. She had a huge heart and was known for her loyalty, doing anything for her friends.

"I'm just a midwestern girl," she always said. "And I believe in giving back."

Benedict put his coffee cup down and took a breath. "You love Cookie, don't you?"

"Of course," said Topher. "I was only kidding when I said I was jealous. I'm thrilled you're seeing so much of her."

"I'm glad. She's a special woman, and she . . . cares about me very much." Benedict paused as Topher felt a sliver of anxiety.

"What are you not telling me?" Topher said quietly. "There's something going on. What is it? Are you sick? Is Cookie sick? What is it?"

Benedict looked back at him. "No one is sick. I am fine and Cookie is fine. But there is something we need to talk about. We need to talk about England."

"You don't think we should go?" Topher's heart sank.

"It's not quite that. I think *you* should go. I don't think I should go."

Topher frowned. "But we're a partnership. I live with you. If you don't want to go, we won't go." Even as he said the words, he felt a pang of sadness. Being with those old friends after so many years, deciding to live

410

together, had made Topher feel young again; it had given him something to look forward to. He wanted to be back in England, with the people who had known him so long, they felt like family. He wanted to be close to his mother. But he wouldn't leave Benedict, not when he had made him a promise.

Benedict reached out and took Topher's hand. "Darling boy. You have been so very, very good to me. Far better than I had a right to expect. I watched you very carefully with your friends on the other side of the pond, and you light up when you are with them in a way I haven't seen you light up with anyone here. There is an ease and a naturalness about you when you are together. It felt like I was seeing the true Topher. Not to mention the not-insignificant fact that your mother is there. It is quite clear to me that you belong there. Perhaps it hasn't always been the case, but at this stage of your life, you need them just as much as they need you."

Topher swallowed the lump in his throat. Benedict was so good to him, but he couldn't let him down, couldn't leave him when Benedict relied on him so much.

"Dickie, I adore you, and you know me well enough to know that I don't break my promises. I have promised to look after you, and I won't abandon you. We will find another apartment in New York, and I will not go to England. My friends will be fine without me, and my mother will carry on visiting New York just as she has always done."

Topher was saying all the words he knew he had to say. He was loyal, and he loved Benedict. He would do the right thing by him, even though there was a sense of real loss at the prospect of not living in that glorious house with his old friends. Topher had always been a committed Anglophile, and the very idea of living in Somerset made his heart sing with joy, not least because it would have been with people he truly adored.

All those movies he watched when he was young, the Evelyn Waugh books he read, Nancy Mitford, Cecil Beaton, the days he spent salivating over Chatsworth and Debo, the Duchess of Devonshire. Ah well. In another lifetime he would perhaps be lord of the manor. Not this one. He wouldn't leave Benedict. He couldn't leave Benedict, even though his mother seemed to need him, even though he had promised her he would be seeing her all the time. The only good thing about her failing memory, he thought ironically, was that hopefully she would forget that he was ever planning to move.

He would have to stop dreaming of the manor house, the garden that could be so beautiful again with some love and care. He had spent a good few hours browsing gardening books in Barnes & Noble, lingering over pictures of topiary yew, clipped box hedges with clouds of cranesbill and alchemilla tumbling behind. This city boy's brain started bursting with ideas as soon as he saw the faded grandeur of Maggie's overgrown garden.

He had pictured all of them going for long walks through the fields. Maybe they would get a dog. The manor house would feel more like a home with a big shaggy dog running around. They would stride through those gorgeous English fields, climbing stiles, Topher in a tweed flat cap, carrying a silver-topped cane. Perhaps the cane was pushing it a little too far.

Sitting here, looking at Benedict, the realization that he would not be fulfilling a lifelong dream of living in England, not as a student in a grotty student house, but in splendor as a fully formed adult, was almost enough to make him want to cry. But he would not let Dickie see how he felt.

"I love you," said Benedict. "You have

been my family, but I don't want you to stay here. Over there is where you are supposed to be. The manor house is exquisite, as are your friends. I love the idea of it, but I'm too old to change my life in this way. New York is my home, and it's where I need to stay. Where I *want* to stay. But not you, darling boy, and who knows, maybe you will find a new love when you are there. You've come so far in therapy and I don't want to hold you back any longer. I know you have dalliances now and again, but you deserve something more. It is selfish of me to expect you to devote your life to me. You are too young. You deserve to have a life filled with happiness. You deserve this, and you deserve to find love."

He put a hand up to silence Topher, who was about to speak. "Not lovers. I know you have those. But as long as you are looking after me, you will not be able to have an intimate relationship. Maybe you don't want one, but you deserve to be able to have one. I won't take no for an answer. I have Cookie, and she and I have discussed this many times. The penthouse apartment in her building is, privately, available. We are going to purchase it together. We will each be able to have our own living space, and there is plenty of room. It is time for us to move on,

414

and it is time for me to let you go."

Topher stared at him, a storm of emotions inside him. Loss, sadness, gratitude, and relief. As much as he didn't want to leave Benedict, he recognized the resolute look in Dickie's eye and knew that Dickie had made up his mind. That Dickie wouldn't be on his own, that he and Cookie had decided to buy something together, didn't feel like a betrayal; it felt like Topher had been set free, and his whole body seemed to exhale with relief.

"I don't know what to say." Topher's eyes were filled with tears.

"Don't say anything. Just get the check and let's go home. We've all got some packing to do."

As they walked out, Topher felt people staring at him, the odd whispering. It wasn't unusual for him to be recognized, and he had learned to stare into the middle distance with a friendly smile on his face, always gracious should someone tap him on the arm and ask for an autograph.

He turned as he felt a hand on his back, to see Alan, an actor he had worked with years ago on a commercial.

"Alan!" He gave him a hug, about to introduce him to Dickie before realizing Dickie had already walked to the front of the restaurant. "I haven't seen you in such a long time! What are you up to these days?"

"The usual." Alan smiled, but seemed awkward. "Auditions and summer stock in the Berkshires. I just . . . I just wanted to say I'm sorry about what's happening. I hope you're okay."

Topher stared at him. "What do you mean?"

"The book drama. You don't deserve this and it stinks. I hate that fucking website. I hope you know it will all blow over quickly and everyone will have forgotten about this bullshit soon."

Topher's heart started beating so fast, he could hardly catch his breath. "Alan, what are you talking about?"

Alan faltered. "Oh my God. You haven't . . ."

Topher frowned. "I haven't seen . . . I don't know . . ."

"Oh my God, I'm so sorry. I wouldn't have said anything."

"Can you just tell me?"

"Absolutely." He was embarrassed, as if bearing the bad news somehow made it his fault. He stepped back to his table and grabbed his phone as the man he was sitting with caught Topher's eye. His look, too, was one of pity. He knew as well, Topher realized. They were probably talking about it before Alan approached him. He turned to look around the restaurant, seeing people still staring, wondering what the hell he had been embroiled in now.

He wasn't unused to bad publicity, but God knew what they'd printed this time. A former lover giving an explicit tell-all to one of the gossip blogs? He tried to think of what it could be, but his mind was blank.

Alan busied himself with his phone, eventually handing it to Topher with an apologetic expression. On the screen he saw the gossip blog that everyone in the business read. He read it, all his friends read it, everyone he knew read it (even if they wouldn't admit it).

The headline made him feel faint. *Soap Star Revealed as Fraud! Author of Behind the Scenes accused of plagiarizing book!*

He didn't read more. He felt dizzy and slightly sick.

"Here," Alan said, gesturing to their table. "Do you want to sit down? I am so sorry. You didn't know about this?"

"I . . . my phone has been switched off. I haven't been online. I didn't know."

"Can I do something for you? Call anyone?"

"I'm fine," he lied, forcing a smile. "Please

don't feel bad for telling me. I'm glad I know." He rolled his eyes. "They'll drag up any old garbage on you."

"I know," Alan commiserated. "Sometimes I thank God I've never been successful." They said goodbye as Topher headed toward Dickie, ignoring the feeling that every single person in the restaurant was staring at him and thinking he was a fraud and a liar.

"Are you okay?" Dickie shot him a look as he approached.

"No. I'll tell you outside."

Topher showed him the story on the way home. It was worse than he thought when Alan showed him the headline. They had printed paragraphs from Topher's book, and paragraphs from the self-published memoir Topher had picked up in Maine, lining up and highlighting the sentences that were the same. The beautiful sentences Topher had copied into his own manuscript to try to inspire him at a time when he had no idea what to write. Sentences, he realized now, he had forgotten to remove.

He was supposed to read through the final edits and approve them, but he was so fed up with the book by that time, he didn't have it in him to read it again. He gave the book to his assistant to approve, figuring she would pick up on any typos or grammatical errors. Which she did. What she did not pick up on were the numerous sections that had been directly copied from someone else's work.

"What do we do?" Benedict asked, not worried, for he had been around long enough to know that these things always blew over. "How do we address this?"

"Maybe with the truth?" Topher said, turning the corner onto their block. Outside their apartment building was a swarm of journalists. Topher slowed to a halt, his mouth dropping open. There were photographers, journalists, even a news crew. This can't be for me, he thought, until he heard his name, and suddenly they were all running toward him.

"Topher! *Daily News* here. Can you just tell us a few words about how you're feeling? We'd love to have an exclusive." Topher kept his head down, looking at the pavement, raising a hand for the first yellow cab, ushering them both in as his heart pounded.

"This is not good," Dickie said, finally looking worried.

"What the hell am I supposed to do?" said Topher. "Where am I supposed to go? And how on earth am I supposed to explain that this was all a terrible mistake?"

Thirty-Seven

- 2019 -

They spent the afternoon holed up in the apartment, speaking to various crisis management PR firms. Topher didn't deny the plagiarism, he honestly had meant to change it, but even that was problematic. While the PR experts conceded that the memoir wasn't necessarily one hundred percent real, adding in full paragraphs that did not belong to you did not bode well.

Perhaps they could spin that it wasn't supposed to be a memoir. That it started as a novel, and it was not unusual for writers to add notes from things that inspired them, that those passages — and they were numerous — were overlooked.

The local cable news channel featured the story, showing the growing press outside their apartment, kept at bay — thank God — by their ferocious doorman, and both Topher and Dickie turned their cell phones off, turning them back on only to make calls rather than to take them.

Topher spent much of the day feeling sick. For years he had been famous, feted, loved. He had been interviewed by everyone, even the *Today* show, and had seen his memoir climb up the bestseller lists. Today, every time he heard his name mentioned by a news anchor, it was synonymous with fraud. A part of him wanted to crawl under the covers and never come out; he wanted to run away from all of it and disappear, but he didn't dare leave his apartment.

The doorman buzzed up early evening. Dickie had left an hour before. He was being honored at a gala dinner and couldn't back out, even though Topher, obviously, couldn't join him. Not tonight, so naturally, Cookie stepped up in his place, leaving Topher all alone.

"I have Evvie downstairs," said the doorman, who was clearly impressed at this former supermodel showing up in his building. "She says you're expecting her?"

Topher wasn't expecting her, but hearing that she was there filled his eyes with tears. "Send her up," he said, opening the front door for when she arrived.

"They are all fuckers," announced Evvie, walking through the door and going straight to Topher, putting her arms around him and

421

holding him tight. And Topher, who for years didn't much like to be touched, sank into her, allowing her to hold him for what felt like several minutes.

"I can't believe you came up here," he said, blinking back tears as he disengaged. "Also, I can't believe the doorman let you in. Everyone's been trying to get in all day."

"He was a fan. I turned on the Evvie charm and he was toast. So, what are we going to do about this? We need to get you out of here. The press won't go away until a bigger story breaks, and God only knows when that will be. As your fairy godmother, I've decided that you should come and stay with me in Westport, and we should move our flights to England to as soon as possible. I've already spoken to Maggie and she's on board. No one will bother you in Westport, and look!" She reached into her giant purse. "I've got baseball hats, dark glasses, spray-in hair color, and a fake beard for us. Well, the beard's for you, clearly. And the hair color."

"Are you serious about me staying with you?"

"Absolutely. You can't stay here with all the crazy press. You'll be trapped in this apartment like a prisoner. And even though it's lovely" — she looked around with approval — "I know you. You'll go stir-crazy."

"How can we get out without them following us?"

"My friendly fan the doorman already said we could use the service elevator to the basement, then go out the back entrance. I can pull my car around and they won't even know you're gone. I'm telling you, in another life I should have been a PI."

"Evvie, you're amazing. But don't I have to face the music at some time? My career's effectively over and I have no idea what to do."

"Honey, you were always leaving your career. That's the point of moving to England. We're all having a redo. It's time for our second acts to begin."

"I have no idea what I'm going to do for my second act. Acting's clearly off the table now."

"You've been wanting to give that up for ages. You'll figure it out. Your soap never aired there. Nobody cares. This story will be done soon and it won't matter in Somerset, where you'll be lord of the manor."

"Gaylord of the manor."

"Even better. Come on." She slipped her arm through his. "I'll pour us a glass of wine while you pack."

"Aren't you going to ask me about the

book?" Topher said, when Evvie handed him a glass.

Evvie shrugged. "No. I don't really care. If you want to tell me about it, you'll tell me, but here's what I do know: that you are one of the most honorable and decent people I have ever known, and I have known you for over thirty years, so I think I'm qualified to say that. If you did what they are saying you did, I'm sure there was a reason. And whatever the reason is, I'm sure it makes sense. We all make mistakes, this one just happens to be in the public eye, but it doesn't make me love you any less. A mistake doesn't change who you are. I know you, and I love you. Don't cry or you'll set me off!" she commanded as Topher blinked hard.

"I know you don't care, but I need to explain. I did copy paragraphs from the book, but not to intentionally steal. They were so beautiful, I wanted to write like that. I planned to use them as notes, to remind me of the kind of writing I was striving for. I never meant for them to be in the finished version. Thank you for not caring. You're amazing," he said. "You really are a true friend."

"I'm sorry we haven't seen each other all these years. But I'm going to make it up to you now." After he packed, she took his hand and they walked to the service elevator, which let them out on the side street, and to the car. By the time they hit 95 and Topher had called Dickie to tell him his plans, the car was toasty warm, the purr of the engine soporific, and Topher was so emotionally drained, he fell fast asleep. When he woke up, they were turning off the highway, and a minute later they pulled up outside Evvie's condo.

"It's not much," said Evvie, climbing out of the car. "But it's been a good place to lay my hat. At least until we get to our real home."

Home, thought Topher. The place he had always felt most at home. Somerset. It had all been a romantic fantasy, one that he was eager to play out, but now, given his newfound place in the public eye, he wanted it more than anything else in the world.

Thirty-Eight

Topher couldn't think of anything else but his humiliation. He slept last night, but not for long. Evvie's Ambien knocked him out, but he was wide awake four hours later. He had promised Evvie he wouldn't go online, but the temptation was too strong. He got out of the king-sized bed he had shared with Evvie and crept into the living room, phone in hand.

His hand was shaking as he opened up the gossip sites he had always loved, and there it was, his name the top story on all of them. He started to read, his heart pounding, feeling nauseated as "sources" were quoted saying how shocked they were, that he wasn't the person they thought they knew.

He felt himself flush as he mentally scrolled through who might have said that, jumping from website to website, all of them proclaiming him a fraud. The more he read, the worse he felt. It was too early to call his agent, but what would his agent say? There was nothing anyone could say to make it better, for it was true, he had plagiarized, and even though it was inadvertent, he couldn't deny what was being said.

After a while, he couldn't take it anymore. He turned his phone off and lay on the sofa, closing his eyes and doing his best to sleep.

When he woke up, he felt as if he hadn't slept at all, but his phone said differently. For a second, he wondered where he was, and then he remembered both where he was and why he was there. The room was piled high with boxes, Evvie having already packed most of her things, and because he was not going back to sleep, and because he needed anything to distract himself, he walked over to a box labeled Photographs, picking one up from the top of the box and turning it over, squinting as he looked.

It was Evvie, looking gorgeous, from the height of her modeling days. Her hair was a thick straight mane, her makeup lifted directly from the sixties as she balanced on a chair in a multicolored caftan-like beaded dress that undoubtedly cost thousands of dollars.

He smiled as he looked at how beautiful she was; still is. She had gained weight, but they were all in their fifty-first year; wasn't that what they were supposed to do? He didn't see the weight when he looked at Evvie; she looked the same to him. They all did, as if their eyes didn't age along with their bodies. To him they each looked just as they did at eighteen.

He put the photo back in the box and had just picked up another when Evvie walked in, bleary-eyed as she yawned and smiled before seeing Topher standing with the photograph. She rushed over.

"Don't look at those," she said loudly. She seemed to catch herself, then said more calmly, "We're not going to revisit the past today. Come on." She strode over to him, took the photograph out of his hand, and put it back in the box before leading him to the kitchenette with a smile.

"Coffee. We both need coffee. We probably need something stronger. How are you feeling this morning?"

"Terrible."

"You went online, didn't you?"

"How did you know?"

"Because I know you. Was it bad?"

"Yes. Terrible. I want to disappear."

"It's okay," she said. "I mean, it's not okay, and I totally understand how you feel, but even in this day and age, it will blow over. I can't say today's news is tomorrow's fish and chip wrappers, not anymore, but another story will break any second now, and this will be forgotten. Do you want a bloody Mary instead of a coffee? We can go across the street to Parker for breakfast if it's not a crazy idea?"

Ten minutes later they were settled at a window table, two bloody Marys in front of them.

"It's five o'clock somewhere. Cheers!" Topher chinked glasses with Evvie. "That's better. Thank you for stealing my phone. I hate you for it, but I'm also grateful. When in pain, bury your head in the sand."

"I agree."

"Can I go through those photographs when we get back? You must have a bunch of us from college."

Evvie blanched. "No," she said, a little too sharply. "I've organized them all and I don't want to pack and unpack."

"Okay. I didn't mean to make you uncomfortable."

"I'm fine."

"You seem a little on edge." He peered at her. "Are you hiding something in that box? Are there porno pics or something in there?"

Evvie seemed to relax as she let out a genuine bark of laughter. "Oh, Topher. No, there aren't porn photos in there. Life may have been hard at times, but it was never *that* hard."

"Okay, good. It just felt like there was something you didn't want me to see."

"Oh my God, no! Well, actually, there are some pretty heinous pictures of me in that box. All fully clothed, I might add, but some of them are dreadful."

"Honey, I've lived with you. I've seen you first thing in the morning, horribly hungover, and with chicken pox. Remember when you got chicken pox?"

"How could I forget? Look. I still have a scar." She leaned forward and showed him a tiny round scar above her eyebrow. "Makeup artists spent years covering it up. I love that I don't have to do that anymore. Especially now, with our fresh start in England."

"England." Topher closed his eyes for a second. "Never have I been more relieved to be leaving this country. Thank you, Evvie." Topher took her hand and squeezed it. "I have no idea what I would be doing if you hadn't rescued me."

"You'd be a prisoner in your apartment," she said. "And spending much too much time on your phone. With any luck, we might be able to get a flight out to England tomorrow. But what do we do about your things?"

"I can get Dickie to send them on. Frankly, the thought of setting foot in the city right now makes me sick with fear."

"Then let's go back after breakfast and start exploring flights."

"Am I going to be okay?" Topher took a deep breath.

"You're going to be better than okay. We're all going to be great. This is our second act, and it's time. And even if we end up not being great, at least we'll all be together."

Thirty-Nine

- 2019 -

It was the little things that irritated the most, Maggie realized. It had been so long since she lived with anyone besides Ben, she had forgotten how easy it was for the tiny annoyances to lodge themselves under your skin and itch.

The sink was empty when Maggie went to bed last night. She made sure she took note. Every morning she thought she was going mad when she found the sink filled with cereal bowls and empty mugs. How hard was it to put them in the dishwasher? Just open the door and pop them in. Why can't the culprit load the bloody dishwasher?

She had said something two mornings ago, and four mornings before that.

"Guys, can we just make sure everything goes in the dishwasher rather than the sink if you use anything?"

They were sitting around the kitchen table, Topher on his phone, Evvie eating toast while scouring the classifieds in the local paper for a job. They had looked up and nodded, which Maggie presumed meant they had heard. And here were the cereal bowls again.

Don't let it bother you, she told herself. These, after all, were the minor irritations that you would expect when a group of adults lived together. Of course they were going to do things that annoyed the others, get on each other's nerves from time to time.

The key was not to dwell on it, not build up resentment. The key was to be mindful of the fact that they were all doing their best.

Still. Was it really too much to ask of the secret late-night cereal eater to put their bloody bowls away? Also, Maggie turned to inspect the glass jar that sat on the counter that was normally filled with granola but now held merely crumbs. Would it be too much to ask the cereal eater to buy more or even just to add it to the shopping list? There were now three people living here, and Maggie would have quite liked some cereal today, which was strange only because Maggie's breakfast had always been two slices of toast with butter and jam, and a cup of tea. She had only ever filled the glass jars with cereal because it looked nice.

It had been a month since everyone moved in, and Maggie still couldn't quite believe how lovely it was — mostly — to have people here. It was as if the house had woken up after a long, deep sleep. She lay in bed at night listening to the sound of footsteps, a loo flushing, the murmur of people saying good night, and she smiled to herself. She wasn't alone anymore, had been waking up every morning filled with excitement at what the day would hold. There was always someone to talk to, to eat with, to sit with. If she didn't feel like being around people, she could take herself off to her little office (but that had only happened once, for she was loving the change).

The energy of the house was completely different. It felt lighter, brighter, buzzing with possibility, even when everyone was out. Maggie had had no idea how lonely she was, how dull and quiet and dead she had allowed her life to become, until her friends moved in. She had no idea how depressed she had been, and how much her life had come to a standstill until now.

During all those years married to Ben, she had hoped that he would take care of her, but now it was quite clear that Maggie was happiest when she was taking care of other people. Having people to cook for, to nurture, to love, was making her whole again in a way nothing else had.

Sometimes she wondered what would have happened to her had she not dragged herself out of bed and gone to the reunion. She shuddered to think.

In a throwback to their time at university, Evvie had once again taken over breakfast. She still made her famous ackee and salt-fish, her johnnycakes, but she added home-made blueberry pancakes, waffles, giant slabs of vanilla-infused French toast, and streaky bacon cooked until it was crispy. She bought bagels, smoked salmon, cream cheese. Evvie introduced them to strata — a sort of gourmet French toast casserole, but savory, with asparagus, mushrooms, and tons of cheese.

And Maggie, who was ever so slightly competitive in the field of cooking (and when *did* Evvie learn to cook so well, for Maggie was always the only cook in the house), had been making decadent cakes and buttermilk scones for tea, and home-made chocolate Florentines with lacy bottoms and thick chocolate tops.

"My God," Topher said the other day, polishing off three scones heaped with strawberry jam and clotted cream. "We're all going to weigh four hundred pounds if you keep feeding us like this."

"I can't help it," said Maggie. "I'm just so happy to have people to cook for again. You don't understand. I haven't cooked for anyone since Ben died."

"What did you eat when you were by yourself?" Evvie had asked.

Maggie shrugged. "Whatever was in the fridge. Sometimes I picked up soup. I ate a lot of toast. Cooking for one isn't much fun, and most of the time I forgot to eat."

"No wonder you're so thin," said Evvie. "I don't think I've ever forgotten to eat in my life. That's why I've got my lovely big belly." She stuck it out.

"We love your big belly," said Topher, who had been slapping Evvie's hand every time she moaned about her weight, telling her to embrace herself, reminding her endlessly that she was gorgeous, curvy, and sexy, and telling her she needed to let go of her former skinny self. "It's feminine."

"That's definitely true. I'd make a great fertility symbol." Evvie pouted and posed as Topher shook his head.

"No more putting yourself down, Evvie."

"Doing my best," she said.

"Meanwhile," said Maggie. "Why am I the only one getting a hard time about cooking delicious food? Those American breakfasts of Evvie's are insane. I'm sure that's why I'm putting on weight."

"Don't blame me," said Evvie. "That's only on weekends. You're making something delicious for tea every day. Can't we just have a cup of tea with no food?"

"I can't do that." Maggie feigned shock. "You can't have a cup of tea without biscuits, at the very least. It's against the law over here."

"You know what you two should do? You should open a café together."

Maggie and Evvie both turned to look at him in delight. "I've always wanted to do that," they both said at exactly the same time before they started laughing.

"Can you imagine?" said Evvie. "We'd have so much fun!"

"It would be a crazy amount of work but I'd love it. We could specialize in breakfast and tea!" said Maggie.

"I think you should explore this." Topher pointed his spoon at them. "I'm serious. It would be amazing."

"We should explore it."

"But not rush it. Let's wait for the perfect place to come up, then we'll strike!"

"Let me help you find the place. God knows there's nothing else keeping this gay man busy. Not that I'm complaining, but where are all the gays? I haven't met anyone since I've been here."

"That's probably because you've been with us the whole time," said Maggie. "I'm pretty sure there's an active gay community in Bath. There has to be, surely? We should Google."

"I'm with all the people I want to be with right now."

Maggie had sat there smiling, feeling her heart burst with love for her old friends, for her good fortune in going to the reunion, for her better fortune in picking the kind of friends that would remain true, and real, and lasting, after all these years.

In the kitchen, Maggie now sighed as she picked up the cereal bowls and mugs and put them in the dishwasher, turning as she heard footsteps and heard someone coming down the stairs.

Topher strode into the kitchen, not in jeans and a casual sweater, as he had been wearing ever since he arrived, but in full head-to-toe English country gentleman regalia.

"Are you auditioning for *Downton Abbey*?" asked Maggie, laughing as she put the kettle on.

"Oh, I wish," he said, taking his phone

and sliding it in a drawer as Maggie watched him.

"I just can't anymore," he explained. "I'm still Googling myself and I can't stand it. I haven't got the willpower to stay off-line, and every time I go on, I discover something else terrible that's been written about me. I'm going off-line, and the only way I can do it is to leave my phone behind."

"I thought everyone had forgotten about it. It's been weeks!"

Topher shrugged. As excited as he was to be with his old friends again, to be in Somerset, to try his hand at communal living, he was still dealing with the shame of his exposure. Evvie was right, another story had broken days later, and he had been mostly forgotten (which he knew from trawling online), but when he thought about it, he felt a shudder of shame.

Terrible things had been written about him, with ghastly one-night stands coming out of the woodwork revealing that they always knew he was a liar. Most of those stories were written by people Topher couldn't even remember.

And then there were the comments. The comments! The comments that felt like someone was stabbing him in the back. Vicious and vindictive, written by anonymous people who didn't know Topher, but wrote as if they did. They described him as a liar, unscrupulous, someone who was ruthlessly ambitious, who would do anything to get ahead.

Topher wanted to respond, even considered creating false identities who would defend him, for so much of what he was reading was patently false, patently rubbish. But he didn't, trying to remind himself that they weren't people who knew him, that he ought to ignore them.

It had blown over now, but he still Googled multiple times a day.

"Would you want to act in something like *Downton Abbey*?" Maggie mused. "I thought you had retired from acting."

"I have, but a sexy butler could bring me back."

"Where did all that tweed come from?" Maggie said, eyeing him up and down. "And a Barbour and Hunter wellies too. Blimey. You really do look like you've stepped out of Hunting and Fishing dot com."

"Is that an actual website?"

"I have no idea," said Maggie. "But if it isn't, it could be. At least you don't have a flat cap."

"I wasn't going to put it on until I got

outside," said Topher, brandishing a cap from the pocket of his Barbour. "Too much?"

"Too bloody much!" yelped Maggie, giggling, pretending to peer around him. "You don't have a lurcher hiding anywhere, do you?" said Maggie.

"A what?"

"Dog. Country dog. Good hunters. It would accessorize that outfit perfectly."

His face lit up. "We actually should get a dog."

Evvie walked into the room. "Dog? Did someone say something about getting a dog? Can we be trusted with a dog?" asked Evvie. "Remember Colin the cat?"

"Colin the cat!" Maggie broke into peals of laughter. "I haven't even thought about Colin the cat for about a hundred years. What ever happened to him?"

"He went missing. That's the point. Maybe we're not responsible animal owners, although I have always wanted a dog. Mind you, if Colin could have talked, I bet he would have told people not to let us have animals."

"I disagree," said Topher, reaching over and taking a bite out of one of Maggie's slices of toast.

"Hey," she said, "make your own." Nobody had eaten her food since she was married. She remembered how Ben always had terrible food envy. Whenever they went out to eat, their food would arrive and Ben always wanted what Maggie had. He always reached over to take the first bite off her plate, and would have done exactly what Topher just did, reached over and helped himself. And she hated it. She would shout at Ben all the time for doing what Topher just did, but it didn't bother her in the slightest when Topher did it, even though she pretended it did. If anything, these small acts helped foster the intimacy they all once had.

"I don't want my own," groaned Topher. "Other people's food always tastes better. The point being, Colin the cat hated us. He hated me, at any rate. He never wanted anyone to touch him. Whose idea was it anyway to rescue a cat?"

"We didn't rescue him," said Evvie. "If I remember correctly, Colin attached himself to Maggie."

Maggie shrugged. "I remember him being lovely. We had dogs here years ago. I love the idea of a dog but what if . . ." She stopped. What if it all went wrong? was what she was going to say. Could she be the only one who was even thinking that? Everyone else seemed blissfully happy, and it wasn't that she wasn't, but that she still couldn't quite believe this was going to be permanent. The last month or so had felt like an extended holiday, without the sand and sea. And sun. And someone else making the beds every day. Obviously.

It still felt temporary to her, as if one day she would wake up and everyone would decide to go back to their normal lives, their real lives, and the house would settle back to sleep under a blanket of quiet.

"What if this doesn't work out?" Topher finished Maggie's sentence for her as she shrugged, apologizing for voicing a thought she felt guilty for thinking. "I've thought about that too. I guess if it doesn't work out, we move on and figure out our lives. I guess this is bigger for me, and Evvie maybe, because we moved from the States, but I needed a change. That is, Dickie had already decided to let me go. And with my mother here, I would probably have come over anyway. If it doesn't work out, we're all grown-ups, we'll figure it out."

"I hate even hearing you talk about it not working out." Evvie's mouth was downturned. "Of course we'd figure it out, but it's been so amazing, living with other people. I had no idea how lonely I was."

"Me too." Maggie nodded.

"I have no idea what I would do. I'm sure I would be fine, but I honestly don't know if I'd stay in England or go back to America. Maybe I'd go to California to be near Jack. But I hope this does work out. Are you having doubts, Maggie?"

"Not doubts. I love every second of it. Apart from cereal bowls and mugs being left in the sink late at night." She gave them both a pointed look.

"That's me," Topher confessed, wincing. "I'm sorry. I'll try to do better."

"Can you also refill the cereal jar?"

"Yes. Of course. I'm sorry, I'm sorry. I'm used to a housekeeper doing all that stuff."

"You did not just say that!" Evvie's mouth dropped open.

"Say what?" he said innocently. "What? It wasn't me, I'm not spoiled. It was Dickie. Oh, okay. So I became spoiled. I'm having to retrain myself, okay? I made my bed this morning."

"Well done," said Evvie, but her eyes were twinkling.

"Sorry." Topher looked at Maggie. "You were saying?"

"I was saying that I love it, but I suppose I'm so used to this house being quiet, to me rattling around in it by myself, I kind of feel like it's all going to end and everyone will go back to their lives, leaving me by myself again."

Topher nodded, musing. "I get it," he said. "In some ways it must be hardest for you because this house is your home. It's where you lived with Ben. It must be filled with memories, and it's also yours. It's not a place you can easily share. It probably would be easiest if we all bought something together, started on an equal footing."

"We could still do that," said Evvie. "Not that I don't love it here, but we're not tied to anything. Now that we're renting from you, we could always look for something else and start again. If it doesn't work out, of course, which I am sure it will."

"Are you?" Topher looked at her. "You look doubtful."

"I'm sure," she said, which was true. As long as the past stayed in the past, it would all work out. She changed the subject. "Where are you going dressed like that anyway?"

"I'm taking my mother out to lunch."

"I haven't seen her in so many years. I'd love to see her. Why don't you invite her over here?" said Evvie, remembering the Dexatrim she was introduced to by Joan.

"I will, but she can't stay. I love my

445

mother, but only in small doses. Speaking of which, I have to go."

"Have a wonderful time." Evvie blew him a kiss as Topher stole the last of Maggie's toast, dropped the flat cap on the table, and left.

"What are you doing today?" she asked Maggie.

"Boring stuff. Paperwork. I have to run into the village to get some coffee and a few other things. Why?"

"Can I come with you? Is there an animal rescue anywhere around here?"

Maggie peered at her friend. "We're not getting a dog."

"Definitely not. But let's just go and have a look." She winked. "Just for fun."

FORTY

- 2019 -

"I do like it at Hadleys," said Topher's mother, eyeing the faux bookshelves approvingly. "It's lovely to have such sophistication at the English seaside. Also . . ." She paused as the waiter set down her roast chicken. "They do lovely big portions. Not that I can eat anything anymore, but I'll take it home and this will feed me for the next three days. It's like being back in America. That lovely Gillian doesn't even frown when I ask her for a doggie bag."

"How often do you come here?" asked Topher, who noted how his mother was greeted like one of the family.

His mother shrugged. "I've never cooked, darling. This is where all my dates bring me."

"Ah yes. And who is the lucky man this week?"

"My gentleman caller of the last six months has been James. He's lovely."

"James? Same name as Dad. How funny."
Topher's mother looked at him blankly.
"He's ever so charming, and handsome. His
people are from Connecticut. Greenwich."

"Mom?" Topher frowned, leaning forward.
"What are you talking about?"

"They're in shipping. Not him, but his
mother's family. Lots of money, apparently.
Such fun!"

"Mom. You're talking about Dad.
He's . . ." Topher gave up, sighing. What
was he supposed to say? If he told her that
the man she thought she was talking about
had been dead for years, would she break
down in floods of tears in the restaurant?
No. His mother was not one for public
shows of emotion, but nor was she one to
be confused. This wasn't like her at all.

"Do you remember our house in Greenwich off Round Hill Road?" Topher said,
and it was like flicking a switch as his
mother nodded, suddenly animated. "Remember the polo club you used to go to?"
And suddenly his mother was back, enthusi-
astically chatting about the polo club, their
life as a family when Topher was young, not
a confused bone in her body.

"And . . . do you remember Dad's funeral?" Topher asked gently.

"Oh God, yes," she said. "The service in

New York. It was standing room only, and there was an overflow that had to fill all the other rooms. We had to bring in screens so they could watch the service. What a beloved man he was."

"You miss him."

"I do."

"So, Mother, you know I've moved to Somerset?" He was treading gently, not sure of the areas in which her confusion struck.

"Of course I know that, darling. You're with all your lovely old friends from university. We can see each other all the time. You can bring me to Hadleys every week for lunch. How's that for starters?"

Topher smiled, relief flooding his body. Whatever happened before, with her confusion, must just be old age rather than anything more serious like dementia. His mother was back to herself, in charge of her destiny, her choices, her life.

"You have to come and see the house," he said. "They would all love to see you, and you'd adore it."

"What house?" she said, lifting the chicken to her mouth and not noticing that gravy dripped down the front of her silk blouse.

"Mother," he said, his heart again fluttering with fear. "Have you been to see a doctor recently?"

■ ■ ■ ■

They managed to get in that afternoon.

"Who says the NHS is rubbish?" muttered Topher in the waiting room, stunned that they got an appointment that day, and that there was no wait.

"It's wonderful here," said his mother, back on peak performance. "London was so challenging for doctors. I once spent eight hours in Accident and Emergency and not one person came to see me."

"What was the matter?"

"Theater!" His mother was distracted by a poster on the bulletin board. "Oh, look, they're doing *Bedroom Farce*! Oh, we must go and see it. Darling, will you get tickets?"

"Of course." Topher took out his phone and took a shot of the poster so he could call for tickets, thinking how unlike her it was to be so easily distracted.

"Darling, I do love having you here," she said, taking his arm and snuggling up to him. "I can't believe my little boy is right here in Somerset. It's going to be so much fun."

"Mrs. Winthrop?" The receptionist called her name without looking at her, even though they were the only ones in the waiting room, and Topher and his mother stood up and walked through to see the doctor.

He joined them almost immediately in what was clearly his consultation office. "I'm Dr. Khan," the young man said in introduction, shaking hands with Topher. "Very nice to meet you. I have heard lots about you from your mother."

"Oh." Topher was surprised. "That's so nice."

"And it's lovely to see you, Mrs. Winthrop. You're looking very elegant, as always." Topher watched as his mother positively simpered at a compliment from a handsome man.

"Please, take a seat," said the doctor, gesturing to the two plastic seats in front of his heavy mahogany desk. Then he sat at the desk and looked at them. "What brings you here today?"

"I have no idea," said Joan, looking at her son. "I'm in perfect health."

Topher cleared his throat. "My mother is, as you can see, in perfect health, but I've noticed some . . . confusion . . . recently. I'm just a little concerned it might be something more serious."

"Confusion?" His mother grew imperious. "I'm not confused in the slightest. I've never felt better."

451

"Mother," he said gently. "Earlier today you told me you were dating my father, who has . . . well." He looked at the doctor. "He's been dead for over twenty years."

"I did?" Rather than being angry, or refuting what she would surely think was a ridiculous claim, his mother seemed meek, unsure.

"You did. And there have been other things that are uncharacteristic. You phoned me the other night, or morning rather, at three, and you didn't seem to realize it was the middle of the night. You said you were about to go out shopping."

"I did?" she said again as Topher felt his heart lurch. His mother had always been so strong, so elegant, so together, and yet now, as he looked at her, she seemed small and confused, almost childlike, as Topher felt a stab of pain, seeing his omnipotent mother seem so fragile, so vulnerable. He reached out and took her hand, giving it a reassuring squeeze as she smiled at him, seeming again to come back to herself.

The doctor asked a series of questions, at the end of which he looked at Topher.

"Mr. Winthrop, I think your mother is in excellent health" — Joan smiled like the cat who got the cream — "and at her age this kind of confusion and memory loss isn't uncommon. Her recall of the past is exceptional, and it may be that there is a touch of dementia, but I'm not seeing any of the other signs — trouble finding the right words, mood changes like depression, or anger and aggression. Often people suffering with these kinds of issues stop keeping up things like personal grooming, but that clearly isn't the case for you, Mrs. Winthrop. I think we keep a close eye with monthly checkups, and I will give you my details so you can contact me with any concerns."

"You don't think it would be wise to maybe start researching . . ." He paused, wondering how to put it delicately. "Some sort of assisted-living facility?"

"I already told you," Joan interjected, "I am staying in my house."

"We could maybe find someone to come and stay in the house with you. To help out a bit."

"Do you remember that lovely Filipina we had?" Joan said dreamily. "She was your Yaya. Baby. Isn't that funny? That was her name, Baby, and her husband's name was Boy. They lived in the guesthouse and made the most delicious food for us. Oh, you loved her, Topher. She indulged you horribly. She'd take you out for walks and buy you every sweet thing you wanted."

Topher shot the doctor a look that said, *See? This is what I'm talking about. Why is she banging on about someone who worked for us fifty years ago?* Dr. Khan just smiled at him with the slightest of eyebrow raises and a nod.

"We will monitor," he said softly, "and if we see further deterioration, we can run some tests. But, Mr. Winthrop, for eighty-five, all things considered I would say your mother is pretty spectacular. Let's keep in touch, but a lot of this is normal. I know it's worrying to see a parent get older, but your mother is in great shape."

"I told you," she said to Topher. "No need to see a doctor after all. When you drop me home, don't forget to get tickets to *Bedroom Farce.* And you should bring all your friends. My treat."

"Okay." Topher shrugged helplessly, his mother back to her normal self. "Will do." He took her arm as they walked to the car, worrying about the future but grateful, so very grateful, that he was able to be there for her now in a way he was never able to before. He had spent all this time resenting her, convinced that she didn't protect him from the abuse, convinced she refused to see what was so obvious because it would have marred her perfect life, but now he knew he was wrong. All the anger and resentment was gone, and he was able to enjoy her in a way he hadn't since he was a child.

And if she needed to be taken care of, he would do that, too, even though, all those years ago, she wasn't able to take care of him.

FORTY-ONE

- 2019 -

Driving along the shaded roads was the first time Evvie and Maggie had been alone with any proper time to talk, the first opportunity for a true heart-to-heart. Evvie hadn't been able to stop thinking about what Maggie said the night of the reunion when she burst into tears claiming her marriage to Ben had been a disaster. Maggie had described it as being filled with deceit and lies, and Evvie hadn't been able to stop thinking about what that might mean.

She hadn't been able to ask Maggie, had to wait until Maggie was ready to talk, even though she was desperate to know. Maybe today would be the day Maggie revealed all.

"I am so sorry we lost touch," Evvie said, thinking about Jack.

Maggie took her eyes off the road for a few seconds to look at Evvie. "Me too. I always wondered what happened, why you just disappeared. I didn't realize how much

I missed you until you came back into my life. What happened, Evvie? Was it Ben?"

Evvie blanched. "What do you mean, was it Ben?"

"I know you never liked him. You saw something in him that I never did. I think you knew what he was really like."

"What do you mean?" Evvie shifted uncomfortably in her seat.

"Did you know about the drinking? You worked with him at that bar, remember. You must have seen it. I saw it myself, but I chose not to believe it was a problem."

"What are you talking about, Maggie? What drinking? Weren't we all drinking back then?"

"Right. But not like Ben. He never stopped." Maggie took a deep breath. "I've never been able to tell anyone this. He didn't die of a heart attack, Evvie. I couldn't bring myself to tell anyone the truth. Not even you and Topher. He died of alcoholic hepatitis."

"What?" Evvie's voice came out in a shocked whisper.

"He tried getting sober. Many, many times. He did AA and various kinds of rehab over the years. He had periods of sobriety, when I thought we had a chance, that we could be happy, but they never lasted." She pulled up at a red light and turned to Evvie. "I don't know why I stayed, and now I don't know why I didn't do more. Our marriage was so broken by the end, but I didn't know what to do. Do you know I joined a bereavement group soon after he died? But I had to leave. None of them had been through the same thing I had. I lost my husband to alcohol long before I lost him to hepatitis. I loved him and I hated him, and on the day he died I finally found the strength to tell him I was leaving him." Tears filled her eyes as she blinked them away, trying to stay focused on the road. "I still feel guilty every day. For sending him that text, for not doing more, for not doing things differently. I don't know if I'll ever be able to forgive myself for asking for a divorce on the day he died."

"Oh, Maggie," Evvie whispered, tears in her own eyes now as she looked out the window, in total shock. "I had no idea." But she did have something of an idea, she realized. That perfect week after she graduated? Ben was drunk every day. But everyone was, back then; she didn't think that was anything out of the ordinary. Granted, Evvie hadn't been drunk. Topher wasn't drunk very much, nor Maggie, but her week with Ben was during his vacation, and wasn't it normal to drink to excess on vacation?

Ben had been an alcoholic. Evvie couldn't believe it. For so many years she had held Ben Curran up as the perfect man. The one who got away. The only one who might have made her happy. The only good man she had ever been attracted to. All the others had turned out to be like her father: abusive, alcoholic, or both. And she had always thought Ben was the one man who was different, the one man who was normal. How wrong she had been! Thirty years of a false assumption disappearing in a flash. He was like all the others. Evvie was the one who had been wrong, in oh so many ways.

She thought of Jack then, how lucky she was that he hadn't inherited his father's alcoholism. Evvie was enough of a compulsive eater to recognize the addiction gene in others — even though she had never figured it out about Ben — but she always felt relieved that Jack didn't have it.

Evvie turned to look at Maggie, putting a hand over hers. "I don't know what to say. I had no idea. I thought you had the perfect marriage. I thought Ben was the perfect man."

"No one had any idea," said Maggie. "I went to great pains to make sure everyone thought we did in fact have the perfect marriage. I felt such incredible shame. We stopped going out, stopped seeing people, because he was always drunk. And the fights we had."

"Why are you telling me this now?"

"Because I don't want to keep secrets anymore. I stayed in a miserable marriage because I thought I needed, I don't know, the status of being married, and because I kept thinking that I could make him change. But the whole thing was a spiderweb of lies, and I don't ever want to lie to people I love again. I needed you to know the truth."

She looked at Evvie with a smile, but Evvie couldn't look back at her. She looked out the window, wishing her heart wasn't beating as fast as it was. Now would be the time for Evvie to reveal her own deceit, her own lies. The very fact that they didn't have a perfect marriage might be enough for Maggie to forgive her. But she immediately realized the alternative was too terrible to imagine. Evvie couldn't tell Maggie about Jack. Not now. Maybe not ever. She had just been offered a second chance at happiness, and she wasn't about to do anything to jeopardize it. This secret was one she had to continue to keep.

By the time they reached the animal

shelter, Maggie was chatting away about other things, Evvie pretending to listen, astounded at how she didn't see Ben's foibles, how she had always assumed he was the one healthy relationship she could have had, relieved Ben never told Maggie, never left her for Evvie, as he had talked about doing that fateful night in New York. Most of all, she felt guilty, guilty, guilty.

She forced her own secret aside, bringing herself back to the present, to Maggie, to be the best friend she could be, given all she now knew.

"Are you okay?" Maggie looked at her as they were about to get out of the car. "You've gone quiet."

"I'm just . . . I'm a little shocked. And I'm sorry. I'm sorry we weren't in touch."

"You're here now." Maggie squeezed her arm. "That's all that matters."

There were only six dogs, and none of them felt right. The only one they both liked needed a quiet home with no men, as the dog deeply feared them. They spoke to the woman in charge and said they were very quiet, in a large house filled with adults, and that there was one man, who was terribly gentle, and were sure the dog would be fine.

The woman shook her head, saying she

461

couldn't bend the rules. Maggie was demoralized, Evvie relieved that they were doing something, anything, to take her mind off the conversation in the car.

"It's probably a good thing," said Maggie as they made their way back out to the parking lot. "This must be the universe's way of telling us we're not supposed to have a dog."

Just then a van swung into the lot at great speed. Maggie threw out her hand and stopped Evvie from stepping in its path. "Whoa. That's fast."

The van came to an abrupt stop as a woman with frizzy hair and red, puffy cheeks rushed out, throwing a cigarette on the ground. She huffed around the side of the car, opened the back, and pulled out a cage containing a small gray terrier that looked less like a dog and more like a lamb. It was the cutest dog they had ever seen.

Evvie and Maggie stared at each other, wordlessly, before Evvie approached the woman.

"Excuse me," Evvie said politely as the woman scowled at her. "Are you dropping your dog off for adoption?"

"What's it to you?"

"They have a huge amount of paperwork," Evvie said, who had no idea if that was true but suspected it might be. "It takes about forty-five minutes to complete."

"Ah shit," said the woman. "I'm in such a rush." Her face fell.

"We came here looking for a dog," said Evvie. "Your dog looks perfect. We could just . . . take him. Or her."

"Him."

"There wouldn't be any paperwork," Maggie said, trying not to smile.

The woman's face lit up.

"Can you tell us anything about him?"

"He's two years old, a purebred Bedlington terrier. He was my daughter's dog but she just had a kid and can't cope, so I ended up with him. My other dog's a Staffie and he hates him so we can't keep him, but he's a lovely dog. He's a lover. Just wants to be cuddled. His name's Scout and he's house-trained. Very easy."

Maggie looked at Evvie, then crouched down to see Scout.

"If you'd be willing to let us have him, we'd give him a lovely home," she said. "We're big animal lovers and I've had dogs all my life."

"I definitely don't have to fill out any paperwork?" said the woman.

"No. We'll take him right now."

"Here you go." She lifted up the cage and handed it to Maggie, and before anyone could say anything else, she was back in the car and zoomed out of the parking lot at high speed.

"Oh my God." Evvie couldn't stop grinning. "Talk about the universe sending a message!"

"I can't believe how easy that was! This is the perfect dog for us. This is the dog we're supposed to have. Hello, Scout!" she crooned through the bars as the little dog wagged its tail. "We're your new family. Let's go home."

They stopped at the pet shop on the way home, taking Scout out of the cage and each picking him up to cuddle, crooning over how cute he was as he looked up at them with large black eyes.

"He's a cutie. Which is a relief, given that we now own a dog we didn't even meet properly. She didn't even take him out of the cage!" Evvie started to laugh.

"I was terrified that stern woman from the shelter would come out and take him away. I just wanted to get him out of there. Look at that face!" Maggie put her face close to Scout's, who licked her all over. "He's adorable."

"He's perfect. We'll have to take him to the vet to get checked out. She took off so fast, I hope there's nothing wrong with him."

"I think there's something wrong with her driving, that's all," said Maggie. "There's nothing wrong with you, Scout, is there?" she murmured.

At the pet shop they bought leads, bowls, a bed, and bags of toys as everyone stopped to pet Scout.

"What a lovely little fella," the shop owner and his two other customers said as Scout wagged his tail for everyone, looking up at them with big black eyes filled with happiness.

"He looks like he belongs to you," said everyone who stopped, after Maggie and Evvie told them they had just adopted him. And they smiled, sure this was true.

"Hello?" Maggie called through the front door as they walked in, Scout stopping to smell all the unfamiliar scents.

"Hello!" Topher echoed from the kitchen. He came out, saw the dog, and stopped in his tracks.

"What the hell is that? Have you brought home a pet lamb?"

"It's not a lamb. It's a dog. A Bedlington terrier called Scout. He's our new mascot."

"Hello, Scout. Aren't you lovely! Come

and say hello." Topher crouched down, extending a hand, which Scout ignored, taking off into the kitchen. "Knows his name then?"

"We don't know very much about him, but he's definitely very clever," said Maggie, who was delighted at having a dog again in the house. "This was an impromptu rescue."

"Honestly, this was fate," said Evvie, bringing the bags into the kitchen. "There were no suitable dogs at the shelter, and just as we were leaving, this grumpy woman showed up with Scout, and we just . . . took him."

"House-trained?" asked Topher.

"Yes," Maggie and Evvie said at the same time. They all turned at the sound of something trickling, and sure enough, Scout was marking his territory on the leg of the kitchen table.

"Oh fuck," said Evvie, giggling despite herself. "I'm not cleaning that up."

"I'll do it. It's not like I haven't done it a million times before. He's just nervous. I can train him," Maggie said. Scout emerged blithely from the laundry room and made his way over to the table. He came straight over to Topher, sat down, and looked up at him.

Topher leaned down and lifted Scout onto his lap, whereupon the dog curled up, snuffling his snout under Topher's arm. "Well," he said. "Aren't you the cutest lamb ever? He is adorable. I didn't know we were getting a dog." He shot a look at Maggie, who shrugged, with no apology whatsoever.

"Don't blame me," she said. "Evvie took me to an animal shelter today and we were supposed to be just looking. For fun."

"No one goes to an animal shelter and looks just for fun. You have to come back with an animal. It's a universal law."

"Shhh. Don't tell her now," said Evvie.

"He seems like he belongs here." Topher stroked him softly. "Can he sleep on my bed tonight?"

"I'll fight you for him," said Evvie.

"We'll all take turns."

Evvie sidled up to Maggie. "You know how earlier you said you were worried that this would all end and we would go back to our lives and you'd be left alone in the same old house? Now it can never be the same again. We've brought Scout in, which means that the future will be different, no matter what."

"You're right. I feel the difference. And I didn't think I wanted a new dog, but already it feels like this house is filled with love again. Thank you for suggesting it, even though I know you didn't really think we'd end up with a dog." She gave Evvie a hug.

"You know me so well!" laughed Evvie. "We should go out to celebrate. Can we go to the pub in the village for a celebratory drink? We'll bring Scout."

"Great idea," said Maggie. "Do I have time for a shower first?"

Evvie frowned. "Why? Is the pub posh?"

"God, no! It's a proper country pub, with a lovely big roaring fireplace, I might add. I just didn't shower earlier. Give me about half an hour, that okay?"

"Sounds perfect."

Upstairs, Maggie took a shower, and threw on some jeans and her old, comfortable boots. It was only the pub, but she paused in the hallway before returning to the bedroom.

It may be the local pub, but she hadn't been there in months, hadn't seen Karen and Pete in months. They were such good friends when she ran the village fete, and Karen was fantastic after Ben died, but Maggie had been so depressed, everyone had deserted her after a while. She didn't blame them. Karen would keep inviting Maggie out to things and Maggie kept declining. After a while she stopped asking, and after a while, she stopped phoning.

Maggie would fix that tonight. She was looking forward to seeing them and was bound to run into people she knew. It would be nice to let them see the new, improved Maggie, the Maggie who had a constant smile on her face. Ever since the reunion, she lost the sad, drawn air that dragged her features down, and thanks to her home dye job, she was no longer a dull ginger streaked with gray, but back to her vibrant red hair.

But the biggest change was on the inside. Maggie, who had spent her entire life feeling older and wiser than her years, was finally feeling her age rather than ten years older. In fact, if she was being honest, she felt ten years younger. Maybe fifteen. Being surrounded by friends from her youth had brought a youthfulness and a levity back into her life.

Last week Topher insisted on taking her shopping to SouthGate. Instead of the conservative country housewife skirts and ballet flats or sensible boots that had been her uniform all her adult life, he had her trying on platform sandals, faux fur vests, and floral maxidresses in shops that Maggie had always ignored, presuming them to be for teenagers and the young at heart, which Maggie had never been.

"It's time for your transformation," Topher had said. "You've spent your life aging up, and now it's time to age down."

"I can't look like mutton dressed as lamb," she'd said, which cracked Topher up.

"Trust me," he said. "I won't put you in anything ridiculous."

He spun around the shops, gathering clothes. Each time she emerged from the fitting room (he insisted on seeing *everything*), he clapped his hands in delight. Maggie felt vaguely ridiculous, but gorgeous, as if she were in a fancy dress she would never wear in real life. Despite herself she loved the black leather biker jacket, would never have thought to pair it with the chiffon maxiskirt, and even though the platform sneakers were the last thing she would ever have looked at, they were comfortable. For the first time since leaving Les Jolies all those years ago, Maggie looked, and felt, trendy.

They drove home, the car piled high with bags from H&M, Urban Outfitters, and Topshop, Maggie stunned at how much they had bought, worried that she would never wear anything.

She had worn everything, and felt beautiful in a way she never did when she was young, and photographs revealed she actually was beautiful.

Topher was right. Even if the reflection in the mirror was almost exactly the same (with better skin — that micro derma roller thing Topher insisted she buy in Boots really had made a difference), she no longer looked fifty going on sixty-two. This new Maggie could pass for forty. Evvie said thirty-eight. The new clothes, the vibrant hair color complete with a shoulder-length, choppy "lob" had made her feel young again and, dare she say it, sexy.

She pulled off the boots and put on the platform sneakers, slipped off the cashmere cardigan, and pulled on the faux fur vest. She grinned at herself before removing the pearl studs from her ears, replacing them with large red beaded hoops. Wiping off the clear lip gloss, she applied red lipstick and pulled her hair out of the bun, shaking it out.

I'm ready, she thought. Not just for the pub, but ready to start living again.

FORTY-TWO

- 2019 -

The unseasonal heat wave had given way to a chill in the air in the evenings, but the village had never felt more beautiful to Maggie, never felt more like home. She hadn't strolled like this, to the pub, in years. She tried to avoid the pub when Ben was home, knowing a quick pint of beer would always end in a binge for him, but they did this in the early days, strolled down the lanes on a summer night. It felt even better now, with Topher and Evvie, and Scout on a lead.

Evvie was walking in front, wrapping her arms around herself, wishing she had brought a coat. "God, it's chilly. When did it get so chilly?"

"Winter is coming," said Topher, putting an arm through Evvie's and squeezing her tight. "Better?"

"A bit."

"Wait for us," said Maggie as Scout stopped every few feet to sniff the unfamiliar smells. Maggie pretended to be irritated, but was clearly delighted at having a dog again.

"Oh, look!" Topher said as they rounded the corner and the pub came into view. "That's like a picture postcard of what a pub should look like."

It was true, the ivy-covered stone building was one of the prettiest for miles. Barrels of geraniums and fuchsias sat outside in summer, with hanging baskets everywhere. Now that autumn was well and truly in the air, the hanging baskets were starting to die off. The barrels were filled with box balls, and every window was alight with a warm, inviting glow.

Inside there was a huge inglenook fireplace with a blazing fire, low ceilings and beams that dated back to the sixteenth century. The bar was full, people perching on stools, bursts of laughter punctuating the air, but there were still empty tables.

"Maggie? Is that you?" Karen came toward her, tentatively at first, before flinging her arms around her.

"You're back!" she said, holding her at arm's length. "Look at you! You look like yourself again. Oh, Maggie. I've been so worried about you but I didn't want to keep bothering you. I didn't know what to do, but I've been thinking of you all this time."

"I've been thinking of you too," said Maggie. "I needed to remove myself for a while, but now I'm back."

"And looking better than ever, might I say! Does this mean you'll come back to us at the village fete? It hasn't been the same without you."

"I'll definitely think about it," said Maggie, introducing Karen to Topher and Evvie.

"These are my oldest friends," she said as they all shook hands.

"Very nice to meet you all. Are you here for the weekend?" asked Karen.

"Not exactly," said Topher.

"They've moved in with me," said Maggie. "We all lived together at university and we've decided to live together again."

"Now that is a good idea," said Karen. "No wonder you look so good. I've been so worried about you, rattling around in that big old house by yourself. It's grand to meet you all. We've got a lovely table by the fireplace that's reserved but they're late so why don't you take it. I'll move them if they show up."

"I don't think we're going to have dinner," Maggie said, looking at the others. But Topher had his gaze firmly fixed on a plate of fish and chips that was being carried out of the kitchen.

"That looks delicious," he said. "Maybe we'll have a little something to eat."

"Either way, doesn't matter. Take the table and first round is on the house."

"Karen, you don't have to . . ."

"I know I don't. I want to. And, Maggie, let's you and I get together this week. I've missed you. Righto, everyone. What will you all have?"

A few minutes later they were cozily ensconced near the fire with drinks in hand. "Now this," said Evvie, sipping her gin and tonic and looking around the pub, "really does feel like we've regressed. I haven't been in a pub since I moved to New York."

"I thought there were tons of Irish pubs in New York," said Maggie. "I've been there. I've seen them."

"They're not like this though. Not proper English country pubs. They're more like bars, with four-leaf clovers and pictures of leprechauns everywhere. I haven't been in a proper, centuries-old, cozy beamed pub with a giant fireplace since college. Cheers!" She lifted her glass. "Here's to many more nights in the pub."

"Here's to bad-taste pub crawls in our future," said Topher, shooting Evvie a look.

"Yes!" Maggie started laughing. "Here's

to Evvie dressing up as a pregnant nun."

"What were *you*?" Evvie looked at Topher. "I remember you were there but I have no idea what your costume was."

"I went as a drunk. I covered my pants with mushy peas as if I'd vomited on them."

"Oh my God, now I remember. That was disgusting."

"That's probably why you forced yourself to forget."

"Excuse me?"

They all stopped talking and laughing to look up and see a handsome, clean-cut man standing near their table — one of the men, Topher thought, that was sitting at the bar.

Maggie squinted at him, feeling her heart plummet. Oh God. Not this again.

"I'm sorry to interrupt but . . ." He looked at Evvie. "Are you Evvie Thompson?"

Evvie nodded. "Do I owe you money?" she joked, not knowing quite what to say, for no one had recognized her in such a long time.

"Oh my God. I thought it was you, but then I thought, what on earth would Evvie Thompson be doing in my sleepy little village? I'm sorry. I'm just, I'm a huge fan. I used to watch you on that TV show where you played Yolanda, and I've just . . . wow. Sorry. I just can't believe you're in this pub.

What are you doing here? I'm sorry, I shouldn't ask. I don't want you to think I'm some kind of stalker or anything."

"No, that's fine," said Evvie, who was glowing, because whoever this man was, and despite the fact that he was wearing a wedding ring, he was quite clearly smitten with her. Evvie, who was still bigger than she would like to be, who still believed the world could only be her oyster if she was skinny, still so hung up on her weight, she didn't think she would ever have this effect on anyone again. "I live here now." She smiled, feeling beautiful for the first time in ages.

His eyes widened in shock. "You do? I know Stella McCartney's nearby but I never heard your name. I'm James Sullivan, by the way." He shook Evvie's hand, then Topher's, before giving an embarrassed smile to Maggie. "Hi, Maggie. Nice to see you in the pub. You're looking well."

"Nice to see you here," she said. "Do you have a permanent roost at the bar?"

He narrowed his eyes. "No. I'm not here often enough. I'm just here for a quick bite to eat while Emily's out with the girls."

"Chicken?" Maggie asked, before she started to laugh. "I'm sorry, I'm sorry. I couldn't resist."

"That's okay. I took your advice and

bought earplugs. Now the children all like the rooster. I'm sorry I was such an arse that day. Can I get you all a drink to apologize properly?"

Maggie was about to say no, but before she had a chance, Topher jumped in. "That would be lovely. Thank you. I'm having a vodka martini with olives." He looked at the others, who all chimed in, with Maggie adding her own gin and tonic.

"He's nice," said Evvie, when he had gone to the bar to get the drinks. "A little young perhaps, but very handsome."

"And very married," added Topher, gesturing to the third finger on his left hand, "before you get any ideas. Although he does seem to be rather smitten, you cougar, you."

"First off, I wasn't thinking that," said Evvie, blushing. "Secondly, he wouldn't be interested in me. I'm not only old enough to be his mother, look at me. I'm hardly the Evvie Thompson of old. Or rather, I'm twice the Evvie Thompson of old. He's just got a celebrity crush."

"Evvie, you are stunning," said Maggie. "Whatever weight you are, you are beautiful. How can we get this into your head? When will you stop beating yourself up about your size? Frankly, I thought you were way too thin when you were modeling. I used to see pictures of you and wish I could fly over and feed you."

"She's right," said Topher. "I think you have to let go of this weight madness."

"I'm working on it," Evvie said, which was true. Rather than avoid full-length mirrors, which she had done since the end of her marriage, she had bought a full-length mirror for her room, and stood naked, looking at herself, every day. She embraced her full breasts, her rounded stomach, her thick thighs, telling herself she was curvy, womanly, and feminine. "I am lush," she whispered to herself, "and luscious. I am beautiful exactly as I am. This belly has held my child. Some women pay a fortune to have breasts like mine." These affirmations felt ludicrous when she started, but the more she said them, the easier it was, and even though she was a work in progress, she had started to feel better about herself.

She was starting to accept that this was the body she was supposed to have now. As tempting as it had been to do keto, paleo, intermittent fasting, to take pills, cut out all carbohydrates and sugar, go vegan, she was fifty years old, too old to get back on the crazy diet roundabout she was on for years when young. Until she started accepting herself exactly as she was, she would never be at peace, and she was starting to get over the shame of no longer being a size two.

"Who is he, anyway, this handsome man who has excellent taste in women?" Evvie said, changing the subject.

"He's our neighbor," said Maggie. "You know all the huge new houses that line our road?"

"The ones you're always taking the piss out of because they're so aspirational?" asked Evvie. "Wisteria Hall?"

"Indeed. That, in fact, is lord of the manor of Chestnut Hill."

"Chestnut Hill Manor? Didn't you say you used to be friends with them but you'd fallen out?"

"We had. Maybe we're falling back in," whispered Maggie as James headed back to the table with drinks.

"May I join you?" he asked. "My friends are leaving and I'd love to have another drink, if that's okay."

Evvie didn't wait to confer with the others. "Of course!" She slid over on the bench to make room for him.

"So I understand from Maggie here that we're neighbors."

"Oh, really? Gosh, how unexpected. Where are you living?"

"We're all living with Maggie," Evvie announced with a flourish.

There was a pause as he frowned, trying to understand. "You are?"

"Please don't tell me you're going to start complaining about the noise." Maggie couldn't help herself.

"I haven't heard any noise. I had no idea. How does that work then? Have you divided up the house?"

"Haven't needed to," said Topher. "Have you seen the place? It's enormous."

"Well, cheers!" said James, raising his glass. "Welcome, new neighbors!"

"Jesus," Maggie said, sliding over to Topher, her head falling awkwardly on his shoulder. "I think I'm a bit drunk."

"I'm not drunk," said Evvie, "I'm completely fucking arsed," and she started giggling.

"We're going to pay for this tomorrow," said Topher, blinking until he could actually focus on James. "James, I blame you. This was supposed to be an hour's quick drink. This is all your fault."

"This isn't my fault! This is Evvie's fault. If she wasn't here, I wouldn't have come over. Evvie, you are a very naughty girl." He wagged his finger at her, and Evvie burst out laughing.

"Stop flirting with her. She's too old for you," said Topher.

"Psssssshhhh," said Evvie, looking at James. "Don't be so rude. Anyway, he's married and that's a road I'm *definitely* not going down again."

"Oh, really? Is there more to this story?" asked Topher as Evvie paled, shaking her head.

"What time is it?" James pulled out his phone and tried very hard to focus on it. "Oh shit."

"Last orders!" called Karen from the bar. She came to the table. "I think maybe you lot should be making your way home. Will you be okay?"

"Karen?" Maggie stood up and swayed a bit. "Have I ever told you that I love you?"

"No, darling, but I love you, too, and I think it's time you all got yourselves safely tucked up in bed. Do you need Pete to chaperone you home? He's upstairs but I can go and get him."

"No," said Maggie, falling on Karen and giving her a hug. "We will be fine. Next time will you do a lock in? It's only eleven. You should do a lock in tonight and let us stay all night."

"Maybe next time," said Karen, steadying Maggie. "You're sure you'll all be all right?"

"Sure," said Maggie as they all stood up and swayed, giggling as they tried to get their coats on.

"James, you walk with me," said Maggie, pulling him away from Evvie. "I don't want you to get into trouble." She slipped her arm through his and they stepped outside into the cold air.

"You're quite nice, you know," she said as they walked. "Even though you drive a Tesla and you're part of the whole new yummy-mummy crowd, you're all right. I like you."

"What have you got against Teslas?"

"Nothing. I haven't got anything against them. You should come over for dinner one night. I'll cook. I'm a very good cook. Bring Emily. Bring your children. Bring your dog. Do you have any cats? Bring them too. Let's all be best friends again."

The two of them started laughing as they turned the corner and wandered down the road, shortly finding themselves in front of Chestnut Hill Manor.

"Oh fuck," said James, patting his jacket. "I don't think I've got the key."

"Ring the doorbell," said Topher, swaying with Evvie at the end of the driveway.

"My wife will kill me," he said.

"She'll kill you harder if you don't come home at all," said Evvie with a giggle.

James paused, then rang the doorbell. Silence.

"Why isn't your dog barking?" said Maggie.

"We don't have a dog," he said, and they started laughing again.

"Try again," she said.

"It's freezing!" Evvie called out, huddling with Topher. "I need to get into bed. I might need to throw up first."

Topher quickly moved away from her.

"I was kidding!" she said.

"Emily's asleep." James suddenly looked very worried, very drunk, and very young. "I could sleep in my car."

"I don't think a Tesla would be very comfortable to sleep in." Maggie turned and stared at the charcoal-gray car in the driveway. "You can come and stay at ours. We have lots of room. But you can't sneak into Evvie's room."

"I wouldn't dream of it. Thank you. I should text my wife and tell her." He patted his jacket again. "Oh shit. I left my phone in the pub."

"You can e-mail her from mine. Come on. Let's go home."

FORTY-THREE

- 2019 -

Maggie woke up first with a pounding headache. She remembered to drink a whole bottle of water before she went to bed. It was an old trick from her youth — match the amount of alcohol drunk with water, and you would be fine. She had no idea how much alcohol she had drunk, but a bottle of water ought to do it, she thought last night.

She crawled out of bed and downed three Nurofen Plus, realizing that she was far from fine, then got back into bed to wait for the headache to subside. A short while later, she heard banging on the front door, which continued on and off for a good five minutes. Eventually, Maggie heard Emily's voice calling through the letterbox.

"James? James? Are you in there?"

Maggie cast her mind back to last night with some difficulty, before remembering that James was in fact *there,* and that she must be the only one awake, given the continued banging at the door.

She was still in the same clothes as last night, she realized as she made her way out of the bedroom.

Topher was emerging from his room as well, holding his head. "Who the fuck is banging on the door?" he groaned.

"I think that's Emily, James's wife. Where did he sleep?"

Topher paused. "He's either on the giant sofa in the den, or in Evvie's bed."

"Are you serious?" hissed Maggie, unwilling to open the door to his wife.

"No, I'm not serious. He's on the sofa. I think."

"Can you go?"

"No," said Topher, backing into his room and closing the door.

Maggie went downstairs and peered into the den, where she saw James, fast asleep on the sofa, covered by one of her cashmere throws. Well thank God for *that,* she thought, going back to the entrance hall and opening the door to find a very angry Emily in large sunglasses and a fur-trimmed parka.

"Hi, Emily," said Maggie. "I'm guessing you're looking for James?"

"Yes, I'm looking for James. What the fuck is he doing here?" Emily looked Maggie up and down, noting her new hair color, the flush in her cheeks. She was clearly furious, her voice loud as Maggie squinted in pain, massaging her left temple.

"It's nice to see you as well, Emily. Would you mind keeping your voice down? Bit of a headache. And if I recall correctly, he left his keys at home, and his phone in the pub. We did try to wake you but we didn't know what else to do. I'm sure . . ."

"Where is he?" Emily cut her off as Maggie realized she didn't believe her.

For all she knew, James spent the night with Maggie, which must have been why she was giving her the dagger glares. Maggie said nothing, just led Emily to the den and watched as she tried to prod James awake.

"Get up!" Emily hissed. "James! Wake up! Oh, for Christ's sake." She stopped shaking him as tears suddenly sprang into her eyes.

"Why don't you come into the kitchen for a minute. I was just about to make tea," Maggie lied, concerned that if she didn't get Emily away from her husband, she might physically hurt him.

Emily paused, blinking at Maggie before looking at her husband.

"Give him ten minutes or so and he'll wake up. Let's go in here." Maggie placed a hand on Emily's arm, amazed as she meekly followed her into the kitchen.

Maggie made the tea as Emily sat at the kitchen table, staring mutely out the window. She brought the cups over to the table, sliding the sugar bowl and milk over to Emily, who added a splash of milk and took a sip.

"I'm sorry," she said eventually. "I didn't mean to take it out on you."

"It's fine. You must have been worried sick."

The tears sprang back into Emily's eyes. "It's not . . . I mean. Yes. I was worried. I didn't know where he was sleeping . . ."

"I understand," Maggie said gently. "I would have had exactly the same reaction."

There was a silence as Emily appeared to be blinking back tears. "Do you think maybe we can let bygones be bygones? Things got weird between us with the trees, and now I wish we could just all be friends."

"It's not just you." Maggie swallowed. "I wasn't in a place where I could be with people for quite a while. After Ben died, I thought . . ." She stopped, seeing Emily's eyes well up. "Emily? Are you okay?"

And Emily started to cry, this time properly, with heaving shoulders, gulping for air. Maggie's first inclination was to put an arm around her shoulders, but she didn't want to overstep her boundaries. She got up and brought over a box of tissues from the kitchen counter, placing it in front of Emily. This small act of kindness seemed to have a calming effect, and blowing her nose hard, Emily hiccupped a little, then looked at Maggie.

"I am so sorry," she said again. "I didn't mean to collapse in tears. It's not just that he slept here. I mean, it is that, but we've been having problems for a while. He's been staying in London quite a bit recently, he says for work, late meetings, but I thought maybe there was someone . . ." She sighed. "And then when he said he was here, I didn't know what to think. I've seen a bunch of people staying here and I just thought I'd find him in bed with someone. I thought maybe he was having an affair with you. I know, it's stupid. It sounds so stupid."

Maggie smiled. "I know I probably shouldn't say this, but I love that you think I'm someone your husband would even look at. I'm an old, boring widow. That's the last thing you need to worry about. But your concerns sound valid. Not that I think he's having an affair, but it doesn't sound stupid. It sounds like you've been really concerned, and you have every right to be angry."

She stared at Maggie. "I do, right?"

"Yes. Ben used to disappear all the time. I'd have no idea where he was, and I'd be a mess. I once spent all night driving around Bath looking for his car."

"Did you find it?"

"No. Which is lucky because I think I would have destroyed it. I don't want to be patronizing, but as someone who's a few years older, the best advice I can give, if you're willing to take advice . . ." Emily nodded. "Well, the best advice is to communicate. Ben and I stopped communicating long before he died, and I always wonder if things would have been different if we had been able to talk to each other properly." She smiled. "On the bright side, I'm glad this gave you a reason to come over. It would be really nice to not be at war with you anymore."

"This is nice," sniffed Emily. "I'm really sorry about the trees. I'll have them cut down."

"Don't worry about it. Honestly? There are far more important things in life to worry about than having a view."

"I don't mind at all. I wanted the privacy when the children were small but I've got a teenager now. Can you believe it? Skylar's a teenager! Where does the time go?" Emily shook her head.

"I know," said Maggie, thinking about all the time she spent trying to find happiness. "I've been asking myself the same question for years."

FORTY-FOUR
- 2019 -

Topher was out in the garden, raking the leaves and pausing every few minutes to breathe in the crisp air, grateful that the pounding headache had finally gone, and that he was doing something to contribute to the household.

They hadn't been very good at designating jobs, treating this more as an extended vacation than a permanent living arrangement, but all that was about to change. Topher had now officially taken on the gardening, including clipping the dreaded hedgerow.

"Have you ever done it before?" asked Maggie dubiously, taking him into the shed and pointing out the hedge trimmer.

"How hard can it be?" Topher had said, immediately taking the hedge trimmer and doing a beautiful job on two small yew pillars, by the end of which his arms were so sore, he was rethinking doing anything else for the rest of the week. Although, he told himself, he hadn't been to the gym since he moved here, and this would get his arms in wonderful shape.

He was fascinated by the garden, and by Maggie's gardening books, which lined the shelves of the den. Topher had been poring over them, studying Penelope Hobhouse's designs, Gertrude Jekyll's color schemes, repeatedly going to the window and looking out, his brain ticking furiously as ideas came into his head.

Last week he found a landscape design course in Bath, taught by one of England's master gardeners, and he was waiting for the brochure and application form to arrive. He had no idea if this was what he had been waiting for, but had a strong suspicion it might be. He wasn't telling the others until he'd been accepted.

Evvie and Maggie were out looking at a building in Frome. It had been a butcher, and was now for sale. Topher was the one who saw the For Sale sign and contacted the estate agent. He went to see it and declared it a distinct possibility for the café they were still talking about.

Topher stayed home, determined to get the garden cleaned up before they returned, when he heard a car pull into the driveway.

It was a Toyota Prius, not a car that belonged to any of them. He wandered over to see who it was, assuming it was either a wrong address or a delivery, perhaps.

The back door opened, and a young man got out, turning immediately and leaning in to the back seat to pull out a large suitcase.

"Thank you," he called to the driver in an American accent. "Have a great day."

The Uber — it was clearly an Uber from the sticker in the window — took off, and the young man looked at Topher, who was about to tell him to call the car back immediately because he had been deposited in the wrong place. But there was something so familiar about this boy, Topher said nothing, just stared at him as the cogs in Topher's brain clicked into place and he was swept back thirty years.

It made no sense whatsoever. For the boy standing in front of him was Evil Ben. Evil Ben just as he looked when they all met him.

"Ben?" Topher whispered, not understanding how this could possibly be. The boy frowned.

"What?" said the boy. "I'm sorry, I didn't hear you." He waited for Topher to say it again, but Topher said nothing, just stared at him, his eyes wide, his breath shallow.

"Okay." Jack shrugged. "I guess it's not

important. Hi. I'm Jack. I'm looking for my mom? Evvie Thompson?"

"Oh Jesus fucking Christ," whispered Topher, the color draining from his face.

FORTY-FIVE

- 2019 -

"I don't know," said Maggie, peering through the dark spaces in the old butcher shop. "It's pretty gloomy. I'm not sure I see this."

"There are all sorts of things you could do," said the agent. "Those walls could come down, and the windows could be replaced with bigger ones."

"For a price," said Evvie, who was as demoralized as Maggie. This was the second place they'd seen, and she had high hopes for this one, given that Topher was the one who found it. "I'm just not sure it feels right."

"I think that's it. I can't see it. I don't know," she sighed, turning to Evvie. "Maybe we should think about it some more. I'm a bit hopeless when it comes to vision."

"I'm not. I've got really good vision and I think this might just be too much money for us to get it right."

"But it's such a great location."

"There will be others. We have to wait for the right one to come along."

They were both a little blue as they left, but by the time they decided to stroll down Cheap Street, all had been forgotten, with Evvie gasping in delight at the medieval buildings — and excellent shopping.

She bought two bags from Amica, a home-made fig chutney (after trying a sample, which was one of the best things she had ever eaten), and, in Hunting Raven Books, a book for Topher on classic English gardens in the West Country.

All the while she had a smile on her face, looking up at the hanging upper balconies that lined the street, down at the crooked paving stones and the leat, the water feature that carried water from the stream beneath Saint John's church.

"This is so charming!" she said. "I can't believe this American gets to live here, among all this history."

Maggie walked alongside her, delighted that Evvie was with her, that she loved it so much, that she was allowing Maggie to fall in love with Somerset all over again.

The disappointment of the butcher's was forgotten as they stopped for smoothies in Café La Strada, and sampled pastries in the

Old Bakehouse.

"If this were in America," whispered Evvie as they stood in front of the glass cabinet admiring the cakes, "it would be Ye Olde Bakehouse."

"Oh, don't you worry," Maggie whispered back. "There's plenty of those to go around here."

"If we open the café, we cannot call it Ye Olde anything, deal?"

"What do you mean 'if'?" said Maggie indignantly. "Surely you mean 'when.' "

"I did. Of course I did."

By the time they pulled in the driveway, both were chattering excitedly about their dream vision of a café. An American-style diner, they had decided, with a twist. The twist being Evvie's famous Jamaican breakfasts, naturally, and an updated, modern take on the classic diner — Evvie insisted on red vinyl stools in an homage.

Maggie opened the front door as Scout came clattering toward her.

"Hi, baby boy." She squatted to pet him as Topher walked out of the hallway leading to the kitchen. He was with someone, but she couldn't see who, the light from the kitchen rendering him in shadow, and she smiled.

"Hi, you. The place was a disaster. The

only thing you got right was location. Is everything okay?" She noticed Topher's face looked pained, and she stopped, looking first at Topher, then at the man behind him as he emerged out of the shadow.

Maggie stared, her brow furrowing as she tried to make sense of what she was seeing, but it made no sense. In front of her, in her house, was her late husband, as he was exactly when she first met him. He stood like a ghost in her hallway, his smile as wide as it always was, the dimples in the same place, his widow's peak as pronounced as it always was.

Evvie walked in behind her, shrieking, but Maggie barely heard.

"Ben?" she whispered, before everything faded to black and she slipped quietly to the floor.

Forty-Six

- 2019 -

"I can explain." Evvie looked at Jack, then at Maggie, who was now lying on the sofa, unable to tear her gaze away from Jack.

"I don't understand," she said. "This is your son? But he's . . . he's the spitting image of . . ."

"We need to talk, it isn't what you . . ." Evvie started before trailing off. Of course it was what she thought.

"What's going on?" said Jack, his sunny demeanor now gone, confusion written all over his face, which made Evvie catch her breath. All these years she'd worried about keeping the secret from Maggie, and now she had to tell her son. She wasn't prepared for this, for him showing up out of the blue. Not by a long shot.

And while she knew she owed Maggie an explanation, she had to first take care of her son, whom she ushered outside, still unable to believe he was even here.

"What just happened?" Jack kept asking, but Evvie was shaking and could hardly speak as she hurried him out the front door.

"Let's go somewhere where we can talk. There's a lot I have to explain to you. I'll tell you when we get there," she said, because she needed some time to calm down.

Hauser & Wirth was a farm that had been transformed into an art gallery. It was the only place Evvie could think of that would be quiet and serene, and she needed some serenity to help her figure out what to say.

When they arrived, Evvie led Jack around the gardens, and taking a deep breath, she explained who his father was, and why she had kept it a secret all these years. Jack said nothing, walked alongside her listening, frowning as he let her talk.

When she told him the whole story, including why she had to keep it a secret, he stopped walking and looked at her, his sunny smile now gone, his tone muted and he had a look in his eye Evvie had never seen before, one that looked suspiciously like distrust.

"I still don't understand why you couldn't tell me. I understand why you kept it from Maggie, but . . . I'm your son. You knew I wanted to know who my dad was." Evvie's eyes were red and puffy as she acknowledged what he was saying.

"I'm so sorry. It seems so obvious now that I did the wrong thing, but at the time I didn't want to hurt Maggie. It all felt so complicated and there was no way to tell you without you wanting to get in touch with him, and then . . . then everything would have been different. I thought I would be enough for you. I know how selfish that seems now, but I thought I was doing the right thing."

"Maggie didn't need to find out." Jack's voice sounded like a child's. "You could have told my father and we could have had, I don't know, a secret relationship."

"It doesn't work like that, Jack. Marriage doesn't work like that. I understand that I deprived everyone by keeping the secret. I deprived you of a father and Ben of a son. I have no idea what would have happened if I had told him. I always thought he and Maggie had the perfect marriage, but it seems they didn't. Maybe it would have split them up, and maybe that wouldn't have been such a bad thing. At the time I always thought I couldn't be responsible for that. But now . . ." She trailed off again, not knowing what the right thing to have done would be, before tears sprang into her eyes again.

"I didn't want to share you with anyone. Oh, Jack, I am so sorry for fucking up so badly. My heart cracked open the day you were born, and everything I've done has been for you, and even though I've made mistakes, it was never to harm you, it was to protect you. I didn't want you torn between me and your father. I didn't want the stresses and problems. I didn't want you to feel that. I thought I loved you enough to fill the hole of not having a father. I thought I could provide everything you needed."

Jack stopped walking and turned to her. "You did, Mom. You were always there for me, and you always supported me. I knew what was going on when you were married to Lance and you always protected me. I guess I have sadness more than anything. Especially when I think back to those years. I hated how scared you were, and I wish I'd had a dad to guide me, or advise me. Even Maggie. I know she was your best friend in college, and I get it. But I wish I'd had the choice. I wish I'd been able to choose to have them in my life, even though I totally understand why you did what you did. It's just . . . I guess I feel betrayed. I always told myself that you probably didn't even know his last name, because if you did, you would have tracked him down and told him, and I could have had a father. I thought you would have done that for me."

Evvie wiped a tear away from her cheek. "I made a mistake. A huge one, and I wish I could go back and do things differently. I am so sorry."

"I'm going to go inside and get a soda. Do you want anything?"

Evvie shook her head, knowing that he needed to be alone, that this was his way of saying he needed a few minutes to breathe, to figure this out. She tried to take a deep breath but she had no idea what she'd done, or what the consequences would be.

When Jack came back twenty minutes later, he was putting his phone in his pocket. He walked over slowly and sat down next to her, looking at his hands.

"I love you, Mom, but I don't know what to do with this news. I think I need some space to try and figure this out."

"Are you furious with me? Do you hate me?"

"I could never hate you, but I'm . . ." He struggled to find the word. "Disappointed. I feel betrayed and I don't know how to get over that. I can't be with you right now."

Evvie wanted to let out a howl of pain,

but she couldn't. She nodded, leaking tears. "Can I drive you somewhere? Where will you go?"

"I don't know," he said. "I've called an Uber. I'll have it take me back to the house to get my stuff, and then I'll . . ." He stood up, still not looking at her. "I'll call you when I'm ready."

Evvie watched him walk away until she couldn't see through the tears anymore. She had spent the last few months terrified of losing Maggie, never dreaming that she might lose her son. And as he disappeared, her heart cracked open all over again.

FORTY-SEVEN

- 2019 -

Topher placed a cup of tea on the table in front of the sofa, looking at Maggie with concern.

"Thank God you didn't hit your head," he said. "Those flagstones don't look very forgiving. I put some whiskey in the tea. It's more of a hot toddy than a cup of tea, but I figured the whiskey would help with the shock."

"Did you know?" Maggie looked at Topher.

"My God, no! I was as stunned as you were. He got out of the car and I just stared at him. I had no idea. I guess this explains why none of us had ever seen pictures of him." Topher shook his head. "I don't know what to even think."

"I want to see her," Maggie said. "I want to know everything."

"She hasn't come back. Do you want me to text her?"

Maggie shook her head. "I'll do it myself. Can you pass me my phone?"

We need to talk, she typed. I'd like you to come . . . Maggie hesitated. She was going to write *home,* but that would be wrong, given what she now knew. This couldn't be Evvie's home anymore. She finished typing, to the house, watching as the three dots appeared on the screen and Evvie said she was on her way.

While they were waiting, a car pulled up outside. Topher went out to meet it, and then returned to the house to get a suitcase, which he carried outside. Maggie realized the boy . . . that boy, must be taking his bag and himself somewhere. But she couldn't think about that now.

Topher waited with Maggie until they heard Evvie walking up the gravel drive. After she had assured him she would be fine, he headed upstairs to give them some privacy.

Maggie sat up and watched Evvie walk in, as if she were watching a stranger. She thought she knew her so well, and yet it turned out she didn't know her at all.

"He's Ben's, isn't he." It was a statement, her voice too defeated to ask the question. "He's obviously Ben's, but I need to hear it from you."

Evvie nodded. "He is."

"How could you?" Maggie said after a pause, her voice cracking with bitterness. "You were supposed to be my best friend. How could you betray me like that? You bloody well slept with my husband, and you had his child! By rights, that's not even supposed to be your son. That's supposed to be *my* son!"

"I know." Evvie blinked away tears as a silence fell.

"Did Ben know about him?"

"No! He suspected, when Jack was born, but I fudged the dates and he believed me."

"He never saw him then."

"No. I was careful to keep everyone who knew Ben away from Jack."

"What on earth were you thinking, moving in here?" Maggie's voice rose in anger. "We're living together in my home, and all the time you had a son fathered by my husband. It's unbelievable." She let out a bitter laugh. "You didn't think it was inevitable that we'd meet at some point?"

"I know. It was selfish. It was stupid. On some level I think I must have wanted to be found out, but . . ." She shook her head. "I don't even know if that's true. I tried not to think about Jack. I just missed you. I missed you, and Topher, and I was lonely. Before the reunion it felt like there was nothing to look forward to. When we all saw each other again and started talking about living together, it sounded so amazing that I stopped thinking straight. I thought I could manage it, with Jack being so far away."

"How long were you having an affair with my husband?" Maggie said.

"It wasn't an affair. It wasn't like that."

"What was it like?"

Evvie sighed. "Can I get myself a drink first?"

"I'll have another one as well." Maggie downed the last of her hot toddy and took the teacup to the bar, this time not bothering with the tea, pouring a large slug of whiskey, and ignoring Evvie, standing behind her. Let Evvie make her own bloody drink.

"So." Maggie sat down again. "What was it like then?"

"It wasn't anything, Maggie. I know that's hard to believe. Remember when I stayed in town that week after graduation? That's when it first happened. I didn't plan anything. I didn't even like Ben, let alone fancy him, but I ran into him while he was doing some kind of scavenger hunt. Honestly, I don't even remember the details, but kissing me was somehow part of the prize. I know it sounds ridiculous, but that's what it was meant to be. Just a kiss for a photo. But then . . ."

"I remember," Maggie said. "I called you dutifully from the South of France every day, and you were never there, and you never returned my calls. That was the beginning of you slipping away from me. Now I know why."

"I felt so guilty," said Evvie. "I didn't know how I was going to face you again."

"Now I know why you were so hard to see or even talk to on the phone," said Maggie. "Keep going. So you holed up with him in your luxury hotel for a week."

"He would go out with friends and come over later, usually. When he was pretty drunk."

"Now that's a scenario I recognize," Maggie said bitterly. "He usually couldn't help himself when it came to drinking. What was your excuse?"

Evvie shook her head. "I didn't have one. I figured it was a weeklong fling, I was leaving for New York, and no one would ever know."

"Thank you for your loyalty." The sarcasm dripped from Maggie's lips.

"Maggie, at that point, he wasn't yours. Sure, you'd had something with him, but he didn't belong to you. He didn't belong to anyone."

"If that had been it, maybe I'd agree with you, but clearly that wasn't it. What happened when you left?"

"I got to New York and got on with my life, until I discovered I was pregnant. I phoned Ben after I had scheduled an abortion, and he . . ." She stopped. She didn't want to tell Maggie, but she didn't want to live with any more lies. "He asked if I would keep it. He said he could come to New York, or I could come to London, and we could make a go of it."

There was silence from Maggie, but her eyes started to well up.

"That would never have happened," Evvie burst out. "It was totally unrealistic."

"He wanted you first," Maggie whispered.

"He didn't. I mean, he may have, but it wasn't real. It was a week."

"So then what? Twenty-one years ago you decided you couldn't avoid him anymore and you had to have some fun with him one last time?" spat Maggie.

"He was in New York for a night. You told him to get in touch with me. He did. I didn't mean for anything to happen but we had a few drinks, of course, and . . . it happened. We slept together. I'm so sorry, Maggie. I regretted it instantly, and it was a one-time thing."

"I don't believe you. Tell me the truth. How many times?"

"I swear to you, Maggie, this time I am telling you everything. It was just that night, just once."

"I suppose you're going to tell me it meant nothing?" said Maggie.

Evvie shook her head. She had spent years thinking about that night, remembering how it felt to be with the only man she thought she had ever loved, a man she'd built up in her head as the perfect man, a man she only recently discovered she didn't know at all.

"No," she said. "It meant everything. I hadn't seen you in years, and I'd spent those years having disastrous romances with the same addicts and alcoholics over and over again. They followed a pattern, which is no surprise, given my father's history. As ridiculous as this sounds given what I now know, I held Ben up as the beacon of goodness; he was the one man who I thought wasn't abusive. He could have been the one man to make me happy. And yet, Maggie, you need to know this, despite that, I regretted it and I felt sick that he was married to you. I would be lying if I said it meant nothing."

"If this was such a big love affair, why didn't he leave me? He could have done. We were desperately trying for children at the time, and I couldn't get pregnant. It would have been easy for him to leave, especially given that you were the one who was able to bear his child."

"First of all, Maggie, he loved you. I'm not saying he didn't have feelings for me, but it's clear to me now that I was telling myself I felt more than I did. I clearly didn't even know him. He was probably telling himself he felt more than he did, too, especially if as you say you were struggling to have children at that time. All we really had between us was chemistry, that was all. And chemistry is never enough for a lasting relationship. As for Jack, he never knew about him. And, Maggie, whatever he may have thought he felt about me, it didn't detract from how he felt about you. I'm not sure either of us could have lived with hurting you. We both loved you too much for that. I honestly don't think I could ever have had a relationship with him knowing he was yours. I'm sorry. I'm so sorry." She paused and took a breath. "Seeing him that time was closure for both of us. I never saw him again."

Evvie closed her eyes. "And I thought I

couldn't see you again either. I couldn't look you in the eye, knowing what I had done. I am so, so sorry, Maggie. I know you won't ever be able to forgive me, even though I hope by some miracle you might be able to in time. I never ever meant to hurt you."

Maggie said nothing, staring down at the ground for a long time. When she reached for her teacup, Evvie saw that she was shaking as much as Evvie was. And Evvie waited. She had never known Maggie to shout, to get angry, but if ever there were a time when anger would be justified, this would be it.

Maggie downed the rest of her whiskey and looked over at Evvie. "I don't know what to say," she whispered, her voice small. "What a betrayal, Evvie. What a huge, awful betrayal. I believe everything you said about not wanting to hurt me, and yet here I am. Devastated."

"I'm so sorry. I'm so sorry." There was nothing else Evvie could say.

"Please stop saying that. If you never meant to hurt me, you would not have slept with my husband. I can just about get my head around your perfect week after we graduated, but I don't understand how you let it happen again when you knew he was married, and not just married, but married to *me.*" Maggie let out another bitter laugh before her eyes started to glisten. "You had his baby, and you never told him. I don't know which is worse. Do you have any idea how much he wanted a son? What he would have given to have had a son? Maybe he would have got sober if he'd known about his son." She gave a short, humorless snort. "God knows he couldn't do it for me."

"You're right about everything," Evvie said. "I can leave. If you want me to leave, I can go upstairs and pack right now." Even as she said it, she felt a mild panic. England may have once been her home, but without this house as her refuge, where was she supposed to go?

"I don't know what I want," said Maggie. "But I think you should leave. I can't have you here. Not now."

Evvie stood up, turning to go upstairs and pack.

"And there's one more thing," Maggie said. "I want to meet your son. Ben's son. Properly. I want to talk to him."

Upstairs, Evvie started to shake uncontrollably. Without warning, a sob escaped, until her entire body was racked with heaving sobs. She opened her mouth in a howl of pain, but no sound came out, and it was a long time until she could do anything other than lie on the bed, arms wrapped tightly around herself, rocking back and forth in a silent scream of pain.

FORTY-EIGHT

- 2019 -

Maggie had been feeling numb for the past
two hours, as if she were trapped in a sur-
real movie, a nightmare that she wanted to
wake up from, but there was no escaping it.
Topher came down and tried to comfort
her, but right now, she didn't want to talk
to anyone, other than this version of Ben,
the Ben she fell in love with all those years
ago.

Topher left with Evvie, piling her suitcases
into the car. She caught sight of his face,
and he looked ineffably sad as he and Evvie
loaded the car, Evvie's face puffy from crying. Maggie watched dispassionately. Good.
She was glad there was a consequence for
her betrayal.

The doorbell rang, and Maggie opened
the door, her breath taken away yet again
by this young man's face, the image of her
late husband before she fell out of love with
him, when she still thought that life held

every possibility, that they would create a perfect family.

Maggie couldn't take her eyes off him as she led him in, not knowing what she wanted to say to him, only that she needed to get to know him.

"Where did you go?" she asked, unable to tear her gaze away, marveling at his face, his hairline, that widow's peak she never thought she'd see again. She drank him in as he crouched down, stroking Scout.

Jack looked up at her question. "To a pub in the village. I needed a stiff drink."

Alarm bells went off immediately. "Is . . . I hope you don't think this presumptuous to ask, but are you a drinker? I mean, is alcohol your thing?"

Jack laughed. "Sadly, no. I'm known as the guy you don't want at your party. I'd like to be able to drink but it doesn't agree with me. I had a beer at the pub, which was pretty awful. It was warm."

"Ah yes." She laughed with relief. "That's how we drink them here.

"You must be in shock," she said. "The last thing you must have expected when you arrived was such a dramatic reaction."

"I don't think I'm in as much shock as you are," he said, offering a small smile.

"Indeed. Are you hungry, Jack? Can I

make you something to eat?"

"Yes, I'm starving. Thank you. I was going to order food at the pub, but then my mom called and told me to come over to talk to you."

Maggie got up and looked in the fridge. "I was about to do a big shop. We don't have too much but do you like eggs? Can I make you an omelet with fresh eggs from the chickens? Spinach? Feta? Onions? I have a homemade cake for after."

"That sounds amazing. All of it."

Maggie proceeded to do what she did best, the thing that comforted her, grounded her: feeding people, nurturing them. Her bones, her muscles, her nerves relaxed as she moved around the kitchen gathering ingredients.

She sautéed the onions, added the spinach and then feta, cracked the eggs into a bowl, whisked them, and seasoned and poured them into a sizzling pan, producing a pale golden omelet, slick with butter, that rolled around the other ingredients.

She toasted her homemade sourdough and slathered it thickly with butter, placing slices on either side of the omelet before sliding the plate in front of Jack. She made herself tea, then sat opposite him at the table as he devoured the food, unable to take her eyes off him, fascinated by every-thing he did.

He held his knife and fork in the same way that Ben did. She shook her head at the memory. How could that possibly be genetic, and yet, watching him eat was exactly like watching Ben.

"This may be the greatest omelet I've ever eaten in my life." Jack's mouth was full as he spoke, as Maggie remembered how much Ben loved her cooking, how, the very first night he had come back to her flat, she had made him an omelet, too, and he had wolfed it down, only pausing to tell her how delicious it was. She hadn't cooked for him for years by the time he died. It was her silent protestation at his drinking. If he didn't love her enough to stay sober, he didn't deserve her food.

A pang of guilt hit her. What if she had continued cooking for Ben, showing him she loved him through food? Would things have ended differently? Could she have saved him?

"Are you okay?" Jack peered at her.

"I'm fine," she said, brusquely pushing the thoughts away as she slid her chair back to bring over a huge wedge of cake.

He forked some into his mouth and briefly closed his eyes, swooning. "What is this?

This is the best cake I think I have ever eaten."

"It's a coffee and walnut cake with a toffee sauce running through it. It was one of your father's favorites."

"My father." Jack laid down his fork, his face serious again. "I look like him then?"

Maggie shook her head. "It's unbelievable. I'm sorry that I keep staring at you. It's just so . . . strange. Your dimples when you smile, he had exactly those dimples. Do you know what he looked like?"

Jack shook his head, following Maggie as she beckoned him to the living room, the two of them flanked by Scout, who seemed to have attached himself to Jack. There were photographs everywhere, and she picked one up, then another, handing them to Jack. The first was one of their wedding pictures, taken on the steps of the church, Maggie and Ben in the middle, flanked by Topher and Evvie, all of them grinning, although with the knowledge Maggie now had, she thought she saw that Evvie's smile was forced, that she must have been putting on an act.

"We look like the same person." Jack's voice was disbelieving.

"Yes."

He looked up at Maggie. "What was he

like? Tell me about him."

They sat on the deep sofa in the bay window, Maggie curled up like a cat, Scout in between them. Ben never allowed the dogs on the sofa, she remembered, feeling the solidity of Scout's warm, furry body pressed against hers, grateful for the comfort as she introduced Jack to his father.

She told him what she knew about his childhood, that his father — Jack's grandfather — was still alive, now living in Scotland, and that she only spoke to him a few times a year, on birthdays, Christmas, things like that; that he would be beside himself to know he had a grandson.

She told him about her crush on Ben at university, how she decided he was her perfect man long before he even knew who she was. She never knew why it was Ben, only that she never had eyes for anyone else.

She described walking into the cafeteria on the first day at her new company and seeing Ben, how they had gone for drinks on the Friday night. She thought back to that night, but didn't tell Jack the details. How Ben was a little drunk, she a little sober, how a tickling fight led to their kiss.

She told Jack how he loved football.

"You mean soccer?" Jack frowned.

"I mean football. Footie. He supported

Sheffield Wednesday." She told him how Saturday afternoons were always spent in front of the television, and how her whole family teased him about it, because no one in her family knew anything, nor cared, about football. She told him that he was a loyal friend, who would help out anyone in need. He would lend people money or give advice without blinking an eye, and he was never frightened of getting involved. If he saw an injustice, he would step in to try and right it, never thinking of the consequences.

Jack grinned when he heard this. "You're like this, too, aren't you?" Maggie guessed, and he nodded.

He was fearless, she told him. And he loved children. He was godfather to three of his friends' kids, and desperate for children of his own.

"He wanted a son," she said. "He wanted a son so badly. He wanted to bring his son to Sheffield Wednesday games, to be his pal. He would have . . ." She trailed off, gazing at Jack. "He would have loved to know you," she said, blinking away the tears.

She thought about telling him about Ben's drinking, but that could wait, she decided. Jack was so overwhelmed at finally discovering who his father was, it would be better for him to find out his flaws later and just let him enjoy getting to know the best of Ben for now. And in telling Jack about the best of Ben, Maggie began to remember it herself, and it was only when she had finished describing him that she realized a sense of peace had settled on her shoulders.

When she had told him everything she could think of, she asked Jack to tell her about himself, and he did. He told her about his childhood, how his mom had always put him first, that he didn't feel he missed out on not having a dad, because she made sure he was loved fiercely, although he always hoped he might find his father. He told her about playing soccer in elementary school, how things had changed when his mom got married. It had been the two of them, a perfect team, until Lance, and in the beginning it all seemed perfect. Lance gave Jack everything he had ever wanted, and Jack loved the idea of a family, until everything changed.

Jack talked about how his mom tried to protect him from his stepfather's rages, ushering him out of the room, trying to keep the fury from him, but he always knew. He wanted to protect her, but didn't know how. Jack's confusion was made worse by the fact that Lance could change in a heartbeat, so charming one minute, so frightening the next. It felt like standing on shifting sands, and as a young boy, he knew he didn't have the power to do anything.

Maggie knew some of this. Evvie had talked about it a little, but had never gone into detail. When Lance's name came up, which was rarely, Evvie had always quickly changed the subject.

A wave of remorse came over Maggie as she listened to Jack. Evvie may have betrayed her in the most terrible of ways, but look at the life she had led, the difficulties she had endured. On the outside she may have seemed glamorous, wealthy, as if she had everything she could ever possibly want, but no one had any idea what was going on behind her closed doors. Maggie had been in touch vaguely, but their friendship was one in name alone by that time. Where was *she* when Evvie was going through hell; where were Evvie's trusted old friends when she needed them most?

Maggie was furious with Evvie, but as she sat here, talking to Jack, she found her anger was transforming into emotions she wasn't sure she even had the words for. There was raw pain for what Maggie was going through, of course, but it was suddenly mixed with empathy and regret; the last things she wanted to feel.

Jack didn't notice. He kept talking, telling her of his relief when his mom left Lance and, standing on her own two feet again, had built a new life for herself. He talked about his college years, his love of computer science, his love of his friends, how he had landed an amazing job while he was still a senior, and that he loved California, but always had a sense that he didn't quite fit in anywhere. It wasn't that he didn't have friends, he explained, but that he had always felt like something of an *other.*

"Is that not having known your dad, do you think?" ventured Maggie.

"Maybe. Although it's more likely to be my own unique crazy mix. Part Jamaican, part American. And now half-English." He looked across at a photo of Ben, his gaze lingering for a couple of seconds before turning to the window. "I know this sounds crazy because I've been here for about five minutes, but . . ." He gazed outside, trailing off.

"You feel like you've come home?"

He turned to look at her. "It *is* crazy, isn't it? I felt it as soon as I stepped into the airport. I just have this sense of belonging."

"I don't know. I think it makes sense." She was staring at him again, catching herself with a quick laugh as she covered her face with her hands. "I'm sorry, Jack. I'm sorry I keep staring at you. Please don't think I'm a creepy old woman. It's just that . . . Ben would have loved you so much."

"I wish I'd known him."

"So do I," said Maggie, even though she had no idea what the impact would have been on their marriage. Now that he was gone, there was no point in being angry with Ben. And what if she had discovered this when they were together? What would she have done? Would she have stayed? Would she have left? She could never have forgiven a long-term affair, but if it truly had been, as Evvie said it was, a one-night stand, would she have been able to forgive that? She would have been devastated, and yet, Ben would have had a son. If she had managed to forgive him, if they had found a way to stay together, she would have had a . . . What would he have been? A stepson, she supposed. How different their life would have been. Jack coming to stay for holidays, Ben wrapping a Sheffield Wednesday scarf around his neck, taking him to the matches. She would have taught Jack to cook. Perhaps the three of them would have formed their own family, even though she was certain that twenty-one years ago, had she known, she would never have spoken to Evvie again.

And now? Now that Ben was gone? Now that Jack was here? A piece of Ben. A reminder of what they always wanted, what they couldn't have, what she might be able to have now. Although what right did she have to this young man? He was her late husband's illegitimate son, *not* her stepson. He was not part of her family, even though he felt like he should be.

Silence fell. Jack got up and picked up photographs, staring at his father as Maggie sat back in the chair, exhausted by the emotions of the day. Jack looked over at her. "What happens now? How do you feel about . . . my mom?"

Maggie shook her head, overwhelmed. "I have no idea. I have no idea how I feel about any of it. Other than meeting you, which feels like the most precious gift I've been given in ages. It's like having a piece of my husband back. It's so strange, seeing you smile, and watching the way you move. Your hairline!" Jack touched his hairline, self-conscious. "It's the Curran hairline. Your grandfather has it, too, that distinctive widow's peak. If it's freaking you out, tell me, but I could just sit here and look at you all day. Oh God, I'm sorry. I'll stop. I think I need a little bit of time to process all of this. We all need some time to sit with this. I can't have your mother here right now. I'm sorry. I hope you can understand that."

"I can." Maggie unfurled herself from the sofa, from Scout, with a long stretch. "I don't know how I feel about what she's done either. I'm pissed, and I don't want to see her now. Thank you, Maggie." He looked suddenly like a little boy. "Thank you for spending so much time with me, and for telling me about my father."

"I'm the one who should be thanking you for being so open with me. You've told me a lot about your family that I didn't know. It helps me to understand." And empathize, she thought. Although she didn't say it out loud.

Maggie wanted to put her arms around him, hug him, but didn't want to cross the line and make him uncomfortable. They stood awkwardly for a few seconds, with Maggie then bending down to pet Scout. "I'm going to go and make some tea." She gave Jack a smile and walked out of the room.

In the kitchen, alone, Maggie sank onto a chair and buried her face in her hands, breaking into sobs, feeling as if her heart was going to either burst with joy or break with pain.

She had no idea which way it was going to go.

FORTY-NINE

- 2019 -

Topher had felt lost ever since Jack showed up, exploding their happy little family. It wasn't Jack's fault, he was the last one Topher blamed, but the fact remained: nothing would ever be the same again.

The house was much too quiet without Evvie, and he had barely seen Maggie. He tapped on her door last night to ask if she needed anything, expecting her to invite him in as she usually would, for him to crawl on her bed and chat like old times, but she just said she was going to sleep. He knew she was lying because the light stayed on in her bedroom for hours.

He stepped into the garden and took out his cell phone. In the old days, he had a myriad of friends to call. He thought back to his life in New York, the parties, the openings, the galleries, the theater. He had a hundred people he could have phoned to accompany him anywhere, to meet for a drink, or dinner. Now, he scrolled through the names in his contacts, all of whom were in New York. There was literally no one in the UK other than his mother. Good God, he thought. This was really too sad that the only other person he could call here was her. He had been lonely since Evvie left, and found himself missing Dickie and reminiscing about Larry. Wouldn't it be lovely, he thought, to have a relationship at this stage of life.

"Darling!" Joan said when she picked up the phone. "This is a lovely surprise. What are you up to?"

"Not much," Topher said, eyeing the lawns stretching ahead of him, the trees, the only sound the odd bird chirruping, and the clucks of the chickens in the distance. He decided not to tell her about the drama that had recently unfolded. "We have a new dog who is lovely. Scout. I was thinking about maybe taking him for a walk. I thought he'd like to see the sea, so I was going to drive over to you. Does that work for you?"

"A dog? How lovely! A walk would be heavenly, but I'm afraid I've got plans this afternoon. I wish you'd called earlier. I'm going out with one of my gentleman friends."

Topher steeled himself. Oh God. Not this again. Please God let this not be his father, or some beau from the fifties. Please God let her not be confused.

"Who's the gentleman friend?" he asked warily.

"You haven't met him. His name is Pierre Van Cate. He's Dutch. Ever so handsome."

"And . . . does he live in Weston-super-Mare as well?"

"He does," she said happily. "We met at my dance class."

"Dance class?" Topher started to smile. Only his mother.

"I know! Isn't it fun? I started ballroom dancing, and this very tall, handsome man came straight up to me when we were asked to find partners. He's taking me out for tea today, and next week he's making me dinner. He looks after me, Topher." Her voice dropped. "When I don't remember things. When I get confused."

"That's wonderful, Mom." Topher felt relieved. "I'm glad you've found someone. Have a lovely time."

"Thank you, darling. Love you," she said, and blowing kisses, she disconnected the call. Topher looked at his phone. Great, he thought. My eightysomething mother has a better social life than me.

He walked around the garden, turning and studying the lawn by the house, the one that ran down from the French doors in the drawing room. It was just flat lawn, doing nothing. He'd been thinking about this lawn for a while now. It was such a pity that the grounds of the house were boring old grass with a few grand trees and the lake in the distance. A house as lovely as this demanded gardens that were equally lovely.

In the outbuildings he pulled out a tape measure and a can of fluorescent paint from a plastic bag and took them over to the large lawn off the terrace. There was a high, old brick wall on one side, covered in ivy and a rambling clematis Montana that, he had learned, bloomed with a profusion of small pink flowers every May. This was the spot he had been studying. It faced southwest, got the sun all day, and the more he looked at it, the more he thought it would be the perfect place for a *potager,* a kitchen garden that was as productive as it was beautiful.

It would be semi-walled, with six symmetrical beds, surrounded by a low clipped box hedge. He had plans for a luscious perennial border on each side, a profusion of whites and greens, à la Vita Sackville-West.

His imagination had been working overtime. He had a spot for a limestone plinth on which would sit an armillary sphere, which would face a bench on the other side, where Topher could see himself drinking tea every morning (he was an avowed coffee drinker, but in his fantasy he was not only fitter and slightly taller than he was now, his middle-aged paunch having magically disappeared, he also, somewhat miraculously, had learned to start his day with tea).

He had been thinking about this all a lot, had even made drawings. He went to WHSmith and bought himself a sketchbook, a set of pencils, and an eraser, and had been sitting at the small desk in his room, sketching out a series of ideas.

But now it was all threatened. Maggie had kicked Evvie out, and now what would happen? Would he even be able to stay here? Wouldn't Maggie sell the house now? If he could talk to her about her future plans, he would, but she had retreated, like a wounded bird.

He suspected she might be annoyed with him because he was refusing to take sides. Of course Evvie did a terrible thing, but Topher was an adult and well aware that people fucked up, they made mistakes. Even though Evvie may have done a terrible thing in having a dalliance with Ben, he couldn't hate her for it, couldn't cut her off. He always suspected Evvie felt more strongly about Ben than she was letting on; he saw the chemistry between them at the wedding. Not that it would have made a difference; it was at Ben and Maggie's *wedding,* for God's sake.

So here he was, living this idyllic life in the heart of the English countryside, with his favorite people in the world, about to do a landscape design course that would hopefully qualify him to turn this newfound passion into a business. And he had such wonderful plans for the garden here, to turn it into a showpiece. And now it looked like it was all coming to an end.

Fuck it, he thought an hour ago. He wasn't going to sit around and cry over something he had no control over. Maybe he'd still do the garden here anyway. Who knows, maybe they'd all leave this house but Maggie would let him do the garden, as a kind of thank-you, a showpiece for the business he hoped to soon have.

He had absolutely no control over what Maggie or Evvie was feeling, or what they were planning to do. But he did have control over his own actions, and he did have control over the garden. Maggie had said that he could do whatever he wanted, and there was no time like the present to get started, before she changed her mind. And if nothing else, it would take his mind off the shit show that had gone down inside the house with the appearance of Jack.

He smiled when he thought of Jack, despite himself. It was the most bizarre thing imaginable, seeing this facsimile of Ben. He had never known Ben well, but because of Maggie's crush in college, Ben had always been a part of Topher's story, and would have remained so, even if Maggie hadn't ended up marrying him. There was something kind of awful and lovely about this surprise reemergence of a part of their past, even though Jack, clearly, was less Maggie's past and more her future, perhaps.

Maybe, he thought. And then he decided not to think about it at all.

It was almost dusk when Maggie came outside. Topher had measured the beds and sprayed them with fluorescent paint, just to check they were in the right place. When he was happy with the placement, he staked the corners with bamboo sticks and string, constantly stepping back to check, amazed how his vision came together so quickly.

He had dug out two beds by the time

Maggie strode across the garden. The Barbour was on the ground, as was his cashmere sweater, and his shirt was not only filthy, but wet with sweat. He hadn't done this sort of physical labor since . . . well, possibly not ever. It felt great in an exhausting sort of way.

"What the . . . ?" Maggie stood in the garden, her mouth agape, as Topher put the shovel down and pushed his hair off his face, leaving another muddy mark on his forehead.

"What are you *doing,* Bob the Builder? What on *earth* is going on out here?"

"I'm building a *potager.*"

"Now?"

"There's no time like the present. I'm thinking of a perennial white border, and then herbs in the beds."

"And you're planning on doing this all by yourself."

"Not really." He grimaced, leaning on the shovel. "I was planning on just marking it out and paying gardeners to do the actual labor, but then I got carried away. Are you okay, Maggie? Do you want to talk? I've been trying to pin you down for days but I feel like you're avoiding me."

"I'm not avoiding you. That's not true, I am avoiding you but don't take it personally. I'm not ready to talk about this with anyone just yet. There's too much going on in my head. I need to let it all settle down a bit."

"Have you heard from Evvie?"

"No! And I don't expect to. I've spoken to Jack though. A few times. Apparently she's staying in a B and B, and he's couch surfing. I have no interest in speaking to Evvie right now."

"I understand. Listen, if you want me to move out, I can . . ."

"Oh, Topher. I'm sorry. I know none of this is going the way we all expected. I don't know what I want right now, and I have no idea what to do. I've decided to take a little break from it all. I'm running away for a few nights to Lucknam Park. I just need a change of scenery."

"Do you want company?"

"No. Thank you. I feel like I'm suffocating a bit with the weight of all this knowledge. I need some peace and quiet. And I need to get away from this house, and all my memories of Ben here. I've booked a few spa treatments and plan on going on lots of long, solitary hikes. I feel like the quiet will help, and I need to be on my own."

"Oh, Maggie. I'm so sorry. You know I had no idea about Jack. You do believe me, don't you?"

"Of course I believe you. But that boy. Man. It's just so confusing. It's like having a piece of Ben back. I don't know what to do about that either."

"I know. It's weird, and awful, and amazing, all at the same time. The similarities are uncanny. I can't imagine what this is like for you."

Maggie let out a deep sigh. "As strange as this may sound, I think I needed this. I was so full of resentment against Ben, and then the guilt when he died. We had been miserable for so long, and I was so angry, and sad, and guilty at not being able to stop him drinking." She paused. "I did tell you about his drinking, didn't I?"

"You did."

"I'm sorry. I am so used to keeping the secret, I can't even remember who I've told. I felt like when he died, all I was left with were miserable memories. But seeing Jack has brought back some of the good memories. Not just university, but the early days of our relationship. This makes no sense to me, but as horrific as this whole situation has been, there's also some healing going on for me. Wherever this leads, the only thing I'm certain of is that this is righting some of the wrongs in my relationship with

Ben, at least in terms of memory."

"Then I'm glad. And I'm happy you're getting away for some alone time. I would give you a hug but I think I'd get you filthy." Topher gestured down at himself as Maggie leaned over and planted a kiss on his cheek.

"Thank you for understanding. I'll be back on Thursday. Take care of the house, and Scout." She blew him a kiss and disappeared as Topher picked up the gardening tools and started to put them away.

FIFTY
- 2019 -

Topher and Jack moved the sofa to the window as Evvie stepped back and considered it, before nodding.

"Thank you. You were right, Topher, that's where it should go." She wished she could feel better about this small apartment, but it felt like she was taking more steps backward than she would ever have wished. She didn't want to be living on her own again, didn't want to be working part-time in the pub downstairs to subsidize her rent. Didn't want to have this strained, difficult relationship with her only son.

But she had no choice. This was her penance, and as such, she accepted it, even as she prayed it wouldn't last. She had felt devastated ever since Jack showed up, ever since she was kicked out of the house.

Every morning she woke up with a small unsettled feeling in her stomach, quickly followed by a wave of grief as she thought about all that she had lost. There were plenty of days when she didn't want to get up and face the world, wanted to bury herself and hide from the pain, but she couldn't. She had a job, and a semblance of a life. However hard it was to push the pain aside, she didn't have a choice.

Evvie hadn't seen Jack. She had texted him regularly, and sometimes he texted back. She believed he would forgive her, because the alternative was not something she could contemplate.

And today, he was here, helping her move into her new apartment above the pub. It was the first time she had seen him since he arrived, and she couldn't stop looking at him, wanting to hug him tight but taking it slowly, tiptoeing around him, knowing he had to come to her in his own time.

"That's it." Jack set down the last of the boxes and looked around. "No more boxes."

"That can't be it." Topher frowned, remembering how many boxes Evvie had when she moved in to Maggie's. "Where's the rest of it?"

"I'm only bringing the bare essentials. Look at this place. I couldn't fit all the stuff." She didn't add that she only signed a lease for six months, by which time she was hoping that Maggie would have forgiven her, and she might be able to move back.

She had tried to talk to Maggie a number of times, but Maggie wasn't interested. She responded to Evvie's texts, but said she wasn't ready, or there was nothing to talk about.

So Evvie had taken a job in a pub in Bruton, which came with its own small flat above. The flat was poky, and dark, with old green carpets and one small window overlooking the pub garden, but Evvie was allowed to paint the burgundy walls white, and throw away the old carpet, revealing wooden floorboards, which brightened it up somewhat.

Topher, with Jack, helped get it ready before moving her in today. There was so much work to do that there was no time for any serious talks, which was good, thought Evvie, who wanted to plead for forgiveness, but couldn't push.

The three of them unpacked the boxes, arranged the sofa, and set up the bookshelves she had found at the local Oxfam store. Evvie was desperate for Jack to stay, but he had hardly looked at her.

"How about dinner?" she said brightly when everything was done. "My treat. We could go downstairs to the pub. They do an excellent burger." The last was said for

Jack's benefit.

"I should go," Jack said, shuffling toward the door. "I've got . . . things to do."

"I'll walk you out." Evvie managed to keep the desperation out of her voice as she walked him down the old, narrow staircase.

"Jack," she said, when they were outside on the pavement. "Please, can we talk? We can't let things stay like this." She knew she shouldn't be pushing him but the pain was unbearable. She couldn't help herself.

Jack looked at the ground with a sigh. "I'm seeing you, Mom. Isn't that enough? I came here today, even though I'm still not ready. I still need more time."

"I understand that, Jack. Or at least, I'm trying to. But I'm your mother. You have to forgive me. I can't stand this tension between us."

"You should have thought of that before." Evvie snapped, her pain breaking through her patience. "I should have, you're right. You're absolutely right, but I did the best I could do and I thought I was doing the right thing. I've always tried to do the right thing by you, Jack. Always. Have I been a bad mother? Haven't I always made sure you've had everything you've needed? And not just materially. I've always been there for you. Do I wish I had done things differently regarding your father? Of course. But I can't go backward, so we have to find a way to move forward. I don't even know when you're leaving. At least tell me what your plans are so I can see you before you go."

Jack stuck his hands in his pockets and looked up at the sky. "I was thinking about staying for a bit."

"What do you mean, *staying*? Where? How?"

There was a pause before Jack spoke. "Maggie said I could stay at the house for a bit."

Evvie stared at him. "Why would she do that?"

"Because she wants me to know about my family. *I* want to know about my family. I have a grandfather who I've spoken to on the phone, and he's coming down from Scotland to meet me. I have an aunt, and cousins. This is the family I could have had all my life, if you hadn't made the decision to keep them from me."

"I'm your family, too, Jack," said Evvie wearily. "I'm the one who has always been there for you."

"You created this," Jack said, before sighing. "Look, I have to go." He turned to leave.

"Jack!" she called out, but he didn't stop

546

walking, and she burst into tears.

Upstairs, Topher tried to comfort her. "He's a young man who's had a big shock. You can understand why he's upset with you."

Evvie's sobs had diminished to occasional hiccups. "Of course, but how long is he going to feel like this? And now he's moving in with you guys? I feel like Maggie's stealing my son to get back at me."

"That's not what's happening," Topher reassured. "I know that's what it looks like, but she's just offering to give him the father, the family, he didn't know. You are always going to be his mother, Evvie. No one can ever replace you. And he loves you. He just needs to get over this, and he needs to find out where he comes from."

"You don't think Maggie's trying to replace me?" She looked up at him with red, puffy eyes.

"Come on, Evvie. This is Maggie. She isn't vindictive. She's a nurturer. She's trying to take care of her husband's son. She's entranced by him, and who can blame her? Not only have you raised a great kid, he's the image of Ben. I can't blame her for wanting to do stuff for him. I think she probably does feel maternal toward him, but she's not his mother. She's very clear about that. And however he's acting now, it's because he's in pain. He still loves you. You're his mother."

Whatever unease Evvie felt, she recognized this as being part of her penance, and she let out a deep sigh. At least she and Jack were in the same county; at least she had a chance to keep asking for forgiveness, to rebuild their relationship.

She nodded. "I guess you're right. As hard as it is, there's nothing I can do, is there?"

Topher sank onto the sofa. "I don't think there is. Not just yet. But give this time. Who knows what will happen? In the meantime, are you sure you're going to be okay here?" He looked around at the dim room. "This is pretty shitty. Not where you expected to end up when you flew over here." He looked at her expression, then winced. "I'm sorry, let me rephrase that. This flat is fine, and it's better than the Airbnb, but . . ." He sighed. "I miss you. The house feels empty without you. I love having Jack around but this whole thing is weird."

Evvie sat down next to him. "Do you think you might be able to work on Maggie? Do you think you might be able to get her to forgive me?"

"I'm trying. I think we may have to let her get there by herself. You know how Maggie retreats when she's hurt. If it helps, I do feel she'll get over it. I don't think this will be forever. And Jack showed up today, which is a start. He'll come around."

Evvie leaned her head on his shoulder. "I hope you're right."

FIFTY-ONE

Maggie still couldn't quite believe that Jack was staying with her. She didn't know whether or not to ask, knowing how much it would hurt Evvie, but how could she not take this boy in? He couldn't stay couch surfing, whatever that was, and God knows she had the room.

Ben's father and Jack had long chats on FaceTime, and he was coming down next week to meet him, overjoyed at having a long-lost grandson. Ben's older sister, whom Maggie never got on with particularly well, had invited Jack to come and stay and meet his two cousins.

And every minute that Jack spent under this roof, he plied Maggie for stories about his father, delighted at the things he found in common, vintage cars for one, awed at the classic Austin-Healey that was in the garage, Ben's pride and joy, which Maggie had never got around to selling.

Maggie was cooking him all the food that Ben loved: roast beef and Yorkshire pudding, chicken Kiev, toad-in-the-hole. Good English comfort food, most of which Jack never had in his life.

She watched him now over the rim of her wineglass as he ate, eating all the vegetables first, just like Ben used to do, saving the best for last. She was aware she was smiling as she watched, embarrassed when she looked over to see Topher watching her.

"Stop staring at him," he said. "You'll make the poor boy uncomfortable."

"Don't worry about me," said Jack, his mouth full. "I'm getting used to it."

"I'm sorry. I'm sorry. I must seem so creepy. I'll try to stop. So what are your plans, Jack? How long do you think you're staying?"

"Do you need me to leave?"

"No! The opposite. You're welcome to stay here as long as you want. I'm just wondering what you'll do."

"I was just texting with a friend in New York yesterday, and he's introducing me to someone who lives over here and needs some consulting work, so hopefully I'll be working soon enough."

"Your dad would have been proud. He loved his gadgets, although I don't know if he would have figured out how to use social media properly."

"It's not complicated."

"Snapchat is complicated," said Topher pointedly. "I have no idea how it works and I've tried. Believe me, I've tried."

Jack laughed. "My mom always said the same . . ." He trailed off, embarrassed at having brought his mother up. "Sorry." He shot a look at Maggie. "I didn't mean to make you uncomfortable."

"I'm not uncomfortable," Maggie said gently, for she wasn't. "How is your mum? Have you seen her since she moved in?"

"Briefly. I'm not sure I know how to get over this and make things normal between us again. Look, she's my mom, and I love her. I guess I'm still shocked that she was capable of this kind of deceit. I know I'll get over it, but I don't know when."

"Jack." Maggie shot Topher a worried look. "I know you must be devastated, and I understand why. God knows I feel betrayed as well, but . . . none of us is infallible. We are all human and we all make mistakes."

Jack looked skeptical. "We don't all make mistakes like *that*. I don't believe you would have kept that kind of a secret." He paused. "And I don't think my father would have either. I'm trying to understand but I can't get there. I just feel so disappointed."

Maggie set her knife and fork down and took another swig of wine, catching Topher's eyes as he shot her a knowing look. She hadn't wanted to tell Jack about Ben's alcoholism. Of course in time she would have to, but she wanted to allow him to believe that his father was perfect, at least for a little while longer. But Ben wasn't perfect. The constant lies he told every day were just as destructive as the one big secret Evvie had kept.

"Oh, Jack," she said softly. "You don't know the whole story."

"I know enough of the story to know that she kept a secret that turned out to be far more damaging than if she had been honest. From everything you've told me, my father was amazing. She deprived me of not just a father, but of an incredible role model."

Maggie sighed deeply. She couldn't let this one slide, could no longer let Jack blame his mother, believing his father was perfect. "That's not true, Jack. There's more about your father I haven't told you."

Jack stopped eating. "What do you mean?"

And Maggie told him. She told him about the drinking, the ugly truth of the disease.

She told him she didn't blame Ben now, believed, finally, after all the reading that she had done, that he had a disease and he couldn't help himself. She told Jack about how his father could be unreliable, would disappear, would hide bottles and drink when no one was watching. She told him about Ben passing out, and all the covering up she did.

She told Jack gently, without emotion, and when she finished, she took Jack's hand in her own.

"I loved him, Jack. He was a wonderful man who was also deeply, deeply flawed. Like all of us, he had so much good, but he wasn't *all* good. No one is, and you can't keep blaming your mother while you put your father on a pedestal."

Jack nodded, taking a deep breath, as if he couldn't quite digest what Maggie had just told him.

"I think." She turned to Topher. "I think perhaps it's time for me to speak to Evvie."

FIFTY-TWO

- 2019 -

Evvie was in the pub, working, astounded that she was managing to get on with her life, despite losing everything and everyone that mattered to her. No one here would know. She was able to leave her grief behind each time she stepped behind the bar. Bartending was a perfect distraction. The locals were all entranced by her, all buying her drinks at the end of the evening, seemingly amazed to have someone so glamorous working in their little pub.

Harry and Ruby were her favorite regulars. An older couple who had run an old-fashioned tearoom in Bruton for years called, naturally, Ye Olde Tea Roomes, they came to the pub every night, a glass of white wine for Ruby, a pint of lager for Harry. They sat at the corner table, holding hands, not talking much but always happy to be in each other's company.

Harry came in by himself and sat at the

bar, the first time Evvie had seen him without Ruby.

"Just a pint for you tonight, Harry? Where's Ruby?"

Harry sighed. "She had a fall this morning. She's fine, but a nasty gash on her leg. We spent the morning up at the hospital, and she's got to keep her leg up for a couple of weeks."

"I'm so sorry to hear that. Are you going to be okay at the tearoom? I know how hard she works. I could help out if you need it."

"We're going to close down. Ruby wanted to close it months ago but I wouldn't, and now I feel terrible. We closed today." He blinked, looking lost.

"Oh, Harry. I am so sorry." Evvie laid her hand on his and squeezed it. "You can't feel guilty. These things happen."

"They do. I just wish she hadn't hurt herself, but it's clearly time for us to sell up. Ruby wants to do a round-the-world cruise for our fiftieth anniversary, so now she's on the couch with a pile of brochures."

"You're selling the tearoom?" An idea started to form in Evvie's mind. It wasn't what she had originally planned, opening a café without Maggie, but maybe she could find another partner, raise the financing to do it herself.

Harry nodded. "I've got the agents coming round next week."

Evvie had been to the tearooms, an old stone building, small in the front, but with a rabbit warren of rooms that stretched back to a small courtyard. The interior hadn't been touched since the seventies: heavy dark beams, a swirling orange carpet, small round tables dotted around, and tea carts piled with cakes baked by Ruby that creaked their way slowly around the room from table to table.

The couple of times Evvie had been, once with Maggie, once with Topher, she couldn't understand how the business kept going, other than the locals' love and loyalty to Harry and Ruby. How she could transform it! Throw out the carpet, knock down the cheap partition walls. Add planking and skylights to the cheap 1970s addition at the rear, banquette seating along the side, French doors onto the courtyard.

"What do you think you're going to ask, Harry?" Evvie struggled to keep her voice calm, excitement bubbling up inside her. "Because I'm interested. I'm very, very interested, and I'd love to talk further."

Harry sat up, more alert than he had looked all evening. "If you mean what you're saying, I'll talk to Ruby." He named the price they were thinking of, which seemed insanely huge to Evvie. She balked slightly, but took a breath. Topher would help her find the money, she was sure of it, and her motto had always been "Where there's a will, there's a way."

"Are you still interested?" Harry peered at her and she nodded. "How about coming over and taking a look then? Sooner rather than later would be best."

"How's later this week?"

Harry nodded. "You just let me know. Do mornings work?"

Evvie nodded, leaving to go into the back room, where she wrapped her arms around herself and took some deep breaths. It would be perfect. It was exactly the space she and Maggie were looking for before . . . Well. Before.

She knew exactly what she would do with Ye Olde Tea Roomes to make it beautiful, and exactly what kind of food she would serve to bring people in. The tearoom would make a perfect breakfast joint. All she had to do was find the money, and she could do it, she thought. She always got what she wanted eventually. She just had to figure out how.

In her pocket, her cell phone vibrated. She pulled it out and looked at the text that had just come in.

I'm ready to talk. Can we meet for coffee tomorrow? The River House at 11?

It was from Maggie. "Thank you, God," whispered Evvie, looking up toward the ceiling, and as she typed back a yes, a large smile appeared on her face.

FIFTY-THREE
- 2019 -

Evvie got to the River House first, unsure of what Maggie would say to her. For all she knew, Maggie could be putting the house on the market, could tell Evvie she needed to get the rest of her stuff out by the end of the week. She could tell her she never wanted to see her again, that their friendship was well and truly over.

But somehow she didn't think so. Not that you can read anything into a text, but Evvie felt that Maggie's text was gentle; she felt that Maggie had found a way to . . . if not forgive Evvie exactly, then to perhaps let bygones be bygones.

Or was that simply her own wishful thinking?

She liked that they were meeting on neutral territory, and in this cozy café, with its whitewashed stone walls and worn, wide-plank wood floors. Evvie took a seat by the window and ordered a flat white, drumming her fingers nervously on the table as she waited for Maggie to arrive.

The door opened and Maggie walked in, and Evvie's first instinct was to rush over and hug her. Maggie was smiling ever so slightly, and Evvie felt a prick of tears — oh, but she had missed her!

"Hi." Maggie bustled over, slipping off her faux fur vest.

"You're still rocking the trendy look then." Evvie attempted levity.

"Topher won't let me go back to what he calls frumpy country maid," she said, and she laughed as Evvie started to relax.

Maggie ordered a cappuccino, then sank her chin in the palm of her hand, looking at Evvie.

"You look well. I've missed you. How's the bartending going?"

"It's going well. I'm surprised at how much I'm enjoying being out in the world. Everyone who comes in is lovely. It's one of the nicest jobs I've ever had."

"And the flat?"

"Pretty grotty. Did Topher tell you? Or . . . Jack?"

"Topher. I think he was ever so slightly horrified." She took a breath. "I want to talk to you about Jack. Well, not just Jack, but

us. Everything. I want to talk about everything."

"Okay. Where do you want to start? I
know Jack's staying with you."

"He is, and you understand why? You
understand that I'm not trying to be a sur-
rogate mother, but that he is desperate to
know the other half of where he comes
from. And . . ." She shrugged. "I love having him there. He's so like the best parts of
Ben. And you. I see so much of you in him
as well."

"Thank you, I think."

"It's a compliment. We were having sup-
per the other night and I know he's been
pretty angry with you, which hasn't been
helped by the fact that he has clearly put
his father on a pedestal. I didn't want to
speak ill of the dead, but it was wrong to let
him carry on thinking that you are the one
at fault when his father was perfect. So I
told him about Ben's other side. The alcoholism. The lies. I told him that none of us
is perfect, that we are all doing the best we
can, and that yes, you have made some huge
mistakes, but so did his father. So did I."

"Okay," said Evvie. "Thank you. How did
Jack take the news?"

"I suspect it was hard for him to hear, but
it's not right that he blames you completely

for this. And I don't think it's right that I blame you completely for this either. Ben was amazing when sober, and made terrible decisions when he was drunk. I'm not saying I can forgive you completely, because you were equally culpable, but I'm trying. I want to try. I've been thinking about nothing else since Jack showed up, and the one thing I've realized is you don't get to make these kinds of friendships at this stage of life unless you are very, very lucky. I don't want to take a chance at making these kinds of friendships again. You and Topher have brought a happiness and contentment to my life that I didn't think I'd ever have again, and now Jack . . ." She trailed off, smiling as she thought of Jack. "Jack has brought me peace. Getting to spend time with him has got rid of the bad memories and brought back so many of the good."

Evvie was smiling as tears ran down her cheeks. "Does this mean we can still be friends?"

"I love you, Evvie. I always will, and I want us to try. Does that sound okay?"

"It does." Evvie nodded. "It does." And as the tears streamed down her face, she took Maggie's hand gently, tentatively in her own. Maggie smiled and waited patiently as Evvie cried.

But eventually, Evvie took a deep breath and wiped her eyes. She looked at Maggie adoringly and said, "And now that we're friends, will you come and see Ye Olde Tea Roomes with me?"

"Why? It's not for sale, is it?"

"Not yet. The agents are going to see it next week. We could get in tomorrow morning. If you still want to?" She took Maggie's hand again and looked at her.

Maggie took a sip of coffee as she thought, and then nodded. "No commitments," she said. "But let's look. Just for fun."

FIFTY-FOUR

- 2019 -

Topher was gathering up his things at the end of class. The others were going to the pub for a drink, but he couldn't join them tonight. He promised Maggie and Evvie he'd help with the styling (he'd also done the painting, but, it transpired, painting was not a skill at which he particularly excelled).

There was a guest lecturer today, Roger Eaves, a well-known gardener who had a number of television shows and was currently hosting a gardening program on Radio 4. Topher was the only one who wasn't terribly excited about him, only because he wasn't a big television watcher, and he didn't know who Roger Eaves was. The rest of the class — a mix of middle-aged women and retired men, with four very handsome younger men who Topher was somewhat fascinated by, even though they were all resolutely straight, with girlfriends and busy social lives — had spent the past week twittering with excitement about actually meeting Roger Eaves.

Roger had walked in this morning, terribly attractive, with thinning sandy blond hair and craggy, weather-beaten looks, and Topher had sat up a little straighter in his chair. Hel-*lo,* he thought. I wasn't expecting *this.* And then: Might he bat for my team? he thought, for there was something about the way he moved, the way he spoke, and the way his gaze kept alighting on Topher, that was, Topher thought, *curiouser and curiouser.*

"Are you joining us at the pub?" Topher looked up to find Roger at his desk, the others all moving toward the door in a large crowd.

"I can't," Topher said regretfully. "I promised to help out a friend with something." Damn, he thought. This was the first man who had stirred his interest in years, the first man who might actually, possibly, be interested in him, but Topher had no choice but to blow him off.

"That's a pity. I know I've been teaching you all day but we haven't been formally introduced. Roger Eaves. How do you do?" They shook hands as Topher introduced himself. "I can hear you're American," said Roger. "Are you here temporarily to do the course?"

Topher shook his head. "No. My parents lived here when I was young, so I went to university here, many, many lifetimes ago. My mother is living here again, and getting older, so I decided to follow her over."

"You're living with your mother?" Roger raised an eyebrow.

Topher laughed. "Most definitely not. She wouldn't have me. Her social life is far too busy. What can I do?" He shrugged as Roger smiled.

"I know this may sound strange," said Roger, "but there's something terribly familiar about you. Is it possible that we would know each other from somewhere?"

Oh, I *wish,* thought Topher, realizing that Roger was becoming more and more attractive as he spoke. Topher shook his head before pausing. He didn't usually mention this, certainly not over here where it meant nothing, but it was possible that Roger may have caught him in something, seen him on television.

Topher cast his mind back to his former life, a life he had rarely thought about since moving here. He started off phoning Dickie every day, just to check on him, but Dickie and Cookie were having such a good time, he rarely picked up the phone anymore. All those years with Dickie, and already it felt like it happened lifetimes ago.

"I used to be an actor. Maybe you've seen me in something? I was in a rather ghastly soap opera for years and years."

"No." Roger frowned and shook his head. "I don't think that's it."

"The steam rooms on Houston in 1992?" Topher said, deliberately making a joke to see Roger's reaction, to see if he was indeed batting for Topher's team.

Roger gave a wry grin. "I wasn't in New York in 1992, but I do remember those steam rooms."

Yes! thought Topher. *Score!*

"I think it's something to do with theater. Is that possible? Were you connected with theater?"

"I did a little off-Broadway but not anything I imagine you would have seen. Although I did have a long-term relationship with someone . . ."

Roger narrowed his eyes then smiled. "It wasn't Benedict Burroughs, by any chance, was it?"

Topher started. "It *was*! Do you know him?"

"I don't know *him* but I have a great friend in New York, Cookie Kempson, who . . ."

"Oh my God! You know Cookie?"

Roger laughed. "We're old friends. What a small world! I can't believe our paths haven't crossed given that you're now living here. How have I not run into you at a dinner party, or a cocktail party? What on earth have you been doing socially, and if you haven't been going out, why, may I ask, have you been hiding yourself under a stone?"

"I live with friends," Topher said.

"Ah." Roger nodded. "You're in a long-term relationship. Still, you have to go out."

"No," Topher laughed. "I'm not in a relationship. I'm single. I do live with friends, but it's been a bit all-consuming. Quite a bit of drama for a while there. Also, I had no idea where to go to meet . . . people like us. I looked online but the only thing I could find were LGBTQ meet-ups that looked like they might have been a bit sad and desperate. I couldn't face it."

"Funny boy. I wish we'd met earlier. I'm going to a dinner party tomorrow night in Frome. Lovely boys, David and Matthew. David's a literary agent, and Matthew's a choreographer. They've been up here for eons, and I think you'll love them. Why don't you come?"

"They won't mind?"

"Absolutely not. The more the merrier."

"This isn't a date, is it?" Topher asked, with a grin and a frank gaze.

"Why, no! It's just a dinner party," said Roger, but he was smiling as he said it.

"That sounds wonderful." Topher tried to contain his excitement at finally finding the people he'd been looking for, the people he didn't even know existed here. Not that he didn't love his old friends, but living with Maggie, and now Jack, had felt like living in a microcosm; it wasn't real life, it wasn't the real world. He adored the house, adored Maggie and Jack, and Evvie, but it would be even better if he had a circle of friends outside of them, a social life with other people! Frankly, he'd spent the last year wondering where all the gay men were.

"I'm going to return the invitation with one of my own." Topher was astounded to hear the flirtation in his voice. It had been so long since he was attracted to someone, so long since he had flirted that he thought he had forgotten how to do it. He had not forgotten.

"If you're not doing anything Sunday morning, I'm helping friends out with a new breakfast spot opening. You should come," said Topher. "It's in Bruton. The old tea-room."

"Ye Olde Tea Roomes?" Roger laughed.

"Of course I know that place! It's around the corner from me. I walk past it every day and I've been dying to know what it's becoming. I heard it was going to be an American-style diner, which didn't sound right."

"It may not sound right for Somerset, but that's exactly what it is. Come and join us on Sunday, and I guarantee you'll eat the best banana pancakes you've ever had in your life."

"You'll be there?"

"I promised them I'd work during the grand opening, so I'll be there, but I'll be working."

Roger narrowed his eyes. "This isn't a date, is it?"

"Why, no! It's just banana pancakes," said Topher, smiling as Roger chuckled.

"Give me your number." Roger took a streamlined leather notepad out of his pocket.

"That's very old-fashioned of you," said Topher, admiring the notepad. "No phone?"

"I'll put it into my phone later," he said. "That's a promise. And I'll phone you later to confirm the dinner party. Does that sound okay?"

"That sounds fine," said Topher, using all the acting skills he had to hide the fact that

571

he was bursting with an excitement he hadn't felt in months. Possibly years.

FIFTY-FIVE

- 2019 -

Maggie was wearing an old smock, touching up the paint around the windows. Topher had finished the painting, but was useless at cutting in, which she only discovered when he finished. It was such a small job that it got put off until now, which was irritating only because they were opening on Sunday morning, and it would have been lovely not to be on a ladder, painting in corners at the last minute.

They learned that Topher was very good at starting jobs, and not very good at finishing them. He had gone into a digging frenzy when Jack first arrived, digging two and a half beds in the garden before getting bored, tired, or some combination of the two, and leaving it looking like hell for the next two months. He refused to bring anyone in to finish it off, saying he was determined to do it himself, but the garden design course then ate up all his time.

Eventually he found a gardening team, and now the garden was exquisite, not to mention the clipped hedgerow down the lane that had made all the neighbors so happy, they were now invited over for cocktails on a regular basis.

In fact, Emily Sullivan had proved something of a godsend in letting the world know about the diner. Because she was in PR in a former life, and ran a local mums' group on Facebook ("like mumsnet," she said, "only *hyperlocal*"), she tapped into every young mother for miles. She featured the diner and got them to offer a kids' special during the week — smiley-face chocolate chip pancakes and an organic fruit juice for every harried mother who didn't know how she'd get through the mornings, and a clown who walked from table to table entertaining the young guests. Emily organized a series of "experts" who gave weekly talks to the mums on, essentially, how to stay sane during those early years. She also came up with the idea of renting the space out in the evening for mums' nights out. Maggie and Evvie had no idea what they would have done without her.

Maggie finished the last of the dodgy paint areas and stepped down.

"What do you think?" she called out.

"Does it look okay?"

Evvie came out from the kitchen, where she'd been making the batter for the pancakes and waffles and soaking the saltfish for the fritters. She stood in the doorway, hands on her hips, and looked around the room. That dark old tearoom, with the beams that were almost black, and the popcorn ceiling, had been transformed into two open-plan, light, bright modern rooms, leading into a conservatory at the back. One wall was horizontal planking; another was chalkboard paint with a low shelf filled with chalk to keep children occupied while their parents ate. The ceiling was now beadboard, the original old beams limewashed, with retro black-and-white photographic prints hanging on the walls.

There was bench seating along one side, the cushions covered in retro red vinyl, with thick modern shelves above, filled with kitsch Americana food items, flour packages, and cookie tins, many from the fifties and sixties with the distinctive type, all of it sourced by Evvie on eBay.

On the other side were diner-type booths, and in the middle, on the wide-planked floor, now limewashed, were tables and red metal chairs. It was part fifties diner, part modern café, and every time Evvie walked in here, she felt a surge of pride at what she and Maggie had created.

Particularly because it so nearly didn't happen. The day after Maggie decided to forgive Evvie, they both came to see the tearoom, and Maggie had looked at Evvie after five minutes and said, "I'm in, if you still want a partner."

With that partnership came their friendship. It started slowly, a little more formal than it had been previously, but they worked well together, and they understood each other, their strengths and their faults. And they shared a love of Jack, for Maggie and Jack had become close, and Evvie found that she no longer worried about being replaced, was happy for Jack that he had found the family she had never been able to provide on her own.

Three months ago she moved back into the manor house, into her old bedroom, and although she never would have believed this, coming through the betrayal had made their friendship stronger. These people weren't just her friends, thought Evvie, standing in the doorway of the kitchen, looking at the tearoom and at Maggie, blinking tears away; they were her family.

"You're not getting sentimental on me, are you?" Maggie laughed from the other side of the room, noticing the tears.

"I'm sorry. I can't help it. Look at what we've done, Maggie. Who would have thought?"

"Especially given the history we've had over the past year."

"Especially because of that, but it's not just that, it's all of it." Evvie shook her head in disbelief. "I feel like I've lived fifty lifetimes, and none of them fit me, none of them have felt right, until this one. I left college thinking I would make my home back in the States because that's where I started, and I ended up in Connecticut, trying so hard to make it feel like home, but it wasn't. I always felt *displaced*. I kept thinking that even though I missed England, I missed the England I lived in when we were at university, not the England of today, and I didn't think I could ever go back. But when we all found each other again . . . it was the first time in my life that I felt like I'd found my home."

Maggie walked over and put an arm around her waist, laying her head briefly on Evvie's shoulder. "I know. I feel the same. Not about being displaced, but nothing in my life went the way I expected it to. I can't say Ben wasn't a good man. He was ill. He was an alcoholic, and I carried the secrets for him. We did have some good times, when he wasn't drinking, but there was no way I could adopt children and bring them into that. I never told him that was why I was so anti-adoption. Maybe if I had, he would have stopped drinking. I just don't know. I'll never know, but I forgive myself for that. I honestly didn't think I would ever have any color in my life again. And now I have all of you, and I have Jack."

"Jack." Evvie smiled. "What would we do without our boy?"

"Speak of the devil," said Maggie as the bell rang and the door swung open. Jack strode in, already getting his iPad Pro out of his messenger bag.

"I've set up the social media accounts." He grinned, opening the iPad and sitting on one of the banquettes as Maggie and Evvie sat opposite him, both looking at him adoringly.

Jack looked up at each of them and burst into laughter. "Can you stop gazing at me like that? It's creepy."

"We can't help it," said Maggie.

"We love you," said Evvie.

"I love you both as well, but we've got work to do." Jack was distracted, immersed in his iPad, tapping away as Maggie and Evvie caught each other's eye and smiled.

"So I gave the name to one of my mates who's a graphic designer . . ." Evvie suppressed a small smile. Since Jack had been living here, he had filled his speech with Briticisms. *Mate,* she thought, was not a word he had ever even thought of a year ago.

"I told him we wanted a retro Americana kind of thing, and he sent this over this morning. I changed it on Insta and I'm going to set up a Facebook page, but it looks really good. Here. What do you think?" He swung the screen around to show a circle design, with three small stars and the title of the diner in heavy block writing.

"My Two Moms," Maggie read, smiling. "I love it."

"It looks fantastic," said Evvie. "It's perfect." And she took Maggie's hand under the table and squeezed it hard.

The bell rang again, and Topher walked in.

"I know, I know, I'm late," Topher said, stopping and looking around. "Maggie! You finished the paint. You did a much better job than I ever could." He grimaced. "Big ideas, bad follow-through. I'm sorry I get so distracted."

"If I didn't know you so well, I'd be cross. Luckily I forgive you. Next time I'll only have you design the garden."

"I did do a good job on the garden, didn't I?" Topher wandered over to the French doors at the back and looked out. It was a small courtyard, surrounded by high stone walls, with terra-cotta pots now attached to the walls at various heights, herbs spilling out of some, silver helichrysum out of others, dark green vinca out of still others. It was simple and beautiful and softened the stone walls, bringing them to life. Square black planters anchored each corner, a long community table was at the back, and a few other bleached teak tables were dotted around.

"The yard looks great." Jack wandered to the back and looked out. "The whole thing looks awesome. Are you ready?" He turned around and looked at Maggie and Evvie.

"Ready as we'll ever be," said Maggie.

"We're going to kill it." Evvie smiled.

Topher walked over and put his arms around Maggie and Evvie, the group huddling by the window, each of them smiling.

"Come on, Jack," Evvie called over. "It's time for a group hug."

"I don't do hugs," said Jack, but he was already taking a step toward them.

"I used to say that, too, but I changed," said Topher, shooting a grin at the girls.

"You have to do this one." He extended an arm to Jack. "We're not giving you a choice."

"Oh all right," grumbled Jack. Behind his pretend frown was a smile and a huge amount of love.

"See?" said Evvie. "This is what it's all about. Because we are a family."

ABOUT THE AUTHOR

A former journalist in the United Kingdom and a graduate of the International Culinary Center in New York, **Jane Green** has written many novels (including *Jemima J, The Beach House, Falling,* and *The Sunshine Sisters*), most of which have been *New York Times* bestsellers, and one cookbook, *Good Taste.* Her novels are published in more than twenty-five languages, and she has over ten million books in print worldwide. She lives in Westport, Connecticut, with her husband and a small army of children and animals.